a life where we work out

Kathryn Basham

Printed in the United States of America

First printed edition: November 2025

ISBN 979-8-218-81229-4 (paperback)

for my own Griffin—the ending I would give us if I could.

(and for Anna, who was very upset that my debut novel wasn't dedicated to her. I love you, bff.)

Contents

Chapter 1

Ellie

October, Age 28

"Okay Ellie, you got this," I mutter to myself, rounding the corner into the old, familiar neighborhood. The pecan trees that line the streets were my favorite as a kid. I used to wander for hours along the shaded blocks, sunlight filtering through where the leaves didn't quite overlap. It felt cozy, and I would daydream that I was in a secret garden, or some forest in a movie where the princess meets her true love for the first time. Now it feels suffocating, like a tunnel slowly narrowing around me until the very last moment when I realize it's actually a monster, not a tunnel, and that monster is going to swallow me whole.

After driving in circles for the last 20 minutes, I've finally forced myself to turn onto the street that holds my destination. Pulling up to the curb in front of the cozy yellow house, I take a shuddering breath as I turn my key in the ignition.

That wasn't so hard, was it?

Stepping out of the rental, I grab my bag from the trunk. When I reach the first step of the stone pathway that leads up to the house, I pause again.

This is ridiculous, Ellie.

It *is* ridiculous, but that doesn't change the fact that I can't convince my feet to move. Objectively, staying at my best friend's new house shouldn't be a big deal. It's a lovely house. Beautiful, even. I've seen it countless times on FaceTime, and being with Abby feels like home no matter where we are.

The problem isn't this house. It's the house across the street that I'm avoiding at all costs–I can't even bring myself to look at it.

"Are you lost, ma'am?"

A wide smile spreads across my face, and I whirl around to face the source of the familiar voice.

"Jack Robbit," I say, instantly feeling lighter than I have in months.

"It's been ten damn years, how many times do I have to tell you to stop calling me that?" He returns my smile, stepping forward to pull me into a hug, planting a kiss on the top of my head.

"You only hate it because Abby came up with it," I say, my voice muffled with my head buried in his chest. With one final squeeze, he releases me from the hug, crossing his arms and looking stern. It only makes me smile harder.

"No, I hate it because it's stupid," he counters. "And it undermines my authority."

"Authority?" I ask, laughing. "What authority?"

"They made me deputy fire chief," he says with a sheepish smile.

"Jack, that's amazing!" I squeal. "So why are you here, shouldn't you be in Dallas?"

"No, I mean *here*. In Larkspur. Old man Ritter plans on retiring here in the next few years, wants to train me up to take his spot. Although the way he's training me now, I'm pretty sure he actually just wants a clone."

My smile falters, the sinking feeling I've had for the past month returning in full force. So Jack Robb is back in Larkspur. I'm the only prodigal who hasn't returned since we all left for college.

"That's amazing," I repeat emphatically, schooling my facial features back into place. "I can't imagine anyone better for the job."

"Thanks, Ellie Bellie," he says softly, his eyes full of an understanding that tells me he didn't miss my reaction. "I'm really glad you came home for this. It's good to see you."

"It's good to see you too," I say, linking my arm through his. "Now, are you going to walk me to the door like a gentleman, or are we just gonna stand at the curb all day?"

It's been ten years since we graduated, five since I set foot in Larkspur, Texas. I would have been happy to stay away forever, but I was told in no uncertain terms that I *would* be the chair of the reunion planning committee, despite my vehement protests.

So here I am, arm in arm with my favorite guy, walking up to the home of my childhood best friend and her husband, Aaron. Before we can even think about knocking on the door it flings open, and a wild mop of auburn curls vibrating with excitement greets us.

"Hi, my sweet ginger angel," I say as she squeals loudly and jumps up, wrapping her legs around my waist. Thank God Jack is standing directly behind me, otherwise we'd be tumbling down the walkway back to the street.

She smacks a big, wet kiss on my cheek, then hops back down, her arms still tightly wrapped around my neck.

"I can't believe you're in Larkspur, I thought you would make me haul my ass to Boston every time I want to see you for the rest of our lives," she says excitedly. With a glance over my shoulder, she adds, "And you brought Jack Robbit!"

"Don't call me that," he says gruffly as we step into the entryway. "And she didn't bring me, you told me to come over, remember?"

"Of course I did, I figured the more of us there are, the less likely Ellie is to hightail it out of here and never look back, *again*," she responds, shooting a pointed look in my direction.

I roll my eyes exasperatedly but don't say anything. She's not wrong– the second I crossed the county line, my brain started screaming at me to run like my life depends on it. Turning around to close the door, I let myself glance at the soft blue ranch-style home across the street. A sharp pang in my chest has me closing the door with more force than I intended.

"Who in the hell is slamming my door?" a booming voice calls from the back of the house. Aaron comes around the corner, wiping his hands on the "Kiss The Chef" apron he's wearing over his bare chest and sweatpants. "Ellie!" he says, all annoyance fading instantly.

"Sorry, Aaron, you know I have violent tendencies," I say in mock contrition, leaning in for a side-hug to avoid getting whatever it is he's making on my clothes.

"Well, let's put them to better use, come help me beat the biscuit dough."

"You are not putting her to work, honey," Abby says in a sickly sweet voice laced with a threatening undertone. "I am going to monopolize her for as long as she's here." Jack lets out an indignant scoff, which makes me laugh as Abby rolls her eyes at him. "Fine, *we* can monopolize her time, Jacky boy." Grabbing my hand, she yanks me down the hall to the living room, Jack shaking his head as he follows behind.

"I would ask if you found the house okay, but you could probably do that drive with your eyes closed," Abby says, sitting cross-legged in the corner of the emerald green velvet sectional. "Lord knows how much time you spent over here."

When Jack shoots her a sharp look, her eyes widen, and she stammers out, "Just in the sense that Larkspur is so small and you lived here your whole life and everyone knows where everything is—"

"It's okay, Abby," I say, cutting her rambling off. "We don't have to avoid it. I know exactly what street you live on."

She gives me a pained, apologetic look. "I'm sorry, if there had been any other house available...but this one was so perfect—"

Plopping down next to her, I lay my head on her shoulder and pat her thigh. "Don't apologize for buying your dream home, my ginger angel. I'm happy for you."

I feel her relax in relief, then immediately tense up again as she asks the question I knew would come, but was dreading anyway.

"Do you think he'll be at the reunion?"

I don't say anything, looking to Jack and holding my breath as I wait for his answer.

"Yeah, he will be," Jack says in a quiet voice, like he's trying to soften the blow. It doesn't help. "We talked about it yesterday."

Jack and Abby are both looking at me nervously, and I inhale a deep, shuddering breath, forcing a smile onto my face.

"Guys, it's fine," I say in an overly cheery voice. "I can handle being in the same room as Griffin Hart for a few hours."

Liar.

Chapter 2

Ellie

October, Age 28

It took me a minute to remember where I was when I woke up in an unfamiliar bed the next morning. I've spent so long shoving thoughts of Larkspur down as far as they would go that it didn't register that I was really and truly *here*.

Beams of the early morning light stream through the lacy curtains, bathing the room in a pale glow I've only ever seen in a Texas sunrise. Boston is beautiful in its own right, but without even seeing it yet, I just know the sky is bigger here.

I feel like I can breathe again.

Before I have time to enjoy it, my chest clenches, because being back home means I have to confront things I've been avoiding like the plague. Memories of the last time I was in this town–when everything went to hell–crawl to the surface, and from the moment I decided to come back, they've been getting harder and harder to ignore.

Pressing the heels of my palms into my eyes, I give myself thirty seconds to feel the crushing weight of anxious dread before forcing it back down, dragging myself out of bed. I follow the smell of coffee to the kitchen and find Abby sitting at the table, engrossed in whatever romance novel she's reading this week.

"Good morning," I say with a yawn, opening and closing the cupboards until I find a coffee mug. I pour myself a cup and take the seat across from her, smiling as she holds up a finger in a silent command of "hold on, let me finish this page."

"Good morning sunshine," she says, placing her bookmark and setting it down on the table. "Sorry, I wanted to finish that last night, but once it hit 2 AM, Aaron made me put it down and go to bed."

"Well don't let me interrupt you, I just needed coffee."

"No way, Jo and Ellis can wait," she says, waving her hand impatiently. "I can't believe you're here."

"Me either, to be honest," I reply with a shrug.

"How have you been, Ellie Bellie? Like, *really* been?"

I stare into my mug, contemplating the lies I've been telling myself for years–*Everything is fine, work is great, I'm really happy in Boston, I don't have time to date, and no, I'm not lonely.* For once, I decide on the truth.

"It's been kinda bad lately, Abs," I admit in a quiet voice. "I'm not doing...well."

She reaches across the table, squeezing my hand.

"Tell me what's going on, my love."

"I just...haven't felt like myself in a long time. Most of the time it's not so bad, but some weeks it feels like I'm going through the motions in a daze, like everything is simply happening *to* me and I'm not an active participant. Sometimes it feels like I'm watching my own life from the sidelines."

"Are you still seeing Dr. Kelsi? Are the meds helping?"

Kelsi, my therapist, who is *not* a doctor by the way, decided about a year ago that I would benefit from an antidepressant in tandem with our weekly sessions. Best decision I've ever made. Maybe the only good one, actually.

"Yes and yes. It's been so much better than it was before, but sometimes the lows get excruciatingly low again, and I just sort of have to ride it out," I explain, drumming my fingers absentmindedly against the side of my mug. "But it gets easier every time."

"I am so proud of you," she says, voice shaky, eyes watering. "You're the bravest, strongest, prettiest girl I know."

I reach up to stroke her cheek, wiping away the errant tear that broke through. "Well, thank God I'm still pretty," I say with a chuckle. "Who knows where I'd be without my devastatingly good looks."

"You'd still be running circles around those jackasses at your firm," she grumbles. "I mean what do they even do around there? It feels like you're never *not* at the office these days."

She looks up, her face guilt-ridden.

"I shouldn't have made you come back," she says, her voice wobbling again. "I should have told them we can do this without you."

"I'm glad I'm here, Abby," I say emphatically. "It's going to be good for me, I can't hide from it forever. I made my bed, it's time for me to lie in it." When she opens her mouth again, I cut her off. "C'mon, let's get ready. We have a party to plan."

"God, it's going to be so weird to see everyone," she says, grabbing both of our mugs and setting them in the kitchen sink. "Obviously I run into some of them around town, but being all together again in the school cafeteria?" She shudders. "It's going to feel like we're fifteen again."

"What a nightmare," I tease, heading to my room to change. Our first reunion committee meeting is today, and despite the nausea climbing its way up my throat, I'm determined to make the best of it.

This will be fun. It's one party, and then I can leave again. There's no reason to panic.

Like hell there's not.

***

Wind whipping through my hair, I take in the familiar town around me as I sit in the passenger seat of Abby's car, windows rolled down and breathing in the crisp autumn air. Flashbacks of driving these streets in a different passenger seat, with a different person behind the wheel, knock the wind out of me like someone punched me in the stomach.

"You want to remind me how I got roped into this?" I yell over the sound of the air rushing past us.

"That's what you get for becoming an East coast hot-shot," Abby yells back. "People here don't know the difference between 'project manager' and 'party planner'."

"This is stupid, I've never planned a party in my life," I counter. "You told them that right?"

"Well I would have, but that would be a damn lie," she says, a wide grin spreading across her face. "Everyone knows you planned the best wedding this town has ever seen."

Now *those* are some memories I could re-live over and over. When Abby and Aaron got engaged, I threw myself into their wedding the way I do with any project–meticulously, wholeheartedly, obsessively, like my life depended on it. I mean really, planning a wedding couldn't be *that* much different than architectural project management, right?

News flash–it is, in fact, wildly different. But that didn't stop the entire town showing up, invited or not, and not to toot my own horn, but it *was* the best wedding Larkspur has ever seen.

"That still doesn't mean I'm the right person for this," I argue, but only halfheartedly. I know deep down that out of all our former classmates, I'm absolutely the right person for this. Determination to manage something flawlessly quickly overrides the painful reminiscing from a few moments ago.

"Shut your mouth," she says, whipping into a parking spot at the front of the school. "You're going to kill it, and everyone is going to worship the ground you walk on."

"That's a bit dramatic," I say, rolling my eyes. Looking up at the stately brick building, a mixture of warm nostalgia and haunted what-ifs washes over me. So many things happened within these walls, good and bad. These days, it's hard to untangle the two. Even the good memories are tainted now—they only serve as a reminder of everything I lost.

Chapter 3

Ellie

August, Age 14

I did it. I survived my first day of high school.

Well, almost.

The only thing standing between me and survival is seventh period Spanish. I weave through the desks and take my seat in the middle of the row by the window.

There's a view of the tennis courts, the practice fields, and the teachers' parking lot–it isn't much to look at, but something about gazing wistfully out the window like I'm in a 1999 Mandy Moore music video makes me feel like I'm standing at the precipice of something huge.

That's exactly what it is, I guess–the beginning of the rest of my life. All of my big dreams about getting out of my small hometown and seeing the world begin with surviving high school.

You're closer than you've ever been, Ellie, I think determinedly as I begin to meticulously lay out my pens, textbook, and journal when my attention is drawn to the door as a group of three very loud (*obnoxious*) boys stumble into the room, laughing about something that I'm sure wasn't nearly funny enough to warrant their current decibel level.

To my annoyance, they take the desks immediately surrounding me, still yammering away. Settling in, they haphazardly yank their textbooks and notepads out of backpacks that look like they've been run over by multiple buses, then—almost as if they rehearsed it—they turn to look at me at the same time.

The one on my right shoots me a mischievous smirk and rattles off, "My family's from Mexico, so I don't even know why I have to take this class, but if you ever need help, I got you girl. Oh, and I'm David."

He's about my height, with dark hair and thick eyebrows, and a face that looks like he's going to be trouble and he's *not* going to be sorry about it. In front of him sits Jack, who introduces himself like this is a job interview and not a mandatory language course.

He looks more like a Kennedy than a high school freshman, I muse, taking in his impeccable posture, perfectly ironed khakis and heather gray golf polo as I grasp his outstretched hand.

The boy sitting directly in front of me turns sideways to look at me, stretching his long legs and cowboy boots out in front of him, and I'm met with bright brown eyes and a wide smile.

"Howdy there, I'm Griffin."

The butterflies in my stomach are as instant as they are foreign. I've never seen someone's entire face light up like that before, but I know I want to see it again. His voice is much deeper than I expect—like his voice got a head start over the rest of him in growing up. His Southern drawl is strong, even for Texas.

"Hi," I say quietly in return, feeling much more shy than usual, "I'm Ellie."

"Ellie," he repeats back slowly, like he's savoring the word. "Is that short for Elizabeth?"

"For Eleanor."

"Alright then Eleanor, it's nice to meet you."

I double-take, looking back up from where my eyes had dropped to my journal, and say "Oh, no, everyone calls me Ellie." He doesn't correct himself, just grins even wider and turns to the front when Señor Flores calls the class to attention.

The class flies by, but I find myself involuntarily glancing at the shaggy brown hair in front of me (*and the tall, lanky cowboy it's attached to*) more than feels acceptable.

With the final dismissal bell, I realize that I did it. Officially. I don't know why I was even nervous to begin with—I've gone to school with most of these kids since kindergarten. But still, high school is supposed to feel like a big deal right?

Everyone stands before the bell finishes ringing, gathering pens and papers and bags hurriedly to bolt as quickly as possible, but when I walk toward the door, head down while distractedly shoving my book in my bag, I stumble right into Griffin.

I quickly stammer out an apology, taking a step back and yanking my bag up my shoulder, but he just smiles that smile again, and the butterflies are back in full force.

"No worries. Have a good day, Eleanor."

I stare at him as he walks out the door without looking back. *Okay so apparently the 'Eleanor' thing is sticking,* I think as I make my way out of the classroom and toward the entrance of Larkspur High.

I spot my mom waving excitedly at me from her silver Toyota Tacoma and push my way through the crowd of students waiting to be picked up. As I approach the door, my eye catches the three boys from Spanish class getting into the car behind me.

I look over and spot the hem of Jack's khakis as he slides into the backseat of the enormous white SUV. Catching my eye, Griffin's face lights up, waving before David shoves him into the backseat and clambers in after him, slamming the door.

"How was your day, sweet girl?," my mom, Susan, asks while I carefully set my things on the floorboard and buckle in. "Was there anything big and exciting? Did you meet anyone new?"

"It was a good day. Nothing big or exciting, it was mostly just teacher introductions and classroom rules, boring first day stuff," I tell her with a shrug, purposefully ignoring the last part of her question. But in the back of my mind, I'm reeling from big brown eyes and a charming grin.

***

I spend the rest of the semester beginning my last class of the day with "Howdy there," and ending it with "Have a good day, Eleanor." Which is totally fine–it's all the words in between the hello and goodbye that are driving me nuts.

I thought that maybe after the beginning-of-the-year excitement wore off, the boys would settle in. Then I thought that maybe they'd calm down once football season ended. Then I told myself that the combination of the excitement of playoffs and the buzz of the holidays was to blame.

But as we start the second half of our freshman year, I realize I could not have been more wrong. Instead, they've cemented themselves as the loudest and most annoying part of my day.

David spends half his time teaching the kids around him every Spanish curse word he can think of, and the other half arguing with Señor Flores because "that's not the way a conversation sounds in Mexico, you sound like a robot."

Jack doesn't talk much, but he spaces out at a level that comes around full circle and distracts me. I don't know why I feel even remotely responsible for him, but when I see him zoning out during a lesson that will surely be on the test, I get so stressed out on his behalf that *I* stop paying attention.

And don't even get me started on Griffin Hart. The butterflies I felt that first day have been viciously murdered by the spark of annoyance that flares up anytime he's in a five-foot radius. I don't think that boy has ever stopped talking a day in his life. If there's room for a sarcastic comment or a wisecrack, he's going to take it.

And if there's *not* room, he's going to *make* it. Sometimes I swear I think he could argue with a brick wall and *win*.

"Do you ever stop talking?" I hiss at him under my breath. "I can't hear Señor Flores over your yapping."

Without turning to fully look at me, he whispers out of the side of his mouth, "Why would I stop talking when everything I say is way more interesting than whatever this is?"

Rolling my eyes, I lean back in my seat again and try to focus on verb conjugation, but I seem to have poked the bear.

"Y'know, if you lightened up a bit I bet you'd actually be fun," he continues in a hushed tone. "Then again," he says as he turns around to look me in the eye, "You sure are cute when you're annoyed with me."

Scowling, I fire back, "I'm plenty of fun when I'm with people I actually like. *You* do not fall in that category."

His eyes light up, like he's excited at the prospect of arguing with me.

"I think you could like me if you tried hard enough. Maybe we could even be friends."

"Hard pass. Does this usually work for you?"

I look past him toward Señor Flores, but I can see his shoulders shaking with silent laughter. It makes me scowl even harder.

The last ten minutes of the class are thankfully uneventful, but the moment the bell rings Griffin whips around to face me, continuing our argument like no time has passed.

"C'mon, give me a chance. For all you know, I could be the most darling gentleman in the history of Larkspur." His face lights up with that stupid smile, and I find myself wondering how I ever thought it might be charming.

"Absolutely not." I try to sound as unbothered as possible, but I can't keep the sharp edge out of my voice. "I don't need more friends, and even if I did, you wouldn't make the list of people I'd consider."

David and Jack look at each other quickly, then continue gathering their things and talking much louder than necessary. Griffin's smile drops a bit, eyes flashing with irritation.

"What have I even done to you?" he snaps. "You can't hate me this much just because you think I'm loud in class or whatever. I thought we got off on a good foot Eleanor, what am I missing here?"

Slamming my bag down with a thud and putting my hands on my hips, I look him straight in the eye. "Well maybe you're not as *darling* as you think you are. Maybe we were never on a good foot, and now we probably- no, *definitely*- never will be."

I know I'm being unnecessarily mean, but I can't help it—there's something about him that grates on my nerves in a way I'm entirely unfamiliar with.

Our voices have raised enough that David and Jack have given up any pretense about not eavesdropping, looking back and forth between us with their jaws dropped.

Griffin's smile is completely gone now, and it's his turn to scowl. "That's how you want to play it, huh? Well great news darlin', I no longer have any desire to be on good footing with you anyway."

"Fine," I snap, storming my way out of the classroom.

"FINE," he yells at me as I walk away. I don't bother to look back at him.

Chapter 4

Griffin

August, Age 15

"Dude, what did you do to piss Ellie off so bad?" David asks, laying on the couch tossing a basketball up in the air absentmindedly.

We've assumed our regular positions in my basement – David on the couch, Jack on the floor with the contents of his backpack laid out on the coffee table, and me in the oversized armchair my dad put down here when my granddad had to get a recliner with more back support.

You'd think they live here with how often the three of us are at my house. It's because my house has "better snacks," according to David.

David has been my next door neighbor since his family moved here when we were both two years old. Our dads started golfing together, and our moms started taking us to the park while they went. I guess you could say we didn't really have a choice in being friends.

Jack joined us in sixth grade. Me and David were riding our bikes around the neighborhood when we saw him sitting on the curb a block over in front of a house with a "Sold" sign on it.

It was just him and his grandma, and something in the awkward one-word answers he had to every question we asked gave us the impression that he'd had a rougher time than either of us combined. He's a year older than us, but in our same grade.

The one time we asked him about school, he mumbled something about his dad missing the deadline for kindergarten registration. We've never seen his dad, and we've never brought it up again. Instead, we forced him into friendship the same way me and David's parents had forced us, and we've been a trio ever since.

"You're going to drop that on your face again, and I'm not driving you to the ER when you break your nose this time," Jack says without looking up from the homework he's diligently doing.

"I don't know, man," I say, yanking my hands through my hair again, like that'll somehow pull an answer out of my scalp. At this point, I probably look like some sort of electrocuted Jimmy Neutron.

What *did* I do to piss her off? When I walked into Spanish that first day, I noticed her instantly. From the moment I saw her nervously twisting a tendril of her long blonde hair, I knew I wanted to be as close to her as possible.

I could barely remember my own name to introduce myself, and the second her deep blue eyes locked onto mine, I was a total goner. I didn't know what or how or why, but I did know that I wasn't going to be learning much Spanish that semester—I was much more focused on learning everything about the girl in the chair behind me.

Unfortunately, all I've learned so far is that she's about as uptight as they get. If you look up "overachiever" in the dictionary, it's just a giant picture of Eleanor Turner, glaring disappointedly at you for not doing the extra credit. And she'll definitely be wearing a scowl, which is all I've seen her since day one.

She's insanely smart, funny in a sort of quiet way that you don't expect, and *everyone* likes her–and she seems to like everyone, myself *excluded*.

Which brings me back to the scowl that seems reserved for me. I might put her next to "overachiever," but I think she'd put me next to "scum of the earth."

David is just as loud, and Jack is just as distracting, so I don't understand why I'm somehow the sole target of her annoyance. It seems like the harder I try to build a bridge between us, the more irritated she gets with me.

I wasn't joking when I told her I might be the most darling gentleman in all of Larkspur. Okay, maybe I was exaggerating. Alright, I was *definitely* exaggerating.

But I've always been well liked. Old ladies love me, all my kid cousins want to hang out with "cool cousin Griff." I have table manners, I hold the door open, I say "sir" and "ma'am", and the smile I inherited from my dad usually wins people right over.

Eleanor Turner is apparently immune to charm–especially mine. And for some reason, I can't stop testing the limits to see how far I can go before she cracks. I guess I found that breaking point today.

"She really laid into you," David continues on. "For a second there I thought she might smack you upside the head."

"You probably deserved it," Jack muses, still laser focused on his textbook.

"I don't understand why she gets so worked up," I grumble, crossing my arms and slumping further into the armchair. "You bozos are just as annoying as me, but *you* never get yelled at."

Snickering, David pauses his one-man game of catch and sits up to look at me with a suspicious looking glint in his eye. "Face it, she just likes us better than you. But..."

"But what?" I ask cautiously. When David gets that look, I know he's about to say something that's going to make my life a lot more complicated.

"But I bet you can change that. You like a challenge, and you've never met a chick you couldn't get to like you."

He's not wrong, but Eleanor isn't like every other girl I've smooth-talked. To be honest, I haven't even tried my normal tactics on her. From the moment I met her, I knew they wouldn't work.

This girl is different.

"Okay so what's your point?"

"Hear me out – what if we make it interesting?"

At this, Jack finally looks up from his homework, shooting David a wary look. "Whatever you're thinking, I'm already voting no."

"Shut up Jack, this is a good one. Okay, what if we put money on it? Twenty bucks if you can get her to be friends with you before the end of the year. Forty if you manage it by spring break."

He pauses for a second, clearly piecing something together in his brain. With a diabolical smile, he says, "A hundred bucks if she wants to go out with you. Like, on a date. Willingly. Without throwing something at your head."

Jack shakes his head, pinching the bridge of his nose.

"Dude, no way," I protest. "Absolutely nothing good can come of this."

Undeterred, David argues, "C'mon Griffin, I know you want her to like you. Or to at least stop hating you."

He's right, but he doesn't need to know that.

"Plus, it'll give us something to do for the rest of the year. I'm already bored out of my mind, and it's only January. Gimme something to enjoy in class," he says in a whiny voice, batting his eyelashes at me dramatically.

"Get that stupid look off your face," I say as I throw a chair cushion at him. "What would your plan be after? What happens if I get her to like me? We can't just tell her it was for a bet and thank her for being our guinea pig in our weird social experiment."

David lays back down and resumes throwing the basketball up in the air. "I don't know, you know I don't think that far ahead. I just think it would be a win-win – I get to have fun, you have incentive to get Ellie to stop being so mean to you, and

Jack gets to focus on school like the dweeb he is because we'll be too busy to bother him."

"I resent that," Jack exasperatedly sighs.

For the next few minutes, we sit in silence while we soak in David's proposal. Every warning bell and siren in my brain is going off right now, but for some stupid reason I'm actually considering going along with it. The way I see it, there's three outcomes here.

Outcome one, I convince Eleanor to be friends with me, but she finds out what we're doing and drop kicks us out of the classroom window.

Outcome two, I might get what I've wanted since day one—to find out everything there is to know about her. As a friend, obviously.

Outcome three, which might be the worst one - it doesn't work at all, and she keeps hating me.

I guess if continuing to hate me is the worst thing that could happen, I might as well try. All I've been thinking about for weeks is how to win her over—at least this gives me an excuse to try without Jack and David getting suspicious about why I want to win her over in the first place.

"Alright fine," I say with a resigned sigh. "Twenty bucks for the end of the year, forty if it's before spring break.

"Aaaaand?" David batting his eyelashes at me again, then quickly ducking and rolling away when I try to smack him.

"And a hundred if I can get her to go on a date with me. But only because I like it when you owe me money. Not because I want to go on a date with her."

Jack and David both level me with a look–it's the same look my mom gives me when I tell her I've cleaned my room and she knows for a fact that I'm lying. But I choose not to acknowledge that.

"And you *can't* tell Eleanor this is happening."

"Excellent," David says with a sinister look of satisfaction. "This year just got a lot more interesting."

As if on cue, he immediately drops the basketball directly in his face, resulting in a gush of blood from his nose.

"I'm not driving," Jack reiterates as David lets out a string of curses.

This year *did* just get a lot more interesting, but I'm not going to tell *him* that. I'll let David think it's about the money all he wants. It won't be about that for me at all. For me, it's about the inherent need to win over the girl who probably wants to stab me with a pencil.

Right now, all I'm thinking about is blonde hair, blue eyes, and a sneaking suspicion that this is going to work out very badly for me.

***

This is not going well. Apparently there *is* a "chick" –David's words, not mine–who simply refuses to like me.

I've been trying everything I can think of. Going out of my way to find her in the hallway just so I can give her a friendly smile, casually making it to class at the same time as her so I can hold the door open, diligently saying "howdy" and "have a nice day" every single day without fail.

I've even made an effort to stop goofing off in class – as much as I can anyway, I can't help my true nature. I was born to be hilarious. Truly, they should study me in a lab.

"You're not a comedian. You're annoying." At least that's what Jack says, but what does he know? It's not my fault he was born without a funny bone.

Anyway, the point is that none of it has made a lick of difference. It's almost like the harder I try to befriend her, the more she seems to hate me. In the evenings, in the time between David and Jack leaving my house and going to bed, my thoughts drift to Eleanor more often than not.

I replay our interactions over and over in my head, trying to pinpoint exactly when she went from being the shy but sweet girl I met the first week of school to being a girl who probably wouldn't save me if I started walking out in front of a bus.

Honestly, if she saw me stepping into traffic, I think she'd give me a little shove to speed things along.

As the weeks wear on, David gets increasingly smug about taking my money, and I get more and more dejected. Spring break is next week, and I've made zero headway. At this point,

I'd happily pay *two* hundred dollars to whoever's able to get her to stop looking at me like I'm a bug that needs to be squished.

Am I really that awful to be around? Has everyone been lying to me my whole life about how lovable I am? She doesn't seem to have a problem with my friends. What is it about me that drives her so crazy?

There's gotta be *something* I can do to change her mind.

But like my granddad used to say–I'm going to do this come hell or high water.

Chapter 5

Ellie

MARCH, AGE 15

Griffin Hart seems to have turned over a new leaf. Oddly enough, it's worse than him being obnoxious. I know how to handle *annoying*. I don't know how to handle... *whatever this is.* I can't exactly put my finger on it, but it's like sometime after winter break he gained consciousness and decided to stop being a court jester.

He actually kind of seems hell-bent on paying penance for being the bane of my existence these past few months. And that's something I have not made easy on him. It almost feels like he's *overcompensating* to make up for some dastardly deed, but he hasn't really done anything bad enough to warrant that, so I'll just chalk it up to an enormous ego being humbled by someone who doesn't immediately fawn over him.

For some reason, every time he says something kind, it makes me want to scream. I bet if anyone looked closely enough they would see the irritated, involuntary twitch in my left eye. Part of me wonders if the change of heart is genuine. Or even possible. That pessimistic train of thought catches me off guard, and stops me dead in my tracks right as I'm approaching the door to our classroom. *That isn't fair, Ellie,* I scold myself. *You haven't really given him a chance. And you haven't exactly been warm and inviting.*

I generally pride myself on being a gracious and patient person, but apparently my subconscious decided to skip right over Griffin Hart when it comes to exercising those traits.

It doesn't help that I'd rather re-create my fourth-grade bowl cut than admit I'm wrong about anything. I can practically hear my grandmother's voice in my head: *"Well, Ellie Bellie, would you rather be right or be kind?"* I really hate when my conscience makes valid points.

Metaphorically squaring my shoulders, I walk into Spanish determined to extend an olive branch. I just hope it doesn't come back to haunt me. Today when I hear a friendly "howdy Eleanor," instead of rolling my eyes and taking my seat as quickly as possible, I look intentionally into Griffin's eyes, which are somehow dark and mysterious without being moody, and give him a genuine smile. "Hi Griffin," I say in a warm tone that feels *very* uncharacteristic before sliding into the desk behind him.

He turns slowly in his seat to face me, and I avoid his gaze as long as possible as I retrieve the maroon journal labeled '*Spanish*' from my bag. I can still feel him looking at me, and when I realize I can't avoid it any longer, I look up at him. It takes everything in me not to burst out laughing at the look of shock on his face.

"Do I have something on my face?" I ask casually, playing dumb while knowing exactly why he looks so flabbergasted.

Pretending to be clueless, I reach up to swipe at absolutely nothing on my cheeks and mouth.

His eyes flicker down to my mouth for a split second, then back up to mine, and all of sudden the monarch butterflies have migrated back from Mexico directly into my stomach. He meets my gaze with a completely new, very unreadable look–like he's looking at me for the first time again. I've seen the way his eyes look when he's being playful, and annoying, and genuine, and irritating–but I don't have a descriptor for *this*.

I'm caught off guard, and feel my carefree façade waver a bit while my brain tries to compute whatever it is that's showing on his face.

"Helloooooo?" I drawl, trying to mimic his own accent and waving my hand in his face in an attempt to snap him out of whatever brain malfunction he's got going on over there.

He shakes his head a little, the way my cat does when I blow on his ears to get his attention.

I wonder if Griffin likes cats or dogs more.

The thought comes out of no where, like someone else planted it in my head.

Since when do I care what Griffin Hart likes?

He assumes a more neutral expression (*or at least it would be if he wasn't squinting at me suspiciously*). "You're being nice to me."

It's more of an accusation than a question. *Have I really been that awful?* I wonder to myself before responding, "Well yes Griffin, believe or not, I am a nice person."

"Not to me, you're not," he fires back quickly. Not accusatory though, more...bewildered. "Why are you being nice to me?"

"Because I've noticed that you've gone out of your way to be nice to *me* lately, and I figured it was time to bury the hatchet between us," I confess with a defeated sigh. "I'll be honest, I can't even really remember why we stopped being friends."

"According to you, we were never friends in the first place, and you said you didn't need more friends anyway," he says, throwing my own words back in my face.

How rude of him to use my own words against me. But it's my turn to turn over a new leaf now.

"I did say that, and it was mean. For what it's worth, I was wrong," I admit. "...and I'm sorry."

To their credit, David and Jack try very hard not to openly eavesdrop when Griffin and I start going back and forth like this. But at my unexpected apology, I find all three of them looking at me, dumbfounded.

After a moment of awkward silence, Griffin breaks into a grin brighter than I've seen him wear in months, and the weight of that smile shifts something inside me. I realize not only that I've missed seeing it, but that it's stirring up more than a simple smile should. It brings up a whole lot of warmth and *feeling* I didn't expect.

That's something for Future Ellie to deal with.

"Why, Eleanor Turner," he gasps in fake surprise, clutching at pearls that aren't there like some sort of old granny down at the hair salon. "I didn't know you knew how to apologize. Is this a first for you?"

Despite my resolution to actively be kinder to Griffin, I can't help but roll my eyes at him and let out an impatient huff.

"Don't push it Griffin Hart, I still have time to take it back."

This only makes him smile even wider, a dazzling and beautiful thing that reaches every corner of his face, including those warm, chocolate eyes that I realize I've never taken the time to *actually* look at.

From this close, I can see flecks of green and gold sprinkled on the inner rim of his irises—more than just brown, and holding something more than I anticipated. They're a deep well drawing me in, the kind I wouldn't expect from a boy who seems to revel in finding new ways to bother me on a daily basis.

"Nope, too late now darlin'. I knew I'd get you to warm up to me eventually," he says with a boyish excitement that has the corners of my own lips twitching upward.

For a split second, I think I see Jack stiffen, and Griffin and David share an undecipherable look before Griffin's attention is back on me. It's so quick I think I might have imagined it, and I don't have the time or care to dwell on it as Señor Flores calls our attention to the front of the room.

With another quick flash of a smile, and a playful flick to my nose, Griffin says matter-of-factly, "I think this is the start of a real fun friendship for you and me, Eleanor."

I can't tell if that sounds more threatening or exciting–but an almost imperceptible shiver runs down my spine as I wonder exactly what I'm getting myself into.

***

He was right. Being friends with Griffin Hart *is* fun. Not just Griffin either - apparently he, David, and Jack are a package deal. Some days it's like having brothers that I never asked for, but I'm secretly glad to have ended up with anyway.

Others...it's like those chaotic videos you see of ducklings who imprint on a cat instead of their mom and follow her around everywhere, except the cat is a fifteen year old girl and the ducklings are tornadoes disguised as teenage boys.

At first it was just goofing around before and after class (but not during–I still have grades to maintain, I can't descend into total anarchy), but over the past month and a half, it's turned into finding each other in the hallways between *every* class, not just Spanish, which then turned into nightly Skype calls, sometimes lasting for hours, comfortably talking about everything and nothing at all.

Without realizing it, I'm laughing more than I ever have, and the highlight of my day has become the time I spend with them.

I'm not sure when I started taking life so seriously. As a kid, I was all about fairies and pirates and adventures. I reveled in knock-knock jokes and campfire stories and running through the sprinklers. I was a windswept, scraped-kneed, constantly giggling force of nature who left joy (and mess) wherever she went. I would spend hours in the hammock in our back yard, staring up at the clouds, daydreaming big fantastical dreams.

Somewhere along the way my wires must have gotten crossed. Sometimes I don't recognize the rigid, anxious perfectionist looking back at me in the mirror. I try so badly to cling to the freedom I felt as a kid, but it's becoming increasingly easier for me to get overwhelmed, and increasingly difficult to talk myself down.

But being around Griffin has started softening edges I didn't even realize were sharp to begin with. I've been so focused on getting out of this town that I haven't been enjoying the life around me.

It's not that I don't love Larkspur, I really do. I can't pinpoint exactly why I'm so set on leaving, but it's all I've been able to think about since I was twelve years old, head buried in a book about a girl leaving her podunk town for the big city. But now the life around me seems a little sweeter every day—a life that might be harder to leave than I anticipated when the time comes.

***

"I feel like I never see you anymore," Abby says, popping another fried pickle into her mouth.

Abby Wheeler is my 'everything' friend–first, oldest, best, you name it. We attached ourselves at the hip in the two-year-old class at The Learning Tree, and shortly after that our dads followed suit. Abby's mom left before she reached her first birthday, so it's been just her and her dad most of her life. There was a brief moment in time where there was an Evil Stepmother involved, but in an ironic (and cruel) twist of fate, wife number two *also* bailed shortly after giving birth to Abby's brother two years ago. Abby was ready to violate the Geneva conventions to exact her revenge, but Mr. Wheeler insisted that she's the only girl he could ever need, and that he should never have tried to add another one in the first place.

The rest was history. More often than not, my childhood pictures include a redheaded angel smiling demurely at the camera, offsetting the whirlwind of blonde always too busy to stop for something as silly as a photo.

Swallowing the too-large sip of milkshake I just took, a brain freeze takes over my mental capacity and it takes a huge effort to choke out, "What are you talking about? We've had dinner on Fridays and sleepovers on Saturdays since we were three, you see me all the time."

It's the Friday evening of spring break, and this one is no different than all the Friday evenings we've had for as long as I can remember.

In a red booth in the back corner of the vintage diner, Abby sits with her usual order—a Diet Coke and an order of fried pickles. Her auburn curls are pulled up into a ponytail, giving her forest green eyes a clear field of vision as she pins me with a look that pierces through my bullshit.

I'm across from her, nursing a vanilla milkshake with much more restraint than I showed the basket of fries that already sits empty at the edge of the table.

"Don't play dumb with me, Ellie, you know exactly what I'm talking about," she shoots back with a stern glare. "When was the last time you waited for me after lunch to walk to biology?"

I try to interrupt to remind her that she switched biology periods so we aren't in the same class anymore, but she's hit her stride and there's no stopping her now.

"Or the last time you called me, well after my bedtime, mind you, to lament about your so-called boredom with this town before admitting that you *actually* called me to help you pick what to wear the next day?"

Once again, I open my mouth to interrupt, but she powers through my protests.

"I know what you're going to say, and don't even try it, Eleanor Turner. Sleepovers are inevitable so they don't count. My point stands that I feel like I never see you anymore."

Hearing my full government name coming out of her mouth is weird. It doesn't sound right when it's not in a deep Southern drawl. But she's on to something. When the school year first started, Abby and I had a built-in safety blanket in each other. We made sure we walked to class together, never ate lunch by ourselves, and made contact in the halls as often as we could.

That's changed since I became part of "Ellie & The Dudes." (David's idea for a nickname, there was no room for argument.)

"I'm sorry for neglecting you, my poor sweet ginger angel," I apologize dramatically, using the nickname that stuck when I first gave it to her in second grade. "I guess I have been a little more absent than normal."

"Probably has something to do with your new boys," she says with a pointed look at me.

"First of all, they're not *my* boys, they're just...boys. And they're my friends. You can't honestly say you haven't made a single other friend in the last 6 months."

I know she has—after our first semester journalism class, Abby dove head-first into the school newspaper sphere. She and the other future Pulitzer winners can usually be found huddled together, talking about whatever subject NPR covered that morning.

"That's not my point at all," she continues. "My point is that you've made friends with *the* boys, and for the first time in our lives I feel like I'm dragging information out of you instead of listening to you monologue about every detail of your current events. Is there something more going on there than just friendship? Perhaps with a certain enemy turned not-an-ene-my-after-all?"

My eyes wander around the diner, looking everywhere except hers. When my gaze makes its way back to her face, she's got her hands folded on the table, looking annoyingly persistent.

"No, not at all. There just isn't much to share, we mostly just goof around. Nothing monologue worthy," I say with a shrug, keeping my eyes down toward my lap while I pick at the hem of my powder blue sweater dress. I absolutely do *not* have anything to monologue about when it comes to a certain brown-eyed cowboy.

"Yeah okay, whatever you say," she says, eyes rolling. "But when you start dating him, I'm going to bake myself an I-told-you-so cake and make you serve it to me."

Before I can argue back, my phone dings. Assuming it's my mom telling us she's on her way to pick us up, I rummage through my bag and pull my phone out. Instead of my mom's name, I see Griffin Hart on the text notification.

> **Griffin:** Eleanor, come over!!!!

> **David:** ELLIE THESE BOZOS ARE SO BORING I MIGHT DIE

> **Jack:** Please free me from this prison.

Laughing, I type out a quick response.

Ellie: Can't, I'm with Abby.

David: You have a sleepover with her every weekend

David: You never hang out with us :(

Ellie: I literally talk to you all day every day.

David: But you've never hung out with us outside of school

David: Do we embarrass you?

Jack: You are embarrassing. That's not her fault.

David: Come over after! We're all staying at Griffin's tonight

David: Pleeeease :(

I don't have time to think of a clever comeback before my phone dings again. It's still Griffin Hart, but this time it's outside of the group text.

Griffin: Come hang out, please

> **<u>Griffin</u>: I'll even kick them out if they get on your nerves**

> **<u>Griffin</u>: It would be fun to hang without Señor Flores in the room**

The way my stomach swoops is foreign, and it must show on my face, because Abby jumps like a shark who caught a whiff of blood in the water. "Who was that from? The boys? Or maybe one boy in particular?"

The thing about being friends with someone for thirteen years is that they can *always* tell how you're feeling–sometimes before you know it yourself. I've been avoiding any sort of critical thinking when it comes to my budding friendship with Griffin, and I can tell Abby is starting to do it for me.

"Yes, it was from the boys," I admit begrudgingly. "They want me to come hang out, but I told them I was with you."

"Okay and I have to go babysit the gremlin in 20 minutes, what does one have to do with the other?"

"I don't know," I say, biting my bottom lip. "I've only ever been around them at school, what if it's weird outside of that?"

"It's going to be weird no matter what because you're there," she deadpans.

Abby and Jack would get along great.

I keep the thought to myself, but make sure to roll my eyes out loud.

"I'm just saying, I think you should go." Her expression turning serious, she continues on, "You've seemed lighter lately. You've been my best friend my whole life, and I know you better than anyone. Certainly well enough to notice that your sunshine has dimmed a little these last few years, my love."

Voice dropping low, she continues, "I get that you want to see the world outside of Larkspur... I just think it's good that you're letting some roots grow here, even if you plan on leaving."

Abby is one of those girls adults call "wise beyond her years"—which usually just means she was a quiet kid who grew up too fast, carrying the weight of being the only-turned-eldest daughter in a single-parent home. It also means that she's usually right.

My mom honks at us from the parking lot, and I realize I missed a text from her while I was lost in my thoughts. Abby and I quickly scarf down the rest of our food, and I shoot off a text before we walk out the diner doors.

Ellie: Fine, twist my arm.

Ellie: We're dropping Abby off at her house, then I'll ask my mom to bring me over.

Jack: Thank God.

Griffin: YESSSSS

<u>David</u>: Tell Susan I said hi ;)

<u>David</u>: And that she looked ravishing in the pick up line today

<u>Ellie</u>: Gross, David. See y'all soon.

On the drive over, I purposefully choose *not* to think about why I responded to the group chat, but left Griffin's texts unanswered. I guess that's an answer on its own.

Chapter 6

Griffin

March, Age 15

I stare at my phone waiting for another text from Eleanor to come through, but it never does. Maybe she didn't feel like she needed to text me back because she told the group she was on her way.

I don't know why that bothers me so much.

It's been ten minutes since "see y'all soon," and I've checked the time about every forty five seconds since then. I know it takes around fifteen minutes to get from the diner to my house, and I figure Abby's house can't be that far out of the way.

Five minutes from now, Eleanor Turner is going to be in my house.

Obviously that was the plan–I literally invited her. But the realization hits me like a freight train. My eyes dart around the room, widening in horror at the current state of my basement.

I launch myself off the armchair, frantically gathering as many empty Red Bull cans and half-eaten bags of chips I can reach in an attempt to make this place look like less of a dump. Jack and David are locked in on Madden, oblivious to my panic. In all fairness, I've never cared about the mess before. We stopped trying to keep things clean a long time ago.

My mom has also completely given up on trying to get us to keep this place looking like a liveable space instead of some National Geographic footage of the after-effects of a natural disaster. Her standards have dropped to "as long as there's no mold growing on anything, I don't care." I think when it comes to the three teenage boys she wrangles on the daily, two of which aren't even hers, she picks her battles carefully.

Right as I shove a whole grocery aisle's worth of trash into the bin, the doorbell rings. "I'll get it," I holler over my shoulder at Jack and David as I bolt up the stairs three at a time. They barely grunt in acknowledgement, keeping their eyes glued to the TV.

When I open the door, it feels like all the air has been unceremoniously removed from my lungs, as if someone has crushed my torso like a soda can.

Eleanor is in my doorway, her heart-shaped face framed in a halo of blonde, wearing a shade of blue that makes her ocean eyes even more vibrant than normal. We stand there just looking at each other for a moment, somehow both caught off guard even though we knew exactly who was on the other side of the door.

Shifting uncomfortably, she laughs nervously as she says, "Well are you going to let me in or not?"

"Oh, yeah, duh," I respond (*very lamely*), stepping aside so she can walk past me into the entryway.

"Shoes on or off?" she asks, and suddenly I'm feeling self conscious as her gaze wanders around the room.

"Uh, it doesn't matter," I mumble abruptly, eager to get her out of my foyer and into the basement, where I'm much more in my element. "We're down here."

She slips off her white sneakers without untying them and follows me down the carpeted stairs into the basement.

"Hi boys," she says in greeting to Jack and David, seeming immediately more at ease once it's not just the two of us. That only makes me more anxious. Do I make her uncomfortable?

Throwing the controllers down immediately, they rush over to sandwich her in a hug. Her laugh is muffled between them, and suddenly I'm overwhelmingly irked that I'm not the one making her laugh.

"Alright alright, get off of me dweebs," she says, slipping under their arms and plopping herself onto my armchair, and I try to hide my smile. Why is the sight of her sitting in my usual spot stirring a warm feeling of satisfaction in my chest?

I shake my head, trying to clear that thought out of my head. I don't even know what it means.

We spend the rest of the evening in comfortable conversation, and it feels like she's always been part of our basement crew. I felt a little guilty inviting someone—not just someone, a *girl*—into our bizarre version of a safe haven, but she fits right in.

Me, Jack, and David take turns telling stories about each other, each of us trying to find something more embarrassing to share about the other than the last.

I scowl furiously, and tears of laughter run down Eleanor's face as Jack tells her about the time my belt loop got caught when we were hopping the chain link fence at the prairie dog park when we broke in after hours. The last thing I need is for her to have a mental image of me helplessly hanging upside down by my britches while Jack and David laughed way too long before trying to help me.

We spend a few hours trying to teach her how to play Madden, and David has to stomp outside to take a breather when she smokes him on her first try. The look of triumph on her face was even more satisfying than David's tantrum.

I like Eleanor at school—she's funny, and smart, and always ends my day on a high. But at my house? I like her even more. That's gonna be a problem.

Before we realize it, it's midnight, and her mom calls to ask her if she plans on coming home anytime soon.

"Shoot, I'm sorry mom, I meant to text you to come get me way earlier. I lost track of time—I'm sorry to keep you up so late," she apologizes on the phone, sounding truly distraught at the prospect of causing her mom even the tiniest bit of inconvenience.

"I can take you home if she doesn't mind," Jack yells loud enough for her mom to hear. "I've had my license for a full year, and I promise to be real careful."

She pauses while her mom responds, and accepts Jack's offer with a grateful smile. "Well boys, it's been a pleasure," she says, saluting in farewell.

The wheels in my brain spin furiously as I try to figure out a way to casually, naturally, invite her back over, but luckily David has no qualms about being direct, and shouts, "Same time next week!" It's more of a declaration than a question, but she says yes enthusiastically anyway.

She gives David a tight squeeze around his middle, and I tag along behind her and Jack as they head upstairs, pretending it's because I'm a good host. It's not. I feel desperate for a few more seconds with her, almost panicky at the thought of her leaving.

She unties the shoes she kicked off earlier, shifting her balance from one leg to the other as she shoves her feet back into them and hastily reties the laces. I don't know why, but I find it insanely cute that she unties and reties them when it's time to put them back on instead of just untying them at the beginning.

She looks up at me with a hesitant smile while I stand awkwardly at the top of the stairs. Jack keeps his eyes glued to his phone, pretending not to notice the awkward silence.

"Well uh, thank you for coming over," I say way too formally, bringing my hand up to rub the back of my neck. "It was a lot of fun."

"Yeah, for sure," she says, her voice much peppier than usual–like the kind of voice my mom uses when she answers a work call. "Thanks for inviting me."

The silence gets even more uncomfortable before Jack clears his throat and asks if she's ready to head out. He pulls the door open, and she takes half a step forward before hesitating and turning back to me abruptly.

She has a conflicted, almost pained, look on her face, and before I know what's happening, she gives me a hug, muttering "goodnight, Griffin" while I stand there like a wax figure, before bolting out the door.

My brain doesn't register what's happening in time for me to hug her back, and by the time the thought comes to me, she's long gone.

Following behind her, Jack turns back to look at me, eyebrows raised, accompanied by a dumb smirk. "Do you want to come with us, Griffin?"

Rolling my eyes, I slam the door in his face, but when I head back down to the basement, I can't wipe the shit eating grin off my own.

Chapter 7

Ellie

April, Age 15

A lot has changed since spring break. Ever since that night at Griffin's, my usual Friday routine includes video games and heated debates with the boys. Abby joins us sometimes, on the nights she isn't babysitting her little brother, Dylan, or covering some event for the school paper.

The first time she came, I thought she was going to have a heart attack. It didn't hit me how much David and Dylan have the exact same chaotic energy until I saw her try to deal with him. I genuinely thought she was going to leave—until Jack sat next to her with a weary look and yelled, "David, stop acting like a toddler who snorted Pixy Stix." They shared a look, then nodded once, and I could tell a silent "we're in this together" passed between them.

She's not there often, but when she is, her and Jack watch like disappointed parents while Griffin and David go off the rails (and I egg them on). Most of the time though, it's just the four of us, and more recently it's been the four of us all weekend instead of just on Friday nights.

The weather has started getting nice again, so I've added an afternoon run to my routine before I meet Abby at the diner. Before I left, I sent a text to the group chat confirming our plans for tonight, and I've gotten so used to our routine that my heart sinks a little as I catch up on the replies I missed.

Ellie: Same as usual tonight boys?

David: Bruh, I don't wanna talk about it

David: But I'm on lockdown for the foreseeable future

Griffin: What did you do???

David: NOTHING.

Jack: :|

David: Except maybe me and my sisters set the curtains on fire

Jack: ?????????

David: Cinco de Mayo prep gone wrong :(

David: Those tiny bitch ass fireworks pack a punch

Griffin: God I would sell a kidney to see footage of your mom's reaction

David: RIP me

Jack: I'm out tonight too. It's granny's birthday and I'm taking her to see Hello Dolly at Magnolia Theater.

Jack: Shut the fuck up David

David: I didn't say anything!!

Jack: Just getting ahead of it

This will be the first Friday in weeks that I won't be spending with the boys, and something about it makes me feel a little lonely.

Walking dejectedly down the hall to my room, I check my phone as it buzzes again.

Griffin: Hey

Griffin: I know David and Jack are out tonight, but you could still come over

Griffin: If you want

My brain short circuits–I know the texts from Griffin are a super normal, friendly thing to send, but they might as well be in ancient Greek.

I must take too long to reply, because another round of messages come through.

> **Griffin:** No pressure though

> **Griffin:** Just thought I'd offer

> **Griffin:** Hello?

> **Griffin:** If you don't want to, that's fine

> **Griffin:** Just let me know

Shoot. I don't want him to think I'm ignoring him. I just can't for the life of me think of what to say.

> **Ellie:** Sorry, just got back from a run!!

> **Ellie:** That sounds fun! I'll ask my mom if she can pick me up since Jack won't be there to take me home.

The way my stomach is twisted up in knots, you'd think my nervous system doesn't know the difference between making plans with Griffin and being chased by an axe murderer.

<u>Griffin:</u> Cool, sounds good

<u>Griffin:</u> See you later.

<u>Ellie:</u> See you soon!

I throw my phone like it bit me and stare at the place it landed on my bed like it's some creature that might come back for more if I don't keep a very close eye on it.

At the diner with Abby, I don't tell her that it's going to be just me and Griffin tonight. I also don't mention that I was late because I changed my outfit three times.

***

I stand rigidly on Griffin's porch, at war with myself. Normally I just walk right in and make myself at home, but that feels weird if it's just the two of us. Should I be more polite? More formal?

I knock hesitantly instead of letting myself in. When Griffin opens the door, he looks genuinely confused.

"Oh it's you," he says, sounding surprised. "I thought you were someone else."

"Were you expecting someone else?" I ask, raising an eyebrow.

"No, but you never knock." His brows furrow as he stares at me like I've lost my mind.

"Well, are you going to let me in or not?" I tease, echoing my words from the first time I came over. Rolling his eyes, he steps to the side and dramatically gestures for me to enter.

With every step we take down into the basement, the silence gets more noticeable. Why does this feel so different from every other time I've come over here?

You have hung out with him dozens of times Ellie, get it together.

Instead of sitting in the armchair like I normally do, I take a spot on the couch, crossing my legs and keeping my eyes fixed on the spot where I'm picking at my cuticles.

I can feel Griffin hovering behind the couch, so I look over my shoulder to face him. He's still standing, arms crossed, brow furrowed even deeper now. The intensity of his gaze catches me off guard. "What?" I blurt out, sounding way more defensive than I should be.

"You don't sit there," he says, gesturing at the couch. "You sit *there*," he says, nodding to the armchair.

"I'm sorry, I didn't realize there was assigned seating."

I'm not the self-proclaimed comedian here, but I'm trying to break the tension anyway. Griffin doesn't move.

After a few beats of silence, he says "You don't have to hang out with me if you don't want to–," at the same time as I say, "You didn't have to invite me over out of obligation or anything–"

"What?" we both say, in the exact same tone, like the other person just said the dumbest thing we've ever heard.

I stand up, turning to face him fully, putting my hands on my hips in a way that reminds me distinctly of my mother.

Yikes.

"Of course I want to hang out with you Griffin, you're my friend," I say exasperatedly.

He takes a deep breath through his nose, gripping the back of the couch so hard I can see his knuckles whiten. Exhaling, he says "You're not an obligation Eleanor, I—" He stops, and clears his throat. "I always want you to come over." His voice is quieter now, and earnest in a way that makes my heart stutter.

"Oh," is all I can manage. I twiddle my thumbs for a few more seconds, then let out an aggravated scoff. "This is stupid, we've spent every weekend hanging out for the last two months, can we stop being weird?"

Griffin gives me a sheepish grin and tosses me a Wii controller. He flops onto the couch beside me without another word.

We spend the next hour trying to decimate each other in Super Smash Bros, quickly escalating from on-screen fighting to throwing real life elbows as we get more and more competitive.

After a poorly placed elbow knocks the wind out of him, we decide to shut the game off and find something less violent to do. We don't argue nearly as much as we used to, but without Jack there as a buffer, there's no guarantee the house survives any sort of escalation.

The silence we sit in now isn't heavy, it's comfortable. We've gone from sitting stiffly with a mile of space between us, to stretched out across the full length of the couch, my feet propped up on the coffee table with his long legs casually draped over mine.

"So what would you do after the diner before you started coming over here?" Griffin asks, arms slung over the arm of the couch behind his head, like he doesn't have a care in the world.

"Nothing really," I respond with a shrug. "I would read, or watch TV, or hang out with my mom. Usually I was asleep by 9:30."

"9:30!? What do you mean!?"

He yells it like I've just confessed to being the zodiac killer.

"What's wrong with going to bed early?"

"What's wrong is that you're fifteen, not fifty. You can sleep when you're dead," he says in the same way someone might explain to a five year old that two and two makes four.

"Well I didn't do that *every* Friday, just sometimes."

"Okay, well what do you do with the rest of your time?"

I begin to share all my favorite hobbies and memories–planting my favorite flowers with my grandmother every spring, summer road trips to the beach, watching a different sports movie with my dad every single week during third grade.

I even share some of the low points (like the one season my dad coached peewee soccer and made everyone on the team cry) and even worse, the embarrassing ones (like how hard I cried when I desperately wanted to be Dorothy in the first grade play but got cast as the Wicked Witch instead.)

When he begins to share stories of his own, I'm overwhelmed by how fascinating I find him.

He tells me about the half sister I didn't know he had—she's from his dad's first marriage, is ten years older, and lives in California with her mom. He doesn't say it, but I can tell from the way his eyes get sad that he wishes they were closer.

He shows me the scar on his chin, and I howl with laughter as he tells me how he got it from trying to ride the goat at his uncle's farm like a bronco when he was five.

I learn so many things I never would have guessed about the boy I never expected to become such a central part of my life. I knew he was funny, larger than life with enough confidence to power a small town—but he's also incredibly kind, loyal, and gentle.

His eyes well with tears when he tells me about his childhood cat that died last year. He talks more animatedly when he shares stories from summers with his cousins at his family's ranch. He tells story after story, and the more I listen, the more I never want him to stop.

After finishing a story about getting chased up a tree by a goose, he bolts upright and looks at me with wide eyes. Startled by the sudden absence of warmth where his legs were, I immediately ask him what's wrong.

"Nothing, it's just late, and I realized I've been talking your ear off." It comes out more like a question, a self-conscious edge to his voice.

"No you haven't, I've loved everything you've told me." I smile at him reassuringly and continue, "You've caught me by complete surprise, Griffin Hart."

"What do you mean by that?" His eyes narrow at me suspiciously.

I pull my phone out of my back pocket, bringing it to my ear as it rings with the outbound call to my mom.

"I mean that when you came into Spanish class like a hurricane that first day of school, I didn't know I'd end up liking you this much." I grin at him, never breaking eye contact while I tell her I'm ready for her to come get me.

"I like you too, Eleanor Turner."

He grins right back at me, and my own smile falters as I wonder if "like" is starting to mean something very different to the two of us.

Chapter 8

Griffin

April, Age 16

Eleanor has been staring at the wall of movie candy at the Dollar Tree for approximately twelve minutes, and if it was anyone else, I'd be losing my mind. But I think I could be happy watching paint dry with this girl.

With how seriously she's taking this, you would think this was a life or death decision, not picking a snack for movie night.

Jack and David are coming over for our regularly scheduled Friday hang, but this week we're making Eleanor watch *Final Destination* since we discovered that she's never seen it. When I volunteered to handle snack duty, I happened to–*accidentally*–text Eleanor separately to see if she wanted to come with me.

I totally meant to send it in the group chat. Scout's honor.

Even though she's nearly scowling with deep concentration, she can't help but hum happily along with whatever pop princess is playing over the speakers.

"What's your favorite song?" I blurt out, suddenly feeling like it might kill me if I don't know the answer.

For a second I think she didn't hear me, but without taking her eyes off the candy, like she's scared it might disappear if she looks away, she says, "Probably *Favourite Colour* by Carly Rae Jepsen."

I don't know what I expected, but it wasn't that.

"Really?"

The shock in my voice is what finally pulls her away from our low-budget Wonka factory, and she looks up at me, her face looking as shocked as I feel.

"Uhhh yes? Why does that surprise you?"

"I don't know, I pinned you for maybe a Frank Sinatra or Fleetwood Mac fan. I can't picture *Call me Maybe* on any of your playlists."

Rolling her eyes, she shifts her attention back to the real task at hand–snacks.

"Don't 'manic-pixie-dreamgirl' me, Griffin. I'm exactly like other girls," she says, with an air like she's trying to explain something I should obviously already know. "Anyway, Emotion is a perfect pop album and CRJ is criminally underrated."

"I...don't really know what those words mean."

"Of course you don't." She doesn't look back at me, but she shakes her head softly and I see the corners of her mouth tilt upwards.

I've never been more confused, but it doesn't matter–I'd listen to her explain anything to me anytime. "Can you elaborate please?"

With a sigh, she grabs Airheads Xtremes, bite-size Kit Kats, and–

"Wait, what the hell are those?"

She holds up a box with a red brick pattern on it, and an old-timey font that reads *Boston Baked Beans*.

"These are my favorite," she says incredulously.

Oh this is about to be so fun.

"There's no way these are *anyone's* favorite–who in their right mind picks something called 'Baked Beans' for a snack?"

"They're just chocolate covered peanuts, don't be dumb. They're obviously not actual beans." She swats my shoulder, and I fight the urge to grab her hand and keep it in mine.

"These were my grandma's favorite, which became my dad's favorite, and now they're mine," she says with a shrug. "I'm just keeping a family tradition going." She crosses her arms across her chest and pops her hip out, giving me a challenging look. "Is that allowed, candy snob?"

"I'm not a snob," I cry in mock outrage. "But this is Texas darlin', I don't want beans in my chili OR my candy."

"Well no one is making you eat them, but I'm getting them," she says, tossing her hair over her shoulder and dropping them into the basket I'm holding. "You can do whatever you want."

"I still don't really know any of those words you said earlier, but that seems like it might be very 'manic-pixie-dreamgirl' to me."

With an indignant scoff, she yanks the basket from my arm and stalks off toward the register–I nearly pull every muscle in my cheeks grinning as I follow behind her.

***

"Are you guys planning on coming over tonight?"

Jack and David's heads both snap up, first looking at each other, then turning to me. David's eyes look like they're on the verge of popping out of his skull. His mouth hangs open, giving me a front-row view of the street taco he was mid-chew on.

We're sitting in the local food truck yard, The Park, like we always do after our Saturday morning disc golfing.

Jack "wasn't raised in a barn," as his granny reminds him on an almost daily basis, so luckily I'm spared the sight of his food, but there's no avoiding the way his eyes narrow at me suspiciously.

"What the hell are you talking about dude?" David asks. "When have we ever 'made plans'? Our default setting is 'at Griffin's house,' where else would we be?"

"I don't know," I mumble. "We did movie night last night, I figured you'd want a night off from my house."

David shakes his head, muttering something under his breath—probably something rude as hell—as he dives back into his food. Jack's attention hasn't wavered for a second, and I'm actively avoiding making eye contact. After the look he gave me the first time Eleanor came over, I don't think I want him paying any more attention to me than he has to.

"Are you going to finish your food or just keep staring at me?"

I'm trying to keep my tone casual, playful even, but he's always been annoyingly perceptive and I don't think I'm getting out of this one that easy.

"Why are you making sure? Is there a reason we *shouldn't* come over tonight?"

This gets David's full attention again, and now I'm looking around the food truck park like it's the damn Louvre to avoid this conversation.

"Yeah Griffin, *isssss* there a reason?"

David draws out his question in a mocking tone, which is annoying because I know he doesn't even know what he's mocking me about yet, he just knows Jack is honing in on something.

"No dude, chill," I mumble irritatedly. "Eleanor was just asking if there was a plan for tonight or if it was boys only, and I was figuring out what to tell her."

Jack's eyes narrow even further, and David gives me a confused look as he checks his phone.

"What are you talking about? She didn't ask what the plan was, she hasn't said anything in the group chat since Wednesday," David says, obviously bewildered by this whole conversation.

I can see the exact moment the puzzle pieces click together in his little pea brain, and I know exactly what's coming. I drop my head into my hands with a groan as David lets out a *very* dramatic gasp.

"Now wait a damn minute! Have you guys been texting outside of the group chat?"

I look over to Jack, silently begging for a lifeline. He raises his eyebrows and crosses his arms, looking at me expectantly.

I guess I'm on my own here.

"Just sometimes," I say with a shrug. "She came over that one Friday when you were both busy. It's not a big deal. "

David gasps again, and even Jack's stoic expression turns into genuine shock. "Funny how you conveniently forgot to mention that for, I don't know, the last month," Jack says, looking amused.

"Hang on," David yells, his tone turning accusatory. "Have you hung out without us more than once?"

I inhale slowly and deeply, trying to buy some time. I knew I'd have to fess up eventually, but I didn't think it would be today.

"Yeah, we have," I begrudgingly admit. "A few times actually. Mostly on Sundays when you have family dinner and Jack has his weird routine—recharging his robot batteries so he can be a human the upcoming week or whatever it is he calls it," I reply, desperately trying to get the conversation off me.

"It's called being an introvert, jackass," Jack says coolly. "I need at least one day a week to recharge my social battery after dealing with you morons the other six."

"Hey, we're not that bad!" I exclaim in offense.

"I am," David says with a shrug.

"Thank you, David," Jack says with a satisfied nod. "Now back to the issue at hand."

"It's not a big deal," I repeat even though my brain feels like it's trying to stage an escape through my ears.

I'm losing the battle of keeping my voice level. I'm frustrated enough trying to figure out what's happening between me and Eleanor on my own—I'm going to snap if they hound me about it.

"I'll put the plans for tonight in the group chat. Can we get out of here now? I would like to end this interrogation and go take a shower."

I storm to the car, clambering into the backseat and slamming the door in a way that makes it very clear I am done with this discussion.

It doesn't take long for Jack and David to find something else to yap about, leaving me alone with the doom spiral occupying most of my mind these days.

This is turning into an actual nightmare. At first Eleanor was more of a fun challenge, but now that we're settling into a real friendship, there's a sinking feeling in my gut that gets heavier every time we hang out.

This stupid bet is looming over me. I know that David doesn't see Eleanor as just a bet anymore either. If anything, he's more attached to her than I am. I have never seen him go out of his way for anyone, but he fusses over her the way my mom doted on my baby niece when she was born.

But there's a nagging feeling that this could still blow up in my face.

I need to find a way to tell her about it that doesn't make us all look like giant assholes. Or make Jack and David swear that we'll take it to the grave.

Every time I think I've worked up the courage to come clean, something stops me. Either we're having too much fun to ruin it, or the moment's too deep to drop a bomb like that. At least, that's what I tell myself.

Or maybe I'm just chickenshit, and I'm scared of losing our friendship.

Or losing something more, I muse, staring out the window of Jack's Jeep on the drive back to my house. Because if I'm being totally honest–I don't know if having *just* a friendship with Eleanor is going to be enough for me.

It catches me off guard at the most random times–we'll be sitting in the hammock in her backyard, and I'll nearly reach up to tuck a lock behind her ear when the wind tousles her golden cascade of hair.

Golden cascade? Since when do I think poetic shit like that?

I wake up and look forward to seeing her. I make up excuses to text her throughout the day–*outside of the group chat,* which I guess is a cardinal sin. I lie in bed at night thinking about the way tears run down her face when she laughs hard enough–the way she harmonizes with songs in the car, the way she's already planning her sixteenth birthday even though it's six months away, and a thousand other moments that draw me in like a magnet.

Jesus, Griffin, dial back the soliloquies.

Or how I swear that sometimes she looks at me in a way that makes me think maybe she spends a lot of time thinking about me too.

Jack parks in front of my house, him and David continuing an argument I haven't heard a word of as we walk inside. I head upstairs to shower, and I stand under the showerhead with my face buried in my hands, wondering how I can keep from screwing this up until the water runs cold.

Chapter 9

Ellie

May, Age 15

I'm staring up at the sky, trying to find shapes in the clouds, when Griffin flops down next to me on the hammock, nearly tipping us both backwards. "I swear to God if you knock me out of this thing I'm never inviting you over again, Griffin."

He doesn't say anything in reply, but his large fist suddenly obscures my view, so close to my face it makes me go cross-eyed when I try to focus on it. Smacking his hand away, I push myself up onto my elbows so I can face him, and find a thousand-watt smile lighting up his face.

My body may not have flipped over a few moments ago, but my heart sure is now.

"What?"

He still doesn't answer, but holds his fist up again at a more reasonable distance, and I see a singular sunflower held in his grasp. "Got you this," he says, grinning even wider.

I can't decide where to focus– the flower, or the smile.

"Would have picked you a bluebonnet, but that's illegal."

I have no idea how to respond, so I blurt out, "No it's not, that's actually a common misconception." My curiosity outweighs my fear of being perceived, so I ask him, "Why?"

"Because it reminded me of you. I wanted you to have it."

I take it from him slowly, dropping my gaze to the petals as I twirl it softly between my fingers. I should be used to it by now, but every time he does something so simple yet so sweet, it knocks the wind out of me.

Shoving those feelings down, I ask, "Why does it remind you of me?"

He shrugs. "It's bright like you." He lies back, putting his hands behind head, his legs long enough that he can stretch them out and still have the heels of his boots dug into the ground.

"And you turn your face up to the sun for a few seconds every time we step outside, without fail," he says matter-of-factly. In a much quieter voice, he adds, "And, it's the prettiest thing I've seen all day. Well, besides you."

He jolts slightly, a surprised look on his face, like he *also* wasn't expecting the words to come out.

My heart doesn't just flip this time, it soars.

***

"You're quiet today."

Abby points it out in a way that leaves it up to me to choose whether to respond, and I love her for it. She knows that sometimes I don't want to talk about things, I just want her to know that there is a *thing*, and sit with me in silence while I work through it.

But I do want to talk about my *thing* today though–and that *thing* is Griffin Hart.

With summer break rapidly approaching, two things are happening. One, Abby and I have resumed our summer tradition of eating pickle flavored sno-cones by Larkspur Lake (which isn't really a lake, but a hole the mayor decided to dig in the 70s to give the town a "water feature").

Two, I need to figure out what to do about Griffin. Or rather, what to do about my feelings for him. Whatever it is I'm even feeling. My chest tightens as I replay the last few weeks on a loop in my head. We've been spending a lot of time together recently–not only with Jack and David, but just the two of us.

I don't even know if they know we've been doing that. I certainly haven't told them. I can't imagine David would be happy about it. That boy has the most severe case of FOMO known to man. I think Jack might already have his suspicions that something's going on, and him asking questions would be worse than any tantrum David might throw about being left out.

Plus, I wouldn't know how to answer any questions he has about my feelings for Griffin. All I know is I'm feeling a lot more than friendship these days, and it scares the hell out of me.

"Yeah," I say, taking a bite of sno-cone to give myself time before I elaborate. "I've been thinking a lot about Griffin."

Abby and I have been friends for so long that it feels like we've talked about everything under the sun—so why does it feel so weird to talk to her about this?

Probably because we never talk about boys. We seem to somehow have managed to skip over that part of girlhood. I've never really done the whole "crush" thing. I'm an only child, fiercely independent by default. I've also never slowed down long enough to have time to develop a crush. My life has always felt so full of love and adventure that I never bothered to consider adding something else.

And there's always that thought lurking in the depths of my brain telling me to get as far away from Larkspur as I can, to see the world. I've never had any intentions of tying myself to this town—or to anyone in it.

That is until a certain cowboy showed up and made himself at home in my perfectly curated routine.

And in my heart.

"Okay," she replies slowly. "Say more words, please."

"Ugh this is so weird to talk to you about."

She looks offended by this, and I can hear the protest coming before she even opens her mouth.

"Not because I don't want to talk to you, my sweet ginger angel," I say soothingly. "But we've never really talked about this stuff."

"Well you've never brought it up before," she says, pointing her spoon at me in accusation.

"Well there's been nothing to bring up! And you've been essentially betrothed to Aaron since birth, so we never need to talk about *your* love life. Even your stupid names match perfectly."

She shrugs simply–she knows I'm not wrong. In kindergarten, Abby befriended the boy who lives three houses down from her, Aaron, and decided then and there that he'd do just fine for the rest of her life. Pragmatic and self-assured even at age five, she approached him on the playground and declared they'd be getting married someday. They negotiated terms (as well as any five year olds can), shook hands, and Aaron has looked at her like she hung the moon ever since.

I don't know if he ever actually asked her to be his girlfriend once we got to dating age, now that I think about it. Everyone just accepts Abby and Aaron as fact the way you accept the sky is blue, or that the sun rises in the east. It's borderline scientific.

"Okay, well now's as good a time as any to start talking about it," she continues. "Again I say–say more words."

Taking a deep breath, I begin to word-vomit all of the thoughts that have been stuck in my brain for the last few weeks. Griffin has caught me completely off guard. He's been everything from annoying to infuriating to charming, and so much in between. Every moment I spend with him I learn more, and every new thing I learn makes me hungry for anything he's willing to give me.

He's got to be the most steadfast, confident, complicated boy I've ever encountered. There are moments where he's every bit of a teenage boy–crass jokes and hyperactivity wrapped in a knack for being something like a Tasmanian devil when he, Jack and David get together.

Then there are moments when it's just us, and I get glimpses of exactly the kind of man he's going to grow up to be. He's kind, and consistent, and dependable, constantly surprising me with the way he listens to me so intently–and even more so with the way he actually remembers what I say.

When I say I like a song, he's got it queued up the next time I get in his car. He remembered my grandmother's birthday, and brought her a bouquet of every flower I've ever mentioned growing with her.

It's like he has a special Ellie box in his brain where he stores every detail about me that I give to him. And he looks at me with such intensity sometimes that I could melt–*or maybe I could shine.*

"So basically I have no idea what I'm feeling, and I have no idea what to say to him, or if I should say anything at all," I conclude at the end of what had to be a twenty minute monologue.

Staring out at the lake thoughtfully, Abby finally says, "With every ounce of peace and love, that's bullshit."

My jaw drops. "What do you mean that's bullshit?"

Turning squarely to face me, she launches into a monologue of her own. "I mean exactly what I said–that's bullshit. You know exactly how you feel, you're just scared to admit it, because for once this is something that you can't control."

She pauses, tilting her head in thought. "You like him, and you're pretty sure he likes you. And that's scarier than him *not* liking you."

I hate it when she's all insightful.

As much as I hate to admit it, this isn't the first time I've been called a control freak. Or the second. Or the tenth. I like fun and whimsy and spontaneity–when I know exactly how it'll turn out.

What's wrong with a girl wanting a guaranteed happy ending?

"Ellie, that boy has liked you since the second he laid eyes on you," she says in a much gentler voice. "I know it, Jack knows it, Griffin knows it–and I think you know it too, but admitting it makes it real."

"So what do I do, Abby?" I can't keep the desperation out of my voice. Probably because I am desperate.

"You find a way to tell him. Or show him enough that he tells you first."

She says it like it's simple. It doesn't feel like anything about this is simple.

When did life get so complicated?

I don't respond, and she doesn't press me on it. She knows that I know she's right. She knows I'll figure it out in my own way. And I will figure it out. Because I want every bit of Griffin I can get—even if I have to risk getting my heart broken in the process.

Chapter 10

Ellie

October, Age 28

"Alright everyone, let's get started, we're already running behind!"

Our former student-body president, Tori, brings the room to attention, twenty minutes after the meeting was *technically* supposed to start. In literally everyone's defense, there's a lot to say when it's been ten years since you've seen each other, and what even is there to run behind on?

Even I, dragged here against my will, metaphorically kicking and screaming, couldn't help the joy that swelled in my chest when I saw all the familiar faces. I've spent so many years trying to block out Larkspur for the sake of Griffin that I guess I must have blocked out everyone else too.

"I wouldn't be surprised if she brought her gavel with her," the guy next to me mutters out of the corner of his mouth. I recognize him, but we never had any classes together and I've been frantically trying to remember his name.

Thankfully, the high school football star turned realtor was perfectly content with my, "Oh my God, hey...you!" and I didn't have to experience the horror of telling him I forgot.

I snort, then quickly try to cover it with a cough when Tori glares at me. She was the peppiest *and* scariest tyrant the LHS student council has ever or will ever encounter.

"Now that we're all focused," she says with a pointed look, the football star's shoulders shaking with suppressed laughter, "I think the most important items on the agenda today are theme and location. Any suggestions?"

"Where are they now?"

"Space themed? Like, Blast From The Past or something?"

"Larkspur Legends?"

After twenty-ish theme suggestions, each progressively worse than the last, we decide to table that conversation for a later date.

"Okay, I see we need to do a little thinking," Tori says with a tone of condescension. "Our resident party planner can't exactly plan a party without a theme," she says, beaming in my direction.

Not a party planner, thanks though.

"How about some venue suggestions?"

"We could do the school gym," the football player suggests.

"Ew no," Abby interjects. "I don't want to spend an evening in a room that smells like gym socks and stale popcorn. What about a restaurant of some sort? Maybe the hibachi place?"

"I don't think that would work either," Sophia, our yearbook editor, says cautiously. She's one of the sweetest souls in the world, and I'm shocked she had it in her to be disagreeable, even on a miniscule level.

"I agree," Tori says. "I think we want more interaction, and if everyone is sitting, you're stuck with whoever is next to you."

"God, imagine being stuck next to Brandon," Tori says, shivering at just the thought of Larkspur's very own stereotypical sketchy, weirdo kid. He was a total creep back then, but now he makes "Dazed and Confused" Matthew McConaughey look like a saint.

"What about the old barn?" Sophia asks. "It got renovated recently. My cousin had her wedding there."

"That's perfect actually!" Tori exclaims, lighting up with relief that we actually made a decision today. "I'll reach out to them to book it, do you think we're still aiming for November 23rd?"

I shoot Abby a sharp look–she conveniently left out that the reunion is scheduled for my 29th birthday.

Of course it is. If there's one thing Larkspur High is good at, it's finding a way to make my birthday wildly uncomfortable.

"It's decided then," Tori squeals, as murmured voices of agreement overlap. "Let's call it for today. Everyone try to think of a theme suggestion before Saturday, and I think we should focus on food and drinks then, as well. Remember, we only have four weeks to pull this off, people! Let's do it!"

Standing up and clapping her hands once, she dismisses us. With a checklist in place for our next meeting, we say our "so good to see yous" and "we should catch up soons" before heading back to the car.

"See, not so painful was it?" Abby asks, in a told-you-so tone. "Well, except for Tori, that neurotic bitch. Some things never change."

"She's reliving her glory days. If she really did peak in high school, we should let her have this," I say, unable to keep the smile off my face. "But no, it wasn't. Not so painful at all."

As she backs out of the spot, my eyes wander to the left side of the steps that lead to the front entrance. An innocuous spot for any average passer-by, but one that holds a rolodex of memories for me–good, bad, and ugly.

"Eleanor, I swear it was never about that for me."

"Griffin Hart, I will never fucking forgive you for this."

Shaking the memory from my head, I stare straight ahead as we head to the diner, determined to recreate a classic Friday night dinner, willing myself to think about anything but that.

Chapter 11

Griffin

May, Age 16

My stomach has been in knots since that day at The Park. Every day that I don't deal with this–every day I don't tell Eleanor how I feel–leaves more room for potential disaster.

And I love them, I really do, but if Jack and David are involved (*mostly David*), it's a *guaranteed* disaster.

I told myself this morning that I would suck it up and tell the guys how I feel about Eleanor before the last week of school. And I'm still technically following through, even if I did wait to send that text until the last Sunday of the school year.

When neither of them reply, I send another text.

Griffin: I know Sundays are sacred

Griffin: I wouldn't ask if it wasn't important

Jack: ...I guess. I can be there in 20.

Griffin: Thanks man

Griffin: David?

Still no response from him. I check the clock and see that it's close to 8:30 PM, so I know his family dinner is over.

Griffin: David, don't be annoying

Griffin: Where the hell are you?

Griffin: Hello??????

Jack: Do you still want me to come over?

One is better than none, I guess.

Griffin: Yeah man that'd be great thanks

> **Griffin:** David, fuck you

If that doesn't get a response of out him, nothing's going to. I don't have time to figure out what he's up to–me and Jack can fill him in tomorrow at lunch.

Twenty minutes later, Jack is sitting on the couch, staring at me while he waits for me to start talking.

"What the hell do you think David is doing?" I mutter, stalling for time.

At this, Jack lets out an impatient sigh, pinching the bridge of his nose.

"Cut the shit Griffin, I didn't disturb my Sunday ritual for you to beat around the bush."

"You and your Goddamn ritual need to be studied in a lab, there's no way you're an actual sixteen year old boy, you've gotta be some kind of social experiment."

All this gets me is a stern glare. Suddenly I feel like I'm in trouble at school. I still don't say anything, picking at the callouses on my hands to avoid looking him in the eye.

"Alright then, I'm leaving."

My stomach lurches with panic as he pulls out his keys and stands to go.

"Wait, no, dude don't–"

Ignoring my protests, he starts heading upstairs.

This fucker is actually going to leave.

"Alright, ALRIGHT–I need to talk to you about Eleanor," I say dejectedly. I've stalled til the last possible moment, and now there's no avoiding it.

Jack whips around with a concerned look on his face and quickly retakes his seat.

"Ellie? Is she okay?"

"She's fine, it's nothing like that," I say slowly.

He already looks annoyed again, so I quickly blurt out, "IthinkIlikeherandweneedtocalloffthebet."

Jack looks confused. Then surprised. Then smug as hell.

"I'm sorry, I didn't quite catch that, could you repeat it?"

"Don't be a jackass." I hurl a pillow at him but he knocks it away as easily as you'd swat a fly. Completely unbothered.

He tries his best to look genuinely confused, but he fails miserably at masking the amusement in his eyes.

"I think I like her, and we–"

"You *think?*"

Oh, so he's going to be annoying about it.

"Fine, I *know* that I like her. And we–"

"Need to call off the bet, yeah I got that part. I just wanted to hear you say it loud and clear."

Saying it out loud makes it feel way more real. One part of me is relieved to finally get it out there–but the other part of me is scared to death because now I have to do something about it.

"Okay, say more words."

"*Say more words?*" I ask, "What the hell is that?"

"Oh, I guess it's something I picked up from Abby–she says it to Ellie all the time."

I didn't know he was spending enough time with Ellie and Abby to pick up the phrases they use.

Filing that information away for later, I steel myself to bare my feelings.

This is so awkward.

"I mean, you know some part of me liked her from the first day we met."

He nods and gestures impatiently for me to continue.

"I think it started for me the first night she hung out with us. Having her here just felt right, and when she took my spot, I thought to myself that I'd give up my seat for this girl every time if she wanted it."

"That's very chivalrous of you, Griffin."

Jack isn't even trying to hide his amusement anymore, and I know I'll be getting a shit ton of "I knew it!"s from him for the rest of my life. There's no unringing this bell I guess.

"Shut up man, this is weird enough to talk about without you giving me shit," I huff out irritatedly.

He mimes zipping his lips and folds his hands in his lap, like he's trying to be the most attentive student in Sunday School.

"It really changed when we started hanging out just the two of us, obviously. Everything I learn about her makes me want to know more. She's...she's something else, man." Heat creeps up my neck to my face and I know I'm blushing, but honestly, I don't care. "She's like...okay, you know when we get the first *real* day of fall, and you didn't realize how hot and miserable it was until the cool air hits your face for the first time, and you feel like you're not just trying to survive the heat anymore? That's her. She's a Goddamn breath of fresh air, a solution to a problem I didn't know I had, someone that makes me want to grow up and try to be worthy of someone like her. She's...she's everything."

"Damn, dude. When did you get so good with words?"

I run my hand down my face in exasperation.

"This is serious, Jack. We either need to come clean about this bet to her, or we need to swear to take it to the grave."

His face quickly changes from smug to serious. He was against this bet from the beginning, and part of me thinks he's going to leave me to deal with it on my own.

"Listen man, I know you didn't want anything to do with this–"

"Yeah but I let it happen. And I think you're probably right," he muses. "We've got to tell her. Maybe we should sit down with her, all three of us."

" I think that's our only shot–hopefully with all of us copping to it and apologizing, she'll forgive us and realize that we all want to keep her around."

"And then you can ask her out."

I can't help but smile at the possibility of me and Eleanor turning into something more. But my smile quickly fades when I think about her reaction. There's no guarantee she'll forgive us.

"And then *yes*, ideally I can ask her out. If she doesn't hate me."

We sit in silence for a moment–he's probably just as scared of Eleanor cutting him off as I am. There's something really endearing in their friendship, like they're both the sibling the other always wanted.

"We need to sit down with David like, yesterday," Jack says sharply. "I don't trust him not to make an ass of himself and say something before we've got a game plan."

I couldn't agree more–that's why it's so damn frustrating that he's MIA tonight. Anxiety suddenly grips me so hard that I feel like I can't breathe.

"Hey man, it's going to be okay," Jack says reassuringly. "I knew something was up that time I drove her home and you slammed the door in my face." Pointing at me, he adds, "Which was rude as hell by the way."

I roll my eyes, then drop my head into my hands. I usually trust Jack immediately when he says something's going to be okay, but I can't shake the sinking feeling I have about this.

"It doesn't take a rocket scientist to see that you guys would be great together. And you obviously both have feelings, but you've been playing the dumbest game of chicken in history."

He leans forward on the couch, looking more serious than he has all night. I know this is the part where he tells me what I have to do, and I don't know if I'm going to like it.

"You need to put your big boy pants on and tell her. The only person suffering because you don't know how to communicate is you."

Looking thoughtful, he adds, "And Ellie actually. You're wasting time that could be spent being happy because you're too scared to be honest. So figure it out and go be happy."

I nod my head–I don't think I can open my mouth right now without throwing up. Being an anxious barfer is the worst.

With the conversation clearly over, Jack once again reaches for his keys to leave, and I don't stop him this time.

Laying in bed that night, I stare at the ceiling and rehearse what I want to say to her over and over. I need to find a way to convince her that the bet was never meant to be mean, and that it's been over for a long time.

My sleep is fitful and peppered with nightmares about Eleanor walking away forever. Getting ready for school the next morning, there's a heavy feeling in the pit of my stomach. If I mess this up, it's not going to be a short-lived argument—I'm risking losing the best thing that's happened to me.

***

The only class me, Jack, and David all have together this year is seventh period–which doesn't give me a lot of time to intercept David before Eleanor shows up.

And apparently Larkspur does end-of-year finals in a block schedule, so today is the last day we'll have Spanish for the year.

Basically, I'm running out of time, and there is zero margin for error.

Of course it's my luck that Eleanor is already in class when I get there, and David shows up right before the bell rings.

Leaning over, David whispers, "Dudes, I gotta tell you what happened this weekend. My mom went ballistic, I haven't had my phone in days."

I swear I actually feel my blood run cold. He doesn't have a single inkling that we need to talk to him.

I need a backup plan.

I barely pay attention to the final, rushing through it as quickly as possible so I have more time to come up with a strategy. I've already got an A in the class, so even if I tank the final, it doesn't matter.

The same can't be said for my (*hopeful*) relationship with Eleanor. I'm getting more and more nervous about tanking something that *does* matter.

I decide that after class I'll ask her if we can hang out that night to talk. David and Jack can come over early, and we can come up with a plan then. I think that's the only way this is going to work.

When all the finals are turned in and the last bell rings, the whole class bolts like the room is on fire. Normally I'd feel that way after a final too, but I don't care about being one step closer to summer.

I care about being one step closer to Eleanor.

I hang back, slowly gathering my things– and to my extreme annoyance, Jack and David hang back too. I know we always leave together, but c'mon guys, read the room.

Eleanor has taken her time to gather her things too, which makes me wonder if she can sense that I want to talk to her. We seem to be in sync a lot recently, and my heart starts to pound–maybe it's a sign?

"Uh, hey Eleanor, I was wondering if we could–"

Before I can finish my sentence she interrupts me.

"Actually, I had something I wanted to talk to you about," she says quickly, a determined look on her face.

I can feel Jack freeze, with David digging in his bag for something, completely oblivious to anything happening.

She lowers her voice and continues, "Listen, we've been spending a lot of time together lately. And, um, well..."

Her eyes on the ground, her hands nervously twisting the lace hem of her pale pink tank top.

God she looks pretty today.

She lets out a huff, steeling herself to say whatever it is she's agonizing over.

"Abby told me I should do it, so I'm just going to do it."

"Okay..." I say slowly. "Do what exactly?"

I've looked into them a thousand times, but when her sparkling blue eyes meet mine, my stomach swoops like I'm free-falling. It catches me off guard every time.

"Tell you how I feel."

All I can do is blink at her. It feels like my entire body has gone numb. Is this actually happening? Did I fall asleep during the final and land in the dream I've been having for weeks?

"And that is...?" I cautiously ask. I don't know if I'm ready to hear the answer.

"You've been an incredible friend."

Oof. Ouch. Yikes.

She scrunches her nose in what must be a colossal summoning of courage, then blurts out–

"But I think I want more. Well, I know I want more. And I think you might too, and I won't know until I ask, and I feel like we've been dancing around it, and I thought maybe I should take it into my own hands, so–" she rambles off at lightning speed.

"So here we are. I like you, Griffin Hart. Like, *like you* like you."

I've imagined, dreamed, *hoped* for this moment a thousand times over. Hearing her say those words is the brightest joy I've ever felt–like fireworks and lightning bugs and Christmas lights wrapped in the sun.

I stand there like an idiot, desperately trying to find the words to convey how much I *like her* like her back.

"This is a really bad time to decide to finally shut up," she says with a nervous laugh.

I manage to get my brain working again, stumbling over my words I'm so fucking excited to tell her how I feel. "Eleanor, I've wanted to–"

"Damn it bro, of course you got it done right at the last minute," David interrupts with a shout. "You better use my hundred bucks to take her somewhere nice."

My heart stops. My breathing stops. Time stops. Everything stops.

I didn't fall into a dream–I fell into my worst nightmare.

Jack punches David square in the chest, looking angrier than I've ever seen him. David's grin drops as he looks from me to Eleanor.

I quickly turn back to her, opening my mouth to try and explain before it goes any further. But I can't get a word out before she slowly asks,

"What is he talking about Griffin?"

David tries to interject, but Jack silences him with a sharp look (and a hand over his mouth).

"Okay I know this is going to sound bad, and it was only a joke for like five minutes before we actually got to know you, but I swear..."

My sentence trails off, and my chest cracks open as her face shifts from confusion to hurt.

"I was a joke to you?"

"No, not a joke, Eleanor," I say desperately. "You hated me so much, and David made this stupid bet that he'd give me twenty bucks if I could get you to be my friend–"

"But he said a hundred. What changed it from twenty to a hundred?"

I've never felt desperation like this in my life. How can I make her understand that it was never actually a bet to me?

"Eleanor, I swear it was never about that for me, it just gave me an excuse to–"

"Why did it change, Griffin?" she demands in a cold, firm voice that I've never heard from her.

I have no choice but to tell the truth, even though it's the last thing I want to do right now.

"Because you want more than friendship now."

This is the most awful scenario I could have imagined. I knew David might do something stupid, but I didn't expect it to go so wrong so fast.

"So I was a bet to you. You've all lied to me from the very beginning."

I can see her lip trembling as she looks at each of us in turn. Jack's pained face shows more emotion than I thought was possible from my stoic best friend, and it makes me feel ten times worse.

David looks horrified, and even though I know he didn't mean to do it, anger burns in my chest and at this exact moment, I don't care if I ever see my oldest friend again.

They both stammer out protests, please, explanations, but she lifts her hand to cut them off and they fall silent immediately.

Her attention focuses back on me, and the tears in her eyes nearly send me to my knees. This beautiful ray of sunshine looks absolutely crushed, and it's all my fault.

"You're not who I thought you were." Her voice breaks, and so does my heart.

In an instant, the hurt disappears from her face and is replaced with a cold, impassive look.

"Well, I hope you boys have fun celebrating your triumph."

"No, Ellie, wait–"

"I swear it's not–"

"Please believe me–"

Without another word, she turns on her heel and starts walking out of the classroom. I look at the clock, and only five minutes have passed since class ended. Is that really how fast your life can be over?

We rush after her, shouting apologies and explanations, and promises that everything we've said and done was real and not just some bet, but she keeps walking without a backwards glance.

When we exit the front doors of the school, we stop in our tracks when she abruptly turns to face us.

"I never want to see you guys again. Don't call, don't text, don't *anything*."

"Eleanor, please." This time it's my voice that breaks.

"Griffin Hart, I will never fucking forgive you for this."

I think it would have hurt less if she hit me with a tire iron. I've never heard her curse like that–it sounds wrong coming out of the same mouth that sings in the car and rants about movie candy.

"And you," she aims specifically at Jack. "I can almost believe this from them, but not from you."

Jack looks nearly as heartbroken as I feel. I've never seen him open up to anyone besides me and David, and the thought of ruining one of his few safe friendships is more than I can stomach.

With one final look at each of us, she whispers, "Please, just leave me alone."

All I can do is watch desperately as the girl of my dreams walks away from me.

Spinning around to face David, I spit out, "What the fuck is your problem dude?"

"Griffin I swear, I didn't think–"

"No, you fucking didn't," I yell angrily. I'm being unfair, and I know it. But I don't care.

"You know what David, I don't want to hear from you either."

"Take a deep breath, man," Jack says, trying his best to calm me down.

"Don't give me that bullshit, Jack," I fire back. "I'm done."

Before they can say another word, I storm to my car. They can find their own damn ride.

I peel out of the parking lot, with no intention of going home. I have no idea where I'm going to go, but I am painfully aware that wherever it is, I'm going alone.

I don't know what's going to happen, but I do know one thing–this is without a doubt, the worst fucking day of my life.

Chapter 12

Ellie

July, Age 15

I might be the first teenager to ever say this, but I can't wait for summer to be over.

I'm spending today the way I've spent the entire first month of break—alone.

Hugging my knees to my chest, I look out at the still surface of Larkspur Lake from the bench I usually occupy with Abby.

I've been avoiding her—and everyone else—since the nuclear fallout that occurred the last week of school. I've been stuck in an endless loop of emotions I don't know how to untangle.

First there's the anger, so visceral sometimes that I can't stop shaking. Then comes the confusion, which always ends with me taking Tylenol to counteract the massive headache that comes when I try to pinpoint how I missed what they were doing.

But the sadness, the loneliness, the absolute *misery* is debilitating. Some days I can't find the energy to drag myself out of bed, so I tell my parents I'm just taking a day to stay home and read.

I haven't cracked a single book open—but I could draw every crack on my ceiling from memory now.

I haven't told Abby. I haven't told my mom either. Every Friday at the diner, I tell Abby to go ahead, that Jack is running late but he's on his way. Then I walk down to the lake park entrance, and sit in silence until it starts to get dark, when I make my way over to the coffee shop in my neighborhood.

I sit there until closing, and by the time I walk back home I know that my parents are asleep, and this is a believable hour for me to come home on a Friday night during summer.

I don't know why I haven't told them—they're usually the first two people I tell about anything and everything. But something about this feeling is so foreign, and so lonely, that I wouldn't know how to begin to describe it. And it feels more daunting trying to explain something I know they won't understand.

So I sit here, alone, again. I can feel myself putting up walls, collapsing into myself, but I can't stop it. All I do is replay that scene over and over in my mind until silent tears run familiar tracks down my face.

I sit, with no one but the birds playing in the water to keep me company, and hope that no one stumbles across me and asks how I'm doing.

I think if someone asked me that question at precisely the wrong moment, I would fall apart and never be able to put myself back together.

The worst part of everything isn't the anger or the betrayal. It's how much I *miss* him. I can control the rage, and I'm no stranger to melancholy, but missing him is the part that makes me feel like a belt is tightening around my chest and I can't do anything to get it off.

Unfolding my arms and stretching my stiff limbs, I slowly stand up, peeling the back of my thighs off the bench they adhered to in the summer heat. No plan for the rest of my day—or for anything, really. It's just me and my thoughts on my walk home.

***

Sitting in my reading chair, staring out my bedroom window, I'm feeling very 'Bella in New Moon' right now. I always thought she was being melodramatic, but I get it now.

I don't bother even looking at my screen when my phone rings once, then twice, then a third time. When it dings again with a text, I finally check it in case Abby needs something. My heart drops into my stomach when I see that it's from Jack, not Abby.

At first I consider just deleting the text without reading it, but morbid curiosity gets the better of me.

Jack: Ellie, can we please talk?

What even is there to say? I can't imagine any sort of explanation or apology that would make things even fractionally better.

Ellie: No.

Tossing my phone over my shoulder onto my bed I go back to watching the blue jays at the feeder in the backyard.

A barrage of non-stop notifications eventually irritates me enough to get out of my chair. Snatching my phone off my bed, I flop down on my stomach and read the five additional texts that just came through.

Jack: Please Ellie

Jack: Come to lunch with me

Jack: Just give me an hour

Jack: I won't even bring him up, I just want to apologize

Jack: I miss you

It's the last text that gets me. I might miss Jack the most–holding a grudge against him has taken the most effort since he was the least involved in the whole debacle. Letting my loneliness get the better of me, and against my better judgment, I finally reply.

> **Ellie: Fine. I'll meet you at The Park.**

> **Jack: Can I pick you up?**

I consider it for a moment, but I don't want to risk any chance of being held hostage if I decide I don't actually want to hear what he has to say.

> **Ellie: No. I'll meet you there in 20.**

I change into a t-shirt and shorts that I *haven't* been wearing for three days straight, and head downstairs to ask my dad if he'll give me a ride.

Twenty minutes later, I see Jack's truck in the parking lot before I see him. Before I get out of the car, my dad gives my hand a squeeze. "I'm happy to see you out of your cave, Ellie Bellie. I was starting to get a little worried."

I attempt a reassuring smile and respond, "I'm okay dad, just feeling a little more introverted this summer. No need to worry."

With a quick kiss on his cheek, I tell him I'll call when I'm ready to be picked up. Then, with knots in my stomach, I nervously walk deeper into the park to find Jack.

I spot him at a picnic table in front of the grilled cheese truck, and he looks up at me with a tentative smile and a wave.

"Thanks for coming," he says, a little timidly.

Good, he should be nervous.

I nod, taking a seat on the bench across from him, focusing on the wood grain of the table so I don't have to look at him. I'm afraid I'll start crying if I do. When he doesn't say anything else, I try to mask my sadness with anger as I look up and demand, "Talk."

"I don't even know where to begin, Ellie. I'm sorrier than you could imagine. If I thought they were actually going to follow through on that stupid bet I would have kicked their asses."

Now my anger is real. "So you did know about it the whole time then."

It's his turn to stare down at the table, looking truly ashamed.

Again, good.

"I did," he admits quietly. "I had no idea it'd go that far. I know they're idiots, but I didn't think David was taking it seriously anymore. Not when things changed between you and Griffin. "

Even the brief mention of Griffin makes me freeze, a muscle in my jaw twitching as I clench my teeth.

When I don't reply, he continues on, "I don't ever expect you to forgive Gr–us. I know you told us to fuck off, but I couldn't take it anymore."

My rage falters briefly when my typically composed deadpan friend (*ex-friend?*) looks up at me with tears in his eyes.

"You're the best friend I've ever had," he says in a whisper so low I can barely hear it over the noise of the trucks and lunch-goers. "I miss you all the time. These have been the most miserable few weeks of my life–I thought we'd be having fun all summer long, but now it's just me and my granny watching Jeopardy and making casseroles."

I roll my eyes and look away. *He can't be serious.*

"Oh stop it, I'm sure you guys have gone back to your normal unholy trinity bullshit."

"No, we haven't," he counters earnestly. "I haven't seen either of them. I've been just as pissed at them as you have."

My eyebrows skyrocket at the audacity of that statement.

"Okay not *as* pissed, but I am furious. They fucked up, and now everyone is suffering."

I meet his eyes again, and the walls I've put up crumble a bit at the look on his face. He's got hollow circles under his eyes, and it looks like he hasn't gotten a haircut since school let out. He's looking much less "Kennedy" and much more "Tim Burton."

"I miss you too, Jack," I say gently, deciding to extend an olive branch. "I think we can probably be friends."

His shoulders drop with relief as he runs a hand down his face.

"But I have conditions."

"Anything you want, Ellie." I fight the smile trying to form on my face. He sounds so excited, and he suddenly looks 5 years younger, but I can't let him off the hook that easily. Not just yet, anyway.

"I don't want to hear about them at all. I don't care how sorry they are, or how much they miss me."

Yes I do.

"And I don't want them to know that we're hanging out. I swear to God if you try to ambush me–"

"I won't, I promise," he says firmly. "Like I said, I haven't seen them either. I just want my friend back."

It's so terrifying to consider letting even one of them back in my life that I almost consider taking it all back, but his puppy dog eyes, so sad and heartfelt, eliminate the last of my defenses.

"Okay," I say with a genuine smile.

"Okay," he says back, with a bigger grin than I've ever seen from him. "How have you been?"

My smile immediately drops, and his eyes go wide with panic.

"That was a stupid question, forget I asked," he stammers hurriedly.

"No, it's okay," I say with a wave of my hand. "It's been hard. I've been really lonely."

It hits me how true those words are as I say them out loud. I don't think I've ever been lonely in my whole life–I've always had Abby, or my parents, or any of the other classmates I made friends with throughout the years.

Even though I know it's objectively not true, this is the first time that I've ever felt like I've got no one. A hot pressure builds behind my eyes and I'm horrified to realize that if I don't stop talking, I'm going to cry. Shoving those feelings down as far as they'll go, I quickly change the subject.

"Anyway, I don't really have anything interesting to share. What's been going on with you?"

We sit there and catch up for what must be hours, because my dad calls to ask whether I've been kidnapped or simply decided to run away from home.

With a laugh, I let him know I'm fine and that Jack will give me a ride home. His face lights up when he hears that, and a tiny ray of light breaks through the cloudy gloom in my heart.

It feels wonderfully familiar to be back in Jack's passenger seat as we take the long way home. I look out the window to hide my smile—I don't want him to know that I've clocked the route he chose. He's not the only one savoring the few extra minutes together.

When we reach my house, he gets out to give me a hug—it's full of regret, relief, and love all at once. As I walk up the path to my front door, I'm on the verge of tears again, but this time, they're happy ones.

Chapter 13

Griffin

July, Age 16

"Griffin, you need to get out of the house."

I roll over to face my dad, who's standing in my bedroom doorway with a severe look on his face that tells me he means business.

"What?"

"I mean it, son. You haven't left this room all summer. Get your ass up and go get some fresh air." His face softens, and he continues in a gentler tone, "Now listen here, I've been giving you your privacy, but don't think I haven't noticed how quiet the house has been."

I stare at him blankly, waiting for him to make his point so I can get back to staring at nothing.

"I don't know what's going on, but I do know that you boys have been friends long enough to figure it out. You need to apologize, or forgive—or both, I don't know the story here."

For a second I think he might let me off the hook about Eleanor, but no such luck.

"I would also strongly recommend you patch things up with that young lady," he says, pointing his finger at me. "She's a darling, and you need to fix whatever you did."

"What makes you think I'm the one who did something?"

Leaning against the door frame, he crosses his arms with a raise of his brows, and he's obviously right, so I just nod.

"Good boy," he says. Pushing off the door frame, he walks over to my bed and ruffles my hair like he used to do when I was small.

I feel pretty small right now.

"You're a good man, Griff, and I–" he hesitates, clearing his throat. "I'm not good with the touchy-feely stuff, but I'm proud of you."

With a final pat on my shoulder, he walks out of my room, leaving me feeling even worse.

He shouldn't be proud of me. I have royally fucked everything up. I'm ignoring David's texts, Eleanor is ignoring mine, and Jack said he won't come over until I'm willing to talk about it.

I push myself up with a groan, and sit on the edge of my bed with my elbows on my knees.

I don't know if I'll ever be able to patch things up with Eleanor, but my dad's right–there's at least one thing I can fix.

***

I ring the doorbell and wait nervously on David's front porch. I don't know if I've ever rang the doorbell. I usually just let myself in with the key I've had for almost ten years.

"Griffin! Hi!"

David's mom, Victoria, looks at me with wide eyes, her mouth open in a surprised *O*.

"David didn't tell me you were back in town! How was your trip?"

My trip...?

She steps aside, and it hits me once I'm inside.

I guess I'm not the only one who's not talking about this.

"Um, yeah, it was great," I respond, trying to sound like I definitely know what she's talking about. "We got back a day early, I figured I'd just come over instead of calling."

"Well, it sure is good to see your face," she says warmly, patting my cheek. "David's upstairs in his room"

I head upstairs, my thoughts working overtime to figure out what exactly I should say here. And *how* I should say it–I viscerally cringe at the thought of another shouting match.

His door is open, but he's got his headphones on, laser focused on his computer. I knock on the door to get his attention, and when he looks up at me his laptop falls to the floor.

"Ah, shit," he curses under his breath, leaning over to pick it up and knocking everything off his bedside table in the process.

I let out a snort of laughter, and sit in the chair at his desk. Once he gets all his stuff back where it belongs, he looks up at me and I can hardly recognize him.

Shit, he looks terrified. Was I that bad?

I don't bother answering my own question–I know I was.

"Hey man," I say in a low voice. "How've you been?"

Still looking like he's scared I'm going to deck him, he swallows before answering, "Uh, okay I guess. I told my mom you were out of town, sorry if you had to explain that."

"Yeah, she mentioned that."

After a few beats of awkward silence, we both start at the same time."Listen man–"

"Bro I–"

He smiles at me sheepishly, and I gesture at him to go first.

"Dude, I'm so sorry. I don't know what's wrong with me."

In all our years of friendship, I've never heard him sound so dejected. I expected my anger to come back in full force when I saw him again, but instead it completely evaporates at the look of shame on his face.

It hits me how much I miss my friend, and I realize I don't even need the apology anymore.

"Hey, man, we all fuck up. Remember when I hit that baseball straight through your living room window and knocked over your grandma's ashes?"

He lets out a low chuckle. "And then my mom made us go to the church to confess our sins even though you aren't Catholic, and our priest told her it doesn't count if she forced us to be there."

All at once, everything feels normal again. It was a lot easier to be mad at David than at myself, but every ounce of animosity fades as we spend the next few hours catching up.

"So," he looks up at me, looking nervous again. "Have you talked to her?"

"Nope," I say with a heavy sigh. "I think Jack has, but he's not talking to me right now either."

His eyes widen. "Dude, why not?"

"He told me he wouldn't hang out with me unless I either made up with you or talked about my feelings," I say with a shrug. "Both options made me want to shove chopsticks through my eyes, so I've just been moping in my room."

"I'm glad you came over, Griffin," he says in an uncharacteristically serious tone. "This whole thing has been such a shitshow, I've felt like ass for weeks."

"Yeah, me too," I say, suddenly feeling exhausted by the weight of the whole ordeal. "I'm sorry I lost my shit on you."

"I'm sorry I messed things up for you with Ellie."

Understatement of the century, but there's no use in pointing that out.

Not knowing how to respond, I just nod my head in acknowledgement.

"Should we go to my house?" I offer up. "You'll have to call Jack though, he won't believe me if I'm the one who tells him we made up."

Breaking into a grin, he finally looks himself again.

"Let's go," he says, throwing the covers off the bed. "I'll tell him we're getting the band back together."

Jumping up with excitement, he knocks everything off his bedstand again.

We bolt down the stairs, laughing loudly and shouting our goodbyes to his mom as we hurdle out the front door.

Smiling to myself, I think, *Maybe this summer is still salvageable.*

But it disappears almost as fast as it came, because making up with Eleanor is going to be a hell of a lot harder than this was.

Chapter 14

Ellie

August, Age 15

The back half of summer has been infinitely happier than the front. Most of my time is spent with either Jack or Abby, and the time I had been reserving for rotting my room is now spent gardening with my grandmother, or at the farmer's market with Mom and Dad.

The suffocating loneliness I felt for weeks eases more and more every day. Sometimes I'll go a whole day without thinking about the reason I'm lonely in the first place.

It never goes away completely, though.

Once Jack and I finally made up, we started hanging out during the day, and I continued spending my nights wandering around alone with my thoughts, trying not to think about who he's with when he's not with me.

When he found out about my little nightly routine, he wigged out at a nuclear level. Despite my protests that this is Larkspur, not Gotham City, he insisted on switching the schedule so that we hung out at night instead.

I about rolled my eyes out of my head at his exasperation with me, but something about the way he was (*very loudly*) protective of me had me so choked up that I pretended to give him the silent treatment so he wouldn't hear the emotion in my voice.

If my parents have noticed a difference in my demeanor, they haven't said anything. To their knowledge I've stayed friends with Jack this whole time, so they're probably chalking it up to teenage mood swings.

July flew by, but once we hit August 1st, dread started creeping in. The start of the school year feels a lot closer on this side of the calendar, and I'm not ready to face Griffin again.

I've almost stopped being angry with David entirely–mostly because I realized that he's just a huge dumbass, not a malicious mastermind.

Maybe when I write my *"What I Did This Summer"* essay, I can focus on my realization that it's a lot easier to get over anger than heartbreak.

But I'll probably just talk about how I broke my personal record for number of pickle juice sno-cones consumed in one summer (*112*).

***

In what feels like the blink of an eye, I'm sitting across from Abby at the diner on the last Friday night of summer. School starts on Monday, and I couldn't be less ready if I tried.

Nothing will ever be as bad as it was in June, but I've felt myself getting more and more introspective this week. I had hoped that a final summer milkshake would put some pep back in my step, but all it's doing is making my stomach churn.

"So," Abby says suddenly, folding her arms on the table. "Are you going to tell me what happened?"

Bewildered, I ask her what on earth she's talking about.

"If I had a dollar for every time I've said *'Don't play dumb with me, Ellie Turner'* in this exact diner booth, my dad could cancel my college fund."

Her talents are wasted on journalism, she needs to pursue the stage.

"I mean it Ellie," she continues, unphased by my scoff. "I didn't push you on it because you straight up looked like a fragile baby bird for weeks, but eventually you need to tell me what happened."

Hurt flickers across her face briefly, and I'm sick with guilt about keeping her at arms length. We've always told each other everything, I didn't even consider that keeping this from her would hurt her feelings.

I shift uncomfortably in my side of the booth, sitting up straight and rolling my shoulders back as I brace myself to relive the nightmare.

She focuses intently on me as I share everything, from the first time Griffin and I hung out just the two of us, all the way through my dramatic declaration that I will never forgive him.

She doesn't interrupt me once as I pour out every stream of consciousness I've had since that day, but the look on her face when I finish is so alarming that even the waitress changes her mind and scurries away when she approaches the table to ask if we need anything.

"I can't believe you let me be nice to Jack all summer," she says through gritted teeth. "I could have focused my energy on ruining their lives."

"Abby, it's okay," I say in the same tone you might use to try and calm down a rabid dog. "Me and Jack have talked through it, and he apologized. We're okay now."

"Okay well he hasn't apologized to *me*," she huffs.

I burst out laughing.

"What on earth does he need to apologize to you for?"

Her sharp look silences my laughter immediately.

"Ellie, you might not have let me piece you back together, but I know when you're hurting," she says with a devastated look. "And when you hurt, I hurt."

She's right–it's always been that way. My whole life I've been called a sensitive soul, but Abby has always intellectualized her emotions. She only loses sight of logic when something has upset me, and when she does she takes on the entire weight of my sadness. And holds on to it for a lot longer than I do.

"I can talk to him," I offer reassuringly.

"No," she barks out fiercely. "I would like to have that conversation myself, thank you very much."

Note to self—warn Jack about a potentially lethal threat coming his way.

I can almost see the wheels in her head spinning as I brace myself for the next explosion.

"Ellie, you really should have told me at the beginning of summer. I could have had months to prepare myself," she says accusingly. "Now I only have two days to figure out how to *not* push them down the stairs the second I see them."

I love my best friend.

"That's not necessary, my sweet ginger angel," I coo at her.

The disgusted look on her face has me doubled over in laughter when the waitress finally works up the nerve to bring us our checks.

Abby pushes her check over to me, her face still scrunched up like a toddler throwing a tantrum.

"You're paying for me."

"What!? I'm the one whose heart got ripped into shreds," I yell indignantly.

A honk from the parking lot indicates that her mom is here to pick her up, and when I look out front, I see that Jack's truck is right behind her.

"Maybe so," she says, sliding out of the booth. "But if I'm going to catch murder charges on your behalf, the least you can do is buy me dinner."

I shake my head as she stalks out of the diner. I watch as she shoots an ugly look at Jack, turning her back to her dad's car so she can flip him the bird without Mr. Wheeler seeing.

Jack's head whips toward me, looking at me through the front windows with such a bewildered expression that I end up clutching my sides and wheezing with laughter all over again.

I have no idea what's going to happen on Monday. I don't know what's more ominous–the thought of Abby causing a scene by committing what the international courts would probably consider war crimes, or the thought of Griffin trying to find me, begging me to forgive him and give him another chance.

Or even worse–the thought that he might not try at all.

Chapter 15

Griffin

August, Age 16

School starts again tomorrow. The last day of summer is always, in my opinion, the worst day of the year. It's like the Sunday Scaries times a million.

But I'd gladly give up every school break if it meant I could work things out with Eleanor.

Today was pretty balmy for August in Texas (*90 degrees instead of 105*), so me and the guys decided to spend our last hours of freedom at the lake.

I thought getting outside would help clear my head–I was dead wrong. To anyone *not* walking around with metaphorical shattered glass in their chest, it would seem peaceful out here. All the "peace" is doing is widening the space for me to be alone with my thoughts.

We always come to the side of the lake where there's no path, since there's less foot traffic out this way. Plus we can watch everyone who sits on the bench directly on the other side of the lake without really being noticed.

That's how we found out our junior high biology teacher was having an affair with the assistant principal–I swear we weren't the ones who spilled the beans, but we *had* to be the first people to know.

That bench is where I've been staring absentmindedly ever since Jack and David started arguing about whether or not you could skip a turtle the way you skip rocks.

"It wouldn't work dude, they'd start flailing their feet and it would drag the momentum."

"Okay fine, but what if it's just the shell?"

I look back over to see Jack's brow furrowing in serious contemplation while David looks at him expectantly, eyebrows raised, "I told you so" just itching to fly out of his mouth.

"Okay, I'll concede that. I bet you could skip a turtle shell without the turtle in it."

Jack crosses his arms with a sour look while David whoops in victory. Shaking my head at the buffoons I call best friends, I turn my attention back to the bench and my blood runs cold.

I see the wild mop of red curls first, distinctive enough to know exactly who they belong to.

Closing my eyes and taking a deep breath, I try to compose myself before I inevitably see her counterpart.

A lifetime of deep breaths couldn't prepare me for this.

When I open my eyes again, I finally lay eyes on the sunlit beauty I would recognize anywhere. If I wasn't already sitting down, I think my knees would have buckled.

The weight of everything hits me all at once. My brain involuntarily flips through the highlight reel of horror from the last three months.

The look on her face when she realized what we'd done.

The visceral hatred in her voice when she said she'd never forgive me.

The dozen unread texts I sent in the days that followed.

The hours I spent staring at my ceiling, full of shame and anger at myself for ruining things.

The dread that's been building over the past week as I get ready to see her again.

After an entire summer of trying (and failing) to run into her casually, I figured I would just see her at school. Now I'm glad it happened out here–the last thing I need is to collapse in the hallway like a dork on the first day back.

My vision tunnels, and there's a tightening, burning sensation in my chest. David and Jack look at me in alarm when I gasp deeply–I didn't even notice I stopped breathing.

"What's wrong with you dude?" Jack asks angrily. I can tell I scared him, but now that my gaze is locked on her, I can't look away from Eleanor long enough to explain myself.

Following my line of vision, I can feel Jack stiffen when he spots the girls. David's shoulders sag–no matter how many times I've told him we're cool, he still looks like a scolded toddler every time Eleanor gets mentioned.

I know they haven't seen us. First of all, they're obviously in a very spirited conversation–at least I think they are from the way Abby is gesturing wildly.

Second, we've tested it ourselves. Even if you were to look directly at the spot we're in, you can't see us from the bench.

Third, I think she would bolt if she knew I was here.

Or maybe I'd be the one to run–my fight or flight has been leaning staunchly towards *flight* since the moment I saw her. Everything in me is telling me to run like hell.

I just can't decide if I want to run to her, or away.

"C'mon man, let's head back."

Jack's comforting hand on my shoulder still isn't enough to tear my eyes away from the stunning creature I'd give anything to be near right now.

He moves his hand under my arm and pulls me to my feet. I finally look away and face him, and there's pain on his face too.

Another stab of guilt threatens to knock me off my feet as I realize that we *all* lost her. She meant something to all of us, and I ruined it for everyone. I let him pull me to his truck, but glancing over my shoulder for one final look before getting in. It doesn't hurt any less the second time.

We drop David off at home for family dinner, and Jack and I drive back to my house in silence. When we get there, he gets out and comes inside with me.

Maybe I need to get checked out by a doctor or something–I must be on the verge of death if Jack is willingly giving up his final Sunday Solitude of summer nearly.

When did I get this emotional?

We continue our silence as we sit in my basement, and I can't help but stare at the spot Eleanor used to occupy every Friday night. It feels like it was just last week, and like it was another lifetime.

I know Jack is waiting for me to say something first, but I don't think there's anything in the English language that would explain the way it feels like a gaping black hole has opened in my chest.

Maybe I can learn something in Spanish II that will help.

I chuckle bitterly to myself, and Jack looks at me with one eyebrow raised.

"It's nothing, man." I've never heard myself sound so defeated. "I don't think I can do this though."

"You can. And you will."

I hope to God he's right.

Chapter 16

Griffin

October, Age 29

"**S**up bitches!?"

Jack and I both nearly jump out of our skin as David bursts through my front door, duffel bag slung over his shoulder, twelve pack of Shiner in hand.

"Jesus, David, maybe knock next time?" I say, Jack swearing under his breath. "And why did you bring your shit inside, aren't you staying with your parents?"

"Bro I haven't knocked on the door of this house since we were six," he says, tossing his bag on the kitchen floor and loading the beer in the fridge. "I'm not starting now just because I'm only here every couple months."

"You need to start locking the door," Jack mutters, mostly to himself.

Unfazed, David flops onto the couch, stretching his legs out in front of him and cracking his neck. "That drive fucking sucks, how do I forget that every damn time?"

"Maybe you should come back to Larkspur now that Jack's back," I say, "I don't know why you stayed in Lubbock in the first place."

"Jacky boy is back? Like permanently?" David asks, like this is the first time he's heard this information.

"You knew that, dumbass," Jack says, rolling his eyes. "We literally talked about it last week."

"I never remember what you tell me," David says unapologetically. "There's not enough room in my brain for all that shit."

"Oh, so what you're saying is you can't hear your own memories over the sound of the clown music. Got it."

A burst of laughter erupts from my chest as David flips Jack the finger. Despite his heart attack of an entrance, I'm glad to see him. The three of us under this roof makes me feel like I'm seventeen again.

"I'm so stoked for this reunion," David says, rubbing his hands together with a diabolical grin on his face. "I can't wait to see who grew up hot. And find out who's in jail."

"Remind me why you came a full month early again?" I ask, pinching the bridge of my nose. Not even five minutes and he's already stressing me out.

"Lubbock is boring as hell man," he groans. "Why *did* I stay there?" He pauses, then continues with a sinister grin, "Maybe I'll move back, like you said.

"I take it back," I joke, lifting my hands in fake-surrender. "Don't threaten me like that."

"God help us all," Jack sighs as David cackles maniacally.

"Anyway, back to this reunion shit," David says. "Y'all know who's coming?"

"Not sure," I say, looking at Jack. "You?"

"I've heard some names, but I don't know who makes the full list."

David looks back and forth between me and Jack before exhaling an annoyed huff. "Okay let me rephrase in a way you bozos will understand. Is Ellie coming?"

My pulse pounds in my ears, breath hitching in my chest–I couldn't tell you the last time I heard Eleanor's name out loud. Hell, I can't even remember the last time I thought about her.

This morning, you lying son of a bitch.

We both look to Jack for an answer. He's the only one who still hears from her, though I don't know if he's talked to her recently. He doesn't bring it up. I don't ask.

"Um." Clearing his throat, he shifts uncomfortably in his seat. "Yeah, she's coming. She's already here, actually."

Pretty sure my heart just stopped completely.

"Wait, really?" David asks excitedly. "What are we waiting for, tell her to come over!"

Jack shoots me a furtive glance–David wasn't here for the shit-show that was the last time Eleanor and I saw each other. It was too hard to talk about for the first few weeks, and by the time I finally stopped feeling like even the thought of her was going to kill me, too much time had passed to bring it up without being awkward. To his knowledge, things simply fizzled out when she moved to the east coast. I fucking wish that's all there was to it.

Mercifully, Jack says something so I don't have to.

"She's part of the planning committee, she's busy," he says. I don't know if that's a lie or not, and I don't care. At least I don't have to revisit that night. Yet.

"How do you know?"

"I saw her the day she got here, she's staying with Abby."

I nearly break my neck as I whip my head toward the front window, where there's a clear view of the yellow house across the street. When Abby and Aaron bought that house, I spent the first year with a pit in my stomach, dreading the day she'd come visit. The second year, I desperately hoped she would. Three years in, I accepted that she would probably never set foot on this street again.

Now she's been here for a week and I didn't even know. How the hell did I not know?

She's probably working damn hard to make sure you don't.

I wrench my gaze from the house back to the conversation happening in front of me, but I don't hear another word. All I can focus on is the fact that Eleanor has been less than 100 yards away all week, and I had no idea.

When David leaves for the night, Jack gives me an apologetic look.

"I'm sorry I didn't warn you about Ellie being here," he says quietly. "I didn't know if it would be better or worse for you to know."

"I don't know if it's better or worse either, honestly," I say with a shrug.

"How are you feeling?" The question is tentative, almost nervous. I guess it is a pretty loaded one.

"I don't know. Weird, I guess?" It comes out more like a question, like I need someone else to tell me how I'm feeling right now.

"Well, I'm here if you need anything. You might not even run into her until the reunion, you barely stay here these days anyway."

For a moment, I'm confused by what he means. Then it hits me like a ton of bricks. He's right–I *don't* stay at this house much anymore. I'm usually at the apartment. Madison's apartment. Madison, my girlfriend's apartment. I haven't thought about her once since Eleanor was mentioned, and the thought makes me queasy. We've been dating for almost a year, shouldn't I think about her when she's not around? I usually do.

Eleanor usually isn't across the street.

"When is this reunion thing again?" I sigh heavily, slumping down in the seat until my chin is touching my chest. I'm already exhausted by the thought of having to endure a night where Eleanor is close enough to touch, but still out of reach.

Out of reach because you have a girlfriend, dickhead.

"The 23rd, I think."

"You're fucking joking," I say sharply, bolting upright. "That's a joke."

"I can assure you, it is not a joke. You're the one who always says I'm incapable of making those."

"The reunion is planned for her fucking birthday?"

"Well I don't think it was planned specifically for that, but yes, the reunion happens to fall on Ellie's birthday."

"I don't think I can do this, man," I say wearily, dragging my hand down my face.

"You can. And you will."

I shoot him a disgusted look–if I never hear those words out of his mouth again, it'll be too soon.

Chapter 17

Griffin

November, Age 16

Well, Jack was right—technically I *am* doing it.

It's been fucking awful.

We're almost three months into the school year, and the dull ache in my chest is pretty much constant. Every time I see Eleanor laughing or talking with her friends, it's a punch to the gut—a daily reminder of how good I almost had it.

The only class we have together this year is, once again, seventh period Spanish. David, Jack, and I took the same desks we had last year.

Eleanor sits as far away from us as possible.

I sneak glances at her as often as I can without being a total stalker, always hoping she might be looking at me too. She never is.

The first week of school, I tried every day to talk to her. To explain. To apologize. And every day, she walked past me like I wasn't even there.

She clearly wants me to give up, but I don't have it in me to do that. Not yet, anyway. Probably not ever.

God as my witness, I will keep trying to get her back until the day I die.

"You can't say stuff like that, dude," David says. We're back to our usual routine–well, our *old* usual routine. The one without Eleanor.

"I hate to say it, but I agree with him," Jack chimes in. "Either she'll forgive you or she won't, but you've got to stop letting it consume you."

I want to argue that it doesn't *consume* me, but that's a lie. It feels like every moment, from sunup to sundown, I'm either missing Eleanor, trying to figure out a plan to get her back, or downright *yearning*, like some kind of Shakespearean sad sap.

"How do I just live with that though?" I look ridiculous lounging on the new, much smaller, chair we added to the basement. I grew about 3 inches over the summer, it might as well be a toddler's seat.

Even though it was technically my spot first, I haven't been able to bring myself to sit in what will forever be, in my mind at least, Eleanor's chair.

Kicking my legs absentmindedly over the arm of the chair, I exhale deeply (and loudly).

"That's it," David stands up and stomps over toward me. "If I have to hear you sigh dramatically again I'm going to scream. You've got to snap out of it."

He grabs me by the collar and yanks me upright.

"It's November, dude. It's been six months. Don't talk about it, be about it. Either that or let it go."

I didn't hear a word he said after "November."

"It's already November? November what?"

"Uhh, it's the seventeenth I think." Jack looks at me quizzically. "Why?"

"That was not the point," David mutter under his breath.

"Eleanor's sixteenth birthday is next week."

They both groan. I know I'm a broken record, but what else am I supposed to talk about when I feel like I lost the love of my life before I even had her?

Love of your life is dramatic, Griffin. You're sixteen. Get it together.

"I know we're not talking," I continue in a subdued voice. "But I still think it would be nice if we did something."

"Like what?" Jack has actually perked up at the suggestion. Even though he doesn't talk about it, I know he still sees her. I don't know if it makes me feel better or worse that I still have some lifeline to her.

I feel like I have some kind of chance as long as Jack is still there, but it's also a cruel joke that she's *right there*, but still so unreachable.

"I don't even know," I say, throwing my hands up in exasperation. "Maybe we could do something in class, something that's not so obviously from m–us."

David's scowl has also changed to a face of concentration. "Yeah, I think that's manageable. Ellie *loves* her birthday."

We get to planning, and I hope desperately that this can be the first step in building a bridge again.

Chapter 18

Ellie

November, 16th Birthday

I'm sixteen today. Anyone who knows me knows that I *love* my birthday, but I usually keep things low-key at school—I save the celebrating for just my family and Abby.

Unfortunately Abby does not operate this way, so everyone at Larkspur High is aware that it's my birthday before the first bell rings for the day.

By third period, I've said 'thank you' so many times it doesn't sound like a real phrase anymore. I'm not a shy person, but I'm also never the center of attention either, so having this much focus on me is a little jarring.

I kinda like it though, I think to myself as what feels like the 200th person acknowledges my birthday. *Maybe I should be the center of attention more often. This is fun.*

This might be my favorite birthday ever. All day long, I've gotten hugs and compliments, and even a red velvet cupcake (my favorite) from my sweet physics teacher.

I'm still riding the birthday high as I head to my final class of the day. It fades quickly though, and walking to Spanish II feels like a death march.

This year, I opted for the desk on the polar opposite side of the room from last year. When the boys walked in on the first day of school, they went straight to their old spots, like they were operating on muscle memory.

Even though I wasn't looking at them, they were as loud as ever, so hearing them was unavoidable–and I could definitely hear when they stopped talking. I tried sneaking a subtle glance, and found the three of them staring at me.

Griffin and David looked away immediately, with the same energy as a dog walking away with its tail between its legs. Jack held my gaze, smiling at me a bit sadly before turning around to rejoin their conversation.

That was the first and only interaction we've had this year. I always get to class first, and make it a point to stare at my desk, avoiding eye contact with anyone until I'm certain they're in their seats.

Today is different. First and foremost, I was nearly the last person to walk into class because I was stopped so many times during my trip from physics to Spanish.

I didn't want to risk catching anyone's eye—especially Griffin—so I kept my gaze on my shoes until I made it to my seat. Once I finally looked up, my jaw dropped.

An arrangement of flowers sits on my desk–a beautiful combination of violet irises, baby pink roses, and white freesias that has obviously been carefully crafted. It's not lost on me that only one person in this room has ever heard me talk about what my favorite flowers are.

Beside it sits a party hat, and when I look around the room, I notice everyone is donning a matching one. I pick up the handmade card placed in the bouquet, and find signatures from nearly everyone in the room. One name is noticeably absent.

Did he do that so I wouldn't get upset? Did he do it because he's hurting just as much as me?

I turn to face the room, and they immediately break out in a Happy Birthday chorus. A burning sensation builds behind my eyes, and I blink rapidly to stop the tears trying to form.

I don't know why I'm suddenly overcome with emotion—maybe it has something to do with the fact that two of the people I *know* orchestrated this surprise are ones I haven't talked to in six months.

I'm still angry and hurt. This doesn't change anything for me. But for the first time this year, I look over at Griffin, David, and Jack on purpose, and the overwhelming emotion isn't anger. It's...something else.

Somehow, it's something worse.

I mouth a silent *thank you* to them with a hesitant smile before finally taking my seat.

It occurs to me later that night when I'm celebrating with Abby that what I was feeling instead of anger was sadness. Except it wasn't sadness exactly—it was more like being homesick.

Earlier this week, my mom asked me if I wanted to invite the boys over to join us for dinner and cake.

I whipped around when she said that, snapping way too harshly, "Why would you say that? It's always just us and Abby."

She looked beyond taken aback at my response. I've never snapped at my mom about anything, let alone my birthday.

"Calm down angel, I just know you've spent a lot of time with them, but I haven't heard anything about them lately."

I clenched my teeth, immediately grimacing and tensing up at the fact that she'd noticed. I didn't tell her anything that happened, and I had hoped that if I never brought it up, she wouldn't either.

Gently, she continued, "I don't know if something happened, but I figured this might be a good way to bridge that gap. But if it's truly that big of a deal, I can leave it alone. I just want you to be happy, my love."

I didn't respond, and she didn't bring it up again.

Tonight, as I blow out the candles on my cake, I find myself wishing for something impossible. I wish for a universe where the bet had never happened–one where it's me, Abby, *and* the boys here laughing. One where my little circle has expanded, and Larkspur doesn't feel simultaneously suffocating and empty.

One with a love story that didn't get its wings clipped before it could fly.

Chapter 19

Ellie

November, 17th Birthday

A lot can happen in a year.

But sometimes what you notice most are the things that *didn't* happen.

Today's my seventeenth birthday, which for some reason, I feel like no one talks about. Everyone raves about Sweet Sixteen, and then you become an "adult" at eighteen. The only thing I can come up with when I think about turning seventeen is Dancing Queen by Abba.

Young and sweet, only seventeen.

I don't know what it is about junior year that has rocked me so hard, but *young* and *sweet* are not words that would make my "describe yourself in three words" list.

I don't know if they'd make a "describe yourself in one hundred words" list.

I don't quite have the words for it, but some days it's hard to even get out of bed and brush my teeth. It's usually only bad like that for a few days–then I feel a hollow kind of sadness for the few days after that, and then I feel mostly normal again. In those moments, I don't have the energy or the care to be sweet, it's all

I can do to manage basic responses. And it makes me feel a deep exhaustion in a way that seems wrong for a seventeen year old.

But like I said, a lot can happen in a year. I got my license, and then a car. I passed my first AP test (*and failed my second one, but we don't need to talk about that*). I got a boyfriend, who I'm pretty sure is throwing me a surprise party tonight.

My worst nightmare—but we've only been dating a few months, I can't expect him to know everything about me yet.

Lots of things also stayed the same. I still have my Friday dinners with Abby every week, I hang out with Jack on Saturday mornings, I garden with my grandmother, I go to the farmer's market with my mom.

Sixteen has been good to me. Mostly. It had country drives, scream-singing with the windows rolled down. It came with braces (*and with getting them off, thank goodness*). It had my first date, and my first kiss.

It started with my favorite flowers from the people who were once my favorite.

But if I'm being honest, what I noticed most was probably the hole where those favorites used to be.

It's been over a year now, and I really should be over it, but there's no use pretending that when I got my schedule on the first day of school I wasn't a little disappointed that I didn't end up in any classes with Griffin.

I guess he decided to stop after Spanish II, and I don't know what I was expecting when I walked into Spanish III, but it never crossed my mind that he might not be there.

Not that it makes a difference to me, obviously. We aren't friends. We haven't even spoken since they threw me a surprise party in class last year.

That realization hits me like a ton of bricks.

That surprise party didn't bother me. I actually kind of loved it.

I shove that thought down, forcing my attention back to the last few minutes of Spanish III. The dismissal bell rings, and on autopilot, I pack up my things, head for the door, and take myself home.

I absolutely do *not* scan the parking lot for a glimpse of three obnoxious but endearing boys.

And when I get ready for my birthday "dinner" with Bennett, I certainly don't consider that my reaction to a surprise party would have anything to do with who planned it.

***

Griffin

November, Age 17

Whoever said time heals all wounds was lying out of their ass.

Maybe I'm delusional, but I really thought that after her birthday surprise that me and Eleanor would rebuild...whatever it was that we had. Or almost had.

Think again, idiot.

Any attempts I made the rest of last year went unnoticed–or blatantly ignored. I really started losing hope when I didn't see or hear from her once over summer break.

And now that we're a few months into junior year, I think I have to force myself to admit that she really meant it when she said she'd never forgive me.

You'd think that would help me move on. Not a chance in hell.

I don't talk to the guys about it anymore, because I don't want to be a pathetic broken record.

Even though that's exactly what I am.

I was so distracted last year that I almost failed Spanish II, so Señor Flores strongly advised me not to take Spanish III. I thought about doing it anyway on the off chance we might be in the same class again, but my GPA has been through enough already.

Now the only hope I have of seeing her is in the halls, and the scheduling Gods must hate me because we never cross paths unless something weird happens with the daily schedule. I'm not exaggerating when I say I've only seen her physically *maybe* twice in eight weeks.

Both times nearly sent me into cardiac arrest.

Not that I haven't checked her Instagram religiously. I don't care if that walks a thin line between regular old pathetic and stalkerish. I'll take any crumb of her I can get.

I don't know how it's possible, but she's gotten even more beautiful. Her blonde waves are nearly to her waist, her smile somehow got more radiant when she got her braces off, and Goddamn she's got some curves on her.

I know I've changed too. When Jack and David started getting really sick of my pining, I took up working out as a way to release my angst. The rest of me has finally caught up with my height, and I get a lot more attention from girls now.

Not that I care. There's only one girl's attention I want. And I'm starting to think I'll never have it again.

I know today is her birthday, and I desperately wanted to do something special for her. When she first told me how much she loves her birthday, I was looking forward to celebrating it with her forever.

I didn't even get to do it once.

Before I could come up with anything, Jack and David talked me out of it. And they were right—there's no way I could have done that in a way that seems natural. I don't want to do anything that might tarnish her day.

I think Eleanor's birthday is going to be the worst day of the year, every year, for the rest of my life.

Chapter 20

Ellie

November, 18th Birthday

I've checked my phone at least a hundred times today. I've called between every class period, but it went straight to voicemail every time. I've sent at least twenty texts. Nothing.

Today is my eighteenth birthday, and I haven't heard from my boyfriend *once*. He knows how much today means to me.

This would be the second birthday of mine that we spent together, but something tells me that's not going to happen. I don't know where he could possibly be.

What I do know is that things between us have changed recently. He's been distant, flaky, and seems disinterested in anything I have to say. The number of times I've heard, "Sorry, what? I didn't hear any of that" recently is making me lose my mind. I can't remember the last time we went on a real date. I actually can't even remember the last time we kissed.

I met Bennett at a book store right after the start of junior year. It felt like something out of a movie–I was browsing the fantasy section, when I looked up and saw someone who looked like he could be in an Abercrombie ad.

Bennett is the opposite of who I usually find attractive–I'm typically into boys with darker features who look a little rough around the edges.

Boys like Griffin Hart.

I shake my head, determinedly ignoring that thought.

Bennett was tall and blonde, with blue eyes like the Texas sky, and he was nothing like I'd ever seen before.

He was wearing slacks and a white polo, with expensive look-ing shoes and the type of fancy watch my mom got my dad for his fiftieth birthday. He looked like he had either come straight from a business meeting or the country club. Either way, my interest was piqued.

He must have felt me gawking at him, because he made direct eye contact with me from across the store. I smiled, embarrassed that I got caught, before quickly turning my gaze back to the shelf. A hand reached over my shoulder to grab the book I had been looking at, and when I turned around, I was face to face with Mr. Abercrombie.

"This one's my favorite," he said with a grin. "Have you read it?"

From there, we talked for hours about books, and he even bought me coffee at the bookstore café. It felt like a meet-cute from a Meg Ryan movie, and I went home with his phone number and the biggest butterflies in my stomach. We haven't gone a day without talking since then.

Full disclosure–he's twenty one. I didn't know he was that much older than me when we met, and I certainly didn't know that when I gave him my number. And yes, I've heard all the things they say about dating older men as a teenager.

And now that this is happening, I've officially become a cliché.

I was so flattered that an older guy was into me that I didn't stop to consider *why* an older guy would be interested in a teenage girl in the first place.

Since that first meeting, everything has been wonderful. He's a perfect gentleman, and incredibly thoughtful. They were leery at first, but once my parents got over the shock of the age gap, they were enthralled with Bennett Campbell.

The day after we met, he brought flowers to my house unannounced. I had never seriously dated anyone before, and this man was sweeping me off my feet. Since then, he's made it a point to bring me flowers at least once a week, even if they are asters and impatiens. He has the worst memory for detail, and can never remember that it's irises I love.

He calls me every night to say, "I love you honey, sweet dreams." The first time he called me honey romantically, I nearly spit my drink out. It's a name I had to get used to, since my grandfather has called me honey my whole life, but I've learned to find it truly very endearing.

Most importantly, last year he worked really hard to curate a perfect birthday for me from start to finish. Like I suspected, he did end up throwing me a huge surprise party. It was a little overwhelming at first, but the gesture was so thoughtful that I pushed past my discomfort to make sure I didn't hurt his feelings after all the effort he put into planning.

Well, he used to do those things, I think to myself bitterly. He hasn't brought me flowers in months, and those sweet late night phone calls have turned into a simple "Night." text sent before 9 pm, letting me know he's done texting me for the day.

Maybe those things have never actually been sweet. Maybe he does things he feels are expected of him. Or does things to give himself the upper hand. Maybe he's never really understood or cared about me at all.

Finally, just as I'm walking out of Larkspur High for the day, my phone starts ringing. Bennett's name and a picture from our one-year anniversary flashes on the screen.

I answer the call, but before I can even say hello, he barks out, "I'm in Houston for the week. Stop blowing up my phone. We can talk when I get back."

Then he hangs up. I feel my jaw drop, and tears prick my eyes almost immediately. This is the Bennett I've been getting lately–a Bennett that's short, impatient, and downright mean to me.

I've been dreading this for weeks, but this is it. This is the moment I recognize it's over for me. And has been for a while.

I realize I've been staring at my phone for a solid minute, and my hands shake with anger as I tuck it away into my bag. Walking to my car, I decide to myself that we're over.

I may not say those words out loud until he decides he wants to talk to me again, but I'm done. Even if he calls. Even if he shows up with flowers. Even if he says he's sorry. We're done.

He didn't even wish me a happy birthday.

As I walk to my car, angry tears begin streaming down my face against my will. It's not just that my relationship is over, it's that my entrance into adulthood feels like a kick to the stomach. I know being an adult is harder than being a kid, but does it really have to start like this?

The worst part is, this is the first birthday I had planned on spending entirely separate from my parents and Abby. My genius thought process was that since I'm turning eighteen and becoming an adult, I should start a fresh new birthday tradition, leaving my old one in my childhood.

Now I have no new tradition–unless you count celebrating alone and buying yourself a cupcake on the way home from school.

As if that isn't awful enough, this is a year where my birthday happens to fall during Thanksgiving week–and because of the new plans I made, that means my parents and Abby made plans of their own.

My parents have gone on a cruise in the Mediterranean. Abby and her dad left for Thanksgiving break early to spend the full week with her grandma in Arkansas. It's just me and my misery left here in Larkspur.

That's just fantastic. I was supposed to spend not just tonight, but the entire week with Bennett and his family. *Now I'm completely alone.*

It's so fantastically awful that a bitter laugh bursts out of me in the middle of the parking lot. Embarrassed, I look around to see if anyone heard me. But I spent so long trying to call Bennett and waiting for him to call me back, I'm one of the last people to leave the school parking lot for the day.

I get into my car–my aunt's old Volkswagen bug, baby blue with tan leather seats–and slam the door behind me. The charm chain Abby made for me swings wildly from my rearview mirror.

I rest my head on the steering wheel, trying to compose myself, but feeling utterly empty and defeated. I sigh, turning the key and bringing the engine roaring to life. I put the car in drive, and when I look up, I find Griffin standing across the parking lot, eyebrows drawn together in concern.

We do actually have an elective class together this semester, but we don't acknowledge one another–I don't know if it's worse or better than when we didn't see each other at all.

He's even taller now than he was when I first met him.

Has it really only been three years? It feels like a lifetime ago.

He's got to be pushing 6'3" at this point. It seemed like overnight the lanky boy with the boyish grin turned into...well, a man. His shoulders are broad, his jawline more defined. Not to mention the biceps constantly trying furiously to break free from the sleeves of his t-shirt.

Not that I've been looking.

Hastily looking away, I pull out of the parking lot without a second glance at him. I don't want to think about how much of that he saw–I'm too busy thinking about how the most anticipated birthday week ever has turned into an utter catastrophe.

***

Griffin
November, Age 18

My heart dropped into my stomach when I opened Instagram this evening. The first photo on my feed was a picture of a cupcake with a single candle on it.

The caption read, *"18 today. Happy birthday to me."* with a pink heart emoji. No smiling face, no friends and family, no presents–just a basic cupcake that was obviously bought last-minute from the grocery store, and a candle that seems left over from the ones pictured on her cake last year.

To anyone else, this might seem like a normal, lowkey way to end a birthday. But I know better.

I could tell something was wrong when I saw Eleanor in the parking lot. I've never seen her unhappy on her birthday, even last year when Mr. Hawkins sprung a surprise chemistry test on us.

I desperately wanted to sprint across that lot and ask her what was wrong and how I could fix it. She looked like she needed to be held, and even though we haven't been friends in nearly two years at this point, I wanted to be the one who was there for her.

So much has changed since that God awful day. My parents got divorced last year after my mom freaked out and decided she wasted her youth on me and dad.

I don't think my dad saw it coming–he'd been divorced before after getting married really young, but the way he described my mom, it was like no other woman had ever existed to him. They had a whirlwind romance, and have been happily in love ever since.

Or at least I though they were.

I used to ask my mom why they never had more kids. *"Because we got it right the first time, my sweet boy,"* she'd always say, sealing it with a kiss on my forehead. Hearing her say that never got old. My chest would always puff out, so proud to have been so good and right that they didn't need anything else. That illusion was shattered the day she stormed out.

I don't think she meant for me to hear, but I swear the whole damn neighborhood heard as she yelled, "I never wanted any of this!" She might not have directly said *"I never wanted you or Griffin,"* but the message was loud and clear.

As a kid, I always wanted a love like theirs. My mom's midlife crisis ruined that, I guess. I thought they were the blueprint–now I have no idea what love should look like.

David and Jack still come over every day like nothing's changed, but the house feels almost haunted now. When things were normal, dad used to come shoot the shit with us in the basement sometimes, but mom barely acknowledged my friends then, and she definitely doesn't acknowledge them now.

Even though mom is the one who blew up their marriage, dad ended up moving out so she could stay in the house. He's in an apartment across town now, and even though I see him two nights a week and on weekends, I still miss him all the time.

Which made it even worse when my mom met her new boyfriend, and they decided to up and leave me too. The day I turned eighteen, she told me I was old enough to fend for myself and left me alone in this house. They still make sure the bills are paid and I have money for groceries, but it's been lonely.

My dad offered to move back in, but I know being here would kill him—she's still the love of his life, even after everything. I can handle a little loneliness if I don't have to put him through any more pain.

So I'm here, alone, sick to my stomach at the idea of Eleanor being alone too. After going back and forth with myself for the better part of an hour, I decide to send her a text.

I don't even know if she still has my number saved.

I try not to think about it. I've worked too hard to climb out of the self-pity hole I fell into when I realized she wasn't going to forgive me.

Don't go back there, Griffin.

Griffin: Happy birthday, darlin'. Thinkin' of you tonight.

I set my phone down, not expecting her to respond. I walk away to grab myself a drink from the fridge, when my phone dings unexpectedly.

With a slightly embarrassing speed, I snatch my phone up and see a reply.

Ellie: Thank you, Griffin.

Simple, formal, straight to the point–but a reply nonetheless.

Trying to tamper down the feeling of hope kindling in my chest, I text back as quickly as possible, as though if I could just send something back soon enough, she might reply to me again.

> **Griffin: Did you have a good day?**

I should have said something more interesting. Something that might keep the conversation going longer. Before I have time to continue kicking myself, she writes back.

> **Ellie: Yeah, it was fine. Can't believe I'm technically an adult now.**

I know the feeling—I turned eighteen eight months ago, and there was a weird bittersweet feeling about it. After everything went down with my parents, it felt like childhood was really over.

After my mom moved clear across the country, I started spending most of my time alone. I go over to my dad's on Tuesdays and Thursdays, and I join David for Sunday dinners now, but there's still a lot of empty space. The nights I spent with Eleanor and the guys feel like a different universe at this point.

Shaking those memories from my head, I send back my reply.

> **Griffin:** Just fine? That doesn't sound like the birthday girl I know.

She takes so long to respond that I worry I've overstepped–after all, she hasn't wanted me to know her in a long time.

Right as I've given up, she sends one final reply.

> **Ellie:** I guess I'm just a birthday adult now. Thanks for remembering. Goodnight Griffin.

I set my phone back on my nightstand, and lay in bed without bothering to change into pajamas. Staring at the ceiling, I wonder if there's still a chance I might get to celebrate with that birthday adult again someday.

Chapter 21

Ellie

November, Age 18

This has been, objectively, the worst week of my life. Apart from a few texts from Abby, and one very glitchy cruise WiFi FaceTime from my parents, I've been alone with my thoughts.

The worst possible place to be.

Realistically, I knew I wouldn't hear from Bennett. I know it's over. But every day that passes without a call or text still stings.

It probably doesn't help that I've re-read the birthday texts from Griffin about a hundred times.

It felt nice to be thought of, to be remembered. We haven't really talked in over a year, minus the texts from a few days ago. And given what happened the last time we spoke...I definitely don't deserve this kind of thoughtfulness.

There have been so many times I've wanted to reach out, to extend an olive branch of some sort. But at this point I've been so committed to holding a grudge, I don't know how to undo it.

There's something deeply broken in me in that regard–I refuse to give second chances, even when I know I'm wrong. It doesn't matter how small the sleight, or how unintentional it was. I think I'm mostly convinced that if I let someone back in, they'll hurt me even worse the second time around.

Not to mention I have no idea how Bennett would react if I started hanging out with the guys again.

I guess I don't have to worry about that anymore.

Besides, one birthday text doesn't mean he even *wants* an olive branch. Maybe he just saw that I looked upset in the parking lot and felt sorry for me. All this time I've been so dead set on holding my grudge that I didn't consider he might have one of his own.

My mouth turns to ash at that train of thought–what if this is some full-circle moment for him, and seeing me spend my birthday alone is some sort of vindication? What if he took some sort of sick pleasure in reminding me of the kind of friendship I missed out on?

I don't think that's in his nature. He's one of the most genuine, earnest people I know. He never does things out of obligation—it always seems to come from some deep-seated need to make sure everyone around him is happy. And he certainly isn't spiteful or malicious–his teasing has always been goodnatured, even when it was driving me nuts.

But then again, I don't really know what his nature is anymore.

I scroll through our texts again, landing on the last thing I sent.

I guess I'm just a birthday adult now. Thanks for remembering. Goodnight Griffin.

A not-insignificant part of me has hoped that he would reach out again.

But if I'm the one who ended the conversation, shouldn't I be the one to start it up again?

Texting Griffin would be a bad idea. I'm still not ready to have a conversation about what happened, no matter how much time has passed. All it does is open a door for more disappointment, and more heartbreak.

Or it could work out.

I stare at my phone, every warning signal in my brain screaming "bad idea!" at me. I'm not going to do it. My parents will be home on Sunday. Abby will be back Monday. I'll be fine. I'm not going to text him.

I'm totally going to text him.

Ellie: Hi.

I toss my phone to the other side of the bed and scream into a pillow. I can't un-ring that bell now—all there is to do is fixate on my anxiety until he texts back.

If he texts back.

I shoot straight up when my phone dings, sending my pillows flying off the bed.

Griffin: Hey darlin'. What's up?

I go numb with shock, like my brain forgot that the whole point of texting someone is so that they *will* text back. But now that he's replied, I have no idea what to do with myself.

Reply, you idiot.

Ellie: Nothing really.

Ellie: It's been kind of a lonely break.

Subtle.

Griffin: What do you mean?

Well, too late to backtrack that.

> **Ellie:** My parents are on a cruise, and Abby is visiting her family in Arkansas

> **Ellie:** So it's just me.

I couldn't sound more pathetic if I tried. Seriously, this pity party is more over the top than any birthday extravaganza I could have planned.

> **Griffin:** What about your boyfriend? Beckham or whatever?

That makes me snort. How did I never notice what a snooty, country club name he has?

This isn't really something I want to get into, so I try to reply as vaguely as possible.

> **Ellie:** We broke up.

> **Ellie:** No big deal, it just ran its course.

I have got to stop double texting.

> **Griffin:** What the hell did he do?

Why would he automatically assume it was Bennett's fault? (*He's not wrong though.*)

> **Ellie:** Who said it was his fault?

> **Griffin:** No guy in his right mind would let you go. He must have fucked up. I'm kind of an expert in this area, darlin'.

This stops me in my tracks. Surely he doesn't still think that highly of me. Most of our history is made up of me being mean, yelling, and holding grudges.

> **Griffin:** Am I wrong?

Might as well tell the truth.

> **Ellie:** No, you're not. He was just…bad at communicating.

Not technically a lie, but not the whole truth either.

> **Griffin:** Is he the reason you spent your birthday alone?

I might as well have stuck a fork in a socket with the way I physically jolt. How on earth does he know I spent my birthday alone?

> **Ellie: How do you know I spent my birthday alone?**

> **Griffin: I saw your post on Instagram and figured.**

> **Griffin: Again, am I wrong?**

No, he's not wrong.

> **Griffin: Wait, is that why you looked so sad in the parking lot?**

> **Griffin: Did that fucker ruin your birthday?**

I'm torn between feeling touched that he noticed and seemingly cares, and feeling humiliated that he, of all people, saw me at my worst moment.

> **Ellie: It's a long story.**

Texting him was a bad idea. I thought telling someone how lonely this week has been would make me feel better, but I feel infinitely lonelier now.

And infinitely more embarrassed.

Griffin: Do you wanna talk about it?

Good question. Do I?

Before I can decide if I actually want to spill the whole mortifying story, he sends another text.

Griffin: You could come over. Anytime. Always.

Griffin: I know it's been awhile, but I don't like that you're lonely.

Griffin: We don't even have to talk. I can just be a warm body in the room.

Griffin: If you want, no pressure. But I'm here for you if you want me to be.

Again, do I? Want him to be there for me?

Before I can think better of it, I send a text I never thought I'd be sending again.

> **Ellie:** Sure, that sounds nice.

> **Ellie:** Be there in twenty.

This is either going to be the best thing to happen to me this week, or the crap cherry on top of a shit sundae.

Leaving no room to talk myself out of it, I hastily slip on shoes and grab my keys.

Even though I've never driven myself to Griffin's, my brain goes on autopilot. I think I'd know the way to his house blindfolded and spun around, like a party goer ready to obliterate a piñata.

I hope this works out better for me than it does for the piñata.

Chapter 22

Griffin

November, Age 18

E leanor is coming to my house. For real.
I think.

I've read her last text at least thirty times, searching for *any* other possible meaning behind "be there in twenty." Honest to God, I've thought of everything. Maybe it's wishful thinking, but I really can't come up with any other explanation. She's actually coming over.

Part of me feels guilty—like maybe I'm taking advantage of her, even if I don't mean to. She's obviously had an awful week. Am I being selfish, inviting her over when she's vulnerable?

The other, bigger part of me? He's just excited to breathe the same air as her again. I feel like I haven't taken a full breath since the wind got knocked out of me when everything went sideways. Over a cliff. On fire.

I know it's not rational to be so wrapped up in this girl. We were only really friends for a few months–even if it feels like life didn't really exist before her.

The thought of her being lonely, even for a second, absolutely guts me. God knows I've been lonely too. I feel a flicker of hope spark in my chest—maybe when we're together again, it'll be like no time has passed and neither of us will have to be lonely again. Maybe she's the solution to my lonely. And hopefully, I can be hers.

Great, a handful of texts and I'm already back to waxing poetic.

I pace up and down the entryway, anxious as hell for her to get here. I'm also trying to figure out a way to tell her my situation without expanding on it—she's inevitably going to ask where my parents are, but tonight is about *her* feelings. My sob story can wait for next time.

Please let there be a next time.

A knock on the door stops me dead in my tracks.

Holy shit. Okay. Don't fuck this up.

I inhale a shaky breath, and when I open the door I damn near fall to my knees.

The backlighting from the porch light gives her a sort of angelic glow—her waist-length blonde waves looking almost fluid, like molten gold. Even in a simple cable knit sweater and jeans, she blows everyone else clear out of the water.

No one else should be allowed to wear cornflower blue again—Eleanor should have exclusive rights to it.

I'm trying not to ogle like a caveman, but I can't help it when I rake my eyes down her body. She's far from the sassy little sprite I met freshman year. Her sweater clings to her figure, showing off the body she's grown into. When I drag my eyes back up to her face and look into those perfect blue eyes, I nearly gasp audibly. I would happily dive deep into those oceans and never resurface.

There's a twinge in my chest when I notice they don't sparkle as bright as they used to.

What did he do to you, darlin'?

The lips usually reserved for some sharp, witty comment–the ones I've wanted to kiss since the day I met her–part silently, eyes going wide at my nonexistent attempt to hide the way I drink in her presence. Without a word, I step back and shamelessly stare at the way her jeans hug what have to be the most perfect hips to ever exist. I can't begin to fathom what her ass looks like in these Levi's. Everything in me wants to pull her close and let my hands roam over every slope and curve.

She came here for company, not so you can maul her like a grizzly bear, you jackass.

Clearing my throat, I break the awkward silence by asking if she wants to go downstairs.

"Where else would we go?" she asks, one of her eyebrows lifting, the smallest of smirks fighting to shine through. She turns and heads downstairs, like no time has passed at all–like she never stopped coming over on Friday nights.

Like David never opened his stupid mouth. Like I didn't fuck everything up before I even got a chance to start something.

I wish I could say everything feels instantly back to normal, but it's hard to pretend when every second without her has been agony.

I follow closely behind, treading lightly like one wrong move might spook her. I'm barely breathing with the fear that I might send her bolting again—not just from my house, but from my life.

I nearly crash into her when she stops abruptly at the bottom of the stairs. At first I think maybe she's seen a bug or something, but once I step around her and get a clear look at her face, I notice her eyes darting back and forth between the couch and the chair.

She doesn't know where to sit anymore.

Trying to make the decision easier for her without actually addressing the giant 2-years-of-silence sized elephant in the room, I take a seat on the couch, leaving the chair open for her.

There's no need to point out that no one has sat in that chair since she stopped coming around.

She looks at the chair almost nervously, pulling her bottom lip between her teeth. I have the sudden urge to launch myself off this couch and see what it would feel like if *I* was the one biting that lip.

The sudden flare of heat is doused almost instantly when I notice the flicker of hurt in her eyes. I've had to stare at that chair daily, but this is her first time back in this room since the bet. I wish I had any idea what might be going through her head right now. I rub my chest, trying to soothe the sharp pain that always comes when I remember how badly I hurt her.

She turns away from the armchair and takes the seat on the opposite end of the couch, crossing her legs and sitting sideways to face me.

I angle my body to mirror hers, and for a moment we just look at each other, neither one of us wanting to be the one to break eye contact first.

"Um, how have you been?" she asks awkwardly.

"I'm fine, darlin'," I say, avoiding the truth. "But tell me what happened with you."

"It's kind of a lot," she says, dropping her gaze to her hands, wringing them nervously.

"I've got all the time in the world for you, Eleanor."

With a deep, shuddering breath, she pours out what's happened the last few weeks, months, years. I didn't think the guilt could sink any deeper, but it turns out I wasn't anywhere close to rock bottom.

When she tells me about that shithead Bennett, I shove my hands into my hoodie pocket so she doesn't see the way my fists clench. If I ever see this clown in public, I don't know how I'll hold back from knocking him straight on his ass.

She tells me about the way she's isolated herself from her mom and even from Abby, and an ache that reaches the very depths of my soul is unbearable. I did this. If none of this had happened, I'd never have let her spend her birthday alone. She wouldn't be this lonely. My beautiful, bright girl has dimmed because I was reckless and stupid.

"...and I just feel like I have no one. So yeah, it's been kind of a bad week."

I can tell she's trying to downplay it, but I don't miss the tears that well in her eyes, or the way her voice broke on the last word. I close the gap between us, extending my arm in an invitation to scoot next to me. For a second I think she's going to get up and maintain that distance, but a choked sob bursts out of her throat, and she lets me fold her into my arms as she finally lets go of the weight she's been carrying by herself.

She buries her head in my chest, and I murmur words of comfort into her hair, stroking her back soothingly as her body is wracked with sobs. Once the tears run dry, she pulls back, and I reach up to wipe the them off her cheeks.

I would kiss every tear away if she'd let me.

"I'm sorry," she hiccups. "Your shirt is soaked now."

She reaches up to smooth my shirt out, and her touch sends lightning bolts all the way down to my toes.

And one other place in particular.

"Well, it's a good thing I live here," I say, trying to lighten the mood (*and to give her an out if she's done talking about her feelings*). "I can go change, it's not a worry. You can ruin my shirt anytime, darlin'."

She reaches up, grasping the hand that's still holding her cheek. I figure she's going to move it, but when I try to pull back she squeezes it, leaning into my touch. The lightning turns to fireworks, and I wouldn't be surprised if she can hear my heartbeat thundering in my chest.

"I've never seen your room," she says, tilting her head like she can't believe she's never considered that. "Can I come with you while you grab a shirt?"

Having Eleanor in my basement has always set me buzzing, but the times I've pictured her in my room? Those daydreams definitely aren't comforting or gentlemanly.

"Yeah, come on," I say with an attempt at a casual tone, but the strain in my voice is undeniable.

She doesn't drop my hand as we stand up, or as I lead her up the stairs, or when I open the door to my room. Once we get inside she finally lets go, and the absence of her warmth feels equivalent to taking an ice bath.

She does a slow turn, taking in all of my knick knacks–framed photos, Lego sets I built with my dad, all sorts of posters plastering every inch of my walls. Every second of her assessment makes me feel more self conscious. I open my mouth to break the silence, but she beats me to it.

"This is exactly how I pictured your room," she says, giving me the first genuine smile I've seen from her in far too long.

"So you've pictured my room before?" I tease, matching her grin with one of my own.

Rolling her eyes, she says "Cool your jets, Griffin Hart. I just meant it feels very...*you.*"

The knowledge that Eleanor didn't shove every thought about me completely out of her mind could have me running straight through a brick wall in triumph.

She steps up to my bookshelf, delicately tracing the spines of the few books I have before picking up a picture of me with my parents. It's one of the last pictures we took together when everything was still happy, and we still felt like an actual family.

With a slight frown, she looks up and asks, "Where are your parents? Are they out tonight?"

Not ready to face that conversation just yet, I give a bullshit answer about having a night away after hosting a big holiday.

Technically not a lie—my mom did host a big Thanksgiving dinner. I just wasn't invited.

Her eyes narrow suspiciously, and I cave instantly, giving her the cliff notes version of the series of events that ended with me alone in this house. To my relief, she doesn't apologize or offer platitudes. She simply grabs my hand again, squeezing it gently before setting the frame back on the shelf and sitting on the edge of my bed.

Do not imagine having Eleanor in your bed under different circumstances.

I lean against the door frame, trying to memorize every detail of having her in my space. After finishing another long sweep of my room, she looks up at me expectantly—except I have no idea what she's waiting for.

"Well are you just gonna stand there, or are you gonna come sit down?" she asks with an exasperated huff.

That's the last thing I thought she was going to say.

"Oh," I say, blinking rapidly in surprise. "Did you want to stay up here instead of going back downstairs?"

Her eyes widen, looking mortified. "Right, duh, of course we would go back downstairs. That makes sense."

She moves to stand up, but I cross the room quickly and grab her by the shoulders, planting her firmly back on my bed.

"Eleanor, it's fine," I say with a chuckle. "We could sit on the kitchen floor for all I care. Whatever makes you comfortable."

She offers a small smile, and I grab a shirt out of my dresser and head to the bathroom to change. When I come back out, Eleanor is sprawled out on my bed, thumbing through the book she found on my nightstand.

I stand at the edge of the bed, unsure of what to do now. I don't have any chairs in my room, and I don't know how she would feel about me climbing into bed with her—even if it's not, you know, *climbing into bed with her.*

She sets the book back on the bedside table, and turns to look at me, eyebrows raised. Without a word, she pats the spot next to her on the bed, giving me the green light to join her.

With a grin, I settle in next to her, the bed shifting under my weight when I reach across her to grab the remote to put a movie on. I pull up Netflix and ask what she wants to watch.

"I don't care, Griffin," she replies with a contented sigh. "Just pick something."

The problem is, once she lays her head on my shoulder, I suddenly forget how to read—all I can focus on is the flowery scent of her shampoo, the way her arm brushes against mine with every rise and fall of her chest, and the warmth coming not just from her body next to mine, but radiating from the core of my being.

My airway constricts as a heavy realization hits me—*for the first time in months, this house feels like a home again.*

Chapter 23

Ellie

November, Age 18

I shouldn't have come up to his room. Or sat on his bed. Or laid my head on his shoulder. It's so much, so fast, and now I'm in too deep to back out.

And it feels *good.* The control freak in me is hyperventilating into a paper bag, but the part of me I don't ever listen to–the impulsive part–is screaming for more.

Boy, do I want more.

I don't think anything has ever felt more intimate than this simple act of watching a movie, Griffin's broad shoulder holding the weight of my head, and the weight of everything I spilled tonight.

My hands are neatly folded in my lap, a desperate attempt to keep from clawing and grasping for every bit of him I can get. The logical part of my brain is begging me to have some shred of self preservation–*hello, this boy ripped your heart to shreds less than two years ago? Have you forgotten?*

I haven't forgotten, and that's what has me so at war with myself. Watching five minutes of some dumb disaster movie with Griffin feels easier and more natural than anything in the entire span of my relationship with Bennett. I didn't realize how hollow that relationship was until I let myself remember how full of life Griffin makes me feel.

That scares the ever-loving shit out of me.

Griffin shifts, scooting a bit lower so that my full weight is now leaning on him, and angling his shoulders so that I'm tucked into him instead of maintaining the distance (*"distance"*) I tried to put between us.

I know this is a disastrous idea, but I don't stop him. In fact, I decide to dig the hole even deeper by shifting my body so I'm practically laying on him, bringing my hand up to his chest and smoothing his shirt out again.

He tenses under my touch, and for a moment I worry I've crossed some invisible line. But then his arm snakes up around my shoulders, his thumb swiping a gentle rhythm on my collarbone.

His breaths turn shallow, almost panicky. Or maybe those are mine. I can't tell over the roaring of my blood in my ears. There couldn't be a more minuscule amount of skin contact, but my whole body feels on fire.

I spent months hoping he would reach for my hand, living for the moments he would tuck my hair behind my ear or wrap me in a hug with the other boys. Now I'm here, being touched by Griffin Hart, and every voice inside my head is screaming that I should run.

I stopped paying attention to the movie a long time ago, so I turn my face up to his, alarmed at how close he is. He leans back to look into my eyes, and my heart rate goes up in a way that would alarm any cardio doctor. His grin reaches all the way to the warm depths of his irises, glittering like he's looking at the most wonderful thing he's ever seen.

No one has ever looked at me like this.

My eyes drop to his lips, just for a second, then back up to his eyes. There's nothing playful or warm about the way he's looking at me now–it's all heat, anticipation, *want.* His gaze fixates on my mouth, and he doesn't look back up at me.

He leans forward slowly, hesitantly, giving me the space to back away if I want to.

I don't want to.

All at once the weight of everything we've been through hits me. This moment feels like it's been planned since the dawn of time–and maybe it has, despite all the pain and anger and heartbreak. From the very first time I heard *"Howdy there,"* I think something deep inside me has known Griffin is inevitable. I don't know if I ever had a choice here.

I don't think I'd choose different even if I did.

I lift my mouth up to his, closing the remaining gap between us. His lips are soft, gentle, and he tastes like some sort of spice–*maybe cinnamon*? I don't have time to pinpoint it exactly, because the hand on my shoulder moves to the back of my neck, his other hand coming up to my jaw, tilting my head back and deepening the kiss.

My hand slides up to his collar, dragging him as close as I can get, the kiss turning from sweet to hungry, and the bed might go up in flames if this gets any hotter. In my entire relationship with Bennett, I never felt like this–like if he stopped kissing me the world would end.

Breaking apart, he presses his forehead to mine, our breathing both heavy and shaky at the same time. He pulls back to look at me again, tucking my hair behind my ear, a dazed look in his eyes.

"I've wanted to do that ever since I met you, darlin'," he says in a hoarse whisper. "I've dreamt it a thousand times. None of those dreams even came close." He presses another soft kiss on my mouth, and pulls me to his chest, holding me tightly like he's worried I might float away.

He hums contentedly, his thumb rubbing circles on my arm as I lay on his chest, the wild thundering of his heart grounding me in the comfort of his arms.

As we lay intertwined in his bed, with the white noise of the movie playing in the background, the butterflies in my stomach drown in waves of anxiety. My thoughts are reeling–we've crossed a line there's no coming back from. We've danced around this for years, and now that it's finally happened, I'm panicking.

Maybe this is real. Maybe this is the right person at the *right* time. I want it so bad it hurts, but my mind is replaying the day I found out about the bet like a scene from a horror movie, and fear overrides happiness before I can stop it.

Clearing my throat, I try to pull away nonchalantly, fighting the urge to run out of his room, his house, this town, and never look back. I would rather deal with the *what ifs* than set myself up for that kind of hurt again.

Oh my God. What if this is another stupid bet?

"It's getting kind of late," I say tensely, trying to keep the panic from my voice. "I should probably go home."

A small crease between his brow appears, and I can tell he's trying to figure out what just happened.

"Are you okay, darlin'?"

"Yeah," I say, sounding overly cheery. "Everything is totally fine, I'm just feeling tired."

"Was that too much?" he asks, his frown deepening in concern. "Did I read that wrong? I didn't mean to make you uncomfortable."

"I'm not uncomfortable! It was great, really. Exactly what I needed."

"What do you mean by that?"

I can hear the worry in his voice, but it doesn't stop me from saying the absolute worst thing I can think of.

"It was a perfect distraction, thank you for helping me get my mind off of things."

I regret the words as soon as they leave my mouth, my stomach dropping when I see the hurt flash across his face.

He recovers quickly, raking his hands through his hair and replacing his frown with a grin—one that *doesn't* reach his eyes this time.

"Anytime, Eleanor," he says casually, his voice still a little hoarse. "Glad I could help."

He follows me as I rush downstairs to gather my things, in such a hurry that my shoes end up on the wrong feet.

I should take it back. I should apologize, tell him I didn't mean it, plead with him to kiss me that way forever. I should tell him that I've felt lighter in the last few hours than I have in the last two years, that I don't ever want to lose him again.

Instead, I wrench the door open and whisper, "Goodnight, Griffin." I sneak a final look at him and immediately wish I hadn't. His composure has slipped, a tortured look now spreading on his face as he begins to say something.

I close the door and half run to my car, before I can give in to the urge to turn around and beg him to say something that might make me change my mind.

Chapter 24

Griffin

November, Age 18

My gut has been in knots since Eleanor all but sprinted out of my door last week. I really thought this was going to be it for us, that I had finally gotten it together enough to deserve her.

Not to mention that was the most mind blowing kiss in my entire life.

I've been on some dates here and there, mostly to distract myself from the way I want Eleanor every second of every day. All I'm saying is I'm no kissing virgin, that's for sure.

But honestly, I might as well have been, considering the way that kissing Eleanor was otherworldly. College is going to be wasted on me–I think I'll skip the partying phase entirely, because no high is ever going to feel as good as having Eleanor wrapped in my arms, her mouth on mine.

Which is why her words cut so deep. *"It was a perfect distraction."* I've never hated a string of words more.

It's my fault. I shouldn't have pushed it. I knew that she was emotional, vulnerable, lonely. But God, I can't help the way I'm drawn to her. It's like there's some force of nature connecting us, and when she was in my arms, *that* close to me, I didn't have a choice. Crossing that chasm that's been between us for so long was literally the only option.

I wanted so badly to show how I've made a real effort to grow up–not just for her, but for me. I don't want to be the dumbass that makes careless decisions and hurts people for the rest of my life. I want to be the type of man people call when they need someone.

I want to be Eleanor's someone.

For a second there, I really thought I did it. When she laid her head on my shoulder unprompted, I was so convinced that she saw the new Griffin–and that maybe she might want him just as bad as he wants her.

But then I saw the panic in her eyes, and she bolted before I could do anything. I don't know what I would have said to get her to believe me, to trust me, to stay, but it doesn't matter anyway. I didn't get the chance. And now that the moment has passed, I'm scared to death that she's going to go back to keeping me at arm's length.

I can't blame her for being scared. I know I fucked up astronomically. But there's also a voice in the back of my mind telling me that she's not scared–she just meant what she said. I was a distraction. Something to get her mind off of her boyfriend, a warm body to fill the void until her real friends were available again.

How many people did she reach out to before texting me? Was I a last resort?

The thought is like a kick to the teeth. But the one that follows is even worse.

Was this revenge? Is she getting back at me? Trying to hurt me the way I hurt her?

My stomach lurches, and I shove that thought down as deep as it will go. There's no way. We may not be friends anymore, but she can't have changed that much. She's everything good and warm and kind in this world, she wouldn't do that to anyone, even me.

Would she?

"Bro, earth to Griffin," David says, snapping his fingers in front of my face.

The guys are here, and I've been trying all night to work up the courage to tell them what happened. I don't want them to give me any grief for it. Even more so, I don't want them to get excited. If they get hopeful, I'm going to get hopeful, and I already have a gut feeling that something is about to go awry.

"Sorry," I mumble. "Listen, I gotta talk to you guys."

David and Jack share a knowing look, and then turn pointedly to face me, completely in sync as they fold their hands in their laps, smirks on their faces as they dramatically give me their full attention.

Rolling my eyes, I bite out, "Don't mess with me guys, I'm really trying to share something here."

This time the look they share is alarmed, and they unwind into more relaxed stances, giving me their genuine attention.

"So, I talked to Eleanor."

They both suck in a sharp breath.

"How did that go?" Jack asks tentatively.

"Good or bad?" David looks nervous. We buried the hatchet a long time ago, but he still gets a guilty look on his face any time she gets brought up.

"That's the problem," I say, scraping my hand down my face. "I have no idea. She kind of gave me mixed signals."

Neither of them say anything, they just raise their eyebrows and gesture for me to continue. I unload everything–seeing her in the parking lot, the birthday texting, having her in my room.

When I tell them how Bennett ruined her birthday, Jack looks murderous, and David jumps to his feet. "I swear to God, I'll go kick his ass right now." Jack grabs his arm and yanks him back down to the couch, shushing him and nodding at me to continue. When I get to the kiss, David whoops loudly, and even Jack cracks a smile. "About damn time," Jack says, sounding uncharacteristically emotional.

My heart physically hurts when I see how excited the guys are, because I know what comes next. The mood is instantly killed when I tell them what she said.

"Damn dude, that's cold," David says, shaking his head in disbelief.

"You know she didn't mean it," Jack says quietly. "She's scared."

"Yeah, I considered that. But what if she did mean it?"

Saying it out loud makes it actually feel real. The more I thought about it, the more convinced I was that none of it was real. If I hadn't read back through our messages a dozen times, I might believe that I actually dreamed it.

"Nah dude, Ellie wouldn't do you like that," David says. "She's an angel."

Shaking my head slowly, I finally admit what's been going through my head the past few days.

"I think I need to let it go."

Their eyes go wide with shock, their mouths opening to argue, but I cut them off. "That was our moment, and she obviously didn't want it. If the only way I can have her in my life is as a friend, I can live with that."

Every word that comes out is a struggle. I don't mean any of it, not really. The thought of having her around without *really* having her is unbearable. But she seemed so alone, and if I can patch things up so we can be "Ellie & The Dudes" again, I'll fall on that sword.

"We can just go back to Friday nights," I say with a finality that makes them both shut their mouths. "She'll move on, I'll move on, we'll all be friends and be happy."

David lets out an exasperated sigh, but doesn't argue. Jack stares me down, a muscle twitching where he has his jaw clenched. I can tell he doesn't want to let this go, but he nods curtly, and I'm grateful that he doesn't make me talk about it more.

David: Ellie, my girl, light of my life. I heard you and Griffin talked.

David: Can we get the band back to-gether? :(

Jack: What he means to say is that we miss you, and would you please come over on Friday?

It's surreal to see that the last text in this group chat was two years ago.

We all stare at our phones silently, fingers metaphorically crossed that she'll reply.

Eleanor: I'll see if I can make room in my schedule.

Eleanor: But not for you David, mostly for Jack. Then for Griffin. Then MAYBE for you. If you're good.

David: So you're saying there's a chance ;)

Eleanor: Just checked my calendar, looks like there's a perfect opening to "get the band back together"

Eleanor: I miss you guys, too.

Jack: See you then. Pick you up like normal?

<u>Eleanor</u>: Sounds perfect. <3

I exhale a rush of air–I have no idea how long I've been holding my breath, but I feel like I can fill my lungs to capacity for the first time in a long time.

"So, what are you going to do now?" Jack asks. "If you're so resigned to just being 'friends' with Ellie." He does air quotations around the word friends, and I can tell he doesn't believe me.

"I don't know," I say. "I'll figure something out."

"OH! I got it," David exclaims excitedly. "You should ask Katie out. She obviously has a thing for you, she's a shoo-in if you want to dip your toes back into the dating pool."

Katie is in the grade below us, but we've had a few elective classes together. She's on the soccer team, a soft-spoken girl with short dark hair, brown eyes and sharp features. She's a stark contrast to Eleanor's soft features and sharp tongue.

Maybe that's what I need–something completely different.

I resolve to ask her out, trying to assure the guys that I'm a lot more confident about this than I actually am. I don't want to move on. I don't ever want to stop fighting for Eleanor. I don't know how in the hell I'm going to be content going back to the way things were after she went and ruined all other girls for me with her perfect lips, and the way her body molded to mine like we were hand crafted for each other.

But I also have too much pride to just be a distraction for her. Being something casual to her is way worse than just being friends.

There's only so much a guy can take.

***

I've been a wreck all day. Eleanor being back in my house after years was nerve-wracking enough–but seeing her back in here after what happened last week? I break out in a sweat every time I think about it.

Jack and David have tried to chill me out, with zero success. Logically, I know that she's been over here to hang out with us a million times, but everything has changed. Now that I know the way she feels in my arms, the beat of her heart, the way she tastes, there's no way I can go back. How am I supposed to be normal when all I want to do is send Jack and David packing and beg Eleanor to give this a real shot?

Stop it, Griffin. This isn't about what you want. Think about your friends.

That's the thought that strengthens my resolve–my best friends in the world are so excited to have their *other* best friend back. Jack might still see her, but even he would admit it's not the same. And while I've had a chance to make up with Eleanor,

David hasn't. He's like a kid on his first field trip, vibrating with excitement at the chance to be around her again.

So I need to stick to my guns. I will not keep trying for more than friendship with Eleanor. Her wit, her charm, her fire–it'll be enough to simply have those in my life. If I can't have all of her...having some of her is better than nothing.

My stomach plummets when the door clicks open and I can hear Eleanor and Jack's voices. David, on the other hand, jumps up like an excited puppy and sprints up the stairs three at a time, shouting with joy.

I decide to wait for them in the basement, and when I hear a loud thud, I don't need to see it to know that David probably plowed into her with something more like a tackle than a hug.

Her bright laughter–music to my ears–drifts down the stairs, making my heart constrict. These are the last few seconds I have to pine for her before I absolutely have to get a grip on myself.

My angst is quickly overshadowed by the three sets of steps coming down the stairs. Jack's confident and even gait, David's thunderous and chaotic footfalls, and Eleanor's tell-tale steps–ones that have more of a swing beat than a steady cadence. The familiarity of it has me grinning ear to ear.

This is how it should be. This is good. This is enough.

Maybe Katie can have a place here too.

"Bro, what's wrong with your face?"

David's question pulls me from my thoughts, and I quickly clear the look of disgust I was apparently wearing.

Hated that thought.

"Stale cheese puff, super nasty," I say, waving my hand dismissively.

Out of the corner of my eye, I see Eleanor busying herself, removing her shoes and jacket, and looking around for somewhere to toss her bag and scarf before finally turning toward me.

When our eyes meet, the nerves on her face overwhelm me with the need to reassure her—*all cool here, I'm not going to make things weird, don't worry.*

"Howdy there, darlin'," I say, standing up and pulling her into a quick (*very platonic, I swear*) hug. I ruffle her hair, taking my seat back on the couch, a silent invitation for her to re-claim her basement throne.

Looking relieved, she drops into the chair and pulls her knees up to her chest, arms wrapped across her shins. She doesn't look uncomfortable exactly, more like she's trying to decide if she wants to slowly dip her toes in or dive head first.

"My boys," she says affectionately. "I've missed you dearly. Tell me everything."

David launches into a monologue about finding his calling (elementary school PE teacher, apparently) and landing on which college he wants to go to. Jack, in a very factual tone, lists off every bit of chaos David and me have found ourselves in over the last two years.

"You already know what there is to know about me, darlin'," I say with a shrug. "Business as usual around here."

I try for a casual, carefree smile, but damn if this girl can't see right through me.

"You doing okay here by yourself? When's the last time you saw your dad?"

I shift uncomfortably in my seat, avoiding eye contact with Jack and David as they whip their heads toward me. I may have failed to mention that my dad *also* moved out, and that I've been here alone. Dudes don't talk about that stuff—and they apparently don't notice it either. I don't know how they've gone months just assuming that he's never home, but I haven't exactly given them a reason to question that either.

"Oh, uh," I mutter, clearing my throat. "I saw him over the weekend, he's good."

When none of them ask me anything else, I ramble out, "Really. I'm good. It's good. Don't worry about me."

"Well I wasn't until now," Jack says, his brows furrowing in concern. "What does she mean by that, Griffin?"

With a sigh, I fill Jack and David in on everything with my parents—specifically about the part where I'm living in this house by myself. Their reactions are what I expected (and what I was avoiding), with David's mouth dropping, eyes widening in horror, and Jack's mouth disappearing into a thin line, nostrils flaring as he reins in his anger.

Eleanor looks at me like a deer in headlights, and I shake my head to let her know it's okay, that she didn't upset me by spilling those specific beans.

"Anyway," she says, a little too cheerfully. "I'm sure Griffin filled you in about my life."

David, who has never missed an opportunity to monologue, jumps into a rage-filled rant about how Bennett is *"the worst fucking rat on the planet"* and *"I swear Ellie, it's not just because I'm trying to suck up, I will drop kick his ass into an alternate timeline if you want."*

It takes my breath away to see her laugh, face lighting up more and more with every outrageous claim, and Jack's quips about the way David should sit this one out since his nine year old sister trapped him in a headlock last week.

This is fun. I can do this. No problem.

"Ellie, me and Jack are great wingmen," David declares. "We'll find you someone way better in no time. There's a guy out there for you."

The room goes eerily quiet, and it feels like a vacuum sucked every last air molecule out. Everyone knows that *everyone knows* what happened between me and Eleanor. There's no avoiding the implications of David's words. "There's a guy out there for you...*and it's not Griffin.*"

"I think the whole point of life is that there's someone out there for all of us," Jack says, something weirdly philosophical coming from him.

Eleanor smiles at him, but I catch a glimpse of sadness in her eyes when she briefly flicks them in my direction.

"Oh for sure," David replies quickly. "Hey wait, maybe you can help Griffin get back in the game!" His eyes go round, obviously hearing the double-meaning in his words. "Wait no, I didn't mean—just that you're a girl, and maybe you can give him advice on girl stuff."

We all stare blankly at him, and he keeps digging himself into the hole further.

"Not like *girl* stuff, Griffin's a dude. But like, advice on stuff girls like. Good compliments, first date ideas, how to ask a girl out, yada yada…" He lets his words trail off lamely, but a pang of panic rips through my chest when Eleanor turns her attention sharply to me.

David, please do not do this to me again.

"Oh?" Eleanor says in a tone that has me bracing for impact. "Does Griffin need advice about one girl in particular?"

I can't tell if she expects me to declare my feelings for her right now, or claim that there's a different girl. I have no idea which is a better idea to say out loud. Probably neither—*I don't think I'm getting out of this one unscathed.*

"Um, yeah," I say slowly, screwing up every fiber of courage I have. "I think I'm going to ask Katie out. We've had some classes together, she's cool."

Her mouth falls in surprise, her eyes shifting from something accusatory to the absolute worst case scenario—filled with hurt.

"Oh," she says again, much more quietly this time. "That's great. She's great. You'd be great together."

I try to concentrate on pretending that is totally my idea, not a new development at David's suggestion. But all I can think about is how we stammer the exact same way when we don't want to talk about something.

"I hope she knows what she's in for," she says, her voice taking on a sharp edge I'm unfamiliar with.

Is she...angry with me?

Suddenly bristling, I fire back, "And what's that supposed to mean?"

I feel Jack tense beside me, and David mutters *oh shit* under his breath.

"I just hope she's not looking for anything serious," she says smoothly. "Since you jump from girl to girl so quickly."

She is angry. For what? She's the one who brushed it off like it was nothing.

"I wouldn't have jumped to another girl if someone hadn't pushed me," I bark out.

"Pushed you?" Eleanor cries with a shrill laugh. "Please do enlighten me. Was it pushing when I cried about my breakup? Was it pushing when I laid in your bed? Was it pushing when I let you kiss me?"

"*Let me?*" I growl, no longer fighting to keep my tone in check. "Don't you dare put this on me, that wasn't a one sided kiss." Smacking my hand to my chest, pointing at myself, "*I'm* not the one who called it a distraction."

Her face turns red as she leaps out of her seat. "Because I was scared, Griffin!"

"Scared of what, Eleanor? That this might be something real between us?"

"Scared that you're going to hurt me again! That I can't trust you!"

"Well I'm not going to be some back up plan to make out with when you're sad, twiddling with my thumbs while you decide if you can trust me again," I say, voice dangerously low. "You don't get to ask me to wait around for you forever."

"Don't worry," she says harshly. "I'll make sure you don't have to be around me *at all.* Enjoy your new girl."

She storms upstairs, slamming the door behind her as she leaves.

"That lasted all of ten minutes," Jack sighs defeatedly, rising to follow her.

"I don't want a new girl," David says in a small voice.

My anger dissipating, I hang my head, shame washing over me. "I'm sorry you guys," I say, shaking my head. "I don't think me and Eleanor can ever go back to the way it was before."

Without another word, I go upstairs to my room, sliding into my bed without turning on the light. An odd combination of numbness and heaviness weighs on my ribs, and I replay her words over and over in my head, trying to pinpoint the exact moment of disaster.

What the fuck just happened?

Chapter 25

Ellie

November, Age 18

My fight with Griffin looks a lot different on this side of sleep.

When I left in dramatic fashion last night, I was so sure my anger was justified. The moment I woke up this morning, reality hit me like a freight train.

To quote the man himself–I fucked up. I'm surprised I'm even admitting it, I'm so used to being right. I'm always on the right side of an argument (*at least in my head I am*), and given our history, no wonder I jumped to the conclusion that I'm the wronged party here.

Newsflash–I am not.

Griffin was right. I'm the one who called our kiss a distraction. I downplayed it because the connection we have scares me to bits.

"Ellie, you're a lot better at forgiving than you are apologizing. And let's be real, you aren't great at either of them. You're going to have to work on that if you want Griffin around."

Abby's words from last night are ringing in my head. I called her the second I slammed my bedroom door behind me, ready to rant and plot his demise.

After I finished unloading, she took so long to respond I thought the call might have dropped. Or maybe she was so appalled by his actions that she couldn't come up with a response. Or she left her phone behind in her haste to follow through on that murder charge she was worried about catching.

Instead she did the worst thing imaginable–she decided to be reasonable. *That traitor.*

"Sweetie, I hate to say it...but I think you're wrong here."

To her credit, she stood her ground when I voiced my outrage. Loudly. At great length.

"He's hurt, Ellie. You shut him out for years, made out with him, then brushed it off. He probably feels used."

Well shit, I didn't think of that.

"I wasn't using him Abby, I just freaked out."

"I know that, but he doesn't. Well I guess technically he does since you screamed at him."

That made me wince. *Not my finest moment.*

"He's allowed to be scared too, my love. Maybe it's time to stop punishing him for one mistake."

"But it was a big mistake, Abs," I choked, tears beginning their familiar path down my face.

"It was. But maybe you let go of that to make room for something wonderful. You like him, he likes you. Let it happen."

"What if everything goes wrong?"

"Not to get too Hobby Lobby canvas with it, but what if everything goes right?"

After considering her words for a few minutes, I grab my phone to call Griffin, but some mental block has my finger hovering over the button without actually pushing it.

Deciding against it, I toss my phone back on the bedside table and bury myself in my comforter with a groan. I'm going to have to apologize. I have no idea how to do that. I don't exactly have a lot of practice.

You're going to have to work on that.

I peek up over my covers when there's a knock on my door. I consider telling whoever it is to go away, but before I get a chance, my mom opens the door and says, "Angel, there's someone here to see you."

My heart leaps with hope that maybe Griffin is here to talk everything out. I can almost feel myself physically deflate when Jack walks in.

"Don't look so excited to see me," he says grimly, closing my door and pulling my desk chair over to the side of the bed.

"Ugh," I exhale frustratedly, yanking the covers back up over my head. "Go away Jack, I know I messed up, I'll apologize."

He firmly, but gently, peels the blanket back, forcing me to look at him. He doesn't look angry, he looks sympathetic. Deciding that he's not here to berate me, I sit up all the way, pulling my knees up to my chin. Hopefully he can say something to make me feel better–or at least feel like less of a psycho.

"How was the rest of the night?" I ask quietly, scared of the answer.

"Well, not good," he admits with a sigh. "When I got back after taking you home, Griffin was locked up in his room and David was pacing like a lunatic trying to figure out how to fix things."

"Sorry I made such a scene," I apologize defeatedly. "The reunion tour is off to a bad start."

He smiles at my attempt at levity, patting my forearm in comfort. "Every great band had some kind of fallout, doesn't mean we can't figure it out."

"You really think so?"

I hate how small I sound. I hate that it's my own fault.

"I do," Jack says with a slow nod. "I think things will be different though."

My heart sinks. "Do you think he'll forgive me?"

In a gentle voice, he continues, "He'll always forgive you, Ellie. In his eyes, you hung the moon. One fight won't erase that."

His tone shifts, his next words sounding like a warning. "But you can't do this to him again. Either be in, or be out. But don't make him feel like a backburner option."

"He's not just an option to me, I swear he's more than that," I reply quickly. Biting my lip nervously, I whisper, "I think I want to be in. All the way."

He nods his head, but doesn't say anything.

"Do you think I ruined everything, Jack?"

"I don't think you blew your only chance, if that's what you mean."

I exhale a sigh of relief, but that relief is short lived.

"But you need to do a lot better than *I think* here. You need to know."

Guilt twists my stomach in knots. Even here, with one of my best friends, I still can't bring myself to be honest about my feelings. I don't know why my knee-jerk reaction is to downplay it.

"And you probably need to give him the space to figure out exactly what *he* wants," he adds, standing and stretching his arms up. "You got to work through your feelings while you were with Bennett."

He extends a hand down to me.

"Maybe it'll be good for him to go on a date with someone else," he says, gesturing for me to take his hand. Yanking me onto my feet, he adds one final thought. "I think it's inevitable that she won't measure up to you. Let's go meet Abby for lunch, I already texted her."

The thought of Griffin on a date with someone else makes me sick to my stomach, but Jack is right. I dated someone else for over a year while Griffin waited around. It's my turn to be patient. I can do that. For him.

***

"Griffin, hey, wait up!" I yell, half-running down the hallway to catch up to him. He turns around, and a fresh wave of guilt washes over me at the residual hurt in his eyes.

We haven't spoken since I, for lack of a better term, lost my shit on Friday. Jack and Abby gave me a combination pep talk slash scolding, and I've been trying to find the words to apologize since then. After my dad told me he was getting whiplash from the number of times I kept picking up my phone and immediately putting it back down at the dinner table, I decided it'd be better to just apologize in person.

Now that I'm here, every word I planned has escaped me.

After a moment of silence, Griffin says, "Okay I waited up. Did you need something?"

Okay, so he's definitely still mad.

"Yes," I say breathlessly, nervously wringing my hands, dropping my gaze to my shoes. "I wanted to say sorry."

When he doesn't say anything, I look up at him, and find him waiting expectantly, eyebrows raised.

"I'm sorry. That was unfair to you. You've been nothing but patient and kind to me, and I had no right to snap at you. If you want to ask Katie out, you should."

Unable to stop myself, I keep babbling on.

"Not that you need my permission, you can do whatever you want. I just want you to know I support you, and I'm glad we're friends again, and kissing you was great, but we don't have to do it again if you don't want, which obviously you don't since–"

"Eleanor, chill," Griffin interrupts with a laugh. "We're all good, darlin'. I appreciate the apology."

He grins at me brightly, and I smile hesitantly in return.

"I'm sorry I lost my temper, too," he says, raking his hand through his hair. "You and me sure bring out the fire in each other."

That's one way of putting it. More like "Fun fact, I've felt like I'm on fire since we kissed."

"I don't know if I'm going to ask Katie out," he continues. "Either way, I hope things can stop being weird. David is gonna be crushed if Ellie & The Dudes are breaking up again."

The smile on my face is no longer hesitant, but full and genuine. "Tell David not to worry, the reunion tour is still on."

He moves to my side, putting his arm around my shoulders as we continue down the hall. My heart skips a beat at the warmth of his touch, but I remind myself that it's just friendly–the same way he would throw his arm around David or Jack.

I feel him tense up, and he drops his arm. I look around for what made him clam up, and spot Katie walking toward us. When she spots Griffin, her face brightens, waving at him with a coy smile.

He waves back, one corner of his mouth tipping up in a smirk. I don't know if he's worried about my reaction, or spiraling about whether or not he's going to ask her out, but there's no denying the way my heart sinks.

He gives me an awkward pat on my shoulder and mumbles out a hurried goodbye before darting inside his classroom.

The rest of the way to my own class, I can't shake the feeling that this is going to be much harder than I thought.

Chapter 26

Ellie

October, Age 28

"Ellie, you're a genius."

Sitting in the crowded coffee house with Tori, my notes are strewn across the table as we hash out some of the reunion details. Once we came to terms with the fact that reunions are inherently cheesy and there's no avoiding it, we finally landed on a theme—A Walk Down Memory Lane.

Today we're focused on how we can reminisce without having some lame slideshow accompanied by Time of Your Life by Green Day.

From what Sophia told me and the photos I've seen online, the venue has a stunning garden, almost bordering on a hedge maze. The idea for the main attraction is to set up some sort of tactile walk down memory lane—with pictures, stories, and highlights, laid out chronologically from freshman through senior year. Not my most inventive idea to date, but certainly not my worst.

"I can start pulling notable stories—things like big sports wins, the time the gym caught fire, the bizarre March blizzard.

Do you think you could reach out to Sophia and see if she can get access to the old yearbook photos?"

"Absofreakinlutely I can," Tori says, nearly bouncing in her seat with excitement. "I'm so glad we convinced you to come back, I don't know what we'd do without you."

"I'm sure you'd be fine," I say with a polite smile.

"No, I'm sure we'd definitely end up with a lame slideshow and a Vitamin C song, but that's sweet of you anyway. Can I keep this?"

"I was stuck on the Green Day song," I chuckle. "And sure, I have copies on my laptop," I say as she begins gathering the scattered designs, to-do lists, and notes.

"Seriously Ellie, thank you," she says earnestly. "I'll see you this weekend for the venue walk!"

Waving goodbye, she weaves through the crowd heading for the door, a polite stranger holding it open for her on the other side. I let out a sigh, settling back into my seat, closing my eyes and taking a deep drink of my coffee. Tori was more peppy than scary today and apparently the crushing weight of adulthood hasn't tampered that side of her one bit.

The bell over the door chimes as it swings closed, and call it fate, intuition, demonic torment–but I feel a shift in the atmosphere that makes me nervous to open my eyes again. Bracing myself, I sit up straight again and cautiously look to see what's caused it.

From where I'm seated in the corner, it's hard to see me from the front door, but I have a clear view of everyone at the counter–including the couple that just walked in.

I recognize Madison first, her silky raven hair nearly to her waist, tall and graceful, olive skin somehow glowing brighter now than it did when we were teenagers. Like the dreaded slow-pan in a horror movie, my gaze slides to the man standing next to her, hand on the small of her back.

I want to scream, to throw up, to run, but I sit here paralyzed by my first glimpse of Griffin Hart in nearly five years. Like it's second nature, my heart warms at the sight of him. He's every bit the way I remember him.

The harsh reality that I'm a stranger to him now follows like a sucker punch.

His hair is longer now, nearly to his shoulders, but has the familiar swoop I was always so desperate to run my hands through. His stature hasn't changed much, but even if it had, I think I'd recognize him anywhere–tall, broad-shouldered, an aura of confidence radiating off of him even as he's just standing there.

He leans down to whisper something in her ear and she lets out a warm, throaty laugh. Suddenly I'm leaning a lot more towards throwing up. He grins at her, and my chest tightens at the memories of all the times that smile was reserved for me.

My brain finally reconnects with my body and I jolt out of my seat, trying to leave as quickly as possible without drawing attention to myself. In my haste to get the hell out of dodge,

I bump into the woman entering the coffee shop, stammering out an apology. In a stroke of horrific luck, my voice echoes in the entryway in the split second that there's silence between the songs playing over the speakers.

Out of the corner of my eye, I see Griffin whip around at the sound of my voice, and although I don't look back, I can feel his eyes on me as I finally clear the glass doors, the tinkling of that damn bell sure to haunt my dreams for the foreseeable future.

Chapter 27

Griffin

OCTOBER, AGE 29

It was inevitable. From the moment Jack told me that Eleanor's back in town, I've been walking around waiting for the bomb to go off–the one where our paths cross again for the first time since my heart shattered all those years ago.

It feels like an eternity and no time at all–some days I miss her so much it physically hurts. Other days, I realize that I haven't thought about her in a week, and somehow that hurts worse. There was never supposed to be a life without Eleanor Turner in it.

But there is. There has been for a long time. Knowing it's over, knowing that I was bound to see her, didn't soften the blow of hearing that sweet voice and seeing those soft blonde waves as she bolted from 8th Street Coffee. Someone could have hit me over the head with a chair and it would have been less of a shock to the system. It didn't cross my mind that I'd be with another woman when it happened.

"Another woman." Like we're not in a fully committed relationship. I'm a jackass.

"Honey? What did you want?"

Madison's voice breaks the trance Eleanor stunned me into. Madison–my girlfriend, my anchor, the sure and steady presence in my life. Madison, who suddenly feels like a stranger now that I've had the slightest glimpse of the woman who just walked out the door.

"Sorry sweetheart, I got distracted. Just a black coffee is fine."

I pay for our drinks, operating on autopilot as my head spins with thoughts of Eleanor. We grab our to-go cups and head back to the car–Madison insists on driving everywhere because she gets carsick. I stoop low, the tiny sedan an uncomfortable squeeze for my long legs, still silent and feeling like I'm a thousand miles away.

When we get to the apartment, I immediately text Jack, quickly coming up with some excuse for leaving even as I'm halfway out the door.

"Okay honey, tell Jack I said hi, I love–"

The door slams shut, cutting her off, and a wave of guilt crashes over me, the way it always does when my subconscious reminds me that she's great, wonderful, perfect for me in every way.

But she's not the love of my life.

I meet Jack at the firehouse, taking the stairs three at a time up to the loft above the station reserved for the fire chief. Old man Ritter would rather drop dead than give up his Sleep Number mattress, so he let Jack take over the space, so small you can barely call it a studio apartment. It shocked the hell out of me when he told me he was coming back to Larkspur, but damn if I'm not glad he's here.

When I open the door, I see that Jack isn't alone–David is lounging on his couch, making himself right at home the way he has a habit of doing everywhere he goes.

"Well, well, well," he says. "Hello traitor."

He doesn't bother standing up as I clap Jack on the back, then move around the couch to shove his legs off and take a seat.

"What are you on about?" I ask.

"What, just because I don't live here anymore, all of a sudden you only text Jacky boy in an emergency?" He lifts a hand to his chest, moaning like a wounded animal. "That hurts, Griff."

He's being dramatic, but it doesn't hide the genuine worry in his face. And given the way I reacted to three measly seconds of Eleanor, maybe he should be worried.

"When?" Jack asks, not needing to clarify.

"Just now, at the coffee house," I say, my voice sounding weary. "She didn't say anything to me, in fact she ran out like the building was on fire. I barely got a glimpse of her."

"Did you want her to say something?" he asks slowly.

"I don't know, man," I say, dropping my head back and closing my eyes. "Part of me wants to get it over with, part of me hopes I can avoid talking to her altogether."

"No way dude, you gotta at least say hi," David says. "It's worse for you if you don't, you'll always wonder 'what if?'"

"What if *what* though?" I say, frustration beginning to boil in my chest. "What if it goes well? What if we fight? What if we have nothing to say?"

Now that I'm on a roll, every bitter thought comes pouring out. "What if we have our movie moment? What if we finally manage a life where we don't constantly rip each other apart? We both know that's not going to happen."

My voice rises along with my temper, and I know it's not fair to take it out on my friends, but that doesn't stop me. "What are you guys even here for? What's the fucking point? Nothing is going to make this less awkward or shitty." Punching the couch pillow in my lap, I mutter, mostly to myself, "I should have gone on vacation and drowned Larkspur out until this stupid reunion is over."

Looking up at my friends' faces, my anger is replaced by regret almost instantly. "I'm sorry you guys, I didn't mean to yell at you," I sigh in that same weary tone. "I feel like shit right now. I was an ass to Madison, I'm being an ass here. Why is it that I become the worst version of myself when my mind gets stuck on her?"

"Because the best version of you wouldn't exist without her," Jack says quietly. "It's soul-crushingly painful when you thought you had forever, but forever walks out the door and doesn't look back."

I tilt my head back, eyes fixed on the ceiling, trying to blink away the burning sensation building behind my eyes. Eleanor was my forever. Part of her always will be.

Patting me on the shoulder, David simply nods his head in agreement. Jack stands up, gripping my other shoulder briefly before heading to the kitchen and grabbing four beers from the fridge, keeping one for himself, handing one each to me and David, and setting the fourth one on the table in front of me.

"Are we expecting someone else?" I ask, brows furrowing in confusion. "No," he says. "But you're going to slam that first one and need another, and I don't want to get up again."

I shrug, not bothering to argue. Cracking the can open, I down half of it in one go, still trying to figure out how one glimpse of her can still turn my world upside down all these years later.

Chapter 28

Griffin

February, Age 18

"**I**'m really glad we're doing this. I thought maybe you'd never ask me out."

After a week or two of things really feeling back to normal with Eleanor and the guys, I decided to ask Katie on a date after all. We've been on a few dates since then, and it's been good.

Okay so maybe I had to talk myself into a second date. I had no reason not to–the first date went objectively well. She's nice, and she's pretty, and she's driven.

And she's not Eleanor.

"Sorry to have kept you waiting," I say with a lighthearted attempt at flirting. Is that flirting? Maybe it's just teasing. Something about it always feels unnatural with Katie. Whatever you want to call it, it makes her smile.

"You seem like the kind of guy worth waiting for."

She's also sweet, albeit a little serious. There's no back and forth, no mutual teasing. Just matter-of-fact communication.

That'll take some getting used to.

I don't have to wonder what's happening between us. Everything is straightforward here. I like her, she likes me, we're having a good time.

This is good for you, Griffin. Just a nice, easy relationship with a girl who's been very clear about her feelings.

Even the thought of the word relationship makes me uneasy, but that's where this is heading. We've spent enough time together now that it's a little weird that I haven't asked her to be my girlfriend.

Every time I get close, something in me freezes up and I can't bring myself to do it. I tell myself it's because it's too soon, and she hasn't met my friends yet, and school has been busy. But I know I either need to commit or cut it off.

Cutting it off opens the door for someone else. But committing is a sure thing here. It's the smart choice, the right choice.

"Listen Katie, we've been on a few dates now, and I think you're great," I say.

To my surprise, her face falls.

"But you don't want to see me anymore," she says in a quiet voice.

Yes.

"No, that's not it at all," I stammer out before I can change my mind. "The opposite actually, I think we should make it official."

The second it leaves my mouth I regret it. I don't really mean it, and this is unfair to her. I know I'm about to be shitty, but

when I open my mouth to take it back, the look on her face stops m
e.

She looks like a kid on Christmas.

"I'd like that a lot," she says excitedly, beaming at me. "God, I've had a crush on you for so long, I never thought this would actually happen."

"I'm glad I made you happy," I say, and I mean it. I am glad she's happy. And I think with time I can be that happy too. This is going to work. This is going to be *great.*

After paying the bill, we make our way out of the restaurant to where my truck is parked. I walk her to the passenger side, opening the door for her like the gentleman my dad raised me to be.

She lingers for a moment, looking up at me, pulling her bottom lip between her teeth.

For a second I can't figure out why she's not getting in the truck, and then it hits me.

She's waiting for me to kiss her.

Despite having gone on multiple dates, I still haven't done more than hug her goodnight. But now that she's my girlfriend...

I tilt my head down, placing a soft kiss on her mouth. I wait for something, *anything.* There are no fireworks, no butterflies, no going weak in the knees.

At least not on my end. But when I pull back, I see a flush in her cheeks, and she avoids eye contact bashfully as she climbs into the seat.

I give her another peck for good measure, hoping that maybe I'll feel a little more of a spark this time. There's nothing. I close the door, walking around to the driver's side less like someone who just kissed his girlfriend for the first time and more like someone walking the green mile.

The whole drive back to her house, I silently berate myself. This is good. This is normal. This is healthy.

Give it time, Griffin. Not everything has to be like wildfire. Slow and steady can be good, too.

No matter how hard I try to shove it from my mind, all I can think about the rest of the drive home is the kiss that altered my entire psyche, and the girl I shared it with.

***

"Bro, when is Katie gonna come to a Friday night hang?" David asks.

"I don't know," I say with a shrug. "I just figured this was sacred 'Ellie and The Dudes' time, I didn't want to infringe on that."

"It sounds so weird when you say that," Jack mumbles.

"What are you on about?"

"The only time you call her Ellie is when you reference the groupchat name, it's unsettling," he says, sounding weirdly irritated. "Just call her Eleanor like you normally do."

Eleanor looks up at him, bewildered. She turns to look at me, and I return her wide-eyed look with my hands raised in mock surrender. I have no idea why he's being so weird.

"I actually don't think I've met her yet," Eleanor ponders. "You should totally bring her sometime."

Her tone is bright, but cool-calm-collected, like she's in a job interview for CEO of nonchalance, not telling a guy she's kissed like her life depended on it to bring his new girlfriend around.

I guess it's not new—we've been dating for a few months now. The longer I wait to bring her around my friends, the weirder it feels, like I missed my window. She would never say anything, but I can tell it's a sore subject for Katie, too.

I wonder (and hope) whether her totally-normal-and-chill attitude is like mine—fake as shit.

"Okay, yeah, for sure," I say, trying to summon even an ounce of enthusiasm.

"Thank God, I've been worried that you're embarrassed by us," David says with a sigh of relief. "Or that maybe you didn't want *us* to meet *her* for some reason."

Jack and Eleanor share a quick look that I definitely *won't* be reading into for hours tonight.

"Nah, you guys are the best. And Katie's really awesome, she's super cool. I think she'd totally fit in."

Am I reassuring them, or trying to convince myself?

***

This was a stupid, terrible, awful idea.

Which makes me internally cringe, because it shouldn't be an awful idea to introduce your girlfriend to your friends. But here we are. The five of us. In my basement.

And it's awkward as hell.

Everyone has made at least one effort to get the conversation going, but nothing has stuck. Katie doesn't get David's humor, so all of his jokes are falling flat. Jack refuses to use words with more than one syllable for some reason. Eleanor has barely said a word, she mostly just smiles and nods.

With a fifth body in the room, our normal assigned seating got all messed up, and not in a way I anticipated. David is sprawled on the floor, even though there's a perfectly fine third cushion on the couch. Even when Katie jokingly said, *"I promise I don't bite,"* David gave a weird pity laugh and settled himself even further onto the ground.

Eleanor is still kind of in her normal spot–she's technically sitting on her chair. But for some reason Jack is in the main seat, and she's perched on the arm. I know they're friends, but the way she's leaned into him to sit comfortably triggers a sharp burning sensation in my chest.

Hello, you have a girlfriend bozo, maybe focus on whether she's comfortable instead of being weird about Eleanor.

I shift and put my arm around Katie's shoulders, but the movement feels forced. She's a lot taller than...other girls...and for some reason she can never quite get her shoulders low enough for this to be comfortable for either of us.

But this is my girlfriend, and if I pull away from her in front of my friends that is *not* going to end well for me.

"So Katie," Eleanor says, her voice much peppier than usual. "How did you guys meet?"

Katie picks at her cuticles nervously, and I should hold her hand to ease her nerves, but I just can't bring myself to do it.

"Oh, it's nothing interesting," she says with a nervous laugh. "When Griffin couldn't fit Spanish into his schedule, we ended up in the same physics class, and then I guess the rest is history from there."

I should add something. Maybe something sweet about the first time I noticed her, or our first interaction. I should say something, *anything*, to rescue her from floundering.

But my eyes are locked on the spot where Jack's hand is resting on Eleanor's knee. He moved it there when Katie mentioned Spanish, and I swear I saw him give her a small squeeze, like he was comforting her.

Nothing's going on there right? There's no way.

"Very cool," Eleanor says in that same peppy tone. David hums in agreement, but Jack only gives one tense nod in acknowledgment.

"Wait a sec," David says, sitting up. "I thought you dropped Spanish because you said it made you sad."

"No, David," I say with a forced laugh, like I'm humoring my dopey best friend and not about to rip his head off. "I said I was bummed I couldn't fit it in my schedule—not that the class made me sad."

"Well obviously I know Spanish didn't make you sad, I meant–" David argues, brows furrowing in confusion, but when I see Eleanor shake her head almost imperceptibly out of the corner of my eye, he snaps his mouth shut.

"Oh, you're probably right dude," he says quickly, trying to brush it off. "You know I never listen to what your dumb ass has to say."

Breaking the uncomfortable silence that follows, Katie asks, "So, I know how Griffin met Jack and David, but how did he meet you, Ellie?"

Katie doesn't clock the way her eyes widen slightly, but I sure do. *And there's Jack gripping her knee again. What that fuck is that?*

"Oh," she says, her falsely cheery shield cracking a bit when the question catches her off guard. "Funny you mentioned it, I actually met him in Spanish class freshman year."

"Oooh, we'll have to hang out sometime so I can get the inside scoop," Katie says, perking up with curiosity. "You must have all the tea about whatever girl from your class broke his heart. He won't tell me who she is, just that they don't talk anymore."

Shit shit shit.

"Oh, totally," Eleanor says, laughing it off like she's genuinely looking forward to some girly gossip hour. "Yeah, she was a real bitch."

David immediately chokes on the gummy worm he's eating, and Jack gives her a sharp look at the same time that I yell, "Watch it!"

Katie jumps, startled by the chaotic reactions, but Eleanor chimes in before any of us can say anything.

"Ignore them," she says with a wave of her hand. "I don't normally curse, they lose their minds every time I do it."

Katie relaxes back, laughing at what she thinks is a well-timed joke. David gasps loudly as he finally dislodges the gummy from his throat, and Jack has readjusted his facial expression, but when my eyes lock on Eleanor's, I can't read the emotions behind them.

I don't think that's ever happened before.

"Anyway, it's getting kind of late," I say, clearing my throat. "Don't you need to be home soon for curfew?" It's only 10 PM on a Friday, and we both know damn well that her curfew isn't until midnight. For a second I think she's going to call me on my bullshit, but whatever she sees on my face when she turns to look at me must convince her otherwise.

"Yeah no, you're right," she says in a small voice, "It was really nice to hang out with you guys."

She gathers up her things, awkwardly waving goodbye before heading upstairs. I mentally kick myself every step of the way behind her, because this was, as I've said, an *awful* idea.

I expected the guys to still be here when I got back, but all I hear is silence. Laying in bed, I try to convince myself my friends are the reason tonight was so awkward. I grab my phone from my nightstand and angrily type out a text.

Griffin: What the fuck guys?

Jack: Pardon?

David: I swear I didn't do it

Griffin: Do what?

David: I don't know, but whatever it is, it's not my fault

Eleanor: Hi Griffin, how are you? I'm fine, thanks for asking. Is there something you wanted to discuss?

Griffin: Hi. Whatever. You guys were so rude to Katie.

Jack: In what fucking universe?

David: It's not my fault I choked, Ellie made me. Blame her.

Eleanor: I know you're not talking to me, I was nothing but polite.

Griffin: Ok ok, rude might be the wrong word.

Griffin: But you definitely weren't welcoming.

David: Bro I tried, she did NOT get me :(

Eleanor: I asked her so many questions about herself, so again, I know you're not talking to me.

Jack: Maybe we weren't the problem.

Griffin: The fuck does that mean?

Jack: Don't make me put it in the group chat.

Ripping my phone off its charger, I call Jack, so angry my skin is crawling.

"Hello?"

Like he doesn't know who's calling him. I might hit him.

"What the fuck is your problem?"

He heaves a heavy sigh, but doesn't respond.

"Hello? Jackass? I asked you a question."

"I don't have a problem, Griffin."

"Acutally, you clearly do."

After another beat of silence, he says, "It's not necessarily a problem, I just don't think you and Katie should be together."

"Why don't you like Katie?" I bark out accusingly.

"I never said I don't like Katie, I just don't like her for you. I actually don't even think *you* like her. And I definitely don't like her for Friday nights. That was the worst."

"It was the worst because you guys wouldn't give it a fair shot," I grumble, ignoring his insinuation about my feelings. Anger flaring again, I continue, "And what the hell was that with Eleanor? Since when have you guys been so close?"

"Since I was the only one she actually talked to for the last two years, don't start with me there," he says with a sharpness to his tone that has me physically recoiling from my phone. "Let's not get into why I'm the one who's close with Eleanor instead of you."

"Is there something going on between you?" I blurt out before I can stop myself. "You sure seemed touchy-feely."

His sigh this time is much more exasperated.

"No idiot, nothing is *'going on'* between us."

"Then why was your hand on her knee?"

"Why were you focused on that instead of your girlfriend?"

Damn, he got me there.

"I don't know, it was just weird." It comes out muffled as I drag my hand down my face.

"Tonight was hard for her too, Griffin," he says, not necessarily angrily, but not friendly either.

Protective. That's the word.

"I'm gonna be frank with you dude," he continues.

"Oh, that was you being polite just then?"

Ignoring the jab, he keeps going.

"Ellie loves you. You love her. You certainly don't love Katie."

He's not wrong, at least about me, but hearing it out loud like that still feels like a baseball bat to the shins.

"What am I supposed to do with that, Jack?"

"I don't know, maybe break up with Katie, make up with Ellie, and get your shit together? We all know it's going to happen eventually, but I wish you'd hurry it up."

Groaning, I sink further into my bed.

"You're right, man. I'll talk to Katie this weekend," I say dejectedly.

"You also need to talk to Ellie, Griffin."

"Okay okay, geez, I'll talk to Eleanor, too."

"Well, she's out of town for spring break, so you'll have to wait."

Fuck me.

"Then why did you even bring it up?"

"To give you time to work out what you want to say to her. Don't fuck it up."

Without another word, he hangs up.

Inhaling a shaky breath, I put my phone back on the charger and stare up at the ceiling.

Ellie loves you. You love her.

Those two sentences play in my head over and over like a twisted lullaby as I try to fall asleep. I almost don't want to believe it. Can we actually work this out? Is this the 'right person, right time' they talk about?

Either way, you still have to break up with your girlfriend.

That thought quickly douses any glimmer of hope that was growing, and I yank my covers over my head, deciding to let that be tomorrow's problem.

Chapter 29

Ellie

> **Tori:** Definitely double booked myself, forgot I was meeting with the caterer today. You think you can handle the walkthrough on your own?

Of course Tori overcommitted–fork found in kitchen.

> **Margo:** Kid emergency! Can't make it, but the contractor will be there, he'll show you around. Sorry!!!!

The second text came through right as I pulled up to the old barn. Tori and I had scheduled a walkthrough of the venue today. I'm hoping that my vision for this reunion is possible. I looked at the photos on the website, but I'm too familiar with real estate photography to trust the space just on pictures alone.

Margo, the on-staff event coordinator, was meant to meet us here and show me around, but given the fact that she has five children, I'm not shocked she also had to cancel at the last minute. Thank God the contractor is here, the last thing I want is to reschedule this. I'm starting to feel the familiar nerves that come when approaching a project deadline–even if this is just a high school reunion and not the high-stakes commercial projects I'm normally running.

My footsteps echo in the enormous ballroom area as I weave through the main building looking for my new tour guide. Sophia wasn't kidding–this place looks amazing. My memories of the barn mostly involve Yeti coolers full of Smirnoff Ice and drunken teenagers tripping over the broken beams scattered across a hay-covered dirt floor. Now it could pass for the type of coveted wedding venue that books out three years in advance.

The dusty floor has been replaced by stunning hardwood, with a checkerboard dancefloor installed in the center of the room. The high ceilings have been expertly restored, the exposed beams maintaining the rustic charm without looking like the roof might collapse at any moment. Twinkle lights have been strung between the beams, with a wagon wheel chandelier providing the majority of the warm glow basking the room. In short, it's every southern belle's dream.

Through the doors at the far end of the main room is the winding red brick walkway that leads to the grounds. As I approach the final curve, I hear a deep male voice. *"Yeah, I'm meeting some event planner here for a walkthrough, one of Margo's kids shoved a dime up their nose. Again."*

Surely this is a joke. That can't possibly be the voice I think it is. But when the owner of the voice finally comes into view,

I freeze–and nearly fall flat on my face. The contractor is none other than Griffin Hart.

Engrossed in his phone call, he didn't hear me approach, and I let myself take him in the way I wanted to at the coffee shop. This is the closest I've been to him since we were twenty three, and good lord has time has been good to him.

In addition to the brown locks and broad shoulders that grabbed my attention a few days ago, I'm close enough now to see the way his arms have only gotten stronger and more toned through years of manual labor.

I swear if he sneezes wrong he's going to rip right out of that t-shirt.

My eyes rake slowly down his body, as if I'm subconsciously trying to memorize every slope of taut muscle, every place the fabric of his shirt clings to him, leaving almost nothing to the imagination. Even though I can only see his back, there's no doubt in my mind that his chest muscles are straining against his shirt the same way his biceps are.

Traveling further south, I suck in a sharp breath when I get a glimpse of what has always been my favorite part of him to ogle–that tight ass in those damn Wranglers.

Thank God that some things never change.

I can feel the critical thinking leaving my brain as memories of deep kisses and hastily removed clothing surface, followed by the alarming thought that I'd like to rip those clothes off him in the middle of this barn and see if he feels as good as he used to.

I take a small step forward, desperately wanting to be closer even as the last sane brain cell in my head is imploring me to get it together. My foot finds a rogue pebble, a scraping noise on the brick finally alerting Griffin to my presence. He turns around, jaw dropping at the same time as his phone goes clattering to the ground. I can hear the voice on the other line yelling *"Bro what was that? Hello? Griffin?"* and recognize it as David's.

We stare at each other in silence for a few moments, his jaw still hanging open as I give a tentative smile and wave. Without taking his eyes off me, he bends down to grab his phone, bringing it to his ear and quickly saying, "I gotta go," before slipping it into his back pocket.

"Hi, Griffin," I say with a nervous laugh.

No response. Clearly I'm the last person he was expecting, and his brain seems to have short circuited with the shock.

"Um, I'm the walkthrough. I guess they didn't give you a name."

He shakes his head twice, still unable to get words out. After another few seconds of silence, he manages to clear his throat and say, "No, they sure didn't." Besides shock, the other emotions on his face are indecipherable. It hits me like a freight train that not only am I the last person he expected, but I might also be the last person he wants to see.

"I can come back when Margo is here," I stammer, cheeks heating with embarrassment. "You didn't sign up for this."

I turn on my heel, ready to get out of here like a bat outta hell, but he says, "No, it's okay, really. I was just surprised is all."

Spinning back around, I force myself to look directly into the dark eyes I spent so much time getting lost in. There's no anger or bitterness–a bit of wariness, but they're still just as warm as they were the first day I met him.

"Are you sure?"

"Yes, Eleanor, I'm sure."

My heart skips a beat hearing my name in that familiar southern drawl. It's been years since anyone has called me Eleanor, let alone Griffin Hart.

"Okay," I say in a near whisper.

He motions his head to the entrance of the grounds, and I fall in step next to him, unsure how to ease the unbearably awkward tension.

"So you're the contractor, huh?"

Sneaking a glance at him, I see him nod his head, features still unreadable. I wish he'd say something–literally anything would be better than this silence. Conversation used to be so easy between us. How did we get here?

You know exactly how, Ellie.

"I took up my old job again when I came home from Tech," he says. "The old man is basically retired, I run most of the major projects now. This was my first big one."

"I didn't know you went to Tech," I blurt, unable to hide the surprise in my voice.

"Only for two years. And that was one and a half years too many. Wasn't for me."

"Oh," I say. "I don't know why I thought you stayed in Larkspur the whole time. I guess I just assumed."

"Don't know why you'd think otherwise," he says, tone taking on a bitter edge. "I told you that's what I wanted, and never told you I tried any different. Doesn't really matter now, does it?"

I've got no response to that. Does it matter? If I had known he was willing to try venturing out of Larkspur, would things have worked out differently?

My thoughts echo his own words—*doesn't really matter now, does it?*

"Well, here it is," he says, arm sweeping across the view. "Fountain and terrace to the right, rose garden to the left. Lighting out here is all solar-powered, first space in Larkspur to do that."

The corners of my mouth turn upwards at the gruff pride in his voice. He's playing nonchalant, but I know this is probably a huge deal to him.

"It looks phenomenal, Griffin," I say emphatically. "Seriously, I can't believe you managed this. I never would have guessed this place had so much potential."

"A far cry from its barn party days, huh?" he says, an amused smirk fighting its way onto his face. "C'mon, let me show you the garden. Margo said you have something special planned for the reunion?"

"I think so," I shrug. "Who knows if it'll turn out, but I think I've got a pretty solid plan."

"I'm sure any idea of yours is going to be perfect, darlin'."

He stiffens, and my stomach drops at the slip of the old pet name. He clears his throat, then continues forward as if nothing happened. "It's a loop, but not a perfect circle. It's easy to get lost in it, in a good way. When there's a party going, the noise doesn't break through the hedges, so it's easy to pretend it's just you out here."

"Sounds peaceful," I murmur, stopping to sniff one of the yellow flowers. "What kind of roses are they?"

"Yellow rose of Texas, wouldn't have it any other way," he says with a half-smile. "There are other flowers around the fountain, but I wanted a true rose garden over here. The landscaper wanted a variety, but I dug my heels in."

"Why doesn't that surprise me?" I laugh, bumping his shoulder with mine. I hear his breath catch at the contact, and immediately step away, worried it was too much for him.

He looks down at me, then grins and bumps my shoulder back. "I learned how to be stubborn from the very best."

"I'm not stubborn," I grumble, crossing my arms in front of my chest. He lets out a loud laugh, throwing his head back at the bald faced lie.

"Sure, and David's not a moron," he says, still laughing. "And Jack doesn't iron his khakis nightly."

This sends us both into a fit of laughter, and I can't remember the last time I felt this light. The initial awkwardness has faded completely, replaced by the comfortable companionship of two people who've known each other for nearly fourteen years.

Well, if you count the five we went without speaking, which I don't know that you can.

We finally stop long enough to catch our breaths, his grin knocking the wind out of me all over again. With all the people I've encountered across the years, I've never found someone with a smile that lights me up the way his does.

We finish the loops through the garden and head in the direction of the fountain. It's nothing ostentatious, but adds a tranquil beauty that makes the expansive grounds feel intimate. He paints a picture of cocktail tables and candles, pointing out where the outdoor bar gets set up and where additional seating can be added if necessary.

From there, the rest of the walkthrough is all business. We talk logistics and lighting, sounds systems and catering tables, and every possible disaster and contingency in place.

It's perfect–I couldn't have dreamed up a better place to execute my vision. Despite all my bitching and moaning, I'm excited to add "best reunion this town has ever seen" to my resumé right under "best wedding."

The tour comes to close as we reach the front door, lingering even though there's nothing else to go over. I don't think either of us are ready to break this spell. For the past hour, it's been like none of the misery and heartbreak happened. We're just Ellie and Griffin, the way it was when we were teenagers, head over heels for each other with no inkling of the turmoil the future would have for us.

"Well, I'll let you get back to work," I say, even though that's the last thing I want to do. "It was good to see you, Griffin."

"You too, Eleanor," he says in a quiet voice. "I've missed you. I do miss you. More than you know."

I think about you every day. I miss you so much it hurts to breathe. I promise I know.

But I don't say that, because I'm a coward. It's been a long time since I was brave enough to give big, emotional, grand-gesture monologues. Instead, I leave without another word, waving one more time before I get into my car.

That went a lot better than it could have, Ellie. Who knows what could happen.

A twinge of hope ripples through me, until I remember that Griffin is with Madison now. Silent tears stream down my face as I force myself to accept that nothing is ever going to happen again for Ellie Turner and Griffin Hart.

Chapter 30

Ellie

March, Age 18

I love spring break.

After a week spent sunbathing, reading, and flirting with college boys *way* too old for us, Abby and I lounge contentedly in the back of her dad's Chevy Tahoe on the long drive back to Larkspur. Abby is laser-focused on her bajillionth college application essay, while I hum along to the song in my headphones, watching Louisiana fly by.

Spring break has sent my excitement for college skyrocketing. Not that I plan on going to college in Florida, but the whole concept of a cliché spring break has me grinning ear to ear every time I think about it. I've decided to stay in Texas for college–I got my acceptance letter to UT Austin about a month ago, and up until now I've honestly been avoiding it.

All I've ever wanted to do is leave Larkspur and see the world, but suddenly even moving five hours south to the state capital makes me feel panicky. How do you leave everything (and everyone) you've known for eighteen years, just like that?

Well, you've got about five months to figure it out.

Just as we cross the state line into Texas, my phone buzzes.

Jack: When do you get home?

Ellie: Miss me that much huh?

Jack: No.

Jack: Wait yes

Jack: But I need to talk to you.

Jack: Can you hang out tonight?

That's weird.

Ellie: We won't be home til like 10 pm

Ellie: I can hang out tomorrow though?

Jack: That's fine. Can I pick you up for breakfast?

Since when do we do breakfast?

Ellie: Is something wrong? Are you okay?

Jack: Yeah, I'm fine, I just need to talk to you

Ellie: Okay Jack Robbit ;)

Ellie: You can pick me up at 9 - NO EARLIER

Jack: Nevermind, I don't want to see you anymore.

Ellie: :(

Jack: And tell Abby to quit telling people to call me that. It's stupid.

Jack: I'll see you in the morning.

"Jack doesn't like your nickname," I say to Abby with a laugh.

A diabolical smile stretches across her face.

"He doesn't like my nickname *yet*," she says.

Shaking my head as she cackles maniacally, I pop my headphones back in, staring right back out the window, wondering what on earth has Jack acting so weird.

***

When Jack picks me up, I can barely get 'good morning' out before he hurriedly gives me a side hug and shoves me out the front door. I try to make conversation on the way to the diner, but he gives one-word answers, white knuckling the wheel like he's worried it might fall off.

"I've never seen this place before 6pm," I muse, sliding into a booth and picking up a menu.

He barely grunts in reply, and when I feel him staring at me, I lay the menu back down on the table, folding my hands together as I look at him.

"Can I help you?"

"Griffin and Katie broke up."

My jaw drops. That's the last thing I expected him to say.

"Did she say why?"

"No, he broke up with her."

The rest of the diner drops away, and all I can hear is my own heartbeat thrumming in my ears.

Don't freak out.

"Oh," I say, fighting to keep my face neutral. "Did *he* say why?"

The waitress brings a pot of coffee, and I pour myself a mug, willing my hands to stop shaking. Bringing the cup to my lips, I look at him, eyebrows raised as I wait for his answer.

He still doesn't say anything as I set my cup down, and re-fold my hands on the table.

"Jack?"

"Don't be stupid, Ellie. You know why."

I suck in a sharp breath, my stomach somersaulting.

Dont. Freak. Out.

"If they got in a fight because she felt like we were mean to her, we can apologize," I say cautiously. "I didn't mean to make her feel–"

"You know damn well that isn't why, and I need you to listen to me very carefully right now."

Taken aback, I mime zipping my lips, sitting back and crossing my arms over my chest.

Clearing his throat, he starts, "Griffin has always been my boy. And now, you're my girl."

Arching my brow at him, he stammers out, "Not like that, like, my sister-girl or whatever."

"Sister Girl is what Abby calls the kid she nannies."

"Can you be serious please?" Pinching the bridge of his nose, he continues, "I love you both. And you love each other. Don't try to deny it," he says sharply, cutting me off when I open my mouth to protest.

"You *love* each other. This has been brewing since freshman year, and you've never gotten it right. Both of you have done some pretty messed up things to each other."

I nod silently, concentrating on where my mug sits on the table to avoid looking at him.

"He broke up with Katie because she's not you. We all know it," he says softly. "But he's scared to death that you're going to shut him down again."

"I don't want to shut him down, Jack," I say quickly, my eyes snapping up to his. "I didn't even mean to shut him down the first time. You know that. You know exactly what I want."

"Yes, I do," he says, nodding. He reaches across the table and gives my arm a gentle squeeze. "And I think if you want this to work out, this is the right time."

I sip my coffee, trying to hide the smile blooming from the inside out. I know I've done an awful job when I look back up and he's grinning at me.

"You've gotta tell him this time, Ellie Bellie."

"Hey, only my parents and Abby can call me that."

"Yeah? Well absolutely *no one* can call me 'Jack Robbit', but here we are."

"You really think this can work out, Jack?"

He nods slowly, seriously.

"I really do. But I think it might be now or never. Don't make him wait for you longer than he already has."

"He wasn't waiting for me, he was dating someone else!"

"Yeah, and you also dated someone else. And then you said he was just a distraction. And before that, he made a dumb bet with his idiot friends. Doesn't mean he hasn't been hoping and waiting for you the whole time."

My heart is racing, the butterflies in my stomach threatening to burst through my chest, my thoughts spinning as I allow myself to hope that the stars might finally be aligning for me and Griffin.

"Okay," I say, unable to contain the giggles bubbling up inside my chest. "Okay. I'll figure out a way to tell him how I feel and that I *want* this, that I want a real shot with him."

"Good," he says, a satisfied smirk on his face. "Can we eat now? I've been up since six and I'm starving."

"Why on earth did you get up at six?"

"I get up at six every day, Ellie, it's called discipline."

Rolling my eyes, we put in our order with the waitress and spend the rest of the morning catching up on our spring break stories. I laugh loudly when my stories of Abby obviously stress him out, and I give him a hard time about how many hours of Jeopardy he watched with his granny.

When he drops me off at home, he gets out of his Jeep and pulls me into a big bear hug.

"Go get your man, Ellie Turner," he says, playfully punching my shoulder. "Let yourselves be happy."

Waving goodbye as he drives away, I turn and bolt straight to my room to call Abby with the news. We spend several hours concocting some sort of grand-gesture, declaration of love that I'm sure will go out the window the second I see him.

Maybe this is our 90s rom-com ending moment. We'll kiss in the rain and live happily ever after, and everything will work out.

One thing's for sure–I love Griffin Hart with all my might. And I'll be damned if I miss the chance to tell him again.

***

By the time Thursday rolls around, I'm convinced the universe hates me. When I wanted to avoid Griffin, he seemed to be everywhere. Now that I actually *want* to talk to him, I haven't been able to find him in the hallways once.

Is he avoiding me?

Maybe Jack was wrong. Maybe breaking up with Katie had absolutely nothing to do with me, and just because he's single now doesn't mean he wants me.

Chewing on my lower lip, I stare at the series of texts Jack sent me a few minutes ago.

> **<u>Jack:</u> Have you talked to Griffin yet?**

> **<u>Jack:</u> Given that he's still walking around like a kicked puppy, I'm assuming you haven't**

> **<u>Jack:</u> What the hell are you waiting for?**

> **<u>Jack:</u> ????**

I wanted to avoid any "we need to talk" preamble, and I *really* didn't want to start anything over text, but I'm resigned to the fact that my current method of passively hoping I run into him at school isn't working.

Ellie: Hi.

Dumb. Boring. I wouldn't reply to me.

Griffin: Howdy there

Exhaling a shaky breath, I send the scariest text I've ever sent. (*Scary for me, not for him, obviously.)*

Ellie: Can I see you sometime soon?

Griffin: You'll see me tomorrow won't you?

Ellie: I meant like, just us

Griffin: Just you and me?

Ellie: Yeah

Ellie: If you want

Ellie: We don't have to

Ellie: I just maybe wanted to talk to you about something

Griffin: Everything okay?

> **Ellie:** Yeah no totally! Just some stuff on my mind that I can't really talk to Jack or David about

> **Ellie:** Nothing ominous

> **Griffin:** That's what someone with ominous news would say

Shit. I'm blowing this. This is exactly why I didn't want to do this over text. Except there's a ninety nine point nine percent chance that I'll also be this much of a bumbling mess in person. Probably worse.

> **Ellie:** Sorry, this is way more dramatic than I wanted it to be

> **Ellie:** Let me start over

> **Ellie:** Hi Griffin, can we hang out sometime soon, maybe just the two of us?

> **Griffin:** Hi Eleanor. I'd like that. When?

> **Ellie:** Maybe tomorrow before the guys come over?

> **Griffin:** Don't you have dinner with Abby?

Ellie: No, we cancelled this week

I'm going to have to tell Abby that ASAP.

Griffin: Okay, that works for me

Griffin: Want to come over here?

Pondering it for a minute, I decide that I'd rather have this talk on more neutral ground, so I can run away with my tail between my legs if necessary. We decide on meeting at the lake for a walk, which is great because it'll give me a perfectly natural excuse to avoid eye contact.

After sending a screenshot to Jack to prove that I'm not backing out, I put my phone on silent, rolling on my back to stare at my bedroom ceiling. It hits me that if things go badly tomorrow, this might be the last conversation I ever have with Griffin Hart. I fall asleep sick to my stomach, that horrifying notion playing on repeat in my mind.

I have no idea how I survive the next day, but before I know it the final bell is ringing, and I'm on the dirt road at the edge of town that leads to the lake. When I see that he's already there, leaning against his truck, my heartrate decides to leave this solar system—I can't tell if it's going a mile a minute or if it's stopped completely.

He's dressed the way he always is, in a t-shirt, jeans, and cowboy boots, but my stomach still flutters when he spots me, his face lighting up as he pushes off the door and walks over toward me. No one has ever looked better in a pair of beat up Wranglers–and no one has ever looked at me the way he does.

I step up in front of him, much closer than I need to be, and let out a breathless, "Hi, Griffin."

His smile somehow gets brighter, and I swear there's an actual twinkle in his eyes when he says, "Howdy there, Eleanor," in return.

Realizing that this is the closest proximity we've been in since we kissed, my face flushes and I hastily take a step back, putting some much needed distance between us. I also realize just how badly I want to kiss him again. And again. And again.

I turn abruptly and head for the walking trail. He swiftly falls into step beside me, hands in his pockets, seemingly very comfortable with the silence between us. Me, on the other hand–my skin is crawling with nerves as I work up the courage to start my carefully planned monologue. The problem is, I can't remember a word of it.

"So, um, how have you been?" I ask, incredibly lamely, failing miserably at sounding casual.

"Same old, same old," he says with a shrug, even though I'm pretty sure he knows that *I know* that's a lie. "What did you want to talk to me about?"

Okay, here we go Ellie.

"Well I was talking to Jack and heard that things, um, ended, with Katie," I continue nervously, "And I just wanted to see how you're holding up."

Out of nowhere, a streak of bravery sears through me, and I steel myself, glued to the spot. I know the next words out of my mouth are going to be as much a surprise to myself as they are to him, but they start tumbling out before I can stop them.

"Actually, that's not true at all."

Not realizing that I'd stopped, he turns around from a few steps ahead of me with a shocked look on his face.

"I don't remotely care about Katie. Actually, I'm glad you guys broke up. Best news I've heard in months, to be honest."

He continues to stare at me wordlessly, jaw hanging open in bewilderment.

"I know I was awful to you after my birthday, and I probably blew my chance, and I have no right to ask for another one, but fuck it, I'm asking."

His jaw snaps shut, his eyes widening. I think it would be enough to just look into those eyes forever, but now that I've started talking, I don't think I could stop if I tried.

"You made a dumb mistake a million years ago, and I have held it against you in the worst way. I've been petty, and stubborn, and scared, and I can't promise that I won't ever be any of those things again."

Taking a step forward, he looks at me warily as I start to close the gap between us.

"I should never have called you a distraction. You are every-thing good in this world, Griffin. You're kind, and thoughtful, and patient. You have this warmth that draws people in effort-lessly, the kind you can't learn or practice. You're better than most of us without even trying, and for the life of me I can't figure out why it took me so long to see it."

I hear the hitch in his breath when I take yet another step toward him.

"I have done absolutely nothing in this world to deserve you," I say in a quiet voice. "But I'm selfish enough to want you anyway. And I do, Griffin, I want you."

This is it. There's no going back now. I look up at him, desperately hoping he can see the truth in my eyes.

"I want the whole damn thing. I want dates, and kisses, and arguments, and laughter, and that comfortable silence you only find with people who really know you. I want it all, and I want it with you. Because I love you, Griffin Hart."

This time he steps toward me, almost involuntarily.

"I love you," I repeat. "And I'm asking if you want to love me back."

He doesn't say anything, just keeps staring, and a terrifying thought occurs to me.

"Unless you got back together with Katie, in which case for-get everything I said and let me know so I can crawl under a rock and never come back out."

He still doesn't say anything, but a slow smile spreads across his face.

"Did you?" I ask timidly. "Get back together with her?"

"Nope."

I breathe a sigh of relief–both because he isn't with her, and because he's finally using words again.

"So you're single?"

"Yes."

"Absolutely, positively?"

"Yes."

"Thank God," I mutter, grabbing the sides of his face and pulling him closer until our lips crash together.

It's better than I remember. In fact, it puts our last kiss to shame. Without hesitation, he grips my waist with one hand, the other fisting my hair at the nape of my neck, drawing me in closer.

My hands leave his face, arms looping around his neck as I fight to eliminate any remaining space between us. Our first kiss was slow, and sweet–this one is all fire.

His mouth leaves mine, my whine of protest quickly turning to a gasp as he kisses down the side of my face, nipping the sensitive skin behind my ear.

I press my body into his, desperately wanting to feel more than just his lips. When I feel him turn hard against me, I whimper softly, heat rushing through me when I hear a low growl in return.

At this moment, nothing else exists–there's only me and Griffin, and the way our bodies fit together perfectly, like they always knew this was right and were just waiting for our brains to catch up.

"On your left!"

We jump apart, startled as a biker whizzes past us. Our breathing heavy, he looks as dazed as I feel. It's everything I ever wanted, and infinitely more.

Without breaking eye contact, he pulls his phone out of his pocket and dials a number, his eyes still blazing as he lifts it to his ear.

"You guys are uninvited tonight."

I giggle, bringing my fingertips to my lips as I hear David yelling on the other end until Griffin hangs up on him.

"My house. Now."

My face heats again, his gravelly voice thick with desire. His tone leaves no room for argument, and all I can do is nod in agreement as his hand slips into mine and he leads me back to his truck.

Chapter 31

Griffin

March, Age 18

I can barely focus on the drive back to my house, but I'm intensely aware of three things–first, as much as I want to fucking *floor it*, getting pulled over would slow me down a hell of a lot more than just going the speed limit. Also I might deck the cop, and that would *really* set me back.

Second, my hand was made to grip the thigh of the girl in my passenger seat. I've never felt anything softer than her skin, or anything that feels more like home than her hand resting on top of mine.

Third, Eleanor loves me.

Oh shit, I didn't say it back.

Glancing sideways, I catch her biting her lip, cheeks still flushed, chest rising and falling with the breath she hasn't quite caught yet–which I know for a fact, because my breathing is just as off kilter as hers.

Pulling my eyes away from her and back to the road takes every bit of effort I have in me, but I've got to get this girl home. *My* girl.

The thought has me grinning like a damn fool, and when I feel her gaze on me, I look over again quickly and see my smile mirrored on her face. She reaches up, running her fingers through my hair, then settling her hand on my face, stroking my cheek with her thumb.

That innocent touch coupled with the memory of that kiss by the lake has my dick straining in my pants. I had sex with Katie a few times, and it was fine I guess—but Goddamn, every cell in my body is lit up right now, and all it took was Eleanor touching my face.

By some miracle, I manage to get my truck into my driveway and park it without losing my mind. She doesn't give me time to be a gentleman and open her door before she's unbuckled and out of her seat, jumping out like she's worried it might grow arms and trap her there. When I get to her side, she wastes no time, fisting the front of my shirt and yanking me forward, slamming her mouth onto mine again.

I didn't think it was possible, but the way she's just as eager for me as I am for her makes me even harder.

We slam through the front door, not breaking the kiss even for a second. Her fingers tug at the hem of my shirt and I rip it over my head, tossing it clear across the room. She pulls back, eyes following her hands as they roam across my shoulders and chest, then down my abs and to the waistband of my jeans. Looking back up at me, eyes on fire, she hooks her forefingers in my belt loops and pulls me back close to her.

Spinning us around, I press her back against the front door, grinding my hips into hers, my hands holding her waist with a bruising grip. She makes the sweetest noise I've ever heard, and I can't help but lean back to look at her in awe.

Her lips are red and swollen, blue irises reduced to a thin band around her wide pupils. I've never seen anything so beautiful in my life.

"Basement or bedroom?" I ask hoarsely, my voice barely recognizable.

Breath hitching, she lets out a barely audible whisper.

"Basement."

She grabs my hand, half-dragging me wordlessly down the stairs. At the bottom, she turns to face me, her self-assurance faltering for the first time.

I instantly close the gap between us, taking her chin between my forefinger and thumb, tilting her head back and placing a gentle kiss on her lips. It somehow drives me crazier than the fierce kissing from upstairs.

I take my mouth off of hers, brushing my lips against her forehead before folding her into my arms, her head buried in my chest.

"I love you too, Eleanor," I murmur, chin resting on the top of her head. "More than you could possibly know."

Stepping out of my grasp, she runs her hands down my arms, grabbing mine as she walks backwards deeper into the room.

I expect her to take us to the couch, but she catches me off guard when she puts both of her hands on my chest, shoving me backwards into the armchair. If I thought I'd never see this chair without thinking of her before, it's set in stone now as I watch her straddle me, sinking slowly into my lap with her knees gripping either side of my thighs.

"This is feeling a little unfair, darlin'," I say, gesturing to my shirtless chest. Playing with the lacy hem of her tank top, I growl, "Shirt off, now." I begin to lift it up, but she swats my hand away and slowly peels it over her head, letting it drop to the floor beside the chair.

My eyes unapologetically rake down her body as she reaches behind her back to unhook her bra. I swallow hard when she lets it fall away, revealing the most perfect tits I've ever seen. Not that I've seen a ton of them, but there's no doubt in my mind that there's not a pair in the world that could compare to the ones in front of me right now.

Now it's my turn to explore her body with my hands, and I take my damn time doing it. I ghost my fingers across her collarbone and down her arms, reveling in the way she shivers under my touch. I slide them back up her sides until they rest on her ribcage, fingers gently stroking the delicate skin just below her breasts. I hear her sharp intake of breath when I finally cup them in my hands, thumbs brushing over the stiff peaks of her nipples.

I move my hands to her hips, but she grabs them and puts them back on her chest, guiding me to knead her tits as she starts moving against me. Settling into a slow, deliberate rhythm, both of us panting heavier and louder as she grinds against the length of my cock through my pants.

Her arms grip my shoulders as she leans down to kiss me, and I *do* grab her hips this time, bucking mine up to meet her with every pass. As she moans into my mouth, I begin whispering in her ear– *"that's it, baby," "God you feel good," "don't stop."*

If we keep at it like this, I'm gonna come in pants at record speed.

Suddenly overwhelmed with the need to feel her underneath me, I stand abruptly from the chair, hands gripping her thighs as she wraps her legs around me as I walk us over to the couch.

Laying her down gently, I crawl between her legs, hands on either side of her head as I kiss her face, her neck, her collarbones, anywhere I can reach her with my mouth. When she starts trembling beneath me, I carefully tuck her hair behind her ear, moving my hand to grip the back of her neck, grounding her here in this moment.

She arches into me, her perfect breasts pressing against my chest, and I let out a guttural moan as I claim her mouth again. I caress my free hand down her body, pausing to palm her breast, swiping my thumb over her nipple again before sliding my fingers down into the waistband of her shorts.

"Fuck," I breathe out harshly when I feel how wet she is through her cotton panties.

"Fuck," I repeat, dragging my finger slowly up her slit through the fabric. "I've never felt anything so perfect, Eleanor. You're perfect."

"Please, Griffin," she whimpers. "Please touch me. I need more."

Don't have to tell me twice.

Moving her panties to the side, I swipe through her arousal, coating my fingers before slowly dipping one inside.

"God, Griffin, that feels amazing," she moans, eyes fluttering shut as she swirls her hips, trying to find more friction. When I add a second finger, she moans even louder, hands flying up to grip my shoulders as I begin to slowly work them in and out of her.

Her cries pitch upward as I begin to circle her clit with my thumb, working my fingers faster as her back arches more, inner walls beginning to flutter around me.

"Are you gonna come, darlin'?" I ask in a low voice. "Let go, I wanna hear what my name sounds like on your lips when you do."

My words send her over the edge, her pussy clamping down on me as she moans my name, riding my hand shamelessly as I work her through every last wave of her orgasm.

When she comes down, I slowly slide out of her. Holding her gaze, I suck my fingers into my mouth, licking every bit of her off before kissing her deeply.

I need her now.

"Wait," she says suddenly, hands stilling mine where they were moving to unbutton my pants. "Can we pause?"

Kissing her face gently, I whisper in her ear, "Of course we can, darlin'. You tell me what you need and it's yours."

I lean back, giving her space as she props herself up on her elbows.

"It's just," she says, biting her lip nervously. "I haven't really, you know, done...this."

I immediately shift off of her so that I'm sitting on the couch, pulling her into my lap, stroking her hair as she hides her face in the crook of my shoulder.

"Things never went this far with Bennett, and I didn't want them to. But I want to go there with you, I really do," she says, voice muffled. "Maybe just not today."

She looks up at me, a fear in her eyes that makes me think Bennett might have pressured her, and I immediately begin plotting how I can kick his ass and get away with it.

"I'm sorry," she continues, "I know it's not fair to be that girl that gets off and then leaves you hanging, but I just need to slow down. Is that okay?"

I grip her tightly, trying to assure her that of course it's okay. "Don't you ever be sorry, Eleanor," I say fiercely, "I'm not keeping score here–anything we do is going to be perfect, every time. How could it not be when it's with you?" With a soft kiss to her temple, I cradle her face, desperately hoping my eyes show just how gone I am for her. "You're perfect. We'll take this at your pace. I'd wait a thousand lifetimes for you, I'm not going anywhere."

With a relieved sigh, she settles back into me, absentmindedly stroking my chest. We stay like this for what feels like an eternity, yet not nearly long enough at the same time, holding each other in comfortable silence. When I hear her stomach grumble, I let out a chuckle.

"Do you want me to order some food, darlin'?"

"Oh my God, that would be amazing," she moans. I set her gently beside me on the couch, grabbing her shirt off the floor and handing it to her. When she pulls it over her head, smoothing the front back into place, I jut my lower lip out, pouting playfully.

"How am I ever supposed to be content seeing you fully clothed now that I know what's underneath?"

Rolling her eyes, she shoves my shoulder lightheartedly. "You'll manage," she says, a mixture of sarcasm and faux sympathy in her voice. "Can you please get me pizza before I Hulk out?"

With another kiss to her temple, I pull out my phone to place an order, pulling her feet into my lap when she stretches out the length of the couch.

I'm never going to get enough of her.

Gently rubbing my thumb over her ankle, my eyes don't leave her face as I place the order, my heart near bursting at the happiness radiating off of her. How the hell did I get so lucky? Never in a million years did I dream that someone so wonderful existed, and that somehow that someone would choose to love me, out of all the people in this world.

As the employee repeats my order back to me, I silently mouth *I love you* at Eleanor. Beaming, she mouths it back, and if the world ended right now, I'd die the happiest man to ever have walked this earth.

Chapter 32

Ellie

June, Age 18

"What's got you smilin' over there, darlin'?"

Turning in my seat, I shift from looking out at the country fields to the cowboy next to me, one hand on the steering wheel, the other on my thigh.

Griffin has taken to wearing his cowboy hat almost every day now that we're free from the shackles of a high school dress code. Nothing turns me on more than the look in his eye when I snatch it off his head and place it on my own before crawling into his lap. Even if he's not technically a bonafide cowboy (a.k.a., he's never worked a ranch a day in his life), I hope he never stops wearing it.

I spend a lot of time in the passenger side of Griffin's truck these days. We do all the cliché things every teenage couple does–mini golf, movies, ice cream dates. But our favorite thing to do lately is to flip a coin at every intersection–heads for right, tails for left–and take those directions until we find ourselves outside the city limits.

From there, we just drive. Drive, and talk, and laugh, and sing, and sometimes just sit in silence. The world feels so big when it's just the two of us out in the middle of nowhere under the big Texas sky. I don't know how I ever felt suffocated here.

"Not smiling at anything in particular," I say, placing my hand over his and tracing soft circles with my thumb. "Just happy."

"Oh yeah?" he asks, his own smile lighting up his tanned face. Griffin year-round is the hottest thing I've ever seen–but *summer Griffin?* He's not just hot, he's devastating.

His entire summer wardrobe apparently consists of nothing but muscle tees that show off his broad shoulders and toned muscles–not gym-bro huge, but the type of strong you get from manual labor, which is exactly what he's been doing. He, Jack, and David got jobs with the local contractor, helping demo old buildings and framing the new ones.

Any time not spent at work, we spend together. Usually it's the four of us, Abby and Aaron joining sometimes. At least until Griffin decides he wants me to himself and kicks everyone out, or sweeps me off my feet, hollering over his shoulder that we're leaving as we're already halfway out the door.

Not that I'm complaining–about the alone time, or the muscle tees. I could spend every hour of the day with him (*and looking at him*) and never get enough.

"Well, what's got you so happy, then?"

Scooting closer to him on the bench seat, I lay my head on his shoulder with a contented sigh.

"You."

He places a gentle kiss on the top of my head, squeezing my thigh before threading his fingers through mine, holding both of our hands in my lap. Tilting my head up, I press a soft kiss to his jawline.

"Can we go home?" I whisper in his ear, goosebumps immediately raising on his neck. Smirking to myself, I kiss him again, this time lower on his neck, my free hand ghosting my fingers up his forearm.

"You're killing me, Eleanor," he says in a hoarse voice.

Laughing softly, I nip at his earlobe.

"Better drive fast, then."

***

"So anyway, once they got the nails out everything was totally fine," David says, finishing a story about how he managed to nailgun his pants *and* boxers to the roof he was working on and had no choice but to either get rescued by the fire department, or get stark naked in public.

Griffin and Jack roar with laughter, rolling on the basement floor. I try to twist my smirk into something much more sympathetic, but fail miserably.

"We go to a different work site for *one* afternoon and you manage to cause mayhem," Jack says, finally catching his breath and shaking his head.

"Exactly, this is totally your fault," David says, pointing an accusatory finger at him. "You know I need constant supervision."

Griffin sits up, wiping the tears from his eyes. "Shit dude, I haven't laughed that hard in a long time."

He climbs off the floor, picking me up out of the chair and settling me into his lap when he sits down. I wrap my arms around his neck, pulling him in to rest his head on my chest, stroking his hair absentmindedly. I never thought I'd be a PDA girl, but I can't seem to keep my hands off of him, no matter who we're with. Even at my house with my parents, there's always some point of contact, albeit much more chaste.

"Should I be more affectionate in public?" Aaron asks with a slight frown, looking from Abby to us, then back to Abby. He and Abby joined us tonight, but Aaron sat on the couch while Abby took the other chair across the room.

"God, no," Abby replies with a scoff. "If you try to touch me like that outside of the bedroom, I'm breaking up with you."

"Okay, good," he says, letting out a relieved sigh.

"No offense, of course," Abby adds, waving her hand in our direction.

"None taken," Griffin says with a wicked grin, one hand sliding up my thigh, playing with the threads of my cutoffs, his other arm snaking around my waist and holding me tighter.

"I do not need to hear about what goes on in either of your bedrooms," Jack grumbles.

"I do," David says, wiggling his eyebrows. "The more detail, the better."

I laugh loudly when Jack smacks him over the back of the head, scolding him to stop being a perv.

David hands Abby the Wii controller and turns on Mario Kart, while Jack and Aaron start a heated debate about the Rangers versus the Astros. I don't hear a word they say–I'm distracted by the way Griffin has been steadily moving his hand higher and higher up my leg, thumb now brushing my skin underneath the hem of my shorts.

In response, I press my ass against the bulge in his pants, which is slowly starting to strain against the fabric.

"Careful there, darlin'," he murmurs, "Keep that up and David's really gonna get a front row seat."

"Not if we're alone, he won't," I whisper in a teasing tone, swirling my hips at just the right angle to have him whispering *"fuck"* under his breath.

"Alright, everyone out," Griffin says loudly, voice straining with the effort to sound positively *not* hot and bothered.

"Bro, we just started a game!" David yells in protest.

"Hey, you can save your dignity instead of getting your ass kicked again," Abby says, standing and dropping the controller onto the seat. "I think our current record is forty five to eight, right?"

"Forty five to nine," he grumbles under his breath, throwing his own controller to the other end of the couch. "C'mon crybaby," Jack says, grabbing David by the collar and pulling him toward the stairs. "We can go practice at my house so you can make it forty five to ten."

"I swear she's cheating somehow," he whines, voice fading as stomps up the stairs, Abby and Aaron following closely behind.

The second the door slams shut, Griffin has me thrown over his shoulder, bolting upstairs to his bedroom.

"Griffin, you're going to drop me," I say, giggling, then letting out a yelp when he smacks my ass.

"Like hell I will," he says gruffly. "At least not before we make it to bed."

Kicking his door open, he keeps his word as he sets me on the mattress, immediately climbing over me to pin me down with his hips.

"I think you get off on teasing me more than anything else," he says against my lips, claiming my mouth in a heated kiss.

"I can't help that it's so fun," I say between kisses. "You get so worked up so fast."

"Because you're the most stunning Goddamn thing I've ever seen," he says, drawing a moan out of me as he grinds his rock-hard erection against the needy spot between my legs. "And I still can't believe you're mine."

Pulling back to look into his chocolate eyes, wide with desire, I stroke one thumb across his cheek.

"I've always been yours," I say seriously. "Always will be."

"I love you so much, Eleanor," he says, voice shaky. "I know we're young, and you have so much you want to do, but you're it for me. *I* will always be *yours.*"

Something about that stops my breathing, a twinge of anxiety stabbing in my chest. I do have so many things I want to see and accomplish before I settle down. I don't want to be one of those girls who gets married right out of high school and never leaves her hometown.

He's not asking you to, Ellie. Just enjoy this.

I fist his hair, bringing his mouth back to mine, trying to show how much I love him rather than saying it back. There will be time to think about futures and logistics later–for now, I want to enjoy the beautiful boy holding me like I'm the most precious thing in the world.

I flip us over so that I'm straddling him with my hands on his chest, looking down at him and marveling as his eyes go from sweet to smoldering. He slides his hands up my ribs, silently asking permission to get rid of my tank top. I lift my arms over my head to let him, and he groans when he realizes I'm not wearing a bra underneath.

"Dirty girl," he says with a dark chuckle. "If I'd known what you had going on under that top, I would have kicked everyone else out hours ago."

Leaning forward, I brush his ear with my lips and whisper, "Wait til you see what I've got going on underneath these shorts."

Quick as lightning, I'm underneath him again as he makes quick work of yanking my shorts down my legs and tossing them across the room. His eyes rake over my naked body, and he lets out a low, slow groan.

"Fuck Eleanor, I'll never get tired of this view," he says before removing his own shirt and jeans, leaving nothing between us but the thin material of his boxers. I lock my legs behind his back, hips rising up to meet him with every stroke of his hard cock against my slit.

"You're so wet already," he moans, kissing and biting at my neck. "Look at the mess you're making on my boxers. The way you respond to me makes me go fucking feral."

We've fooled around more times than I can count since that first night together, but we still haven't taken that final step yet. He's been so unbelievably patient with me–I can't explain why, but every time we get close, my whole body tenses up and my heart starts racing, and not in a good way.

I think it's lingering anxiety from the way Bennett weaponized physical intimacy–saying things like "Getting off is the only thing that helps me unwind after a long day," and "I'm obviously going to be short with you if I'm stressed out and you won't do anything to help me." When I told Griffin about the way he would manipulate me, I had to hold him tight and reassure him that I'm okay now, that I feel safe with him, until finally he stopped shaking with rage.

I still get choked up when I think about how upset he was on my behalf. He was more than that–he seemed truly distraught that anyone would treat me that way. Every time I've pumped the brakes or asked to slow down, he's stopped without hesitation, gently wrapping me in his arms and repeatedly telling me that he'd wait for me forever, that he's not going anywhere.

He moves his hand between my legs, slowly circling my clit before slipping two fingers inside of me. I don't know how he manages to make it feel so good, but everytime he hooks his fingers to hit my most sensitive spot, I shudder and moan his name over and over, a reverent prayer that won't ever leave my lips. It feels otherworldly every single time, I wonder if it'll ever stop feeling like magic.

I writhe against his hand, pressure building in my core as he works in and out of me, still grinding against me with his hard length.

"That's it darlin', ride my fingers, make yourself feel good."

His words do just as much for me as his fingers, and before long I'm seeing stars, back arching off the bed as he works me through my orgasm.

When I come down, I lift up to meet him, stroking my tongue against his as he runs his hands up and down my body. He grabs my waist then cups my breasts, still rocking against me, his breaths harsh and shallow.

"I still don't think I'm ready," I whisper, guilt constricting my throat. "I'm sorry I keep doing this."

With a kiss on my forehead, he lays down next to me, pulling me into his chest.

"You have nothing to apologize for, darlin'," he says, nuzzling into my hair. "No need to rush when we have the rest of our lives ahead of us."

There's that pain in my chest again.

"But there is something else I wanted to try," I say slowly. We also haven't ventured into the world of oral yet, but every time I think about having his dick in my mouth I'm instantly wet. I've been trying to find the perfect moment to bring it up, and this feels like it.

"What's that?" he says, one eyebrow cocked as he waits for me to explain.

But I don't explain myself, I just kiss his face, down his neck, his chest, his abs–those fucking abs, I've been dying to lick every ridge since the first time I saw him shirtless. He props up on his elbows, both eyebrows raised now. When I reach the waistband of his boxers, I hook my fingers and begin to pull them down. Before I can, his hands stop mine.

"You don't have to do this if you don't want," he says earnestly. "Don't feel like you owe me anything."

"Griffin," I say firmly. "You have no idea how many times I've touched myself to the thought of taking you in my mouth. Believe me when I say I want this."

He audibly swallows as I remove the last barrier between us, freeing his cock. It's my turn to swallow–I have no idea how I'm supposed to fit that entire thing in my mouth.

Use your hands and your mouth at the same, Abby told me. We've never explicitly talked about it, but I know her and Aaron go at it like rabbits when they're alone. Once the initial shock of me asking for sex advice wore off, she gave me very, very detailed instructions on how to give an A+ blowjob.

I grip the base of his cock, pumping slowly a few times, using my thumb to swipe the bead of precum off the head and work the wetness down his shaft.

He shudders, hips bucking into my hand as he mutters a string of curses under his breath.

Emboldened by his reaction, I slowly lower my mouth to him, taking the tip in my mouth and swirling my tongue around it, still working the rest of him with my hand.

"Fuck me Eleanor, that already feels so fucking good," he moans. Looking up at him with a wicked grin, I flatten my tongue against the bottom of his shaft, licking slowly from base to tip before taking him deeper into my mouth. I settle into a steady rhythm, bobbing my head at a quicker pace when his moans grow louder.

His fingers weave through my hair, gripping it at the back of my head. "I've gotta move, darlin' girl. Is that okay?"

Nodding eagerly, I hollow my cheeks out as I slowly lift up, his cock escaping my mouth with a soft pop. "Whatever you want, babe," I say breathlessly. "I want to make you feel good."

"Fuck, you're perfect," he says hoarsely. "Tap my thigh if you need me to stop."

I nod my head, lowering my mouth onto him again. Holding my head in place, he begins to pump up into my mouth, making me gag when he hits the back of my throat.

"Shit, are you okay?"

"Shut up and fuck my mouth, Griffin."

With a moan, he begins working himself in and out of my mouth, his movements growing jerky and less controlled.

"Keep it up and I'm gonna come, darlin'," he says, moans growing louder with every thrust. His words have me moaning, the vibration from my low hums causing him to move faster. "If you don't want me to come in that pretty mouth, you better tell me now," he says through ragged breaths. In response, I open my throat as wide as I can get it, tears streaming down my face as I gag around his length again.

"Look at me," he says harshly. I do what he says, nearly coming from just the sight of the wild desire in his eyes. "I'll never get enough of those eyes, pretty girl."

I bob my head faster, desperate to get him off, turned on beyond belief knowing it was me that made him lose control.

I might come again just listening to him.

"Fuck, darlin', don't stop. I'm coming."

He yells a loud, guttural moan, and I feel the hot ropes of his orgasm hit the back of my throat. I fight to swallow every last drop even with him still in my mouth, working his cock fiercely until he stops shuddering and releases his grip on my hair.

"You are the sexiest Goddamn thing I've ever seen."

I beam up at him, unable to keep the look of satisfied pride off my face. After licking the last bit of him clean, I press a soft kiss to his lower stomach, then allow him to drag me back up the bed, intertwining our naked limbs until I'm not sure where I end and he begins.

We lay in silence, our heartbeats returning to normal as we bask in that post-orgasm haze. Looking up at him, I see his eyes closed, brow furrowed in concentration.

"What are you thinking about?"

"Shh," he whispers. "I'm trying to memorize every detail so I can relive that for the rest of my life."

Giggling, I lay my cheek against his bare chest, breathing in his scent–some woodsy body wash coupled with Old Spice, a slight hint of sweat and musk present as a result of our…exertions.

"So I did okay then?" I ask, still feeling a little self-conscious about the whole thing.

"Are you kidding me?" he says hoarsely. "That was fucking perfection, Eleanor. Where the fuck did you learn how to do that?"

"You don't want to know," I say, letting out a deep sigh.

"It wasn't because that piece of shit made you, was it?" he said, anger immediately flaring.

"Worse," I say, my lips meeting his in a comforting kiss. "I asked Abby."

"You're right, that is worse," he groans, dragging his hand down his face. "I don't want to think about her doing any of those things. Next time just tell me you watched porn or something."

Giggling again, I snuggle in even tighter next to him, trying to remove any space between us. I could stay right here in his bed, in his arms, forever and be happy.

No, you couldn't. Not really.

That anxious voice in the back of my head has been getting louder with every mention of a forever with Griffin. I've been diligently shoving it down where I can ignore it for weeks, but the closer we get to the end of summer, the harder it's been to keep it at bay.

You have so much you want to do. Griffin's words weren't meant to cause turmoil. But where his breathing slows as he drifts into sleep, my thoughts begin to race, and I can't seem to draw in a full breath under the weight building in my chest.

Chapter 33

Griffin

July, Age 19

"I want you to come meet my family."

The thought blurts out of my mouth in the middle of dinner at the only Italian place in town, where I'm celebrating four perfect months with Eleanor.

"What do you mean?" she asks through a mouthful of pasta. "I've met your parents like a thousand times."

"Not my parents, my aunt and uncle, and some cousins," I clarify.

"You've never talked about them before."

"I haven't really seen them since my mom left," I try to say nonchalantly. "It's my mom's sister, and that side of the family was never crazy about my dad."

She reaches across the table and squeezes my hand, a knowing look on her face. As much as I try to pretend that I'm totally fine with my mom being gone now, it still stings every time she gets brought up.

"I'd love to meet them," she says gently. "When are you thinking?"

"They're doing some kind of mini family reunion next weekend, and they asked if I wanted to come. I said I would, but only if I could bring you."

She smiles, my heart nearly bursting in my chest the way it does every damn time she looks at me.

"I would love to go. I need more dirt–I mean stories–about baby Griffin," she says, smile turning wicked.

Mental note–bribe your cousins to hide all the family photo albums.

As shocked as I am that Aunt Lizzie invited me, I can't wait for them to meet this girl–woman? Angel on earth?

And honestly, I can't wait for her to meet them. Some of my happiest childhood memories are from the summers we spent at the lake with Lizzie and Ryan, and their boys, Harrison and Hunter. Harrison is two years younger than me, and Hunter two years younger than him. We were thick as thieves, until Ryan's job moved them an hour north of Larkspur and they took up permanent residence in the lake house. In reality it's only about fifty miles, but it might as well have been on the other side of the world for how far away it felt. Still feels.

Gazing across the table, transfixed by my golden ray of sunshine, I realize that it doesn't hurt like it used to–the way it felt like an entire half of my family dropped me as soon as my mom bowed out. Between my dad, David and Jack, and my darlin' Eleanor, I've got all the love and support a guy could dream of having.

"Do I have something on my face?" she asks, and I realize I've been silently staring at her for the better part of five minutes. She doesn't, but I reach across and swipe my thumb along her chin anyway, desperate for any excuse I can find to touch her.

"Your face is perfect," I say, my voice surprisingly thick with emotion. "Most beautiful sight in the world."

She shakes her head in amusement, setting down her silverware and folding her hands under her chin to prop her head up. "You sure are a smooth talker, Griffin Hart."

"I mean every word."

"I never said I didn't like it," she says, "I'm just waiting for the day you run out of sweet things to say to me."

Now it's my turn to shake my head at her. I could talk non-stop, twenty four hours a day, every day, for the rest of my life, and never hit the bottom of the well of how I feel about her.

"Never gonna happen," I say with the same assurance as I would saying the sky is blue. "I'll even make sure to write it all down so it's recorded in history when I'm dead and gone."

"Well I'll never be reading that," she says. When I raise my eyebrows at her, she continues, "I fully intend on dying first. No way I'm doing any of this by myself."

We pivot back to more lighthearted topics for the rest of dinner, then take the long way back before I drop her off for the night. Parked out in front of her house, we make out in my truck for a solid twenty minutes before her porch light flickers on, signaling that her parents know we're here and *absolutely* know what we're doing.

With one last quick kiss, she leaps from my truck, yelling "I love you, cowboy" as she walks backwards toward her house, only turning away from me once she reaches the front door.

I can't wipe the grin off my face the whole drive home. Or as I get ready for bed. In fact, I'm pretty sure I fall asleep with a smile on my face, memories of days spent with Eleanor far better than any dream I might find in sleep.

***

"Do I look okay?" Eleanor asks nervously, spinning around in a baby blue sundress, completely knocking the wind out of me. The thin straps have her freckled shoulders on full display, the swell of her breasts barely visible above the modest sweetheart neckline. The soft fabric cinches in at her waist, accentuating her curves before flowing down to just above her knee. Between the hue of her dress and her sun-kissed skin, her blue eyes sparkle brighter than I've ever seen.

"You need to change," I say flatly.

"What?" she says, eyes widening in fear. "Is it too much? Or too casual?"

"I can't focus on my family reunion if all I'm thinking about is tearing that dress off of you and taking you to the nearest bed I can find."

Her expression immediately turns from nervous to exasperated.

"Griffin, you scared the shit out of me," she scolds. "I'm already nervous enough, don't do that to me."

"I'm sorry, darlin'," I say, pulling her in close and pressing a soft kiss to her forehead. "You look beautiful. Don't change a thing."

"Thank you," she says, almost begrudgingly. A low laugh rumbles in my chest and I squeeze her tighter.

An hour later we pull up to the lakehouse, my heart instantly warming with nostalgia and excitement. I've always loved this place, and didn't realize how much I missed it until right now.

"You ready, darlin'?"

She nods, nervously chewing on her bottom lip and twisting the fabric of her dress in her hands. I reach out and take her hand in mine, bringing it to my mouth for a quick kiss, then step out of my truck and move around the front to open her door.

"Aw hell, who invited this jackass?"

Grinning so wide it makes my cheeks hurt, I turn toward the voice bellowing from the porch.

"They still haven't given you back to the orphanage yet, huh?" I yell in response.

Hunter bounds down the steps, gripping me in a tight hug once we reach the house.

"Y'all might have gotten me with that when we were kids, but it'd be a lot more believable if I wasn't a carbon copy of my mom," he laughs. "I missed you dude, how the hell have you been?"

"I've been good," I say, clapping his shoulder. "Eleanor, this is my second-favorite cousin, Hunter. Hunter, this is Eleanor, my girlfriend."

"First of all, I'm definitely his favorite." His expression turning grave, his next question comes out in a low, somber voice. "How long does he have?" he asks, looking at Eleanor.

"I'm sorry, what?" she says, smiling nervously, a confused look on her face. "He's sick, right? That's gotta be why Make-A-Wish assigned you to be his girlfriend. Because I know you can't be dating him voluntarily."

He ducks quickly, cackling as he narrowly avoids the hand I raised to smack him upside the head.

To my surprise, Eleanor frowns deeply, slowly nodding her head and patting me on the arm. "He doesn't have long, but he's being very brave about it."

He lets out a roar of laughter, wrapping his arms around Eleanor and lifting her off the ground in something more like a tackle than a hug.

"I like her. Can we keep you even after you get rid of him?"

"I'll talk to my supervisors and see what I can do," she says teasingly as she tucks in to my side and wraps her arms around my waist.

Hunter leads us inside, shouting for everyone to come say hi as we follow behind him. Eleanor yelps when I give her a playful smack on this ass.

"You're supposed to be on my side here," I murmur, low enough so only she can hear.

"I need to win them over," she says out of the corner of her mouth. "I'll make it up to you later."

Music to my ears.

The rest of the afternoon is a blur of introductions, yard games, and repeatedly answering "how have you been?" and "what's your father doing these days?" and "I can't believe you're old enough to have graduated!" until my head spins. Eleanor and I got separated when Hunter dragged her into a game of cornhole against Lizzie and Ryan, and my gaze swivels to seek her out more often than not.

Everyone adores her, like I knew they would. She's effortlessly charming, her quick wit and natural kindness winning them over just as fast as they reeled me in. The few times she's happened to look up at me the same time I'm looking at her, she smiles so brightly that I go weak in the knees. She's currently standing by the drinks table with Lizzie, her lemonade sloshing precariously in her solo cup as she talks animatedly, Lizzie's shoulders clearly shaking with laughter as she shoots me a furtive glance.

I don't think I want to know what she's saying, actually.

When the first lightning bugs make their appearance with the setting sun, the whole group makes their way inside to a makeshift dining table made up of about four folding tables lined up end to end. I don't know how we manage it, but soon enough all thirty-ish of us are seated, passing dishes along as we fill our plates. After passing a dish to Ryan's brother, my Uncle Tim, Eleanor leans in close, whispering in my ear.

"I'm having so much fun. Do you think they like me?"

"They love you," I whisper back, squeezing her thigh under the table. "Who wouldn't?"

She kisses me softly on the cheek before turning back to the table to resume her conversation about books with my cousin Carter.

The table is boisterous, but not overwhelming–it just sounds like a group of people that love each other deeply (and loudly).

"So Ellie," Uncle Tim starts. "You guys just graduated?"

"Yes, sir," she says, nodding. "Just before Memorial Day."

"Congrats, kiddos," he says, tipping his glass in my direction. "What's next for you?"

My stomach drops, Eleanor's smile faltering as she shifts uncomfortably in her seat. We haven't talked about that yet. Frankly, I've been actively avoiding it. I don't know what comes next for us. Eleanor is headed for the University of Texas, and I've been accepted to Texas Tech, although I haven't decided if I'm going to enroll or not. Working in construction this summer is the first time I've ever actually felt *good* at something. More and more, I've been thinking I might be built for doing something with my hands, not studying in a classroom.

College has always been this abstract thought –I never had a dream school in mind, or a dream career, or a dream town outside of Larkspur. I love our little corner of Texas. I like being in a town where everyone knows everyone, and we help each other out. The thought of living somewhere surrounded by thousands of strangers makes me feel like I can't breathe. A steady, quiet life sounds a hell of a lot more comfortable than one that's fast-paced and always busy.

But Eleanor's not that way. She dreams of traveling, of not just undergrad but a Master's program, of a career in the city. I wouldn't ever even consider asking her to compromise any of her dreams for me.

Could I live with myself if she did it anyway?

"Well the plan has always been to leave Larkspur but, um, I'm not entirely sure yet," she says, taking a sip of her lemonade. "I know I'm headed to UT Austin to study business admin in August, but I don't have much figured out beyond that."

"UT Austin!" Aunt Lizzie yells from her spot a few seats down, the table suddenly going quiet. "That's amazing, Ellie, you must be so excited!"

"I am," she says with a smile that doesn't reach her eyes. "It's a great opportunity."

"What about you, Griff?" Uncle Tim asks, turning his attention toward me. "Where are you headed?"

"I'm still deciding," I mumble. "I got into Tech, but I've also been working with a contractor this summer and I'm good at it. I might save myself on student loans and just go straight to working."

"Well," Lizzie says in a sickly sweet, fake-as-shit tone. "It's certainly not for everyone. I'm sure you'll find the best fit for your...talents."

There's a moment of awkward silence before Hunter and Harrison start arguing about football and conversation resumes again.

I try to catch Eleanor's eye out of the corner of mine, but her eyes are fixed on her plate, and my stomach knots up, because I'm pretty sure she's avoiding me. I hope she knows that I'd never hold her back from anything she wants to do–I would move heaven and earth for her. But there's a small voice in the back of my head wondering if I'm going to be enough for her.

My appetite now nowhere to be found, I push my food around my plate halfheartedly and try not to borrow trouble before it happens.

The rest of dinner went by at an excruciating pace–at some points painfully slow, because holy shit I need to get out of here. On the other hand, it also went too fast. Walking hand in hand with Eleanor back to the truck, I realize that a week-long dinner still wouldn't be enough time to gear up for the conversation that's coming.

We walk to the truck in silence, the knots in my stomach tightening with every step. When I open her door, she gets one foot in before changing her mind and spinning back around. She wraps her arms around my waist, face burrowing into the soft fabric of my shirt, and inhales a shaky breath. I pull her in close, my chin resting on the top of her head while my mind tries to piece together what just happened. When she lifts her gaze to mine, there aren't any tears in her eyes, but there's *something* there that chokes me up anyway.

Stepping up onto her toes, she whispers *I love you*, kissing me softly before unwinding her arms and finally hopping up into the truck.

Her hand immediately finds mine once we've made it down the long drive and back onto the county road that will take us home. Neither one of us have said anything, but that's done nothing to stop the lump building in my throat. Everything was perfect not even twelve hours ago–why do I suddenly feel like she's slipping away?

"Eleanor, I–"

"Please don't," she whispers. "Please. I know we need to, and we will, but can we not talk about it tonight? I'm just...not done being happy."

Her voice cracks on the last word, along with my heart. I want to scream, to beg, to plead, to do everything I can to convince her that leaving for college doesn't have to change anything, that we don't ever have to stop being happy. That I love her big enough to cover any distance. That if she's scared, I'll be brave for the both of us. That if she really asked me to, I'd follow her anywhere. That no matter what the world might throw at us, it's me and her forever.

But I don't say any of that. Instead, I just pull her into my side, kiss her forehead fiercely, and pretend to scratch my nose while I swipe away the single tear that spilled onto my cheek.

Chapter 34

Ellie

November, Age 28

God, this takes me back.

Between the crackle of the fire, the buzz of the crowd, and the smell of hot dogs and s'mores, it's like I've been catapulted back in time. In a town as small as Larkspur, there's not much to get excited about–but boy do these people love high school football.

The homecoming bonfire is this town's most anticipated event of the year, since the homecoming game is basically our Super Bowl. Two weeks ago I would have rolled my eyes at the mention of it. But after a fortnight of planning and combing meticulously through memories of homecomings past, I'm buzzing right alongside the rest of the town.

The only thing that's different now is I'm actually *allowed* to be drinking the beer in my hand, as opposed to sneaking it in. "Kinda takes the fun out of it, don't you think?" Abby mutters, clinking the necks of our bottles together in cheers. "Drinking was way more fun when it wasn't allowed. And when I wasn't an old maid who wakes up with raging hangovers."

"You're twenty eight, stop acting like you're one foot in the grave," I say, rolling my eyes.

Apparently it hasn't gone unnoticed that I've stayed away for years—everyone and their mamas have been grilling me about where I've been, what I'm doing, and why I don't come visit more. The townsfolk of Larkspur don't need to know the intricacies and nuances of my complicated relationship with my hometown, so I simply smile politely and say that work keeps me busy.

A loud burst of laughter catches my attention while I'm mid-conversation with Patsy, the owner of the local salon. We both turn our heads toward the noise, and my heart leaps into my throat when I see Jack, David, and Griffin across the fire from us. Griffin grips David's shoulder with his head thrown back in laughter, and Jack is doubled over, hands on his knees, shaking his head. In a strange vision, all I can see are the fifteen year old boys laughing and stumbling into Spanish class, and there's a burning sensation in my waterline.

What I wouldn't give to go back to a time where life was that simple.

Almost as if he can sense my presence, Griffin's laughter cuts off abruptly as his gaze fixes on me. I smile at him with a small wave, and he takes a step toward me before tan, lithe arms loop through the crook of his arm, pulling his attention away from me. My heart drops from my throat to the pit of my stomach, smile fading into a grimace as I quickly avert my gaze. The last thing I want to see is Griffin looking lovingly at Madison, knowing he's never going to look at me like that again.

"I always thought the two of you would end up together," Patsy says. I startle, having forgotten that she was there. "I think everyone did. Whatever happened with y'all?"

"Nothing dramatic. Distance, timing, growing up," I say with a shrug.

"That's a shame." Her tone indicates clearly that she doesn't believe me.

"Well, it was really good to see you Patsy, but I've got to find Abby," I say quickly, desperate to get out of this conversation.

I weave through the crowd, pretending not to hear my name called over and over by people I haven't been cornered by yet. I heave a sigh of relief when I spot Abby, who's in animated conversation with my dad.

"Mr. Turner, you know good and well that Aaron is dead set on opening a café. There's no way in hell he'd willingly work in an office, even with you."

"Foiled again," he says, snapping his fingers. "You can't blame a man for trying. Hey there, Ellie Bellie!"

"Hi Dad," I say with a kiss to his cheek. "Abby, can we go? The smoke is giving me a headache."

Abby's eyes narrow suspiciously, then lock on something over my shoulder. Following her line of sight, I see the boys ten feet away from us, Griffin's arm slung over Madison's shoulder, but looking sullen. Her face is tight, arms crossed over her chest. They're both silently watching Jack and David argue, and whe n Griffin's eyes flicker over to mine briefly, I spin around to face Abby again.

Her expression softens, and she moves to my side, arm looping through mine. "Of course we can, my love. I'll tell Aaron you're still trying to poach him, Mr. Turner!"

Shouting a goodbye to my dad, Abby drags me by the arm toward the parking lot. "I'm sorry," she says quietly. "I know that can't be easy."

"It's okay, my sweet ginger angel," I say, laying my head on her shoulder as we cross the lot and find her car. "It's inevitable."

"For what it's worth, he looked fucking miserable," she says gleefully. "They might be in the running for unhappiest couple in Larkspur, and that's saying something when Principal Burnett and Wife Number Three are right there."

I laugh, squeezing her arm tighter before letting go and climbing into the passenger seat. "I'm sure they're perfectly happy, Abs."

"Yeah, yeah," she says sarcastically. "You know what we need?" The wicked grin on her face tells me whatever it is, we absolutely do *not* need it.

"We need some Denim, and perhaps even some Diamonds."

Twenty minutes later, cocktails in hand, we slide into the last open booth at the biggest country bar in the county. Denim & Diamonds opened our sophomore year of high school, and we counted down the agonizingly long days until we turned eighteen and were allowed to come two-stepping, black X's on the back of our hands barely fading before we'd come right back and get fresh marks.

"When's the last time you went two-stepping, east coast girl?" she shouts over the cover band in the corner.

"Your wedding," I yell back, watching the couples spinning deftly around the dancefloor.

"You need a refresher then!"

Without warning, she grabs the arm of the cowboy in conversation with his friends next to our booth. "My friend here is a little rusty, think you can help her out?"

"Oh I'd be honored," he says, tipping his hat with a grin. I glare at Abby as I take his outstretched hand and let him lead me to the dance floor.

"It's been a long time," I shout. "I don't know if I'll remember the steps."

"Don't you worry about that darlin', just follow my lead!"

I fight to keep the look of disgust off my face–hearing anyone but Griffin call me *darlin'* feels wrong, and from someone else's mouth, it's honestly a little condescending. The feeling quickly fades as the moves come back as easily as riding a bike and I lose myself in the joy of twirling, feet moving in sync with the beat of the music.

The song ends before I'm ready to stop, so when he asks me to dance with him again, I let him take the lead. Flashes of dancing in fields of wildflowers and empty parking lots hit me like an unexpected hail storm, but I squeeze my eyes tight, shutting them out of my brain as I let this unfamiliar cowboy spin me around. By the time the second song ends, I'm desperate to get back to the booth, and to my drink.

I need something a lot stronger if Griffin is going to haunt my every waking moment here.

I slam a tequila shot at the bar before ordering two more and heading back over to Abby. She lets out a triumphant whoop when I set the glasses down in front of her, and I barely give her time to cheers me before throwing the second shot back.

I've lost count of the number of drinks I've had when Abby mutters, "Oh shit." Twisting in the booth to see who just walked through the door, I yell a little too loudly, "You've gotta be fucking kidding me."

Jack, David, and Griffin are moving through the crowd to the bar, and it's too late to hide before David spots me and shouts, "ELLIE! MY GIRL!"

Half-running over to us, he shoves himself into the too-small booth, wrapping his arms around me and kisses the top of my head with an exaggerated *mmmmwah*.

"I missed you! I thought I'd never run into you, why the hell haven't we gotten the band back together yet?" I avoid looking at Griffin, instead making eye contact with Jack. He mouths a silent *sorry*, and yanks David out of the booth.

"Don't suffocate her, bozo," he scolds him. "She has better things to do with her time than hang around a bunch of dorks."

"I'm not the one wearing khakis to a country bar, dweeb," he yells, punching him in the shoulder.

"C'mon guys, let's go grab drinks," Griffin says. "Can I get you ladies anything?"

I bark out an emphatic *no* at the same time as Abby says, "Two tequila shots please! And bring salt and lime!"

With a tip of his hat, he drags David with him over to the bar and Jack pulls up a chair next to us.

"Hi Jack Robbit," Abby says sweetly, dramatically batting her eyes at him. "Fancy meeting you here."

"Don't call me that," he grumbles as she cackles loudly. "You know this shit wasn't my idea."

"And yet, here you are, khakis and all."

"Why is everyone so damn obsessed with my khakis?"

"Ta daaaa," David says with a flourish, setting five shots down on the table. "Cheers to being old enough for a reunion, but young enough to still get shitfaced!"

"Speak for yourself," Jack grumbles as we all throw our shots back, slamming the glasses back down on the table, shuddering at the burn of the alcohol.

"Ellie, tell me about your life," David shouts, turning his attention back to me. "Any men I need to intimidate?"

"Alright, dork," Abby yells, sliding out of the booth and shoving him toward the dancefloor. "Let's see if you grew out of your two left feet."

"Okay, but you have to actually let me lead, control freak."

Jack, Griffin, and I sit in awkward silence, and now I wish I had a beer just so I could have something to do with my hands.

I consider going to the bar, but my head is swimming with all the tequila, and standing up right now is definitely a bad idea.

"So, did you guys enjoy the bonfire?" I ask, all my energy focused on not slurring my words.

"It was alright," Jack said, looking at Griffin. He simply shrugs his shoulders, mumbling in agreement. "I wasn't sorry to get out of there."

"Me either," I say. "The smoke was giving me a headache." I don't know why I've decided to double down on this particular lie, but I'm operating at about forty percent brain power right now and it's the best I can come up with.

"How long have you and Abby been here?" Griffin asks. His brow is furrowed in mild concern, and I can't help but think that I'm not doing a very good job at hiding how plastered I am.

And holy shit, am I plastered.

"Long enough to have had about three too many shots," I say, mimicking Abby's fluttering eyelashes and mischievous smirk.

Jack shakes his head, chuckling, but the lines between Griffin's eyebrows deepen. "How are y'all getting home?"

"Don't worry, dad," I say with a dramatic roll of my eyes. "Aaron is picking us up in an hour. No drinking and driving, scout's honor." I hold up three fingers with one hand and cross my heart with the other, taking a deep drink of the water Abby just set in front of me.

"He's hopeless," she says, jabbing her thumb at David. "No sense of rhythm whatsoever. What do they even teach you in Lubbock?"

"No way ginger, I am not the problem out there," he protests. "How come you only know the guy's steps?"

"Years and years of Ellie Bellie being my dance partner," she says, blowing a kiss at me. "You need to hydrate, my love, you have drunk eyes."

"I do not," I hiccup, punctuating my sentence in a way that does nothing to support my argument.

"I texted Aaron, he should be here in thirty."

"I'm going to use the bathroom, I'll be right back," I say, cautiously getting to my feet.

"Are you okay to get over there?" Jack whispers in my ear. "Need me to walk you?"

"I'm fine, Jack Robbit," I say, kissing his cheek. "But thank you for checking." I barely make it five steps to the bathroom when I feel someone fall into step beside me. "I'm fine, Griffin," I say in a singsong voice. "You don't need to chaperone me."

"I'm not chaperoning you, darlin'," he says, and my stomach flutters. *That's* how the word is supposed to sound. "I just happen to also need the bathroom right now."

"Sure you do," I say, swinging the saloon doors open and stumbling to the first open stall I see. There's nothing that makes you realize how drunk you are quite like sitting on a toilet in a bar bathroom.

Shit. Maybe I did need a chaperone.

Despite all odds, I manage to successfully wash my hands and exit the bathroom without incident. No part of me is surprised to see Griffin waiting for me outside. "You didn't have to wait for me," I say, breezing past him and heading back to the booth.

He grabs my arm gently, pulling me back until we're close enough that I can smell the lingering bonfire smoke on his shirt. "No, but I wanted to," he says softly. He hesitates, and I see some unnamed internal battle raging behind his eyes. His jaw sets, clearly having come to some sort of conclusion.

Ghosting his fingers down my arm, he delicately takes my hand, and whispers so low I can barely hear him. "Dance with me before you go?" As if on cue, a slow, romantic ballad begins to play, and partners make their way onto the floor.

I should say no. Being close to him at the barn was painful enough. Letting him touch me, letting him *hold* me, is a catastrophically bad idea. But somewhere along the way my wires get crossed, and the "no" turns into "okay" as the words travel from my alcohol soaked brain to my mouth.

Placing his hand on the small of my back, he guides me out and settles us into place, taking my hand more firmly in his and placing the other at my hip. We begin the slow country waltz, the sounds of the bar fading away as our eyes lock. I let him pull me in closer, the connection between us magnetic as ever.

"I remember the first time we danced in that parking lot," he says, leaning down to whisper in my ear. "I watched so many videos on YouTube to practice before I had the nerve to try."

"Really?" I say, a shocked giggle bubbling out of me. "I never knew that. You seemed like such a natural."

"I was a bull in a china shop. That's why I took you somewhere wide open, so I could eliminate all possible death traps."

"Always so thoughtful," I muse, reaching up to brush his hair back so I can see his face clearly. "My sweet southern gentleman."

"I wanted to impress you," he says, chuckling lowly. "I would have done anything you asked me to, darlin'."

"Please don't call me that," I whisper, pulling away slightly.

"Why not?" he asks, voice thick with alcohol and emotion.

"Because I'm not a darling," I respond. "And you have a girlfriend."

He stiffens at the mention of Madison.

"Who I noticed isn't here, by the way," I say, irritation flaring. "Why'd you ditch her between the bonfire and the bar?"

"I didn't ditch her," he snaps. "She didn't want to come."

"So you thought I'd fill that hole for the time being? Be your temporary girl for the night until you go back to the real one?"

"You don't get to be mad at me for finding someone, Eleanor," he says, voice taking on a dangerous edge. "You're the one who left me."

"Doesn't mean I have to like it," I snap. I'm being childish, petulant even, but the alcohol has lowered my inhibitions (*and my maturity apparently*).

The song ends, and I jump back out of his hold. He opens to his mouth to respond, but I turn with a pout and storm out of the back doors and into the empty parking lot.

"Eleanor Turner, you come back here," he shouts angrily. "What the hell is your problem?"

"My problem is that one minute you're telling me you miss me and reminiscing, and the next you're throwing it in my face that you found someone new," I spit, my words feeling like venom in my mouth. "That's not fair to me."

"Not fair to *you?*" he says with a hollow laugh. "No, what's not fair is you showing up here five years later, no call, no text, no warning, and then getting mad at me for having a life after you ripped my heart out of my chest."

"I did that for you, Griffin," I say, voice shaking with anger. "You would have been unhappy with me."

"Don't you dare do that," he growls. "None of that was about me, and you know it. You were scared, and you bolted. Over and over again."

"Oh, whatever," I yell, turning away from him and walking back to the bar doors. "No one made you wait for me, Griffin. Go home to the life you worked *soooo* hard to build after I left."

"Classic Eleanor," he yells after me. "Walk away, avoid this conversation. Shouldn't be surprised, that's what you do best." I slam the door behind me, leaving Griffin in my wake like I have every time before.

Chapter 35

Ellie

August, Age 18

I've been sick to my stomach for weeks. After meeting Griffin's family and the almost-conversation on the drive home, everything seems to be spiraling out of control.

Except it's not. *Nothing* has changed. I have dinner with Abby on Fridays. We hang out with the boys. Griffin and I still spend as much time together as we always have, laughing and talking and loving the way we always do. My school plans are the same, my dreams well within my reach. And yet, it feels like I'm in one of those nightmares where you're desperately trying to hold onto something and it keeps *just* slipping through your grasp.

I have everything I've ever wanted—dear friends, a clear goal, a boy so perfect I couldn't have dreamt someone better if I tried. When I truly look at it, really and *objectively* look at it, all of those things are screaming at me that they're here, and attainable, and not going anywhere.

So why does it feel like my life is imploding?

"You look like you're about to cry. Or throw up. Or both."

In a horrific turn of events, the diner was rented out for a private party tonight, so Abby and I are eating ice cream for dinner in my backyard, cross legged on the grass in the golden glow of the sunset.

"What's going on in that head, Ellie Bellie?" she asks when I don't respond.

"Do you ever feel like something catastrophic is about to happen and no one will believe you?"

"Well, no," she says through a mouthful of rocky road. "What kind of catastrophe are we talking about here?"

"I feel Griffin and I have an expiration date, and I'm the only one who sees it."

She whips her head around, her expression saying that she clearly thinks I've lost my mind.

"What on earth are you talking about?"

"He wants to stay here and I don't. How does that work?"

"He wants to stay here and you don't *for now,*" she says, eyes rolling in exasperation. "Who knows what's going to happen in the next four years? Who's to say where either of you will end up?"

"But I can't just bank on one of us changing our minds."

"Okay, but you also can't bank on you *not* changing your minds," she says, pointing her spoon in my face. "I know you're my little worrier, but don't work yourself up over a problem you don't actually have."

I stare down at my bowl, my mind warring between what Abby's saying and my own anxiety.

"I don't know why this feels so big to me," I say, fighting back the tears gathering in my waterline. "Nothing has changed, except my brain is convinced that *everything* has changed, and I need to cut and run."

"Do not cut and run, Ellie." Abby's tone turning sharp, she sets her bowl down and grabs my face so I'm forced to look into her eyes.

"As your best friend, it's my duty to tell you when you're making a mistake. This is me telling you."

When the first tear falls she wipes it away gently, but doesn't stop her admonishment.

"I know you, Ellie Bellie. You get Big Scared, and your instinct is to hurt your own feelings before someone else can. With peace and love, cut that shit out. If Griffin isn't scared of the distance, why do you need to be?"

"He's a romantic, and an optimist, and a dreamer, Abs. I need to be pragmatic for the both of us, someone has to plan for the worst case scenario."

"Babe, I love you, but you're talking nonsense. Your worst case scenario isn't happening to you, you're creating it yourself. It's going to be a self-fulfilling prophecy, and then you're going to use it as an excuse to say *I told you so* and wall yourself off. You think it'll prevent heartbreak, but it's just going to prevent your own happiness. I'm telling you, you do not need to do this."

She finally releases me and I look away quickly, anxiously chewing on my bottom lip. Everything she's saying makes sense. Logically, it should be calming my nerves. But it's not.

I can feel myself losing the battle against my own mind. I don't want to feel this way. I don't want to do this. I want to trust that we can make it through every life change together.

I want to tell myself to shut the hell up, but the more my mind reels, the more I accept the inevitable. Even if I have to drag myself kicking and screaming, I have to do the right thing, for both of us.

This is the right thing. Don't talk yourself out of it.

"You're going to do it anyway, aren't you?" Abby mutters so low that I can barely hear her. I nod my head in response, unable to bring myself to say anything.

With a heavy sigh, she scoots over to me, laying her head on my shoulder and gripping my hand. "I think you're going to regret this, my love."

The small crack that's been building in my chest splits wide open, a hollow chasm threatening to consume me from the inside out. I'm going to lose him, and no matter what Abby says, there's nothing either of us can do to stop it.

***

Later that night, after the boys have gone home, Griffin and I lay wrapped together in his bed, my head on his chest as he slowly strokes my hair. I lose myself in the steady rhythm of his heart, wondering if I can actually bring myself to break it.

"You're quiet tonight, darlin'," Griffin muses. "Everything alright?"

"Yeah, just tired," I say, nuzzling my cheek against the soft fabric of his shirt, tightening the grip I have around his torso like if I can just hold him tight enough I'll finally be convinced that I don't have to let him go.

Move-in is next weekend, which means doomsday has officially arrived. Despite my efforts to dig my heels in and force summer to stay forever, August has arrived with a vengeance. Between packing and making sure my schedule is in order, and spending as much time with friends as possible, and slowly drowning in my own turmoil, I end each day feeling like I've run a marathon.

"Do you want me to take you home?" he asks.

"Not even a little bit," I say, tilting my head to look up at him. He's the most beautiful thing I've ever seen—brunette locks of hair lightened by the summer sun, freckles dusting across the nose and cheeks of his tanned face, brown eyes somehow full of stars looking at me like I've hung the moon.

"I was hoping you'd say that," he murmurs, slowly leaning in until our lips just barely touch. Savoring the closeness, our breaths mingle for a moment before crossing that final distance, sealing our lips together in a kiss that I feel down to my toes.

"I'm ready," I say, eyes flicking up to his, all the air whooshing from my lungs at the realization. He may not be my last, but I can't stand the thought of someone else being my first. If it has to be over, it needs to be everything.

"To go home?"

"No," I say, bringing my mouth to his, urgent and hungry for him. "I want you. I want you to have me. And I know we only have a week left, and it's not fair to do this right before I leave, but I want it to be you."

His eyes widen, hand gripping the back of my neck where he'd been gently fingering the long waves of my hair.

"Are you sure?" he says, gently clearing his throat. "There might only be a week left of summer, but that doesn't mean we have to do this now. We can wait."

No, my sweet boy. We can't.

"I don't want to wait," I murmur, peppering kisses along his jawline. "I don't want to go another second without having all of you."

His eyes darken with desire, shifting our bodies until I'm underneath him, looking up at the boy I want so badly to keep.

Make it count, Ellie. If this is it, give him something to hold on to.

I reach up to stroke his cheek, and he leans into my touch.

"I love you, Griffin Hart," I whisper, hoping he chalks the tremble in my voice up to anticipation.

"I love you back, Eleanor Turner," he replies before claiming my mouth with his, our tongues swirling together as our bodies begin to move against each other.

I let myself turn to putty in his hands, shutting my brain off and focusing on nothing but the feeling of his touch. If these are our last moments together, I never want to forget them. If this is goodbye, I want it to feel like forever.

Chapter 36

Griffin

August, Age 19

From between her legs, I pull us both up until she's straddling my lap, frantically ripping our clothes off until there's no barrier between us.

I know what this is. I've felt it coming for weeks. I kept hoping that if we just never talked about it, it wouldn't happen. But it's here, and I don't think there's anything I can do about it.

I don't know what it is that scares her so bad, or why she thinks this can't work. I've watched her fade a little bit every day since the lake house, trying desperately to change her mind but knowing I'm powerless to stop it.

Rising to my knees, my hands grip the back of her thighs, steadying her until she's on her back again. When her blue eyes look straight into mine, I nearly give in to the urge to scream, beg, plead with her not to do this. Instead, I kiss her fiercely–her mouth, then her jaw, down her neck and the valley between her breasts. Settling between her legs, I hook my fingers into her panties and yank them down, spreading her thighs open until she's fully exposed to me.

I look up at her with a wicked grin, careful not to let my own heartache show on my face.

"What are you doing?" she whispers, eyes widening in shock. She lets out a soft whimper as I slowly trace one finger down her slit, humming with approval when I feel how wet she already is.

"If we're doing this, we're doing it right," I growl. "I've felt you come around my fingers, and I fully intend to make you come around my cock."

Her eyes flutter shut, moaning as I slide a finger deep inside her entrance.

"But first," I say, nipping at the sensitive skin of her inner thigh then soothing it with a kiss. "I need you to come on my face. Can you do that for me, darlin'?"

"Griffin, please," she whines, chest heaving with gasps of anticipation.

"I need to hear you say it," I say, grinning as she whimpers in protest when I remove my finger. "Say you'll be a good girl for me and ride my tongue."

"Yes, fine, please," she babbles. "I'll be a good girl, I'll do whatever you want, please touch me."

"Yes ma'am," I say, relishing the way she shudders when I slowly lick from her entrance to her clit, flicking the bundle of nerves with my tongue in a way that has her arching off the bed.

"Oh my God, Griffin, that feels so good."

I let out a dark chuckle, sliding my tongue back down and inside her, one hand holding her open while the other takes over working her clit.

"You taste like heaven, darlin'," I moan against her, still fucking her with my tongue. "Seriously, how am I ever supposed to eat anything else ever again?"

Her fingers lace through my hair, holding me in place as she grinds against my face. Flattening my tongue against her, I lick up every drop of her arousal until my lips find her clit, sucking it into my mouth while I work two fingers in and out of her.

"Oh my God, right there," she cries. "Don't stop, please."

I double my efforts, hand splayed across her lower stomach to keep her in place, licking and sucking and nipping until I feel her inner walls start to pulse around my fingers.

"That's it, baby," I say, pumping them harder and faster. "Grind on my face, make yourself feel good."

Her legs begin to tremble, hips bucking faster, her grip on my hair tightening as she reaches her climax.

"Good girl," I say, my own voice thick with desire. "Come for me."

A heartbeat later, she shatters, clamping down on my fingers as she screams my name. I don't stop working her clit with my tongue until she's practically begging for mercy, completely wrung out by her orgasm.

With one last kiss to her inner thigh, I crawl back up her body until her hands grip my head, pulling me down to her face until she's tasting herself on my tongue.

"You did so good, darlin'," I whisper, kissing her forehead. "You think you're ready for me now?"

Pulling her plump lower lip between her teeth, she nods nervously, but looks determined. I grip her chin between my thumb and forefinger, bringing her gaze to mine.

"If it gets to be too much, you say stop and we stop. You can change your mind at any point, no questions asked."

She nods again, eyes softening. "I trust you."

I wish you'd trust me enough to keep me.

Shaking the thought from my head, I reach into my bedside table and grab a condom. Ripping the foil with my teeth, I watch Eleanor as her eyes are fixed on where I slowly roll it down my shaft.

Bracing myself on either side of her head, I kiss her deeply as I position myself at her entrance. I pull back and rake my eyes down her body, then back up to her face, trying to memorize every curve, every freckle, every detail while I still can.

"You ready?"

She nods, exhaling a shaky breath. I slowly push forward, watching in awe as the head of my cock disappears inside of her. Her hands grip my shoulders, my eyes snapping up to her face when she sucks in sharply.

"Is this okay?"

"Yes, keep going," she says, voice trembling.

I groan as I sink deeper–nothing has ever felt this good. Nothing will ever feel this good again.

"Jesus Eleanor, you feel incredible."

Once I'm nearly all the way in, I pause, letting her adjust to the feeling. When I finally bottom out, she whimpers, grimacing.

"Too much?"

She shakes her head, eyes still squeezed shut, brows furrowed. "No, not too much. Just, different."

"Take all the time you need, darlin', I'm not going anywhere."

After a few deep breaths, she rocks against me, giving me permission to start moving. I slowly slide out, then back in, until I'm fucking her in a steady rhythm, her nervous whimpers turning to moans as the initial pain turns to pleasure.

"Holy shit," she breathes out. "Why did no one tell me how good this is?"

I laugh softly as I begin to pick up the pace, her legs locking behind my back as she rolls her hips, matching me move for move.

"You're perfect, Eleanor," I murmur against her ear, her moans growing increasingly louder. "Nothing will ever compare to you."

Her eyes meet mine, suddenly full of tears and heartbreak. She knows that I know, and that I'm not going to stop her.

It's okay darlin'. I'd do it all again a thousand times over.

I flip us both over, Eleanor now straddling me, looking down at me with wide eyes.

"You wanna try this?"

She nods eagerly, leaning forward to put her weight into the hands she's placed on my chest. She grinds against me, perfect tits bouncing as she works my cock.

"Oh my God, Griffin," she moans. "It feels so different from this angle."

"Different bad or different good?" I say, panting with the effort to keep my cool.

"Different good," she says breathlessly. "Definitely good."

She begins rolling her hips faster and faster, inching towards another orgasm. My balls are clenching, and I want to blow so bad, but not before my girl comes again.

"Darlin', I'm real close," I groan. "But I need you to come on my cock first. Can you do that?"

She nods vigorously, grinding her clit against me while she works me in and out of her.

"Fuck," she cries out. "Oh my God, I'm gonna come."

And then she does, my vision blurring around the edges as she clenches around me over and over, until my own climax hits me. I grip her hips, still grinding her against me as my dick twitches inside her, still stroking me as she coaxes every last drop into the condom.

She collapses against my chest, and I roll us onto our sides, holding her tightly against me as I softly sing her praises.

That's my girl. You did so good. I love you. I love you. I love you.

After a few moments of perfect bliss, I get up to clean myself off and find a washcloth for Eleanor. I don't stop telling her how much I love her as I clean her off, then slide back into bed next to her. She tucks in to me, back to my chest, grabbing my arms and putting them around her, gripping me like I'm the only thing holding her to earth.

"I love you," she says in a hoarse whisper. I inhale deeply, trying to commit the scent of her shampoo to memory. I don't ever want to forget this moment, even as I feel the tears dripping off her face onto my forearm. I pretend not to notice, the same way she's pretending not to notice how my own eyes are leaking into her hair.

We lay like this until her breathing evens out, sleeping peacefully in my arms. I wrap even more tightly around her, willing myself to be grateful for the time I had her instead of regretting the time I won't.

When I wake up to an empty bed the next morning, I'm not surprised. The pillow still smells like Eleanor, knocking the wind out of me as my very last glimmer of hope is snuffed out. I sit up, throwing the covers off and gripping the edge of the bed, my bare feet not even registering the chill of the hardwood underneath. Hanging my head, I finally break down.

***

Griffin–

This is shitty and selfish, and I'm sorry. I'm shitty and selfish and a coward, and you won't believe me, but this has nothing to do with you. I promise. I can't stay here, and I can't ask you to come with me, and you deserve someone as kind and brave as you are. I'd give anything for it to be me. For what it's worth, I really thought it could. Please don't try to change my mind, it'll just make it worse for us both. I love you more than anything. I'm sorry that wasn't enough.

–Ellie

"Fuck dude," David says, wiping tears from his eyes and handing the note to Jack. "Fuck."

"Yeah," I say miserably. When I finally dragged myself out of the bed Eleanor left me alone in, I found her note on my bathroom counter. I read it once, then twice, then tucked it away in a drawer. I couldn't stand to look at it again, to see my name in her handwriting. Or to see the way she talked about herself. I don't know how it got into my beautiful girl's head that she's selfish or unkind when she's anything but, and it shattered my heart all over again.

I don't know what made me do it, but the first person I called was Abby. I needed someone who might understand, who might be able to explain it to me. She told me that she's tried to talk her out of it, to convince her that she can have her dreams and keep me at the same time, but apparently nothing either of us could say could change her mind.

"She's scared, Griffin," Abby said, the pain in her voice an unexpected punch to the gut. "I don't even know what she's scared of, but I see it when I talk to her. She's scared and she's sad, and I don't know what to do."

"Do you think she'll ever change her mind?"

I wasn't sure I even wanted to know the answer.

"I don't know," Abby whispered. "I'd like to think she will. You mean everything to her, Griffin."

"Apparently that's not enough."

"No. I suppose it isn't. For what it's worth, I think she'll regret it."

But will she regret it enough to come back to me?

I really didn't want to know the answer to that one, so I didn't ask. I just listened to Abby apologize on her best friend's behalf, and tell me that I can still call her any time.

After murmuring a thank you and goodbye, I hung up the phone and texted Jack and David, then sat in silence on the basement floor, not bothering to turn the lights on as the sun went down.

When they came down the stairs and flipped on the lamps, all I could do was point at the note on the coffee table and hide my face in my arms, like if I could just bury myself deep enough the truth wouldn't be able to reach me anymore.

"This doesn't make any sense," David says, now pacing around the room. "Did she get kidnapped or something? How do we even know this is her handwriting?"

"Stop it," Jack says harshly. "This isn't a joke."

"I never said it was," David replies angrily. "But there's no way she just changed her mind and left, just like that. I don't believe it."

"Well, she did," I say with a humorless chuckle. "Just like my mom did. Maybe Hart men just aren't worth sticking around for."

"It's nothing like your mom, Griffin," Jack says in a gentle voice. "Your mom's a selfish bitch."

"No offense," he adds quickly, and I wave him off. My mom *is* a selfish bitch.

"But Ellie is not, and you know that," he continues. "She's confused, and overwhelmed, and probably just as miserable as you are right now."

Not a chance in hell.

"What am I supposed to do now?" I ask, hating the desperation in my voice.

"Can you do late enrollment at Tech? Tell them you had a family emergency or something," David suggests. "Come to Lubbock with me, get the fuck out of here."

The irony is so ridiculous that I'd laugh if I wasn't so Goddamn sick to my stomach. She's leaving me because she can't stay in Larkspur. But I can't stay in Larkspur now that everything will just remind me of her.

What was the fucking point of any of this?

"Yeah, okay, I'll look into it."

Jack opens his mouth like he might say something, but closes it without a word. What could he even say at this point?

"I don't know what to do without her, Jack."

"I don't either, Griffin. I guess we figure it out."

Two weeks later, my things are packed in next to David's in the bed of my truck as we head out west. By some miracle they let me squeeze in on the last day of the late registration window, even if it did cost a chunk of change to do it. Looking in the rearview one last time, I decide it was worth every penny. I don't know if there's anything for me in Lubbock, but there's sure as hell not anything left for me here.

Chapter 37

Ellie

November, Age 28

"Hey, look who's back!" David cheers, holding his drink up to me as I storm toward the table. His eyes widen, arm sinking back down when he gets a good look at my face. "Wait, are you okay?"

Leaning in close to her ear, I plead, "Abby, we need to go now." Without hesitation, she grabs both our bags from the hooks under the table and slides out of the booth.

"What happened?" Jack asks, but when his eyes meet mine I know I don't need to tell him. There's only one person who gets me worked up like this.

Yeah, yourself. Don't act like this is his fault.

Extremely unwilling to deal with that self-reflection right now, I spit out, "Go ask Griffin. I'm sure he'll tell you all about how I wasted his life." Both boys jump up, reaching out for me to stay and explain, and I struggle to wrench my arm from Jack's grasp. "Let me go, Jack."

"Ellie, please–"

"No." My voice is shrill and unfamiliar in my own ears. "I need to get out of this bar, I need to get out of this town, I need to get out of this *life*. I never should have come back to this stupid town and its stupid people in the first place."

He releases his grip on my arm, the flicker of hurt in his eyes sobering me up quicker than a bucket of ice water over the head.

"Jack, you know I didn't mean you. I shouldn't have said that."

There's a lot I shouldn't have said tonight.

"Go home, Ellie Bellie," he murmurs into my ear, patting me on the shoulder as he passes behind me and heads toward the back door. "Sleep it off."

"Jack, I–"

"I know, Ellie. It's okay. Go home."

I stand frozen in place as I watch them weave through the crowd. Abby tugs gently on my arm, leading me out of the chaos to the front parking lot. I wrap my arms around myself and close my eyes, shivering while I try to adjust to the frigid November air from the heat of the crowded bar.

Aaron pulls up in front of us, and I clamber into the backseat in complete silence. He briefly glances over his shoulder at me, then turns his attention to where Abby is buckling her seatbelt.

"Don't," she whispers, leaning over to kiss his cheek. "Just take us home."

I let my forehead thud against the cold window, staring at the streetlights on the drive home without really seeing them. Regret is already settling in–except, can something really settle in if it's had a permanent spot in my psyche for ten years?

Why do I always do this?

Therapy must really be paying off, because the second the thought crosses my mind I can hear Kelsi's voice in my head.

"You treat these things like a self-fulfilling prophecy, Eleanor. You think it will hurt less if you can convince people that you're awful and unlovable before they come to the conclusion on their own. The problem is that neither of those things are true—you are the only one who believes them. But you are unwilling to give people the chance to prove you wrong. You rob yourself of the opportunity to be happy."

Mental note—email Kelsi to set up a virtual appointment as soon as possible.

I told her, and myself, that I'd stop doing that. And for the most part I have. I'm more honest with my friends, and I'm more honest with myself. But there's something about being around Griffin that yanks me back to the Ellie who treats self-sabotage like a full time job.

Maybe it's that he has been so unwavering in his love for me. He is so inherently good and kind that I can't help but feel small and unworthy around him.

You are the only one who believes those things.

Griffin has never believed those things about me. The one time he even remotely suggested it, right before I went to Boston, he texted me immediately apologizing.

Griffin: I didn't mean what I said, Eleanor.

Griffin: You're not selfish or awful. I never should have said that. I wish you'd stop saying it about yourself.

Griffin: I love you darlin', no matter what.

Back then, I read that text over and over as some sadistic kind of punishment. As a reminder of just how badly I messed everything up. After I started therapy, I read it over and over as a reminder that not even the best person I've ever met thinks horribly of me.

Well, he didn't then. But as my own words from tonight echo through my mind, I can't possibly fathom how he wouldn't think that now.

You and me both, Griffin. You and me both.

Chapter 38

Griffin

November, Age 29

"**F**uck!"

I slam my fist into the back alley dumpster right as the door slams shut behind Eleanor. I regret it instantly, because I'm pretty sure that I now have some broken fingers to go with a broken heart.

How many times can a Goddamn heart break?

"Fuck," I swear again under my breath, running my fingers through my hair wildly. What the fuck just happened? How did we go from laughing in the rose gardens to screaming at each other in a parking lot?

Taking a deep, steadying breath, I head back inside to find Jack and David. When I wrench the door open we nearly collide–they must have been coming to look for me. I shake my head at them, then close out at the bar and storm out, blood still roaring in my ears.

"Griffin, wait up," Jack yells, jogging to catch up to me. "Let's go back to your place and talk this out."

"Can't," I say bitterly. "Told Madison I'd be over at hers by midnight."

"No offense dude, but do you really think you should be going to your girlfriend's house after a public fight with your ex?" David asks breathlessly, coming to a halt next to Jack.

"No offense *dude*, but it's none of your damn business."

"Cut the shit, Griffin." Jack's teeth are gritted, words sharp enough to cut glass. "It is our damn business, and you need to cool off before you go anywhere. Let's just go to the house, and you can rage at us all you want."

"He's right." David's voice has gone soft and reassuring, and all it does is piss me off more. "We all know that things are over with Madison, and probably have been since Ellie came back. But she deserves better than whatever you're going to say in this state."

Well fuck. He *is* right. I think I've always been one foot out the door with Madison—no matter how hard I tried. "I feel like a jackass," I spit out harshly. "I wasted a year of her life, just like I've wasted nearly fifteen years of mine."

"Nothing about your time with Ellie was a waste," Jack says, voice rising. "I get that you're pissed, but I'm not going to let you talk about her like that. Ellie is the best thing that's happened to any of us, don't you minimize that."

Glaring at him, I wrench the truck door open, turning the key and barely giving them time to get in before peeling out of the gravel lot.

I slam every door from the car to the basement, Jack and David following behind in grim silence.

<u>Madison:</u> Are you on your way?

Shit. I forgot to text her. Not only was I a complete dick at the bonfire, but now I'm standing her up.

<u>Griffin:</u> Sorry, not gonna make it. Gonna hang with the guys at my house.

Gonna hang out with the guys and brainstorm how to end things with you without being the world's biggest asshole.

<u>Madison:</u> Ok. We should talk tomor-row though.

<u>Griffin:</u> Yeah I know. I'll call you in the morning.

Throwing my phone into the chair with way too much force, I sink onto the floor and drop my head into my hands.

Five years. I've spent five years getting my shit together, putting myself back together piece by piece until I finally felt like a functional human being again. All it took was two weeks for all that work to go up in flames. I'm twenty eight years old and already feel like I've got nothing left to give. I gave every-thing, heart, body and soul, to a girl who didn't want it and still managed to walk away with it. Eleanor Turner is my only chance at happiness, and the singular source of all my agony.

"You gonna tell us what happened now?" David demands, crossing his arms. "Things looked good, and then y'all were just gone."

"Eleanor did what Eleanor does," I laugh, the sound bitter and hollow. "She builds a bridge then sets it on fire, and leaves me with the ashes."

"Give us more than that," Jack urges. Heaving a deep sigh, I stand and pace, forcing myself to share every miserable detail from the bathroom to the fight.

"Jesus, Griffin, that was a bit cruel, don't you think? Throwing it in her face like that?"

"Me? What about her? *No one made you wait for me, Griffin.*" I say, mimicking the words that felt like a dagger in my chest. "*That's* fucking cruel. As if I had a choice? Does she think I wanted to spend the last five years pining after her?"

"I think you both said some things you didn't really mean."

"Oh I meant every word of it," I snap. "Stop being diplomatic for once in your life, Jack."

"I will not," he snaps back. "I don't think you've ever said a mean word to her, and you're going to regret it like hell once the alcohol and temper have worn off." That sobers me up real quick.

Little does he know the regret is already climbing up my insides like a demon from hell.

"Even if I do, she sure as hell won't," I say, sliding back down to the ground. "You didn't see her face. Everything she said came straight from the heart." Heaving a sigh, I continue, "Why is she even mad? She doesn't want me. She should have just brought whatever guy she's dating back in Boston with her."

And I should never have asked her to dance.

"What do you mean? Is she dating someone?" David looks accusingly at Jack. Jack shakes his head no.

David continues on slowly, clearly scared of setting me off again. "That's what I thought. I didn't think she was seeing anybody. And from what I've heard, life hasn't exactly been sunshine and daisies for her."

"What do you mean?"

"The past five years didn't just happen to you, Griffin," Jack says. "She's been through a lot. I think we saw glimpses of it in high school, but she's been battling her own brain for a long time. She never wanted to run, but she didn't know how to stay."

"She told you that?"

"In her own way. I guarantee she carries a lot of regret and shame around, and she does it on her own." His face darkens, and it once again catches me off guard that I'm not the only one who's spent years caring for Eleanor. "I watched for years while she shut herself away. Depression is a different kind of beast. Abby and I have given her space where she needed it, and support when she finally started asking for it. She's starting to come back to herself, with a little help and a lot of grace."

"Why haven't you told me any of this?"

"You needed to come back to yourself too, man," David interjects, sitting next to me and gripping my shoulder. "You got the Big Sad. You wanted to help her so bad that you neglected yourself. That didn't do either of you one bit of good."

"When did you get so touchy-feely?" I say with a watery laugh. "Those are some big therapy words you got going there."

"Bro, I have three sisters studying psychology," he says. "You think I haven't absorbed some emotional intelligence through osmosis?"

Jack takes a seat on my other side and pats me on the leg. "It's okay to have big feelings, Griff."

"Alright, pack it up, Mr. Rogers," I mutter, knocking his foot with mine. "That's enough psychoanalysis for one night."

Groaning, I pull my knees up and rest my forearms on them. "What do I do about Eleanor now?"

"With peace and love dude," David says, getting to his feet and offering his hand. The phrase catapults me back to high school. I can picture it crystal clear–Abby attempting to soften the blow of whatever harsh words are about to leave her mouth. "You have some more pressing matters at the moment."

"Like what?" I ask, frowning.

"Like breaking up with your girlfriend."

Fuck me.

"You're right," I sigh. "You're right. I'll go talk to her in the morning."

"You know what else you need to do?"

"Damn David, do you just keep a running list of things you think I should be doing?"

"No, but speaking from personal experience," he says pointedly. "You have *got* to stop mixing alcohol and Ellie."

Chapter 39

Ellie

MARCH, AGE 20

"Ellie? ...Ellie. ELLIE."

The shout yanks me unceremoniously back to reality. I'm not sure exactly how long I've been zoned out, but I can tell from Jenna's face that it was long enough for her to get annoyed. "I'm sorry, what were you saying?"

Jenna rolls her eyes in exasperation. "I was *saying* that physics is stupid and Dr. Hayes clearly has a vendetta against me."

Right. We're supposed to be studying for our midterms. Something I have not thought about once in the...however many hours we've been sitting in the courtyard, enjoying what will probably be the only true spring weekend we get before we go straight into summer heat.

It's the weekend before spring break, but Texas is Texas, so it's 75 degrees, even though it snowed on Monday—the warm respite would be much more enjoyable if finals weren't threatening to melt our brains out of our ears.

Jenna narrows her eyes, shooting me a suspicious look. "What's the matter with you today? Normally *you're* the one keeping *me* on the rails. If you've lost focus then what hope do we have of passing this final?"

Tossing her textbook to the side, she flops back onto the grass and lets out a dramatic huff, her silky dark curtain of hair fanning out around her.

"You might as well tell me what's going on. You've been weird all day, and you know I'm going to bug the living daylights out of you until you tell me."

Despite the inner turmoil I'm trying very hard to avoid, I can't help but smile at the use of the southern colloquialism she used to make fun of me for. I've been rubbing off on her.

"Nothing is going on, I think I'm just fried from all of this studying," I say casually, looking down at where I'm picking at the grass.

She probably already thinks I'm lying, but if I look her in the eyes she will know it for an absolute fact.

Her eyes narrow even further, which doesn't actually seem physically possible. "Eleanor Camellia, you've got to be the worst liar in the history of the universe, I don't know why you even try," she says, propping herself up on her elbows to face me.

I wince at the sound of my full name.

No one calls me that anymore.

Shoving that thought out of my mind, I brace myself for her to press the issue, but instead she lets out a defeated sigh and says, "But I also know that if you've made up your mind not to talk about it, no amount of bugging from me is going to make you tell me any faster. It's just going to make me batty, and Dr. Hayes, who absolutely *does* have a vendetta against me, is already doing that so I'm at max capacity."

I jerk my head up to see her lying back down on the grass, arm draped over her eyes to block out the sun.

I met Jenna Wilbanks during first semester move-in week when she came barrelling down our hall with a bright turquoise suitcase and started unpacking her things, talking a mile a minute before I managed to get a word in to tell her that she was in the wrong room.

She's down the hall in her actual room now, but we've been attached at the hip ever since. She's from the Pacific Northwest, so we couldn't have grown up more differently, but she's my kindred spirit in every way. She even begged to visit Larkspur with me over fall break, spending the full week squealing every time she saw even the most mundane of small town clichés.

"It's just like Friday Night Lights, I didn't think shit like this was real!"

At first I was nervous about introducing her to Jack and Abby—I've never had to mix friend groups before, and I was convinced that somehow my three favorite people would hate each other. Even though Jack and Abby have also been friends for years, and Jenna has never met a stranger.

To my immense surprise, Jack and Jenna have eerily similar niche interests, and talked about how scientists use samples from the ice caps to determine when volcanic eruptions have occurred for the better part of an hour until they remembered that I was, in fact, still at the table with them.

When Abby came over for a sleepover, it was a huge relief that they instantly clicked. It then became a huge nightmare, because the two of them together is akin to every version of the Joker teaming up, but instead of destroying Gotham City, they force me to talk about my feelings.

Something I have been adamantly opposed to since I broke my own heart, as well as his.

To Abby's credit though, she didn't bring up Griffin at all, and Jenna was fascinated by my personality as a child, so she didn't even notice that the topic of boys never came up.

That's why it's so jarring to see her back down so quickly. Jenna is studying psychology, and by that I mean she's taken Psych 101 and has been locked in on determining exactly where all of my anxieties stem from ever since. (The conclusion is nearly always sexual frustration, obviously.)

Is she trying to lull me into a false sense of security before she really pounces?

"I can feel you looking at me," she says without bothering to move her arm to look at me. "Believe it or not, I do know when to pick my battles. You've got that look on your face that you get when you think about home, and I know better than to push you on that. Just know it's going to haunt me forever and I will hold it against you until the day we die."

Even though I know she can't see it, I'm certain she can feel the way I roll my eyes dramatically, even as my stomach clenches at the tangential mention of Larkspur.

"Have you ever considered toning down the drama for one day in your life?"

Mirroring her movements, I lay down next to her and throw my arm over my face.

Without missing a beat, she snarks, "No I haven't, and that's a stupid question and I resent it."

I laugh out loud, realizing it might be the first time I've laughed all day as Jenna joins in.

***

Earlier today, my morning had started off the way it has every day since we switched back to Daylight Savings Time– with the sunlight peeking through the curtains in my dorm room directly onto my face, very rudely waking me up well before I'm ready to be awake.

When I rolled over to grab my phone from under my pillow to check what time it was, two notifications made my heart skip several beats before I could even register how early it was.

[1 Missed Call & 1 New Voicemail]

Frowning at my phone, I was still half asleep as I checked to see who called me in the middle of the night.

[Griffin Hart]

Surely not, I thought to myself, bringing my phone up to my ear to listen to the voicemail. *It had to be a pocket dial.* My heart stopped entirely when I heard the southern drawl coming through the speaker.

> *"Uh, hey darlin'.*
> *Listen, I'm sorry to call you.*
> *I actually don't even know why I'm calling you.*
> *Uh, basically I fucked up and I don't know what to do.*
> *And things always make more sense when I talk to you.*
> *Or maybe they don't anymore. I don't know.*
> *Shit, this was a bad idea."*

He was very clearly drunk, and ended the call with a humorless chuckle without saying goodbye. I listened to the voicemail three more times, and before I could start to process it, my phone buzzed with a new notification. This time, I get a text that reads:

<u>Griffin:</u> I shouldn't have called you. That was a mistake. Ignore it.

My heart plummeted into my stomach as I read the text over and over and over. An onslaught of a million different emotions sent me reeling– I still can't tell if I'm more shocked, sad, or angry.

As I lay next to Jenna on what should be a perfectly lovely day, I decide to hone in on anger, fists clenching so tight I can feel the crescent moon indents from my nails that will probably linger for hours.

The problem is I can't tell if I'm upset that he called me in the first place, or that he so flippantly said it was a mistake.

Ironic, coming from me.

And even worse, that I should forget it. I haven't heard from, or spoken to, or even talked about Griffin since I left for college. It pisses me off that he told me to ignore it, even though that's exactly what I planned to do when I showed up here–ignore and forget everything to do with Larkspur High and the cowboy I left behind. Jenna has badgered me relentlessly about what she refers to as my "mysterious sordid past," but I know if I talk about it, that means I have to think about it, and I've worked painstakingly hard not to do that exact thing. To think about it. To think about *him.*

All it took was a voicemail and a text to crack open the vault in my heart where I shoved everything to do with Griffin Hart the moment I left his house that morning—left, and never looked back.

Chapter 40

Griffin

March, Age 20

I fucked up. Actually worse than that. I double-fucked up.

The first fuck up happened last month. I was dragged to a frat party by David–simultaneously my best friend and bane of my existence.

When he convinced me to come to Texas Tech after Eleanor ripped me to shreds, I regretted the decision the moment we crossed the county line. I've already decided that I'm not coming back next semester, despite David's attempts to convince me that he might die if I leave.

You know what, maybe I've actually hit some sort of unholy trinity of mistakes.

The first mistake was going to the party in the first place. The second was getting so belligerently hammered that I hooked up with a random sorority girl in the bathroom without even asking her name.

And this isn't a Cinderella "oops, I fell in love and forgot her name" type of disaster. This is a "the girl I hooked up with while blacked out texted me that she might be pregnant, except I never saved her name in my phone and can't really confirm if the text was even meant for me" type of disaster.

Which brings me to the third–and probably not final–problem.

I thought that college was supposed to make you smarter, but David decided that the best way to cope with my drunken disaster was to get even drunker this weekend, which, admittedly, I didn't think was even possible.

When I woke up this morning with the hangover to end all hangovers, I wracked my brain trying to remember the events of the night before. Flashes of fireball shots, mechanical bulls, Crunchwrap Supremes, and even more fireball shots were making my head spin until one very clear flashback stopped me cold.

There's no way I did that, I thought to myself as I pulled up my call history log. I'm not that dumb. When I see the most recent outgoing call, I realize that I am, in fact, that dumb.

Eleanor Turner - 1:37 AM

Fuck. Of all the people in the world I could have called, I picked the worst possible option.

Before I can think better of it, I fire off a text.

I stumble out of bed, and pull on the first pair of sweatpants I can find before heading straight to David's room. After pounding on the door for a solid two minutes, he finally opens it.

"Uhhh I'm sorry, did the world end? Is there a reason you're yelling at the ass crack of dawn?" he groans, looking nearly as bad as I feel.

Pushing past him into the dorm, I say "It's 12:30, it's not early–you're just hungover." He mumbles something under his breath that I can't hear, and then lets out a strangled yell when I open the blinds. I turn toward him and bark out, "What did you let me do last night?"

It comes out more accusatory than I intended, but I'm too pissed that this whole semester has been spent with a David-shaped devil on my shoulder convincing me to make bad decisions to care.

With a wicked grin on his face, he says, "I don't know what you could possibly be referring to. I didn't let you take rapid shots and then get on the mechanical bull, you did that all by yourself, buddy."

I roll my eyes and collapse onto his couch. Why am I friends with him again? "I'm not talking about that, bozo. What happened to friends not letting friends dial drunk?" I shoot him an accusatory look, and watch the wheels in his head spin until it finally clicks.

"Wait, you drunk dialed someone? Was it Maggie? Because Sarah told me that her pregnancy test came back negative so you don't even need to worry about that anymore."

Maggie, that was her name. "No, this isn't about Maggie." I drop my head into my hands and sigh. "I called Eleanor."

He's quiet for a beat, then lets out a low whistle. He looks genuinely sympathetic when he asks, "What'd she say, dude?"

"She didn't say anything. She didn't answer." Right? Using every single brain cell that wasn't drowned in alcohol last night, I try to remember how that call went. I pull my phone out to check the duration of the call, and when I see that it was under 90 seconds, my stomach unclenches a bit.

Until I remember the voicemail.

Uh, hey darlin'....
....Uh, basically I fucked up and I don't know what to do.
And things always make more sense when I talk to you.
Or maybe they don't anymore. I don't know.

I drag my hand down my face, then bite my knuckle hard enough to leave a mark. Regret and shame crawl up my spine with the same determination to make a reappearance as the Crunchwrap Supremes apparently have.

Maybe I'm imagining it, I think to myself hopefully. Maybe I didn't actually make a complete ass of myself after working so hard to shut out every thought of her for the last two years.

My phone dings with a text notification, and that hope is gone even faster than it came.

<u>Ellie</u>: Hope everything is okay. You know I'll always be here if you need me, Griffin.

I lurch myself to the trashcan just in time to empty last night's contents from my stomach. But I don't think it's the hangover making me feel sick now.

Chapter 41

Ellie

May, Age 20

"Thank God you're home," Abby sighs, taking a drag from her milkshake like it's a drunk cigarette. "I've been losing my mind."

"You only got home two days before me," I say, pointing my french fry in her face before popping it in my mouth. "I thought I was supposed to be the dramatic one."

"I had to take up your mantle in your absence."

"My forty eight hour absence."

"Forty eight hours too many."

After somehow surviving sophomore year, I've made it home to Larkspur for the summer. I always dread coming home, but after Griffin's drunken voicemail and subsequent radio silence earlier this year, my stomach is in particularly painful knots. I didn't see hide nor hair of him last summer, but I doubt I'll be that lucky again.

The knots in my stomach tighten even further at the thought of my well-kept secret—I'm not going back to school in the fall. Well, I'm not going back to campus at least. I've accepted an internship program with an architectural firm in Boston, and plan to take my next year online (maybe my last two years if my internship goes well). I haven't shared it with anyone yet, including my parents. I have this horrible feeling that everyone is going to be mad at me for going even further away, and I can't handle that. Even worse, I couldn't handle someone accusing me of running away from my feelings. Again.

Because they'd be right. I thought Austin would be far enough, but after that missed call, I immediately started researching internships–the farther away, the better. When I stumbled upon this one, I applied on a whim, and was shocked when I got the acceptance email three days later.

All it took was one voicemail and a short text to send me into a spiral, desperate to flee with my tail between my legs. When I think about Griffin, and the way I left things, it feels like my lungs might collapse. My chest caves in even further when I remember that I have no right to feel this way. I did this to myself–and worse, I did it to him. I don't get to wallow in self pity when I'm suffering the consequences of my own actions. I've been selfish enough.

The worst part of me wants to be selfish. It hopes that I run into Griffin, and I can beg him to forgive me and tell him I changed my mind, and he'll kiss me and sweep me off my feet, and I can have him back without having to make any sacrifices. And I think he would let me do that to him–which makes it that much more awful, and that much more tempting to give into the fucked up life we'd have if I let him drop everything he's ever wanted to be with me.

Selfish. Awful. Mean. You never deserved him.

Those words play on a constant loop in the back of my mind. Even when I'm not consciously thinking about him, the part of my heart that I tarnished two years ago is still palpable.

"When are we seeing Jack?" I ask, desperate to get out of my own head. "Are he and Aaron still attached at the hip?"

"I swear Ellie Bellie, my boyfriend got himself a boyfriend," she says, rolling her eyes. "I'm a third wheel in my own relationship. Reiterating my point–Thank. God. You're. Home."

Laughing, I thank the waitress as she hands me our bill, quickly tipping and signing the receipt as Abby stands. "We can see him tonight," she says with a toss of her auburn curls over her shoulder. "He'll probably be there when we get home."

My heart swells in anticipation of being reunited with my dearest Jacky boy. We text pretty often when I'm away, but it's not enough. I haven't even told him about the phone call. My smile falters as Abby slams her door shut and turns the key in the ignition. Talking about Griffin is going to be unavoidable–hopefully *seeing* him won't be.

***

My jaw drops, eyes blinking rapidly as I stare dumbfounded at the notification on my phone.

> **David:** *Poltergeist gif"

> **David:** We're baaaaack >:)

> **Jack:** Sorry, who's this?

> **David:** Don't be a dick

> **David:** Me and Griffin just got back for the summer, when are we getting together?

I must be dreaming. Or David must be experiencing some sort of amnesia, because there's no way he's reactivating this group chat after two years of being dormant.

More importantly, getting back from where?

> **Griffin:** Wait what

> **Jack:** I didn't even know we still had this group chat

> **David:** Oh shit *gif of Homer Simpson disappearing into the bushes*

Heart in my stomach, I wait for another text that doesn't come. Then I realize that David just meant to text the boys. It wasn't some chaotic attempt to make us all be friends again–he just used the wrong group chat. Somehow that's infinitely more painful.

Well, we know that Griffin's phone does in fact work.

After March, I had this monumentally stupid hope that we might be able to rebuild something, anything, between us. When I never heard from him again, I tried to kid myself into thinking that maybe his phone broke, or he finally changed his number, or he accidentally deleted mine. Now I know the harsh truth with certainty–he has *no* desire to talk to me.

And for good reason.

My phone dings again with another text from David, but this time it's just us.

David: Sorry Ellie Bellie

David: I'm an idiot

David: I do wanna see you though

Collapsing back onto my pillows and releasing a heavy sigh, I respond.

Ellie: You're not an idiot

Ellie: Well, sometimes

> **Ellie:** But not always

I hesitate before adding–

> **Ellie:** I'd love to see you, my darling David

> **Ellie:** Name a time and place.

> **David:** Any chance you'd come over to Griffin's and hang with us like we used to?

> **David:** Enough time has passed that it's not weird, right?

> **David:** I miss the band :(

A wave of nausea floods my body as I force myself to type out the words.

> **Ellie:** David, he doesn't want to see me

> **Ellie:** We haven't spoken in two years

> **Ellie:** There's no reunion tour this time

> **David: That's not true**

> **David: He called you in March for a reason, even if he said it was mistake**

> **David: What is it with you guys and saying that shit to each other?**

My eyes widen in shock. I had no idea he told David about it. Or anyone, for that matter. I certainly didn't.

> **David: If he says yes, will you come?**

> **Ellie: Leave it alone, David**

> **Ellie: Don't ruin his summer on day one by dragging me into it**

I don't bother waiting for a reply before putting my phone on silent and setting it on my bedside table. I don't need to see it in writing that Griffin doesn't want to see me.

"Are you fucking kidding me," I mutter as my phone buzzes on the hard wood. I should have expected it–David notoriously (*and shamelessly*) refuses to accept the end of a conversation.

With an annoyed huff, I roll over to grab my phone, but when I see the notification my breathing stops.

Griffin: Howdy Eleanor

This must be a dream. I must have fallen asleep.

Ellie: Hi Griffin

I'm starting to feel lightheaded–I think my body has forgotten how to breathe.

Griffin: So you're home for the summer?

My breathing resumes in shallow, anxious inhales.

Ellie: Yes, I got home a few days ago.

Ellie: You?

Griffin: Yup.

I desperately try to scrounge up a follow-up question when another text comes through.

Griffin: Well not just for the summer

Griffin: Got a full time promotion with the contractor

Ellie: Oh, that's great

Ellie: How have you been?

The typing bubble pops up, then disappears. Pops up again, then disappears again. After an agonizing five minutes, he finally replies.

Griffin: We don't have to do this

Griffin: I don't really know why I texted you

Griffin: I guess that stupid group text scrambled my brain

Tears well in my eyes, instantly spilling down my cheeks. This is my worst-case scenario. I've daydreamed a thousand times about what he might say to me if we ever spoke again. I can't daydream anymore. Now it's a waking nightmare.

Ellie: It's okay, I get it, I really do

Ellie: I was surprised you texted me

Ellie: I promise I'll leave you alone this summer

Ellie: I know I'm the last person you want to see

Ellie: And I don't blame you. Have a good summer, Griffin.

The tears are coming in earnest now, a sob choking its way up my throat as I bury my head in my pillow.

Griffin: I always want to see you Eleanor

Griffin: Lord help me, but I do

Griffin: I think about you constantly

Griffin: I miss you so much it hurts

My breath hitches mid-sob, but another text comes through before I can begin to reply.

Griffin: I'm sorry, that wasn't fair

Griffin: I'm the one who needs to leave you alone

Panic rises like bile in my throat. The last thing I ever want is for Griffin Hart to leave me alone. Even if I'm the one who left him alone to begin with.

> **Ellie: I don't want to be left alone**

> **Ellie: I miss you too**

> **Ellie: What if we hung out? Just lunch or something casual, no pressure**

I chew anxiously on my lower lip, silently pleading for him to say yes.

> **Griffin: Yeah, I'd like that**

> **Griffin: How about I pick you up tomorrow?**

I reply as fast as possible before he has a chance to change his mind.

> **Ellie: That sounds perfect**

> **Ellie: Let me know when you're on your way, and I'll see you then**

This time when I set my phone down, I'm genuinely giggling and kicking my feet as my tears dry up. Maybe hope isn't monumentally stupid after all.

Chapter 42

Griffin

May, Age 21

This is a huge mistake. But the second that group chat popped up, I knew it'd be impossible *not* to talk to her. I wasn't lying when I said I miss her so much it hurts. I walk around with a metaphorical limp, heart never having fully healed from being shattered two summers ago.

Inhaling a shaky breath when I park my truck in front of her house, my equally shaky hands text her to let her know I'm here. When she walks out of the front door, I can't tell if my chest is trying to explode or implode—all I know is this girl is going to unravel me until my last breath.

My eyes try to soak in every detail, from the red tank top and cutoffs, to the high ponytail and the bangs framing her face—*she has bangs now*—to the quirky swing that hasn't left her step. It's like no time has passed and I'm eighteen again, picking my girlfriend up for a casual summer Tuesday. God, I wish that were true.

She opens the door and hops up into the passenger seat, slowly and carefully buckling her seatbelt before finally, *finally* looking at me. My stomach bottoms out as my eyes meet the bright blue ones I've dreamed about every day since I last looked into them.

Without a second thought, I grab her face and pull her in, kissing her fiercely. My lips move against hers, and *God I've forgotten how soft they are.* I pull back, my breath ragged as I search her face for any sign of what she's feeling.

"Griffin..." she whispers softly, a single tear running down her cheek.

"I know, darlin," I whisper back, reaching up to swipe it away. "I just couldn't help myself."

Looking so sad and guilty that it breaks my heart all over again, she reaches up to stroke my cheek before leaning in to place a soft kiss on my mouth.

After staring at each other in utter silence for what feels like an eternity, I tear my gaze away and put the truck in drive, heading down the street without another word. Muscle memory takes me to the lake, my stomach clenching at the memory of the first time she said *I love you* on this exact trail. We step out of the truck without a word, walking down the path as if pulled by a magnet, straight to the bench that will always be ours. We spent so many summer evenings at the spot where we began. I never thought we'd end up here again.

Eleanor stares at the folded hands in her lap, knuckles white from gripping them tightly. I reach over and pry them apart, taking one in my hand and rubbing gentle circles on the soft skin. Despite the front she puts on, everything about her has always been soft—even the snark and stubbornness and wit. Not soft in a weak way, but the kind of sweet softness that starts in the heart and radiates outward.

She's her own harshest critic, and looking at the turmoil on her face right now, I wish I could pick every negative thought out of her brain and replace them with the thoughts I have of her.

You're the most wonderful girl I've ever met.
Everyone you meet is better for having known you.
You didn't hurt anyone on purpose, we know that.
I still love you.
I'll always love you.
I love you. I love you. I love you.

She squeezes my hand in response, laying her head on my shoulder without looking at me. I kiss the top of her head gently, reaching up to smooth her hair after.

"Why'd you wanna see me, Griffin? I've been nothing but awful to you."

"That's not true, darlin'," I murmur against her hair, kissing her again. "When I called you earlier this year, you were ready to jump right into whatever mess I'd cooked up for myself."

"It's the least I could do," she whispers, and I feel a wet spot on my arm as a stream of tears runs down her cheek and drips off her chin. "I owed you that much."

"You don't owe me anything," I say, tilting her chin up so she's forced to look at me. "I have nothing but love for you in my heart. No grudge, no resentment, no anger. Just love."

"But you shouldn't," she says through gritted teeth, furiously wiping the tears from her face. "You *should* hold it against me, Griffin. I was a coward, and I hurt you, and I'm as selfish as I ever was."

"You're not selfish, Eleanor, you're human."

"Yeah, an awful one," she says with a bitter laugh. "Even now, I'm pissed at you for *not* being pissed. I wish you'd yell at me, or hurt me back. That's so much easier than this."

"Not gonna happen," I shrug. "And I'm not sorry about it. Does that count?"

"No, it doesn't," she sighs, laying her head back on my shoulder. "I just have to accept that you'll always be a better person than me."

I'm only a better man because I met you, darlin'.

"So what do we do now?" she asks, sneaking a timid glance at me. "Is this our closure? I know I didn't give you any that summer. Is this how we say goodbye?"

"Over my dead body," I bark, harsher than I intend. "Eleanor, this is me wanting to say hello again. We've lived more life, we know ourselves better. At least I do. Would it be so awful to give it a shot again? See if we can work this out?"

She looks at me full-on, face stricken.

"Griffin, I–"

"Before you say no, just think about it. We can take it slow, see how the summer goes. You don't have to promise me forever." I sound desperate, but I don't care. "Please don't make me spend another minute without you."

She opens her mouth, then hesitates. Something like dread passes over her face, so quick I might have imagined it. She closes her mouth again, then nods slowly. For the first time in a damn long time, the weight in my chest isn't so heavy.

"Okay."

I pull her into my chest without another word, breathing a sigh of relief as I look out over the water, so still it looks like glass reflecting the blue summer sky.

"Okay," I say back, gripping her tightly.

Maybe this time I won't have to let her go.

Chapter 43

Ellie

May, Age 20

"Can we keep this to ourselves for now?"

Laying in bed later that night, I absentmindedly stroke the patch of hair on Griffin's chest, still unsure if this is a good idea. I look up at him nervously, waiting for his answer.

He frowns, and my stomach sinks. Six hours into trying this again and I'm already bringing him down.

What the hell is wrong with me?

"Is that what you want, darlin'?" he asks quietly, running his fingers through my hair and tucking it behind my ear.

"I just want this to be ours," I say, already feeling a tightness in my chest returning. "If everyone knows, there's so much pressure. I want to get to know you again on our own terms."

I tilt my head up, placing a gentle kiss on his jaw. "I don't want to share you just yet."

A smile tugs his mouth back up, and the iron grip on my insides loosens. He leans down to kiss me, then pulls me in tighter. We settle into the bed further, and I relish the feeling of being in his arms again.

"So it's not because you're ashamed of me?" he asks, his tone turning playful.

"As if." Rolling my eyes, I look back up at him and my heart skips a beat at the unrestrained joy in his grin. "You're the one who should be ashamed of me, I'm a nightmare."

"Don't you talk about my girl like that," he teases, flicking me on the nose. "You're an absolute dream, darlin'."

The tension coiled so tightly inside of me slowly unravels with every word out of his mouth. I've been a nervous wreck all afternoon, dreading the moment he comes to his senses and realizes he should want nothing to do with me. But after a round of *insane* makeup sex and whispered sweet nothings, I'm starting to believe that we might make it through after all. And maybe, just maybe—all of that heartbreak will have been worth it.

***

"Griffin, you couldn't have picked a worse spot, I can't see a damn thing."

He hands me the movie snacks and clambers into the bed of his truck, scooching up next to me on our make-shift blanket pallet.

"It's a drive-in, darlin', it's about the experience." Flashing me a wicked grin, he shoves enough popcorn in his mouth to make him look like a chipmunk, and I laugh so loud that people in front of us turn to give us a death glare. "Movie's starting Eleanor, don't you know it's rude to be noisy at the movies?"

"Sorry," I whisper-yell apologetically, elbowing Griffin in his ribs. "You're going to get me in trouble," I hiss in his ear.

"I'm betting on it," he hums softly, biting my lobe gently and sending shivers all the way down to my toes. He chuckles darkly and snakes a hand around my waist, pulling me in closer. "I felt that."

"Can you just watch the movie? It literally just started and you're already distracting me," I huff, but he nips at my ear again and suddenly I don't even remember what movie we're watching.

"We've seen it ten times," he breathes, trailing kisses down my neck. "Danny and Sandy are still going to ride off into the sky, don't you worry. My attention is on something much more interesting."

His other hand plucks the popcorn bucket out of my hand and flings it to the side, lips now focused on my exposed shoulders, dusted with freckles from the summer sun.

"Is this why you parked all the way in the back corner?" My breathing has turned shallow, legs parting automatically as his hand slowly drags up my thigh and under my sundress. "I think you had some ulterior motives, Mr. Hart."

"With you?" He smirks in satisfaction at my sharp inhale when his fingers ghost across a thin layer of cotton, the moisture between my legs undermining my half-hearted scolding. "Always."

A soft whimper escapes me when his thumb applies the slightest bit of pressure to my clit, sweeping in slow circles that already have my hips lifting in search of more.

"Now, now, darlin'," he whispers, fingers hooking the fabric and pulling it to the side. "You're gonna have to keep it down if you don't want to bother the fine folks in front of us. Think you can do that for me?"

No.

Nodding my head vigorously, I clamp my lips shut as he slowly sinks a finger into my soaking entrance. Any slight sense of satisfaction I might feel from the way he groans *fuck* under his breath is instantly overshadowed when he adds a second finger, hooking them in a come-hither motion at the exact same time his thumb brushes over my clit again.

I reach up and grab his jaw, bringing his mouth to mine in an effort to muffle the sounds I have *no* control over. I rock against his hand as he pumps his fingers in and out of me, and a low growl in his throat has my toes tingling.

He fists the fabric of my dress, now entirely hiked up to my waist, and I cling to his shirt for dear life as he winds me up tighter and tighter.

"Goddamn, Eleanor." His voice is deep and hoarse, and when my hand slides down the front of his body to find the rock-hard bulge in his jeans, it's his turn to let out an uncontrollable moan. "Even the way you rub me through my jeans makes me see stars."

"Shh, baby," I croon in his ear. "You're gonna have to keep it down. Think you can do that for me?"

"Fuck no," he growls, his hand covering my mouth just in time when I let out a shriek as he pulls me from his side and into his lap, settling me between his thighs with my back to his chest. "But good thing we're not focused on me right now."

He wraps one arm across my shoulders, holding me to him while his other hand snakes back down between my legs, resuming the excruciating rhythm that has me on the precipice of exploding.

"Griffin," I whimper, desperate for release. "Don't stop."

"I wouldn't dream of it," he promises, head dipping low. His fingers hit just the right spot as he bites me softly on the tender skin just above my collarbone and my vision goes blurry, legs shaking as he coaxes me through my orgasm.

My breathing levels out as my soul finds its way back to my body, and I twist to face him, my core clenching again as he brings his fingers to his mouth and sucks them clean. Everything this man does is sexy. I can't even be mad at the triumphant smirk on his face—boy did he earn it.

"We'll have to come back in the fall when it cools down," he murmurs, pressing a kiss to my temple and brushing my sweat-slicked bangs out of my face. "I bet we can get away with a lot more bundled up in blankets. I sure as hell want to try."

Guilt constricts like a tight band around my heart as he winks at me. Because I know I won't be here in the fall. I know we have an expiration date. And I know I'm the sole cause of another catastrophe to add to the list of things I've ruined for myself.

I run my fingers through his hair, pushing it back off his forehead and kissing him deeply. We snuggle into each other without another word, turning our attention back to the movie just as John Travolta hits the high note of *Summer Nights*.

In what feels like the blink of an eye, the end credits begin to roll, and my body is still on fire. Everything about Griffin lights me up from the inside out. Not only does he give me earth-shattering orgasms on a near daily basis, but just being around him makes everything feel brighter, myself included. When I'm alone with my own thoughts for too long, I find myself sinking inward to a place where everything has grey undertones and something I can't quite put my finger on makes it hard to breathe. But every time he looks at me, everything is golden again and I forget about the dark part of me that's always clawing to drag me back into the grey.

When I'm with him, I'm just...better. A better person, a better version of myself—a version that starts to believe that maybe I could be the person he sees when he looks at me. But right as I get comfortable in the warmth of being loved by this wonderful man, the cold, inescapable reality of Boston fights its way to the front of my brain and everything dims again.

I have to tell him. I *want* to tell him. But every time I get close to getting the words out, that horrendous, selfish part of me wins out.

Just a little longer. Let me live in this dream a little longer. Let me keep him a little longer.

He would tell me I could have both—I can have my dreams, and my sunshine boy. But I know myself well enough to know that I can't. As much as I'd want to, I would get frustrated and bitter at having to keep one foot in Larkspur, and I'd turn into an absolute monster. I want him to always remember me as his darling Eleanor. I don't want to let him watch me turn into someone he might not love anymore.

And what about what he wants?

I shake the thoughts from my head as we drive back into town, his hand holding mine in my lap. I bring it to my mouth and kiss his fingers, and the smile he gives me cracks my heart clean in two. I never wanted to, but from the moment he kissed me in his truck I knew I was going to break his heart again. He's going to hate me.

But in this moment, with the warm summer air whipping through his hair while he looks at me like he can't quite believe I'm real, no one could possibly hate me more than I hate myself.

Chapter 44

Griffin

July, Age 21

These past weeks with Eleanor have been heaven. I never thought anything would top the feeling of that first summer—the feeling of being young and free and wildly in love. But this is different. Every moment is so much sweeter after having loved and lost her. For the first time in my life I feel like a praying man, like I should hit my knees first thing in the morning and thank whatever God might be out there that I have a second chance with her.

I have brief pockets where my chest aches from the sadness of missing out on two years with her, but I have to remind myself that she needed to figure herself out. And the fact that she went out into the world and still came back to me? Nothing comes close to that.

"Alright, that's it," Jack yells, slamming his controller on the coffee table. I jump, my own controller falling to the floor as David falls off the couch in alarm.

"What the hell, dude?" he moans, massaging the spot where his elbow connected with the floor.

"I can't do it anymore," he says, crossing his arms in front of his chest and turning to face me. "Spit it out."

"What in God's name are you talking about?" I ask, bewildered by his outburst.

"I don't know, but there's something you're not telling us," he grumbles. "Your schedule is suspiciously full all the time, you space out and get these shit-eating grins on your face, you always meet us places now instead of carpooling. Are you on drugs?"

"What?" I half-laugh, half-shout. "No, Jack, I am not on drugs. Scout's honor."

"Hmmm," David hums, eyes narrowing in suspicion. "But there is something. I can't quite put my finger on it, but you're definitely being weird."

"I am not being weird," I scoff, picking my controller back up. "You guys are being paranoid freaks right now. Are you sure *y'all* aren't the ones on drugs?"

"So you are on drugs!" David gasps, dramatically pointing an accusing finger in my face.

"No dipshit, no one is on drugs." I swat his hand away and turn my attention back to the TV, determined not to make eye contact.

"Oh ho ho," David cackles maniacally, rubbing his hands together like a cartoon villain. "I bet it's a girl."

I can feel Jack's eyes boring holes in the side of my head as my cheeks heat. Eleanor still hasn't said anything about being ready to tell our friends yet, and I'm not going to push her on it. I'll gladly take whatever she wants to give me, and we can figure out the rest later.

"I think you're right," Jack muses, shifting his body so he's angled toward me, resting his forearms on his knees. "See the way he got all flushed there? That's gotta be girl related."

"My face is not flushed," I mumble. "It's July in Texas, I'm sunburnt twenty four seven."

"AH HA!" David shouts, leaping up and sticking his finger back in my face. "He didn't deny it!"

"Time to start talking, Griffin," Jack says, settling back in with a smug grin on his face. "Who is she?"

"No one," I say, unable to keep the exasperation out of my voice. "It's none of your business."

"Well, which is it? Is it no one, or is it none of our business?"

"I'm going to slug you."

"C'mon Griffin," David whines. "We just wanna know who's making you happy. You haven't been like this in ages."

"You haven't been like this since Ellie," Jack says slowly, his sharp look giving me the distinct feeling of being under a microscope.

"Okay listen," I stammer. "I'm just not ready to talk about it yet okay? It's new, and I'm figuring it out. Can we drop it?"

"Hell no," David says, smile widening. "Who's the lucky lady?"

"I'll tell you when I'm good and ready." I'm starting to lose my patience, but if I don't keep my cool, they're really going to figure out that something's going on. "Listen," I say with a sigh.

"I've only ever brought two girls around. And both times ended in disaster."

They glance at each other then back at me, looking a lot more sympathetic than they did two minutes ago. The last two girls in this basement with us were Katie and Eleanor, and we all remember exactly how that went.

"Can you let me have this one for now?" I plead. "I promise if it gets serious, I'll let you know. It's just not there yet."

If they caught on to the fact that I said *it's* not there versus *I'm* not there, they don't let it show. The fact of the matter is, I've been there from the second she was in my passenger seat again. I'm *shout it from the rooftops, take an ad out in the local paper* levels of there. If it were up to me, I'd paint "Property of Eleanor Turner" on the side of my truck and make it my full time job to give her the world.

But it's not there yet. She's not there yet. All I can do is show up every day and hope I can convince her to join me.

***

"Griffin!" Eleanor squeals gleefully, flinging her arms around my neck and leaping up to wrap her legs around my waist. "What are you doing here? I didn't think I'd see you tonight."

After Jack and David left my house, I couldn't stop thinking about the way keeping a secret from my best friends has been gnawing at me–particularly because they're catching on, even if they don't know what they're catching on to yet. When I couldn't stand it anymore, I texted Eleanor to ask if I could come pick her up.

The knot in my stomach melts the instant her lips are on mine, her hands threaded through my hair. Her eyes lit up like fireworks when she stepped out her front door and skipped across the yard to me, and erased every other thought from my mind.

"Howdy there, darlin'," I murmur against her lips. "I missed you something fierce."

"You saw me this morning," she giggles, leaning back to look at me.

"I fail to see your point."

She drags her bottom lip between her teeth, cheeks turning visibly pink even in the nighttime shadows. "I missed you, too," she whispers, pulling my face toward hers until we're connected again. The kiss turns heated, and in the blink of an eye we're all lips and tongue and teeth, our breathing rapidly growing ragged. I spin her around so her back is pressed against the passenger door of the truck and grind my hips into hers, letting out a groan when she whimpers softly against my mouth.

Focus, Griffin.

Breaking the kiss, I press my forehead to hers and try to catch my breath. "You wanna come over, darlin'?" She nods vigorously, hopping down gracefully as I open her door and help her step up into her seat.

Once we're curled up in my bed, her head on my chest while she wears one of my oversized tshirts, I work up the courage to broach the subject. "So, Jack and David were over here earlier."

"I know, that's why I thought I wouldn't see you tonight."

"Well," I say slowly. "The thing is, I don't know how much longer we can keep this between us." I hear her breath hitch, and dread washes over me. She says she wants to keep me to herself, but I can't shake the feeling that she's embarrassed to be with me, or doesn't plan on sticking around again.

"What makes you say that?" Her voice is timid, and I want so badly to find the right words to convince her that this is going to work, that we don't need to worry about anything.

"They asked me why I've been weird this summer. And they guessed it was a girl." I feel her tense up, and my heart sinks. "I told them I'm not ready to share it yet, given how things went the last two times I brought a girl around." The second it leaves my mouth, I know I've said the wrong thing.

"That's why I didn't want to tell them," Eleanor whispers, voice trembling. "I was so awful last time, they're going to tell you to run. They're going to say I don't deserve you, and that you shouldn't trust me again." A tear rolls off her cheek and onto my chest, and I drag her on top of me, tightening my grip and kissing the top of her head. "And the worst part is, they're probably right. I'm just waiting for the day you realize that." She looks up at me, eyes full of tears and fear and guilt. "I'm scared to death that you're going to change your mind about me."

"Never in a million years," I say fiercely. "First of all, they love you. They've never held a grudge against you, and neither have I. Second, you are *not* awful, and I'm the one who doesn't deserve *you*." She chokes out a sob, burying her head in the crook between my shoulder and neck. "Don't cry, darlin'." I hold her close, murmuring promises and reassurances until her tears run dry. I don't know how I didn't realize how much guilt she's been carrying–it never occurred to me that she wanted to keep it a secret because she thinks *I* should be embarrassed of *her*.

With a shuddering breath, she lifts her head up and looks into my eyes. Her eyes are the most incredible shade of crystal blue, even as they're red rimmed and puffy.

"You really think they'll be okay with this? If the shoe was on the other foot, Abby would never speak to you again. What makes you so sure they'll forgive me?"

"Neither of them stopped being friends with you, Eleanor. There's nothing to forgive."

"Maybe not as Ellie their friend, but as Ellie their best friend's ex-girlfriend? There's a lot to forgive there."

"Well, if they handle it poorly I'll kick 'em to the curb. It's you and me forever, darlin'." Her tears start to flow again, the pained look on her face bringing a different kind of sinking feeling to my stomach. Lately when I've talked about the future, she looks like she wants to say something but stops herself every time. I'm trying not to let past wounds taint what we have now–but I'd be lying if I said I'm not afraid that she's holding something back again.

She nods, laying her head back down as she snakes her arms around my abdomen and holds on like her life depends on it. "Do you mind if I tell them? I'm having dinner with Jack and Abby tomorrow, and I think I should be the one to say something."

"If that's what you want, that's okay with me."

"It is what I want." She presses a soft kiss to my chest, inter-twining her legs with mine until we couldn't be more closely knit together if we tried. "I'm the one who wanted to keep this between us, I want to be the one to tell them. I don't want them to blame you for keeping a secret."

"Okay," I say, squeezing her gently. "Whatever you want, darlin'." I stroke her arms gently until her breathing turns even and I know she's fallen asleep in my arms.

As if I could ever deny her anything.

I fall asleep with a grin on my face, heart full to bursting. This is my girl, and now everyone gets to know it.

Chapter 45

Ellie

August, Age 20

"I need to tell you guys something."

Abby and Jack are sitting across from me at the diner, currently locked in a heated discussion about why Aaron can not, in fact, miss his anniversary dinner with Abby to go to a Rangers game with Jack.

"Jack, Abby–I need to tell you guys something," I repeat loudly. They stop mid-sentence, looking at me in surprise.

"Geez Louise Ellie, do you need to tell the whole diner or just us? I think they could hear you on the other side of the county," Abby says.

"Sorry," I say in a softer tone. "But I do. Need to tell you something."

"We're all ears," Jack says, brows creasing. "Everything okay?"

"I think so." My eyes are locked on the spot where I'm twisting my napkin nervously in my hands. Without making eye contact, I manage to quickly breathe out, "Griffin and I have been seeing each other again. All summer, actually. And I asked him to keep it just between us, because I was worried that everyone is still mad at me for how I left things and would tell him to run for the hills. But I wanted to tell you." I look up, my heart stuttering at their bewildered faces. "So, um, this is me telling you," I finish lamely.

They look at each other, then back to me. "I fucking knew something was going on," Abby yells, looking back at Jack. "How did we miss this?"

"You rat bastards," Jack says, but I can only see joy on his face. There's no hint of anger or accusation in either of their voices, and I might cry with relief. "Why didn't you say anything? Everyone wants this. You two belong together. It's about damn time."

"I'm sorry I didn't tell you sooner," I say. "I was just scared. I don't even know if I know what I was scared of."

"I feel like you're scared a lot these days, Ellie Bellie." For the first time in this conversation, concern flashes across Abby's face. "Is something going on? Have you considered talking to someone about it?"

"I don't know," I shrug. "I think life is just more overwhelming as we grow up. It's not a big deal, I'll figure it out." I pause for a moment. "But there is another thing I need to tell you. Something I haven't told Griffin yet."

"Okay," Jack says slowly, a leery look on his face. "What is it?"

"I got an internship in Boston." Silence. "I leave in a few weeks." More silence. This time, Jack and Abby stare at each other for a lot longer, and I shift uncomfortably in my seat as whatever silent conversation they have going on seems to bring anger to the surface that wasn't there a few minutes ago.

"What do you mean you haven't told him?" I've known Abby long enough to know that she's trying, and failing, to stay cool. "You know that's bad. Like, really bad."

"I know," I whisper, feeling about two feet tall. "I know it is."

"What exactly are you planning to do about it?" I recoil at the sharpness in Jack's voice–I don't think he's ever talked to me like that. "I swear to God, Ellie, you can't do this to him again. You can't just leave."

"I don't want to," I plead. "I don't want to just leave, I don't want to hurt him again. But I don't know what to do, things are exactly the same as last time. He doesn't want to go, and I can't stay."

"Like hell it is," Jack bites out. "Like hell things are the same. They're not the same Ellie, because this time you know better. You know exactly what this will do to him. You know what it will do to *you*."

My face flushes, a vortex of conflicting emotions beginning to rise up. I know it's completely unfair that just last night I was all but begging him not to leave me–knowing full well that I'm leaving him. "I don't know what's wrong with me."

"You know what, that's the problem," he says, standing abruptly. "I don't believe you. I think you *do* know, and I think you're going to do it anyway. It's not enough to just say that you don't want to do it. You need to actually *not* do it." His hands clench at his side, the tick in his jaw betraying the anger he's trying to keep at bay. "I don't know if I could forgive you if you do this again. I can forgive the girl who was eighteen and scared. But I won't feel sorry for the girl who's twenty and selfish. Selfish and cruel." He turns to leave, but stops to look over his shoulder at me. "Do not do this, Ellie Turner." He walks away, letting the door slam behind him on his way out.

Abby stares at me from across the booth, arms folded in front of her.

"Abby," I begin before she raises her hand to cut me off.

"Dammit Ellie, you're making me take a man's side. He's right. I'm afraid you've made a downright mess again, my love." Her tone is soft, but her eyes are stern. "You need to fess up, and you need to own it. Griffin is going to be hurt, and probably pretty angry. You need to let him be." We both slide out of the booth and head for the door. "I know you, Ellie," she says. "Don't get defensive. Don't be impulsive." She opens the door for me, following behind as we walk to the car. "Jack is right. If you leave him without warning again, it's going to destroy him. And there won't be any coming back."

I grab her arm and turn her to face me, silently begging for any reassurance or help she can offer me. "I don't know what to do, Abby."

"Just be honest," she implores. "And don't make another unilateral decision. For as scared as you are, he's probably equally terrified of history repeating itself. So don't let it." She gets in the car without another word, and we drive home in tense silence. We both know what's going to happen, and at this moment, even though I'm her best friend in the world, we both hate me for it.

Chapter 46

Griffin

August, Age 21

Something's wrong. I don't know what it is, and I don't know if I want to. All I know is that as we sit silently on the basement couch, it's not a comfortable silence–it's heavy and full of dread, like when someone is walking toward you and you just know they're bringing bad news with them.

"Hey Griffin?" she whispers softly, a hint of anxiety in her voice that makes my stomach drop.

"Yeah, darlin'?" I ask, feeling as anxious as she sounds.

"I need to tell you something."

My mind is reeling. One of the things I love most about her is when she blurts out what she's thinking without preamble–if she feels like she has to preface a conversation, it can't be good.

"Okay," I say hesitantly. "Tell me something."

With a sigh, she moves from where she was leaned into my side, turning on the couch to face me.

"I'm not going back to campus in the fall."

Wait, is this a good conversation? Is she staying here with me?

"I got offered an internship," she continues. "In Boston."

"Boston," I repeat.

"Yeah, Boston," she says, gaze dropping to her hands. "I leave at the end of August."

"But that's in two weeks," I say, panic rising in my throat like bile. "Why didn't you say something?"

She looks back up at me, tears welling at her waterline.

"Because I wanted to keep you for as long as I could."

Is that what she's worried about?

"Darlin'," I say with a relieved chuckle, scraping my hand down my face. "You can keep me and have Boston. I'm not going anywhere."

The tightness in my chest immediately loosens. As much as I hate the thought of my girl being on the other side of the country, I love her bigger than any distance between us.

My smile falters at the pain-stricken look on her face as she shakes her head no.

"No I can't," she says. "Because I need to do this on my own. I need to find myself, to belong to myself. I can't do that if my heart belongs to you."

Her voice breaks on the last word, right along with my heart. There's no way this is happening again. There is *no* way she just gave me the happiest summer of my life *again,* just to leave me in the dust *again.* The ache in my chest turns to rage, and I jump to my feet.

"So let me get this straight," I say, fighting to keep my voice steady even as my hands shake with anger. "You knew about this all summer. You knew you were leaving Texas. And you knew you were going to leave *me.* And you did it anyway?"

"Griffin, I–"

"I'm not done," I say sharply. "I barely survived the last time you left me, Eleanor. You've gotta know that. Why would you do this again?"

She shrinks back at the rise in volume in my voice, and I should feel bad, but Goddamn it I don't. I'm pissed. I'm more than pissed. This wasn't fear or confusion–this was on purpose. This was a conscious decision to keep me out of the loop for the second time. This was betrayal. For the first time since I met her, I look at her and the rose colored glasses are cracked.

"I didn't mean to," she pleads, tears beginning to spill onto her cheeks. "I thought I could make this work, that I could be okay with the way things are. But I can't."

"And what way is that, Eleanor?"

"Nothing has changed, Griffin," she says miserably. "You still don't want to go, and I still don't want to stay. We're in the exact same spot we were two years ago."

"No actually, we aren't." I'm fully yelling now. My voice doesn't sound like my own anymore–and after this, I don't think it'll ever sound the same again. "*You* are in the same spot again."

She opens her mouth to say something, but the words are tumbling from my mouth and I couldn't stop them even if I wanted to.

"*You*, once again, have made a decision without talking to me about it. *You,* once again, are running away from your problems instead of dealing with them." My voice is starting to go hoarse, but I'm not done. "You didn't stop to think about what I want? How I might feel about this?"

"Of course I thought about you," she says, eyes pleading with me to listen to her. "Of course I care how you feel."

"Did you consider that if I knew you were leaving again, I wouldn't have wanted this? You didn't give me a fair shot. You used me up *again,* and now you're leaving me behind *again.*" My voice falters, the anger giving way, not to sadness, but a bitterness that swallows me whole. I sink back on to the couch, elbows resting on my knees and dropping my head into my hands.

"Maybe you're right," I say dejectedly.

"I really think I am," she murmurs softly, reaching over to touch my arm. "I think this is better for both of us."

"No, not about that," I say, yanking my arm from her and looking at her with more contempt than I've ever felt for any-one.

Her eyes go wide, face draining of color as the meanest words I've ever said leave my lips. "Maybe you are selfish, and awful, and a coward," I bite out, words laced with venom. "Maybe you don't deserve me, Eleanor Turner."

She chokes out a sob, and we both stand, knowing this conversation is over. There's no point in dragging it out—nothing is going to change her mind, and I don't have anything left to give. "I know I sure as hell didn't deserve this."

"I'm so sorry," she whimpers. "I didn't mean to do this again. I really do love–"

"Don't you dare," I cut her off, my tone dangerous enough that she takes a step back from me. "Not now, not ever again."

She's sobbing freely now, and in spite of everything, all I want is to wrap her in my arms and kiss every last tear away. But I don't. I let the anger keep my feet firmly planted as she goes up the stairs. I stand frozen in silence until I hear the front door slam behind her–walking out of my house, and out of my life, just like she did two years ago.

This time, I don't fight it.

Chapter 47

Ellie

September, Age 21

Boston is...lonely. After my initial internship ended, I decided to stay and finish my degree online. Because that's what makes the most sense. It's the best way to fast track my career. I'm out of Larkspur. Well, I guess I'm out of Texas entirely. About as far away as possible actually, even if that wasn't necessarily the plan. I'm doing what I always said I was going to do. I'm out in this big old world, finding myself.

And I'm desperately miserable.

"How ya doin', Ellie Bellie?" Every time I hear Abby's voice on the other end of the phone, I nearly burst into tears. I've made some friends here, and I like my coworkers, and the locals are perfectly friendly. But they aren't my best friend.

"I'm alright, my sweet ginger angel. How are things there?"

Dead silence.

"With peace and love, shut the hell up."

"Ma'am?"

"*I'm alright.*" Oh boy. She only mocks me like that when she's gearing up for a full tirade.

"That's not what I sound like."

"It sure fucking is," she says. I hear her draw in a deep breath and pinch the bridge of my nose, bracing myself. "You can't even bring yourself to say 'I'm good' anymore. I ask you how you're doing every time I call you, and every time you either say 'okay' or 'alright.' You are very clearly neither of those things."

"I'm good, Abby, really."

"I'm good, Abby, really."

"Will you stop doing that?"

"I certainly will not," she huffs. "Can you just acknowledge that you hate it there? Can we have an honest conversation for once? Please?"

"I don't hate it."

"Okay, but you don't love it."

She's right. I'm ambivalent at best, and at worst, maybe I do actually hate it. But I will never admit that to her—or to anyone else, for that matter.

"It's just growing pains. I'm still adjusting to being on my own, and balancing work with school. I'm not like you Abs, things don't just come easily for me."

"Oh stop it, you don't even believe that."

"I could feel that eyeroll from halfway across the country."

Another long pause.

"It's not a failure, you know." Her tone has softened, and the lump that's always half-formed in my throat comes in full-throttle. "If you decide you want to come home. It's okay if your plans change. No one is going to give you grief about it."

Yes please, I want to come home. Now.

"I don't want to come home, Abs."

I'm lying. Please come get me.

"It's good for me out here, I'm learning so much."

I'm miserable.

"It really is just growing pains, I promise. I'm happy here, you just caught me after a long day."

Lie. Lie. Lie.

I recognize the sigh she makes–it's the one that says she knows I'm lying, but she's not going to push me on it.

Please push me.

"Okay, my love," she says wearily. "I just worry about you. You know you can come home whenever you want right? Just say the word and I'll come get you, and you can move in with me and Aaron. I won't even tell anyone, if you don't want. You can live in the closet under the stairs, Harry Potter style."

I force a chuckle through the tears threatening to spill over. "You don't even have stairs. But I promise I will, my darling, precious angel. But I'm seriously okay right now." I hear her inhale to say something, but I beat her to it. "I'm *good*. Even though that's not grammatically correct. I'm good."

This time when she pauses, I can almost hear the wheels turning in her mind while she tries to decide if she wants to ask me about it.

"Ask the question, Abigail."

"Do *not* use my government name."

"Abby..."

"You promise it has nothing to do with Gr–the boys?" It comes out so fast it almost sounds like one word. Like if she rips the bandaid off, it won't hurt as much.

It does.

"No, of course not," I say, cringing at the awful attempt to sound upbeat. "We actually had a good long talk a few months ago, and we buried the hatchet. I talk to them plenty, it's not about avoiding them."

"Really, Ellie?" Now it's my turn to take a long pause, and I know she doesn't believe me. Because of course I don't talk to them. Jack hasn't spoken to me since that day at the diner. David sent a few memes, trying to act like this wasn't happening, but eventually those stopped too. Griffin–well, we know where Griffin stands.

"Yeah, we still use our group chat all the time!" The lie feels like ash in my mouth.

"Okay," she says quietly, and I physically flinch at the hurt in her tone. I've never blatantly lied to her like that before. Sure, I'll tell half-truths about my feelings, or commit lies of omission. But never like this. "Well, I love you, Ellie Bellie. I'll call you tomorrow."

"I love you, my sweet ginger angel. More than anything in the world. I promise."

We mumble our goodbyes and end the call. The silence that follows makes my tiny studio apartment feel enormous–or maybe it just makes me feel small. Chewing on the skin inside my cheek, I pick my phone up and type out a text. No part of me wants to send it, but the guilt from lying to Abby outweighs my pride.

Ellie: I miss you guys! Hope everyone is doing well :)

I set my phone face-down on the couch next to me and bury my face in my hands. That was monumentally stupid. "Why, why, why?" I whine out loud, for only me and the one house-plant I've managed to keep alive to hear. Dread drops like an anchor in my stomach when my phone vibrates.

David: I MISS YOU

David: YOU GOTTA COME BACK

David: I DEMAND IT

Jack: Miss you, Ellie. Really and truly, I promise.

Jack: But *I* demand that you make your own decisions. And that David shuts up.

Jack: ...but also please come home.

Something between a sob and a giggle bursts out of me. I miss them so much it hurts. I miss everything about Texas, about Larkspur. I wish it was as simple as packing up and moving back just because David demanded it.

Griffin: All good here *thumbs up emoji*

My jaw drops so hard it pops. *Fuck, that hurt.* Rubbing at the tender joint, I read Griffin's text fifty times over. I didn't expect him to reply. Not after the way we left things. My heart feels like it's short-circuiting as it speedruns through a wide range of emotions. Surprise that he responded. Joy at seeing his name light up my phone again. Guilt when I remember why it's been so long. Grief at the reminder of what I lost. Panic at the thought that I may never get another text from him.

It's too much. I shoved all Griffin-related feelings deep in a drawer in the back of my mind, and have diligently made sure it never gets opened. But it's like Pandora's box—now that it's open, there's no hope of locking it back up again, no matter how ugly those feelings might be. So because I'm apparently a masochist now, I send another text.

Ellie: Hi Griffin

Ten long, miserable minutes pass, but the thing I didn't dare let myself hope for actually happens.

Griffin: Hi Eleanor.

Another sob-laugh. I have no idea what to say, but I need to keep this conversation going like I need oxygen.

Ellie: How are you?

Griffin: Like I said, all good here

This is not promising. But it's also not *not* promising. At least he's responding.

Ellie: That's good, I'm glad

Ellie: I miss you

Griffin: Yeah, you said that

Okay, so I guess things are a lot worse than "not promising."

Griffin: I miss you too

A dam inside of me breaks, and the floodgates are wide open now. I have tried so hard not to miss him, have done everything possible to keep myself busy so I don't have time to think about him. I was so stupid to think that was even possible. Every movie night is one I wish was with the boys. Every lunch is one I wish was at The Park. Every date is just another man who doesn't call me *darlin'* in a thick Southern drawl. I hate every second of it.

Ellie: Could I maybe call you?

Griffin: Can't, busy

This time it's all sob, no laugh. God, I wish I could go back to twenty minutes ago and throw my phone out the window before I had the chance to tell the stupid lie that led to the stupid text.

Griffin: But I can call you tomorrow

All laugh, no sob–I'm going to have the worst emotional hangover.

Ellie: Tomorrow is great. Call me any time, I don't have any plans

Griffin: No plans on a Saturday?

Shit.

> **Ellie:** Long week, just wanted to hang at my apartment tomorrow

I shift uncomfortably on the couch. The lies are coming a little too easily these days.

> **Griffin:** Alright then

> **Griffin:** I'll call you tomorrow

For the first time in months, I sleep like a baby.

***

September

> **Ellie:** I'm glad we got to talk

> **Ellie:** It was nice to hear your voice again

> **Griffin:** Me too, darlin'. Me too.

> **Griffin:** Don't be a stranger.

November

Griffin: Happy 22nd birthday, darlin'.

Ellie: Thank you for remembering :)

Griffin: Like I could ever forget anything about you

Griffin: What'd you wish for this year?

Ellie: I'd tell you, but then I'd have to kill you

Griffin: C'mon, tell me

Griffin: I'd die a happy man

Ellie: You, Griffin. I wished for you.

December

Griffin: Are you coming home for the holidays?

Ellie: No, my parents are coming here

Ellie: I'm on a big project at work and can't get away

Griffin: Breaking my heart, darlin'

Ellie: I wish I could see you

Griffin: Name a time and a place, and I'm there

February

Ellie: I miss you already

Ellie: I can't believe y'all came up here

Griffin: Best 3 days of my life

Griffin: There's no way I'd miss a chance to see you

Ellie: Sorry we didn't get any time

Ellie: Just the two of us, I mean

Griffin: If I never hear David attempt a Boston accent again, it'll be too soon

Griffin: Next time I'll come see you by myself

Ellie: I would love that

March

Griffin: Did you mean what you said?

Ellie: When?

Griffin: When we were on the phone last night

Ellie: Oh, when I said I think left hand- ed people are faking it?

Griffin: No, but I still think you're in- sane

Griffin: I mean what you said when you thought I'd fallen asleep

Ellie: You were awake??

Ellie: And you let me ramble like that??

Griffin: It was cute

Griffin: So did you?

Griffin: Mean what you said?

Ellie: Of course I did.

Ellie: I've always meant it, Griffin.

Griffin: Say it again

Ellie: I love you. Always have, always will.

Griffin: I love you, darlin'. Always.

April

Griffin: I miss you

Griffin: Everything okay?

Ellie: Yeah, sorry I went MIA

Ellie: I've just been really busy between work and school

Ellie: I love you.

Griffin: Music to my ears. I love you.

June

Ellie: I'm sorry I fell off the face of the earth

Ellie: Please don't hate me

Griffin: I could never hate you, darlin'

Griffin: Are you alright?

Ellie: Yes, I promise

Griffin: That's all I care about

Griffin: If you're ever not alright, please tell me

Griffin: I'd be there in a heartbeat

Ellie: I know you would, and I love you for it

September

Griffin: Hope everything is okay.

Griffin: I miss you

Ellie: I'm the worst person

Ellie: I miss you

Ellie: I swear I don't go a day without thinking about you

Griffin: Call me next time you think about me

Griffin: I miss your voice

October

Ellie: You're the only person in the world I could stay on the phone with for six hours

Ellie: And it still doesn't feel like long enough

Griffin: I never get tired of you, darlin'

Ellie: Sorry that I talk so much

Ellie: I feel like all I do is talk about myself

Griffin: I would go the rest of my life without saying another word if it

meant I never had to stop listening to you

Ellie: I don't deserve you

Griffin: You deserve the world.

Ellie: I love you.

Griffin: I love you.

November

Griffin: Did you get anything delivered today?

Ellie: No, not that I've noticed. Why?

Griffin: Maybe you should check your door.

December

Ellie: I still can't believe you surprised me on my birthday

Griffin: I'll never forget the look on your face

Griffin: It makes my top five favorite moments for sure

Ellie: No one has ever made me feel as loved as you do

Griffin: I'll do it for the rest of my life if you'll let me

Ellie: I think I'd like that very much

March

Griffin: I heard the good news

Griffin: When's the big day?

Ellie: I can't stop freaking out

Ellie: They're leaning toward December

Ellie: Abby has always wanted a Christmas wedding

Griffin: Maid of honor?

Ellie: She's got me on maid of honor and planner duties

Ellie: I swear this is all I'm going to think about for the next nine months

Griffin: Hopefully you can spare a few moments for me

Ellie: Always.

June

Griffin: How's planning going?

Ellie: Holy shit, there's so much to do

Ellie: I didn't know there was so much to do

Griffin: I don't think I want to know

Ellie: I'm never having a wedding.

Ellie: I'm eloping.

Ellie: I wouldn't do this to my worst enemy

Ellie: But I've never been happier, I would do anything for Abby and Aaron

Griffin: I know, darlin'. Eloping sounds great to me

Ellie: Who says it'll be with you?

Griffin: You wound me.

Ellie: You know I can't picture it with anyone else.

Ellie: I love you, cowboy

Griffin: You gotta stop calling me that, I don't work on a ranch

Ellie: Yeah but you wear the hat and have the accent

Ellie: That's good enough for me

Griffin: You're something else

Griffin: I love you too, darlin'

August

Ellie: I'll be in Larkspur for a few days at the end of this month for the bachelorette party

Ellie: Can I see you?

Griffin: I'd move heaven and earth to see you, Eleanor

September

Ellie: Will you be my date to the wedding?

Griffin: You tell me when and where, I'll be there

Ellie: I can't wait to see you

Griffin: I can't wait to see you in that dress

Griffin: The picture you sent damn near knocked me on my ass

Griffin: You're gonna put the bride to shame

Ellie: If Abby hears you say that she'll cut your head off

Griffin: I won't let her hear then

December

Ellie: I'll see you tomorrow :)

Griffin: Counting down the seconds, darlin'

Chapter 48

Griffin

December, Age 24

I've never really been a big wedding guy. Not that I've been to many–I think my experience begins and ends with being the ring bearer in my aunt's wedding when I was six years old, which ended in catastrophe. But what's a boy to do when a kite bird decides we're a little too close to its nest and starts divebombing the guests? If you answered, "launch the pillow with the rings at the bird and run away screaming," you'd be correct.

But this wedding? I don't know if it's because Aaron and Abby are close friends, or because I know how much work Eleanor put into this, but I've been damn near in tears for most of the day. Of course I didn't say it out loud, but I was right–Eleanor blew everyone out of the water, even the bride. When she came down that aisle arm in arm with Aaron's brother, red wine satin dress hugging her in all the right places, my heart just about stopped. A vision of her walking down a different aisle, this time in a white dress with her dad on her arm, made me weak in the knees. The rest of the ceremony and all through the reception, when everyone else's gaze was fixed on the happy couple, my eyes were locked on the blonde beauty with tears streaking down her cheeks from the joy of watching her best friend start her future with the love of her life.

"You ready to head home darlin'?" I step up behind Eleanor, wrapping my arms around her shoulders and bringing her back flush with my chest. She just finished a conversation with the venue coordinator, closing out the final details of the night and declaring the wedding officially over. "I sure am ready to get you there."

Eleanor hums in approval, leaning her head back against my shoulder and gripping my forearms. "You look sexy as hell in that tux," she murmurs, low enough so that only I can hear. "But I'd be lying if I said I haven't been dying to get you out of it from the moment I saw you earlier."

Lord have mercy.

"Okay, time to go," I growl, unwinding my arms and placing my hands and her shoulders, marching her out of the ballroom while she throws her head back with laughter. I glance over my shoulder one last time, taking in the empty dancefloor and the venue crew starting to clean up the remnants of the reception. It makes me think the same thing I've been thinking all night.

This is going to be us someday.

Sooner than later if I have anything to say about it.

And I do. A solitaire emerald cut ring has been burning a hole in the inside pocket of my tux jacket since I tucked it in there this morning. I know it's taboo to ask someone to marry you at a wedding–which is why I'm waiting until we get home. I've known from day one that I wanted to marry this girl, and I don't want to wait another second. We've talked about forever so many times over the last year, and every time she brings it up I light up like a Christmas tree.

When we first started talking again I went into every phone call, every text, with a pit in my stomach, wondering if this was going to be the conversation when she changed her mind again. Two years later, even through some long periods of silence brought on by the busyness of adulthood, she's still here. And *she's* the one talking about the future.

"I love love," she sighs, curling into my side as we walk to the truck. "I've never been happier than I am today."

That's my opening. Holy shit. Okay, this is it.

"You know, I was thinking the same thing." She leans against the side of the truck, turning to face me when she notices that I haven't moved to open her door. "But I think that every day. Every time I talk to you, I've never been happier than I am at that moment."

She smiles sweetly, tilting her head up and dragging me down by my tie until our lips touch. The kiss is slow and gentle–the kind that makes me soar even higher than the needy, passionate, downright *feral* ones. "I love you, Griffin Hart."

"I love you, Ellie Turner." Inhaling a shaky breath, I continue, "I always have. And I always will. And watching Abby and Aaron tonight has made me more sure than ever that you're the only one I'm ever going to want." Reaching into the pocket against my chest, I pull the ring out and hold it between us. "I know I shouldn't do this at a wedding, but I don't think I can wait another second."

When I look up at her face, her eyes are wide with shock. But she's not smiling. She looks like a deer caught in headlights, desperately wanting to run but rooted to the spot in fear. "I know we're young," I say reassuringly, reaching for her hand. "And there's a lot to figure out. But I don't want to figure it out with anyone else."

"Griffin," she whispers. "Please don't do this."

My blood runs cold, and everything stops. My hearing, my breathing, my heart. I've seen this look on her face before. It's the one that's haunted all my nightmares for years.

This can't be happening again.

"Why, darlin'?" My voice is hoarse and desperate. "Why not?"

"Because I...I can't," she breathes, and I can hear the panic rising in her voice. "Your life is here, my life is in Boston, we're so young. Why do things need to change? I thought everything was fine."

"We're the same age as Aaron and Abby," I counter. "And you're making it sound like I'm breaking up with you, not promising to love you forever. What's scaring you so bad, Eleanor?" I finally start to breathe again, but it comes in quick, shallow pants. "I thought we were past this."

"I thought we were, too." She looks at me, eyes miserable and full of tears. "I don't know what's wrong with me. I know I love you. I know I want you. But then you stand there so sure of everything and I'm just...not."

"But you're the one who started this," I mutter, mostly to myself. "You're the one who reached back out to me, you're the one who didn't let me go."

"I know I did," she replies in a small voice, gaze dropping to the gravel parking lot beneath our feet. "I know."

"Then why? If you didn't mean it, why'd you do it?" Hot tears prick my eyes, and I swipe at them furiously to keep them at bay.

"I meant it when I said I love you, I swear," she pleads. "I just don't know if I could say 'forever' and mean it."

I take a step backward, sliding the ring back into my pocket and staring at the spot over her shoulder. I can't look her in the face, not right now.

"Griffin, this has to stop." Her voice breaks on the last word as she looks up at me. "We can't keep doing this. You can't keep letting me do this to you."

"Then stop doing it to me, darlin'. Please don't run again, please don't rip us apart."

"I don't want to," she whispers. "I don't want to be the girl who calls you up when she's lonely, then disappears again. But what if that's all I am? What if I'm not as wonderful as you think I am? What if you deserve better?"

"I don't want better, Eleanor. I want you."

"I know," she continues in the same hushed tone. "And I want you, Griffin. But I also can't say yes to you. I can't give you what you want right now, and I don't know if I'll ever be able to."

My eyes squeeze shut, finally allowing the tears to run freely. This is not what I thought was going to happen. I thought we'd both be crying happy tears. But we're right back where we always end up–me placing my heart in her hands, and her handing it right back.

"I have to ask the worst thing of you," she sobs. "Something is...wrong. In my brain. I never want to hurt you, and yet I can't stop doing it. I need you to do it this time. I need you to be the one to walk away. I need you to cut me off, block me out. I am selfish, and awful, and cruel, and I'm asking you anyway. Please let me go. And don't let me come back again."

This is different. This is a thousand times worse than anything we've been through before. Even when we didn't talk for years at a time, I think both of us knew we'd find our way back to each other. But this doesn't feel like that. This feels...final. Like we've really reached the end.

"Please don't do this," my words echo hers from earlier, but completely opposite. "We can figure this out. We don't have to get married, it's fine. I just want you. Please don't give up."

"Oh, my sweet man," she says, reaching up to wipe my tears away and cupping my cheek. "I don't want to give you up, please believe that. But you deserve so much better than what I do to you over and over. I think we're at the end of the line here."

"But we were supposed to be forever. We were meant to have a life together."

"I really thought we would. And I know it's my fault that we won't, and it kills me. But this is it."

I scrape my hand down my face and clear my throat. "Okay. Okay, if this is really what you want. I'll let you go." *Even if it kills me.*

"It's not what I want. But it's what you need, even if you don't see it yet."

"It has to be the last time." Something inside of me has shut down. My voice is hollow and monotone, as if I've hit the bottom of some well and have no emotion left to give. "You said it yourself–we can't keep doing this. I cannot do this again Eleanor. If you walk away again, that's it. I really mean it this time. We can't come back from this."

"I know," she says defeatedly. "I know."

"I'm always going to love you, you know?"

"I know," she nods. "And I will never love anyone but you. I don't think I'd even know how. It's just not enough."

I nod in silent agreement, backing further away so she has a clear path back to the venue. And for the last time, I watch the love of my life walk away from me.

She doesn't turn to look back.

Chapter 49

Ellie

November, Age 28

When we get home from the bar, I go straight to my room, not stopping Abby when she follows behind me and closes my door. I fling myself face down onto the bed and let out a muffled scream.

"There, there," Abby soothes, taking my boots off and setting them neatly in the corner. "Let it out."

And I do. I throw a bona fide hissy fit. I slam my fists into the bed, kicking my feet in unison, screaming into the down throw pillow the entire time. Once I've exhausted myself, I go limp, and Abby slides into the bed beside me.

"Feel better?"

"No," I pout, voice still muffled by the pillow. I toss dramatically onto my side, looking up at her with my lower lip jutted out. "I certainly do not feel better."

"Well, at least you tried," she says, stroking my hair. "You wanna tell me what happened?"

"No," I sigh heavily. "But I will anyway."

She chuckles, fingers still running through my hair as she waits patiently for me to begin.

"You know how when you're watching a romcom, and you just know two people are meant for each other, but there's a character who makes the wrong choice over and over, and you think to yourself, 'No one could possibly be that stupid in real life'?"

"Yes, we lament this frequently."

"Well, apparently I am that character, and yes, I am that stupid in real life." I heave myself up and sit against the headboard, grabbing Abby's hand in mine. "My sweet ginger angel, please tell me what's wrong with me."

"You self-sabotage, my sweet," she says, pinching my cheek. "And you've spent years telling yourself that he's better off without you. Which is ridiculous."

I frown at her. "Is this really the time to call me ridiculous?"

"You did, quite literally, ask me to tell you."

"Fair enough, continue."

"Anyway, as I was sayinggg," she says, drawing out the last word with a flourish. "It's ridiculous, because not once has anyone been a better person for *not* having you in their life."

I open my mouth to argue, but nothing comes out. I rack my brain trying to pinpoint exactly when the idea that Griffin was better off without me took root. I try to think back through every fight we've ever had, and I can't seem to find a time when I didn't believe that. Instead of arguing, I give a play-by-play of what happened from the time I left our table to the time I returned.

"Hmm," she hums, pursing her lips. "Do you wanna say it, or should I?"

"Counteroffer–what if neither of us says it?"

"I'm afraid that's not an option," she protests.

"Fine, go ahead."

"You should probably apologize."

With a groan, I bury my face back into the pillow while Abby rubs reassuring circles on my back. This is a tale as old as time–I self-sabotage, Griffin tries to cope with the consequences of my actions, and I get mad at him for it, flying off the handle even though he's done nothing wrong. I wish I could somehow reach through a mirror and shake my reflection by the shoulders until I knock some sense into her.

"He's not going to want to hear it, Abs." Muffled and miserable, my voice is barely audible through the pillow. "Plus, he blocked my number, I wouldn't know where to find him."

"If only you were friends with someone who could talk to him. If only he lived, oh, I don't know, across the street from your best friend's house. Oh, wait…"

"This is not the time for sarcasm."

"It's always the time for sarcasm," she argues. "It's also the time to face the music, my love."

"I don't like music."

"Shut the hell up."

Pushing up onto my elbows, I glance over at her. She's smug, and expectant, and determined, and worst of all–she's *right.*

"Fine, I'll text Jack and see if he can get Griffin to meet with me. But don't hold your breath."

She nods, clearly satisfied that I'm at least going to attempt it, and I plop face-down back into my designated Wallowing Pillow.

"Have you guys ever actually had a closure conversation? Or apologized? Or has it just been the same old song and dance of–and you know it pains me to say it–you fucking things up, ignoring each other, then getting back together like nothing happened?"

"I tried once. During college. Somehow it went from, 'Okay, here's the closure we need' to 'Wow, makeup sex is next level.'"

When she doesn't answer, I look up at her again. She's staring off into space, fingers pensively drumming on her chin.

"Abby?"

"Sorry," she says, looking at me with a wicked grin. "I was trying to think of a fight to pick with Aaron so we can have some of that makeup sex you mentioned."

"Gross, dude," I groan, using the spare pillow to smack her in the face. "Back to the *actual* conversation at hand, no I don't think we've ever gotten real closure. Maybe that's why we can't let each other go."

"Is it though?" She glares at me skeptically, one eyebrow cocked, arms crossed across her chest.

"What do you mean?"

"Is that why you can't let each other go? Is it the closure, or is it maybeeeee..." She draws out the last word slowly in a lilting voice. "That you're meant to be together and you keep getting in your own way."

"Abby, I think if we were meant to be together, it would have worked out by now."

"I would agree with you if I didn't know you so well. I know you're resigned to defeat, and that you think it's going to end the way it always does. But think about how far you've come in the last five years, Ellie Bellie." She lays a soft hand on my forearm and squeezes gently. "You recognized that you needed help, and you got it. You're actually willing to apologize instead of doubling down. Y'all have been textbook *right person, wrong time*, but if it was ever going to be *right person, RIGHT time*, I think you're in the headspace for it now.

"You're forgetting that he has a girlfriend. Madison? Ring any bells?"

"Ellie, I saw how he looked at you while you danced. If they aren't broken up by the end of the weekend, I'll get your face tattooed on my ass."

"I'd give a kidney to see that," I chuckle. "But really, Abs, I don't want to be that manipulative bitch that apologizes just so she can gain something. I want to apologize for the simple reason that I really *am* sorry."

"Well, first of all, manipulative is never a word I would use to describe you," she says with a sad smile, patting my arm. "But do you see what I mean? That's growth, my love. You're all grown up now, and I'm so proud of you."

"I meant what I said, though," pushing the rest of the way up until I sit cross-legged on the bed. "I don't think there's any future for us. He told me so when I turned him down five years ago. But I want to do this, to apologize, because he deserves it-and because I want to prove to myself that I've grown into someone that *I* can be proud of."

And deep down, I hope he'll be proud of me too.

Chapter 50

Griffin

November, Age 29

Hungover and loitering in the hallway outside of Madison's apartment, I probably look like the world's biggest loser. Several passersby have given me odd looks, probably because they've seen me come and go from this apartment a thousand times. It makes no sense that I'm standing awkwardly on the doorstep, but here I am. I've been going back and forth for the better half of five minutes about what to do. Do I knock? I have a key–do I let myself in? Do I call first?

I knock three times, wincing at the sharp sound as it echoes through the empty hallway. I hear muffled footsteps and the swing of the metal peephole cover, but the door doesn't open.

"Madison, can I please come in?" I ask through the door. After a few moments of silence pass, I really start to think she might leave me out here.

Would serve you right, jackass.

Just as I turn to leave, I hear a heavy sigh and the turn of the lock. When the door swings open, I'm surprised to see that Madison doesn't look angry–she just looks tired.

"You have a key Griffin, there was no reason to make me get up," she grits out through her teeth, sweeping her arm dramatically in a sarcastic gesture to usher me inside.

Okay, maybe a little angry.

"Come sit down," she says with a defeated sigh, pointing at one of the barstools at her kitchen island. "Let me get you some coffee, you reek of tequila."

"Sorry," I mumble.

She waves me off, pulling two mugs from the cabinet and filling them both to the brim. The one she sets in front of me has a picture of the two of us on it, and my chin falls to my chest, shoulders curling inwards in shame.

"Madison, I–"

"No, Griffin. I'm going to talk and you're going to listen."

I nod sheepishly, feeling distinctly like a kid caught with his hand in the cookie jar. But when I look up at her, it doesn't look like she's winding up for an explosion. She looks more like she does when she's preparing for an important business deal at work. Sharp, focused, and kind of terrifying.

"We've been together for a year," she says, matter-of-factly. "And it's been good. Great, even."

"Um, yeah, it has. Been great, that is. You're great," I stammer, fumbling over my words. "Listen–"

"Shh, I'm still talking," she says, holding up a finger. "But let's be honest with ourselves. It's run its course. This was never going to last forever, and as much as I wish it was ending differently, here we are."

"Ending?"

"Yes, Griffin, ending."

I was not expecting this.

"I know you walked in here thinking you were going to deliver the death blow," she continues. "But I think it's only fair that I get to have this on my terms. I'm not an idiot." She gives me a pointed look that tells me she might know me better than I thought.

"The second I heard that Ellie was back in town, I knew this was coming. Anyone with half a brain knows that you're going to carry a torch for her until the end of time."

Fuck. She's reading me like a book.

"I'm not mad," she says, patting my arm reassuringly. "I was shocked when you asked me out to begin with. But I knew she hadn't come home in a while, and I figured if you were going to make a real effort to move on, I'd let you do it with me."

My jaw drops. "So you thought this would happen from the beginning? You didn't ever think I actually liked you?"

"Oh, stop it, of course you liked me, Griffin. I'm incredibly likable. We made an excellent pairing. I just knew I wasn't going to be some great, big love for you."

"And you were okay with that?"

"When have you ever known me to do something I wasn't okay with?"

I can't help the way the corners of my mouth quirk upward. Madison *is* likable, she always has been. A big part of what drew me to her was her independence and self-assuredness. I should have known she'd be three steps ahead of me, even in this.

"The longer it lasted, the more I convinced myself that you really had moved on," she continues. "It was nice having companionship. And to be frank, it was real damn nice to get laid on a regular basis. But I think part of me always knew we were on borrowed time."

"Why did you let me waste your time like that, Madison?" My voice comes out hoarse, a combination of the hangover and the guilt.

"You didn't waste my time, honey," she says softly, squeezing my hand. There's no anger or betrayal in her eyes, even though she has every right to feel them, and a thousand other things. I think she genuinely means it. "Just because it didn't last doesn't mean we didn't gain anything from it. At the very least, you know for sure that no one is ever going to fill the Ellie-shaped hole in your heart."

"I really didn't mean to do this," I murmur. "I wanted this to work."

"I know you did," she hums, coming around the island to stand behind me, wrapping her arms around my shoulders. It doesn't feel like she's trying to hold on to me—if anything, it feels like she's holding me together. "And I thought I could help fix that broken heart of yours. We were both wrong."

"How are you being so chill about this?"

"Don't worry, I spent last night raging," she says, shrugging her shoulders. "Got it out of my system before you came over."

"You deserve so much better than this, Mads. I'm so sorry."

"You're a good man, Griffin Hart. I don't need better, I just need different. And we both know what *you* need."

I turn to look up at her, and I can tell she means every word she's saying. I was so wrapped up in my own dread about breaking up with her that it didn't occur to me that she might want to end things with *me.*

"I don't know if I'm going to get it," I whisper. Even if we're both single now, I don't know if Eleanor and I can piece ourselves back together.

"I think you will," she says simply. "I know soulmates when I see them. And anyone who has been around y'all for two seconds could figure out the two of you are the textbook definition of soulmates. You'll get it. Buck up."

"I really hope you get what *you* want," I say, pulling her into a hug. "I'm sorry it ended like this."

"I'm not," She pats me on the cheek before adding, "I get to tell everyone that I broke up with you. That makes me feel much better."

Chuckling, I give her one more squeeze before heading for the door. "Feel free to talk as much shit about me as you want. You've earned it."

"Don't you fret, honey," she says, a warm smile on her face. "I'm already rehearsing my vitriol in my head. Go get your girl."

I shake my head in amusement, tossing my key into the bowl on the entryway table and stepping out of Madison's apartment for the last time, her words echoing in my head.

Just because it didn't last doesn't mean we didn't gain anything from it.

I didn't realize just how true that was until she said it out loud. I gained so much in my time with her–probably more than I know.

No one is ever going to fill the Ellie-shaped hole in your heart.

She's right. Eleanor has had my heart from the very beginning, and no matter how much she infuriates me, no matter how many times she runs away, I'm never going to stop chasing her. I'll never stop waiting for her to be ready to come home.

You didn't waste my time, honey.

For years, I've been bitter. Carrying around misery, stubbornly holding on to a grudge in the hopes that anger might drown out the constant ache I have for Eleanor. Told myself over and over that she wasted my time and tried to hate her for it. But Madison and Jack were both right. Nothing about my time with Eleanor was wasted.

In my truck, I lean my head against my folded arms, the steering wheel holding my weight up. I can't fight it anymore. I still love her as easy as breathing, and I need her like the air in my lungs. But even if we never work it out, even if she never loves me back again, it'll have been worth it.

But God, what I wouldn't give for a life where we work out.

Chapter 51

Ellie

November, Age 28

I need to get my nails done before this weekend.

Staring down at the nails I've ripped to the point of bleeding, I absentmindedly pull my phone out to schedule a manicure appointment for tomorrow morning. My nervous system is thanking me for the brief reprieve–for even thirty seconds not spent hyperfocused on the front door of the coffee shop. Every time the bell rings, I jolt like I've been hit with a taser. Not that I actually know what being tased feels like, but I'd imagine it's something close to this.

I jerk in my seat as the bell chimes again, and this time my muscles do *not* unclench as Griffin walks over to me. I'm so anxious that it barely registers how unfairly good-looking he is right now–especially considering I'm on hour 36 of the hangover from hell and look like the third step in an Animorphs transformation.

He pulls out the chair across the table from me, sliding in smoothly and crossing his ankle over the opposite knee. "Howdy, Eleanor."

"Hi, Griffin," I mumble, my focus back on shredding the nail on my right thumb. "Thanks for meeting me."

"Of course. Wouldn't miss a chance to see you, darlin'."

I look up at him, my eyes narrowing suspiciously. If there's any sarcasm or contempt there, I can't find it. His tone is sincere, and his eyes are twinkling like he's trying to suppress a smile. A far cry from the face I shouted at a few nights ago.

"I didn't expect you to respond, let alone show up. I'm kind of surprised, actually."

The spot between his eyes creases as he furrows his brows. "Why is that?"

"I'm not sure if you're aware of this, Griffin," I joke, "But the last time I saw you, we were screaming at each other in a parking lot."

"Oh, that was you?" His eyes light up fully, the smile he was fighting breaking through. "I thought it was someone else. That makes more sense now."

"Yeah, I wish I could say it wasn't me, but it sure was," I say, smiling sheepishly. "Hell hath no fury like Tequila Ellie." I lean forward, resting my forearms on the table and locking my eyes on his. "And I'm sorry for that. I'm sorry for everything."

"We really were on our worst behavior, huh?"

"Diabolical behavior, really." A deep chuckle rumbles in his chest, warming me from the inside out. "I didn't mean any of it, Griffin," I say in a low voice. "I know you weren't throwing anything in my face. And I know you weren't using me." His hand twitches like it might reach for mine, but stays where it's rested on the oak finished table. "And I'm happy for you, truly. You deserve to be happy."

"Don't beat yourself up, darlin'. You and I are okay. You and I will always be okay."

"Do you think," I start, anxiously chewing on my bottom lip. "Do you think we could be friends? I know things will never be like they used to, but I hate not having you in my life."

"I'll be whatever you want me to be, Eleanor Turner," he says, the sweet words leaving a bitter taste in my mouth because that's not true. I want him to be mine. But that's not fair of me. He has a completely separate life now, and a woman who doesn't change her mind or run away.

"Friends, then," I say with a smile. "Unless Madison isn't okay with that, I totally get not wanting your partner to be buddy-buddy with his ex."

"Madison and I broke up this morning," he responds simply, shrugging his shoulders. He said it the same way you might say you went to the dentist or gave the dog a bath—like it's no big deal. Some mundane, minor detail as opposed to the end of a long-term relationship.

"Wait, huh?" My jaw falls open, and I stare at him dumbly, waiting for additional information. When none comes, I ask, "Is it because of last night? I can talk to her, I'll clear the air. This is all my fault, I'm such a psychotic bitch when I get drunk."

"Hey, don't talk about my girl like that."

His girl.

I blink rapidly, at a complete loss for words after his slip of the tongue. It's something he used to say all the time when I was hard on myself. Old habits die hard, I guess.

"I'm serious, Griffin," I plead. "Let me call her and explain. You didn't need to break up because I threw a tantrum."

"We didn't break up because of that, darlin'." This time, his hand does find mine, gripping it reassuringly.

"Really?" I frown in confusion. " It wasn't because of me?"

"Oh, it was definitely because of you." His hand leaves mine, and he tilts his chair back, locking his hands behind his head with a smile the size of Texas blooming across his face. "But not because of the bar. We just came to the conclusion that no one is ever going to be you, and I need to stop pretending like that's ever going to change." He purses his lips pensively. "Well, she figured it out way before I did. But she helped me get there."

My jaw drops. What does that mean? The difference between his words and his demeanor is short-circuiting my brain. "So you definitely broke up because of me," I repeat back slowly. "Why are you acting like that's a good thing?"

"Because, darlin'," his voice shaky from holding back laughter. "It's such a damn relief to not have to pretend like you aren't the only girl I'm ever going to love."

Going to love. Not loved, past-tense. Going to, future, future-tense.

"I don't really know what to say to that, Griffin." I'm beyond bewildered.

"Ahhh, I love keeping you on your toes," he sighs, shaking his head. I scowl at him, and he laughs loudly. "You're so damn cute when you're annoyed with me."

"Can you quit making fun of me? I had things I wanted to say, Griffin."

He sobers up, setting all four chair legs back on the floor. "I'm not making fun of you, Eleanor. I mean it. But I'm sorry, please continue."

"Thank you," I huff. "As I was saying, I really am sorry for what I said. For everything I've said, for every time I strung you along, for every selfish decision that hurt you." He nods silently, the look in his eyes encouraging me to continue.

"I was a mess. Not just with you, but with my whole life." He opens his mouth to argue, but I do it for him. "Well, not a mess. I was doing the best I could with what I had. I have better words for the way I feel sometimes now."

Something like pride gleams in his eyes, and I avert my gaze before the emotion wells up. "But it doesn't change that those feelings made my actions hurtful, especially with you. And I've never truly apologized for that. I wasn't a mess, but I sure was good at making them. You didn't deserve that, and I'm sorrier than you could ever know."

"I won't minimize your apology by saying you didn't need to do that, but I will accept it. I forgive you, Eleanor. And no mess you've ever made has ever made me love you any less."

I can't stop the well of emotion in my waterline now. Even now, knowing what I know and hearing the words from his mouth, I'm still tempted to argue and tell him in great detail exactly why he should hate me. But I am so tired of beating myself up.

Maybe Kelsi really is right. Maybe it would be so much easier to let people prove me wrong—to just get out of my own way and let them love me.

"Thank you," I whisper, fighting tooth and nail to keep the tears from spilling over. "You've always been so much kinder to me than I am to myself. I can't thank you enough for that."

"If you're not gonna do it for yourself, someone has to," he murmurs, taking my hand in his again and bringing it to his mouth to swipe a gentle kiss across my knuckles. "No matter what, Eleanor. Together or not, in the same state or thousands of miles apart, even if we go another five years without speaking—I will never stop being a kind voice in your life."

All I can do is nod. If I open my mouth right now, I'm going to turn into a huge blubbering mess, and the last thing I need is another public outburst. I grip his hand tightly for a few minutes, not letting go until I feel like I can speak again.

"I think we really did it this time," I say with a watery chuckle as I gather my things. "We finally had the grown-up closure conversation. Look at us go."

"Is that what this is, Eleanor? Closure?"

"I think it is. Right?"

"If that's what you want it to be."

"Is that what *you* want?"

"You know what I want, darlin'," he says with a shrug, standing up when I rise from my chair. "It's what I've always wanted. But it's up to you." I hesitate, opening and closing my mouth several times as I try to find the right words.

No, I don't want closure. I want you.

"You don't need to know what you want right this second," he says, graciously letting me off the hook while I fumble around my own mind, still looking for something to say. "You don't even need to tell me when you do figure it out, if you don't want to."

He holds the door open for me as we step into the pale autumn sunshine. I point over my shoulder at my car, and he gestures wordlessly toward his truck on the opposite side of the parking lot. He pulls me into a hug, the familiar scent of him wrapping around my soul the way his arms wrap around my body.

"But for what it's worth," he says as we untangle our arms. "I unblocked your number the second you left the barn a few weeks ago." He takes a few steps backward, keeping his eyes on me as he heads in the direction of his truck. "If you *do* want to tell me, call me anytime."

He flashes a boyish grin at me, then turns away, shoving his hands in his pockets and half-skipping across the parking lot. "I will, I promise," I yell after him, laughing.

"I love you, darlin'," he hollers back, slamming his door shut before I have the chance to reply. Whether it's from fear that I won't say it back or trying to let me off the hook, I don't really care. I do love him. "Always have, always will," I whisper to myself before getting in my car.

Pulling out my phone, I click on Abby's number and bring it up to my ear. She answers on the second ring.

"How did it go?" She sounds breathless, like she might have been holding it from the moment I told her I was meeting Griffin today.

"I need your help planning something." I can hear the smile in my voice as much as I can feel it on my face.

"Oooooh," she says excitedly. "I like the sound of that."

Chapter 52

Ellie

29th Birthday, The Reunion

Everything has gone off without a hitch. In spite of my insistence that I am *not* a party planner, I do a damn good job at it. After hours of running around frantically, convinced that there was surely a disaster somewhere that I was missing, I've finally taken a moment to soak it all in.

"Ellie, you crushed it," Connor, the footballer-turned-realtor whose name I have finally internalized, says, bumping my shoulder and handing me a glass of prosecco.

"No way, *we* crushed it," I say, bumping him back. "You're basically the Picasso of balloon arches."

"Yeah, well, that's what happens when you've got three kids who decided that balloon arches belong at every event, not just birthdays. You should have seen the turkey arch I made for Thanksgiving, that shit would have gotten me on Ellen back in the day."

The balloon arch over the entrance truly is a work of art—we decided to lean into an elevated school dance aesthetic after coming to the realization that there's simply no way to do a reunion that isn't cheesy. Streamers are twisted and hung artfully across the exposed wood beams, intertwined with fairy lights to add a soft glow. But in lieu of a DJ, a live band in the back corner of the room plays classic country hits as people two-step around the black-and-white checkered dancefloor. Instead of crappy punchbowls begging to be spiked, there are champagne flutes and whiskey glasses, and where there would typically be a corny photobooth, we've rented a 360 slow-motion video cam. It's not a desperate attempt to recreate the glory days—it's a reminder of how we've grown, and the people we did it with.

"Well, I'll know who to call for any of my balloon-arch related needs from now on."

He squeezes my shoulders in a side-hug, grinning and waving as he walks away to join the boisterous group I'm assuming is the rest of the former Larkspur High varsity team.

My gaze sweeps slowly around the rest of the room, warmth blooming in my chest at the sight of so many familiar faces laughing and reminiscing. It's exactly what we intended it to be—a walk down memory lane.

"Remember when—"

"Oh my God, that time you—"

"Can you believe we used to—"

I can't help the smile that seems to be perma-plastered on my face. I make my way across the dance floor, stopping to say hi and begrudgingly accept praise from my classmates as I approach the food table.

"Have you seen Abby?" I ask Aaron—who knocked the catering out of the park, by the way.

"She was looking for you, I think," he says, swapping fresh platters of hors d'oeuvres and mini desserts for the empty ones.

"There you are!"

I spin around and nearly get knocked to the floor by the wild mane of red curls that are clearly on a mission.

"I was just coming to find you," I say, grasping her arm and regaining my footing after side-stepping less than gracefully to avoid a collision. "Do you know what time it is?"

"Time for you to get a watch!" Aaron yells from behind us, a bellow of laughter bursting from him as he slaps his knee gleefully at his own joke.

"You have got to give him a kid as soon as possible so he at least has an excuse for the dad jokes," I tease.

"Yeah, okay," Abby says, rolling her eyes. "Give it a few years, then we'll talk."

"More importantly," she continues, her expression suddenly full of intense focus. "It's time for you to go work your magic."

My stomach swoops with nerves, and I swallow roughly. I have one final surprise in store for the night–but this one isn't for the whole class. It's for the boy I loved then, and the man I desperately want to love now.

"Okay," I nod. "Can you hold down the fort? Find Tori if there are any emergencies."

"There won't be, now go on and get," she says, shoving me toward the door that leads to the gardens. I laugh, but before I can exit, she grabs my wrist.

"You're going to be fine," she whispers in my ear, pulling me in for a hug. "There aren't two people in this world more destined to be together than you two."

Emotion rises in my throat, threatening to spill over when she fixes me with a stern look. "Don't tell my husband I said that."

I mime zipping my lips, walking backward toward the exit with my eyes still locked on hers.

"And don't do anything I wouldn't do!"

"That isn't a very long list, my sweet ginger angel!" I yell over my shoulder, pushing the door open and stepping out into the cool evening air. I pause for a moment, closing my eyes and inhaling a shaky breath before I square my shoulders and walk determinedly toward the rose gardens.

I reach the entrance, an arrow pointing to the right hanging beneath a sign that says *Memory Lane.* Glancing quickly around, I slip past the easel blocking the left side, a *Do Not Enter* sign propped up on it. Originally, memory lane was supposed to be a full circle through the gardens, but I've commandeered the entire western half of the loop for one more Ellie Turner grand gesture.

I just hope to God it works.

Chapter 53

Griffin

Age 29, The Reunion

I meant what I said to Eleanor. I'll never stop loving or wanting her–and I'll be whatever she wants me to be. Things are different now, though.

After our conversation, I realized that no matter what she wants, I'll be okay. Loving her has been the most painful, joyful, soul-draining, life-giving, *wonderful* thing, and I wouldn't change a second of it. Because when I picture the two kids who met 14 years ago and the two adults who sat across from each other a few days ago, everything feels worth it. All of it was worth it to see that beautiful, radiant, sunshine girl look so sure of herself, to know that she found what she was looking for, and found herself.

Just like she always wanted.

So I'm okay with whatever comes. I'm just happy to have been a part of it.

But for the first time in years, instead of actively avoiding her, I'm actually *hoping* to run into her, which naturally means that I haven't seen her once tonight. It doesn't help that David has been weirdly plastered to my side all night, dragging me into conversation after conversation with classmates I barely remember, and making me redo his 360 video seven times.

"I haven't seen Jack in a while," I yell over the music. "I'm going to go find him."

"Good idea, I'll come too!" David yells.

"No, it's fine, you stay," I say hurriedly. "I'll be right back."

He shifts on his feet nervously, biting his lower lip and looking distinctly like a little kid who's about to get in trouble.

"What?" I ask, pinching the bridge of my nose. "Why are you being weird?"

"I know something," he says, "And you're not supposed to know about it, and you're not supposed to know there's anything *to* know, and I'm not supposed to let you out of my sight."

Letting out an exasperated huff, I try to keep a patient tone. "What are you talking about, David?"

"That's the thing, man, I can't tell you."

"Tell me what?"

"Nothing. Nothing to tell. Anything you wanna tell me?"

I'm going to hit him.

"Hey man, do you have a sec?"

David's saving grace comes in the form of Abby's husband, Aaron. I hear David audibly sigh in relief behind me, and I close my eyes for a second to regain my composure.

"Sure, what's up?"

"They want me to set up a second drink table out in the gardens, but all my guys are swamped right now. Think you could help me?"

"Yeah, no problem," I say, shooting David a glare to let him know he's not off the hook about...whatever it is he's not telling me. I follow Aaron to the kitchens, taking the box of glasses he hands to me before making our way to the gardens.

After setting the glasses out on the table, I turn to head back inside, but Aaron stops me.

"Uh, hey, wait," he says, stepping in front of me to block my path. "Have you uh, seen the rose garden yet? They did a pretty cool job with all the blast-from-the-past stuff."

"Nah, but I'll make sure to check it out before I leave," I say, moving to step around him when he grabs my arm.

"No, you should definitely go do it now. Like right now."

What the hell?

Every step I take, he follows suit, continuing to block me until I say, "Okay, fine, geez, I'll go check out the gardens if it's that big of a deal to you. Did you help set it up or something?"

"Uh, no," he stammers, looking around wildly like he's trying to find something to stall for time. "But uh...Abby did. Yeah, Abby helped. Gotta support my wife and all, you know?"

Shooting him a bewildered look, because he's clearly lost his mind, I give in and begin down the path to the hedges. When I get closer, I see Jack and Abby standing at the entrance like guard dogs, whispering to each other furiously.

"Howdy," I say, announcing my presence with a wave. "Abby, your husband has gone insane. He basically held me hostage and forced me to come out here to support you."

"Support me?" she says, brows furrowing in confusion.

"Yeah, since you helped with the memory walk or whatever."

She and Jack share a look that I can't quite read, and I get the feeling that it's not just David who knows something I don't.

"What the hell is going on? David's stuck to me like a barnacle, Aaron trapped me, you guys are clearly plotting something. Anyone care to clue me in?"

"Oh stop it, you drama queen," Abby says, rolling her eyes. I swear, she rolls her eyes more than anyone I know.

I wonder if it ever gives her headaches.

"You'll find out soon enough," Jack says, the corners of his mouth twitching upward, which is the equivalent of jumping for joy for him.

"Okay, weirdos." I shake my head and move in the direction of the arrow sign.

"No wait," Abby shouts. "Go this way."

I look past her to the left side entrance, my brow arching skeptically.

"Go the way that's blocked by the giant *Do Not Enter* sign?"

"Um, yes," she says unconvincingly.

"Do it, man, trust us," Jack says, a mischievous glint in his eye that makes me infinitely more nervous than anyone else's weird behavior tonight.

"Okay, now I'm scared. Am I being punked?"

"March, mister," Abby says, pointing down the hedge path.

"Alright, alright," I say, raising my hands in surrender. "I'm going."

Jack and Abby beam at one another, then hurry back toward the barn as I take my first step into the roses. Strings of bulb lights have been hung along the hedges, bathing the flowers in a warm glow. Looking ahead, I notice there are frames hung along what looks like the entire path.

I approach the first frame, doing a double-take when I realize it's a picture of me. Well, a picture of me, David, Jack, and Eleanor from freshman year. I didn't even realize we had pictures from back then—it looks like this one was taken by David during Spanish, his face smiling at the camera, Jack scowling behind him, with Eleanor and me in heated conversation, completely unaware that we're being photographed.

I notice a folded note clothespinned to the frame with *Griffin* written on the front. Unclipping and unfolding it, I immediately recognize the handwriting as Eleanor's.

Griffin and Ellie, age 14
photographed on a Nikon Coolpix by Mr. David Romero
She didn't know it then, but she was made to love him. And *boy, did she.*

Pocketing the note, I step up to the next frame. It's a photo of two people in a hammock, but their faces are hidden behind their knees. All you can see is a pair of cowboy boots planted firmly on the ground next to a set of bare feet dangling several inches above the grass.

Griffin and Ellie, age 15
photographed by Mr. Rick Turner
The sweetest moments of her life were the ones she spent with
him.

I move hurriedly to the next frame, grinning when I see a photo I recognize. It's one I took the year we did a surprise party for her in Spanish class.

Ellie Turner, 16th Birthday
photographed by Mr. Griffin Hart
Every birthday from that year on, she wished for him.

I continue down the winding path, reliving memories and collecting notes, a pirate on the world's most incredible scavenger hunt. There are so many moments that I didn't know had been captured, and so many thoughts from Eleanor's head that she never shared with me.

When I approach the final corner, just before the path twists back toward the entrance, the photo in the frame makes my stomach turn. I'm in a tux, one hand holding a glass of champagne, the other wrapped around the waist of a stunning blonde in a maroon dress.

Griffin and Ellie, age 24
taken by the photographer at Aaron & Abby's wedding
The moment she wishes she could go back to most.

She would change it if she could.

This was the last photo we took together. Staring down at it, the grief is unavoidable as tears prick the corners of my eyes. Hastily wiping them away, I set the frame back and absent-mindedly tuck the note in a separate pocket from the rest.

When I turn the corner, I'm stunned by what must be hundreds of flickering candles, their light dancing off the hedges and turning a simple garden into an actual fairytale.

"Don't worry, they're all battery powered," a voice in front of me says. "I wouldn't dare risk burning down your Texas roses, cowboy."

I slide my gaze from the candles to the woman standing in front of me—ethereal, angelic, so beautiful it hurts. For a moment, I stand completely still and silent, unable to comprehend exactly what it is I'm looking at. I know this is something huge, something life-altering, but all I can think to say is—

"Howdy there, darlin'."

Taking a deep breath, she takes a step toward me.

"When I was fourteen, all I wanted was to leave this town, and everyone in it. And then I met you," she says, lifting her eyes to reach mine. The candle flames reflect off her deep, blue eyes like starlight, and all I want is to lose myself in them forever.

The sound of fingers snapping brings me back to attention, and she whispers, "Can you pay attention? I'm trying to do something here."

"Sorry," I chuckle, making a show of planting my feet firmly and standing at attention, focusing on her face with intense concentration.

"As I was saying, I met you. And you changed everything, Griffin. You changed the way I looked at things, the way I thought about life. You changed my hopes, my dreams, my idea of love. You changed *me.* You are in every fiber of my being, in every piece of my soul–and I am so much better for it."

Taking another step closer, she continues, "I spent so long being scared. I don't even think anything happened, I just knew that I felt scared, so there must be something to be scared of. And I thought that thing was you. But I was wrong." She steps forward again.

"I'm not scared anymore. You were–*are*–the best thing that ever happened to me. You make me want to be steady, to be sure of things the way that you are. And it took me a long time, a lot of mistakes, and *several* apologetic monologues, including this one, but I think I've really got it figured out this time." She moves toward me until there's only a foot and a half between us.

"So here it is, *again,* hopefully for the last time–I love you, Griffin Hart. In every way one person can love another. I always have, and I always will, if you'll let me."

Without a word, I take the last step, crossing the final distance between us.

"You don't have to have an answer for me tonight," she says, eyes dropping to where she's anxiously twisting her hands between us. "I know I've done this before, and I've hurt you, and there's no taking that back, so you can take as much time as you need to figure out what you want, if you want anything at all."

I gently grasp her chin with my thumb and forefinger, lifting her gaze to mine. When our eyes meet, her breath hitches, and I'm completely and utterly *gone* for her. I press my hand to the small of her back, pulling her to me until there's no space remaining between our bodies. I lower my face to hers, my mouth hovering over hers for the briefest of moments, then we're all lips and tongue and breath and *fire*.

"Everything. I want everything. You can have *everything*," I whisper raggedly, my forehead pressed to hers. "And I'll take whatever you want to give me, Eleanor, for as long as you want to give it."

"Okay, everything it is then," She giggles, tucking her head beneath my chin and wrapping her arms tightly around my middle. I press a kiss to the top of her head, murmuring against her soft hair. "As far as 'how long' goes, I was thinking maybe...forever? How does that sound?"

"That sounds perfect to me, darlin'–I'll take it."

Epilogue

Epilogue - 1 Year Later

"Ladies and gentleman, it's my pleasure to present to you for the very first time–Griffin and Eleanor Hart!"

I grin widely at my husband before we walk hand in hand through the old barn doors into our reception.

Husband. I will never get tired of saying that.

Everything about the wedding was perfect. Abby and Jenna stood by my side, with Jack and David by Griffin's. The old barn–the same one where we had the reunion that brought us back together–overflowed with irises and roses from the gardens Griffin planted on the grounds, long before he had any hope that we'd work out. Each bouquet and boutonniere was made of the same flowers, which was his idea. He let me (*and Abby*) take the reins on wedding planning, but was adamant about the flowers. It took me back to my sixteenth birthday and the flowers on my desk that told me fully knew me, even then.

Griffin's dad got ordained so he could officiate the wedding, and my dad cried the whole time walking me down the aisle. I had the jitters all morning–excited ones, not cold-feet ones–but the moment I locked eyes with my sweet cowboy, the world fell away. No one has ever looked more handsome in a tux and a cowboy hat, and with each step toward forever, my love for him somehow grew even deeper.

As we take the floor for our first dance, the first notes of A Life Where We Work Out by Flatland Cavalry play over the speakers.

In a life where we work out there's a house up on the hill...

"Well, Mrs. Hart," Griffin says, leaning down to whisper in my ear. "How are we feeling?"

A front porch going all the way round, and a flower pot on the windowsill...

"Like the luckiest girl in the world," I whisper, kissing him on the jaw." A shiver runs through his body, and my heart stutters. It's been nearly fifteen years since we met, and I never get tired of the way he reacts to every little touch.

We sit and watch the sunset while the kids play in the field...

"I'm the luckiest man alive," he says, stars in his eyes as he studies my face. "You've never looked more beautiful than you do right now, darlin'."

'Cause in a life where we work out, there's a house up on a hill...

It's been a little over a year since the reunion, and I'm still amazed every day that this is my life. We've gone back and forth between Boston and Larkspur, each of our dreams that much sweeter for dreaming them together. David has taken over temporarily as Griffin's right hand man at the contracting company, and my firm has been graciously flexible with letting me work remotely for months at a time.

If life is only ups and downs, maybe you'll come on back around...

I've agreed to two more years at the firm, after which we'll come back to Larkspur permanently, and I'll join the business as a project manager.

Never in a million years did I think I'd end up in Larkspur for the long haul–I thought I knew what I wanted out in this big old world, desperate to escape and find myself. But life has a funny way of showing us that it's not what we do, but who we do it with. Even if that means circling right back to where you came from.

Save me from what I've become...

Griffin has seen every part of me, good, bad, and ugly, and loves me fiercely all the same. As we sway to the music, eyes locked, captivated by the love we've found in each other, I couldn't be more grateful. I couldn't be more in love.

I couldn't be more excited for whatever the future might hold, so long as I get to do it as Mrs. Ellie Hart. I pull Griffin's lips down to mine, kissing him deeply without a care in the world that everyone and their mother is watching us. I smile against his mouth as the crowd whoops and cheers, whispering "I love you, husband" with my lips still on his.

Lord knows I can't keep losing sleep dreaming about...

"I love you, wife," he whispers back, kissing my forehead as the final lyric sings us into our forever.

A life where we work out.

Author's Note

What began as a therapy assignment unexpectedly turned into the book you have in your hands. Hours of self reflection, and years of blood, sweat, and tears went into this story, and I couldn't be more proud of this book or myself.

When I turned 30, I was in a complete panic about life–I had no sense of direction, no passions, and not a damn clue what I wanted to do with the rest of my life. I was desperate for any sort of sign or spark that would give me some meaning. Then came 'A Life Where We Work Out'.

I'd always said I wanted to write a book, but I thought it would be a memoir, or some other non-fiction book. Writing a romance was never on my radar, but sometimes life has a funny way of throwing these things in your lap and going "here, damn."

Now, at 31, I've never been so in love with my life. There's an abundance of joy, creativity, and love in my life that goes well beyond my wildest dreams. Like my dear, sweet Ellie, I have learned that dreams can change or look different than you thought, and that's okay–it's wonderful, even.

At the risk of sounding like a cringey self-help guru, I do want to leave you with something I have repeated to myself a thousand times over: you are *not* too old, and it is *not* too late. If a girl from small town Texas can lose herself, find herself, and achieve something she never imagined could be possible, so can you.

Acknowledgments

I could probably write another 400 pages entirely dedicated to the incredible people in my life that made this book possible. I may have been the one to write it, but in no way was this a singular effort.

Thank you to my dearest, very best friends and biggest cheerleaders: Anna, Boy Logan, Alex, and Ellee–you believed in me when I didn't believe in myself, and this book would not exist without your love and support.

To MacKenzie, the first person to read any part of this book–your encouragement and excitement kept me going when I was ready to snap my laptop in half.

To my book girlies: Meagan, who listened to my sob stories and my wildest dreams over a Chili's triple dipper and a cocktail more times than I can count; Madison, who changed the game when it comes to read & rot sessions (pregnancy pillow for life); Girl Logan, who introduced me to the joy of audiobooks and is infinitely cooler and more knowledgable I could ever hope to be; Erin R., who went from a stranger to a dear friend at the wildest book signing experience of my life; and Emily, who befriended a crazy customer and spent Thursdays drinking far too many margaritas with her.

To my book club girls: Lacey, Madi, Michaela, Kelly, Claribel, Elise, Erin K., Treasure—I live and breathe for our conversations, our fancasting, our drinks (especially when Kelly makes them), and our friendship.

To Lane and Jolie, who let their weird college friend dress them up and take photos–I will be forever grateful that y'all humored me and my vision. You are immortalized on my bookshelf, and in my heart.

To every other friend who cheered me on and helped turn this dream into a reality–there are too many of you to name, but there is infinite love in my heart for you all.

The biggest thank you to my fellow creators who supported me from day one: to Cleo White, who took the time to sit down with a baby author and answer one million questions–I want to be like you when I grow up; to Jackie (ChapterOne Graphics), you are incredible, and we will always be Swifties first, creatives second; to Della Monroe, whose voice memos kept me sane during the self-publishing process–I will be your number one cheerleader for life; to Kylie Skye, the first author I connected with when starting my author's page, I cannot thank you enough for the support; and to Kristi Joy, who has been a constant source of sweet encouragement.

To my beloved em dash–they will pry you out of my cold, dead hands.

And to you, the reader of this book. I am beyond humbled and eternally grateful that you gave this lil' nobody a chance.